Sharon Kendrick started story-telling at the age of eleven and has never stopped. She likes to write fast-paced, feel-good romances with heroes who are so sexy they'll make your toes curl! She lives in the beautiful city of Winchester – where she can see the cathedral from her window (when standing on tip-toe!). She has two children, Celia and Patrick and her passions include music, books, cooking and eating – and drifting into daydreams while working out new plots.

Sherelle Green is a Chicago native with a dynamic imagination and a passion for reading and writing. Her love for romance developed in high school after stumbling across a hot and steamy Mills & Boon novel. She instantly became an avid romance reader and decided to pursue an education in English and Journalism. A true romantic, she believes in predestined romances, love at first sight and fairytale endings.

USA TODAY bestselling author **Jules Bennett** has penned more than fifty novels during her short career. She's married to her high school sweetheart, has two active girls, and is a former salon owner. Jules can be found on Twitter, Facebook (Fan Page), and her website julesbennett.com. She holds contests via these three outlets with each release and loves to hear from readers!

Christmas Confessions

SHARON KENDRICK

SHERELLE GREEN

JULES BENNETT

MILLS & BOON

First Published in Great Britain 2022
By Mills & Boon, an imprint of HarperCollins*Publishers*
1 London Bridge Street, London, SE1 9GF

www.harpercollins.co.uk

HarperCollins*Publishers*
1st Floor, Watermarque Building,
Ringsend Road, Dublin 4, Ireland

CHRISTMAS CONFESSIONS © 2022 Harlequin Enterprises ULC

His Contract Christmas Bride © 2019 Sharon Kendrick
Her Christmas Wish © 2019 Sherelle Green
Holiday Baby Scandal © 2016 Jules Bennett

ISBN: 978-0-263-31788-6

This book is produced from independently certified FSC™ paper to ensure responsible forest management.

For more information visit: www.harpercollins.co.uk/green

Printed and Bound in Spain using 100% Renewable electricity at CPI Black Print, Barcelona

HIS CONTRACT CHRISTMAS BRIDE

SHARON KENDRICK

This is for the magnificent Joan Bolland, whose wisdom and wry sense of humour are greatly appreciated. xxx

PROLOGUE

DRAKON KONSTANTINOU LOOKED around him, unable to hide the disgust which swamped his body like a dank, dark tide. But hot on the heels of disgust came regret, and then guilt. Regret that he couldn't have done something sooner and guilt that he couldn't have prevented this terrible outcome.

But the trigger to these grisly events had been pulled a long time ago and he couldn't control everything, no matter how much he had spent his whole life trying to do just that. Sometimes control just slipped beyond your grasp and there was nothing you could do about it. His brother had gone now and so had the woman he'd married—the sordid paraphernalia strewn around the room the last testimony to their degenerate lifestyle.

But life went on.

Life *had* to go on.

As if to confirm that indisputable fact, he heard an unfamiliar cry coming from an adjoining room, quickly followed by a voice and the sound of footsteps.

'Drakon?'

He glanced up at his business partner's face as she walked in from the adjoining room. Gingerly, she walked towards him, clearly uncomfortable as she carried her precious cargo—as if unsure just what to do next. *Join the club,* thought Drakon grimly.

'Are you ready, Drakon?' she asked.

He wanted to shake his head. To tell her he wasn't prepared for this latest responsibility which had come slamming at him like a weighted curve ball. To protest that he'd done enough of shouldering other people's burdens and their problems and he needed a break. But that was impossible. He could do this. He *would* do this. He just hadn't quite worked out how.

He needed a woman, that was for sure, but a quick flick through his memory bank of females who would be willing to do pretty much anything he asked of them failed to come up with anyone remotely suitable.

And then, as if in answer to the turmoil of his thoughts, a face unexpectedly swam into his mind. A face with soft blue eyes the colour of the bluebells which had grown beneath the trees in those long-ago English springs, in the heady days before he'd discovered how much his father liked hookers.

Forcing his mind back to the present, he thought about the face again. Not a beautiful face but a kindly one. He felt a faint beat of remembered desire, but far stronger still was his sudden sense of purpose as he allowed his mind to linger on Lucy Phillips for the first time in many months and his eyes narrowed speculatively. Maybe fate was cleverer than he'd imagined. Maybe the answer had been staring him in the face all this time.

'Neh,' he said, his harsh Greek accent echoing around the marble-floored villa. 'I'm ready.'

CHAPTER ONE

AT FIRST SHE didn't recognise him, which was pretty amazing when she stopped to think about it. Except that Lucy had done her best *not* to think about it. Or him. She'd tried to blot Drakon Konstantinou from her mind, the way you did when you were on a diet and didn't want to focus on cream cake, or chocolate, or toasted teacakes swimming with melted butter.

Because only an idiot would want to remember the man who had introduced them to pleasure then walked away so fast his feet had barely touched the ground. Or to recall her own participation in what could only ever have been an impossible fantasy.

But it *was* him. Lucy's heart slammed against her ribcage as she opened the front door of her tiny cottage and peered out through the protective chain at the figure standing on the step, silhouetted darkly against the fiery orange of the winter sunset. It was definitely him. And the first thing she thought was how different he seemed from the man who had seduced her on the beautiful Greek island of Prasinisos, an island which he actually *owned*.

It wasn't just that his features were ravaged and his

shoulders hunched, as if a heavy weight were pressing down on their muscular breadth, but his black hair was longer, too. Instead of being neatly clipped to follow the shape of his head, ebony waves were kissing the collar of his dark overcoat and there was a dark layer of stubble at his angled jaw. His appearance hinted more at recent neglect rather than his usual pristine perfection and it was an astonishing transformation. Suddenly Drakon Konstantinou bore more resemblance to a rock singer who'd spent the night on the tiles, rather than a powerful oil baron and shipping magnate, with the world at his fingertips.

Unwanted feelings flooded through her body and started making her skin feel as raw as if someone had been attacking it with a cheese grater. She told herself she shouldn't be so sensitive. Wasn't that what her former colleagues at the hospital used to tease her about? But sensitivity wasn't something you could just turn on and off, like a tap. Her memories of Drakon were mixed and...*complex*...and the overriding feeling she'd been left with when he'd walked away was that it would be better if she never saw him again. Better for her, certainly. Better to forget those three blissful days and nights which she suspected had ruined her for all other men. To try to get back into the groove of a life which had seemed very dull after her brief glimpse into *his* world.

But he was here now. Standing in front of her with all that dark, brooding power and she could hardly ignore him. She couldn't really shut the door in his face and tell him she was busy—something which her scruffy jeans and swimming club sweatshirt suggested was untrue. Because that would run the risk of making her look vulnerable and that was something she wasn't prepared to do. Okay, so he had taken her virginity. No, Lucy corrected herself sternly. She had *given* him her virginity—with an eagerness which had taken her completely by surprise. And him, if the look on his face had been anything to go by when he'd thrust deep into her body, while, outside, the inky waters of the Mediterranean had gleamed silver in the moonlight.

Just because they'd shared a passionate few days together and it had fizzled out like a spent firework didn't mean they should now be enemies. Or was she deluded enough to have expected that the amazing sex they'd shared would end in some sort of *relationship*, when they came from completely different worlds?

And yet…

She cleared her throat, trying to quell the foolish hope which was spiralling up inside her, knowing how foolishly persistent hope could be. False hope could raise you up and then dash you down again, making the pain even more intense than it had been before. And she was done with pain for the time being. Hadn't she been given more than her fair share of it during her twenty-eight years?

So she forced as wide a smile as she could manage and when she spoke, her breath rushed from her mouth like billowing smoke as it hit the cold winter air. 'Drakon,' she said. 'This is…unexpected.'

He shrugged his powerful shoulders. 'Maybe I should have rung first.'

He said it as if he didn't really mean it. As if any woman should be falling over herself with gratitude that the famous Greek billionaire had deigned to pay her an unexpected call. She wasn't really feeling it but Lucy attempted indignation. 'Yes, you should. You were lucky I was in.'

Dark eyebrows were raised. 'Oh?'

And despite everything, she found herself offering an explanation. As if she needed to prove herself to a man who hadn't even cared enough about her to lift up the phone and check she was okay after their long weekend together. She began to talk. 'Because this is a busy time of year in the catering industry. There are a lot of pre-holiday functions coming up and normally I would be working. In case you don't remember I work for Caro's Canapés and people eat more canapés at Christmas than at any other time of the year.'

'Of course. Christmas.' Drakon tensed as he said it, knowing he needed to choose his words with care— not a normal occurrence for him, since people always hung onto whatever he had to say with an eagerness which sometimes repulsed him. Like many powerful men he demanded servility while secretly despising it, but Lucy was different. She had always been different. Wasn't that one of the reasons he was here today? There were countless women who would have bitten his hand off to accept what he was about to offer—but only Lucy would understand the truth.

Only Lucy would accept the limitations of what he was about to ask her.

But first he needed to gain entry into her mini-fortress of a cottage. He fixed his gaze on the chain which was still stretched tautly across the door and wondered why she hadn't released it.

'Can I come in?' he questioned.

There was a pause. Not long enough to be insulting, but a pause nonetheless and he noted it with surprise and a faint flicker of irritation he knew to be unreasonable.

'I suppose so,' she said at last.

He watched her fiddle with the chain before pulling the door open and stepping back to let him in. He noted that she was keeping her distance but maybe he couldn't blame her for that. He hadn't behaved particularly well after that surprisingly erotic encounter which had taken place back in the summer and afterwards he'd cursed himself for allowing it to happen in the first place. He couldn't understand why he'd behaved in a way which had been so uncharacteristic, because usually he chose his lovers as carefully as he chose his cars—and normally someone like Lucy Phillips wouldn't have even made the cut.

He hadn't rung her or asked to see her again, because what was the point of meaningless phone calls which might have left her fabricating unfulfillable dreams about the future? She was way too unworldly to spend any time with a hard-hearted bastard like him. Not for the first time he found himself wondering what had possessed him to invite someone he'd known from his schooldays to his Greek island home, though deep down he knew why. It hadn't been because of the way she had looked at him with those soft blue eyes, nor the way she had blushed when she'd seen him again after so many years. It hadn't even been about her somewhat old-fashioned attitude, which had been obvious in pretty much everything about her—from the way

she wore her hair to the polite way she'd tried to refuse his offer of a lift home after the reunion, saying
it would take him miles out of his way—an attitude
which had undoubtedly charmed him.

He'd done it because he'd felt sorry for her because
she was hard-working and poor and had been through
a tough time. And yet, against all the odds, he had
seduced her, even though she was nothing like his
usual choice of bed partner. He was not and never had
been a player, for reasons which were rooted deeply
in his past. In fact, if anything, he'd been described
as not just formidable but indifferent to the charms of
women. He was not indifferent, of course. Far from it.
He loved sex as much as any red-blooded man but it
took more than physical attraction to engage his interest. Throughout his life he'd been able to have his pick
of any woman he wanted, but he was much too fastidi-
ous for that. When he did engage in a relationship, he
liked women who were experienced. Sexual equals
who were willing to experiment. Intelligent women
more focussed on their career than on the idea of marriage, who treated sex like an enjoyable form of exercise. Not someone soft and gentle and full of wonder,
like Lucy Phillips.

As she closed the door on the freezing winter afternoon, he was able to study her. Nobody in the world
could ever have described her as pretty, although her
soft brown hair was shiny and her skin was clear, and
she had a way of looking at you with that misty blue
gaze which was more than a little unsettling…

He narrowed his eyes. And, yes, she had a body
made firm by youth and exercise but the grey jeans

she was wearing did her curvy derrière no favours. Neither did her sweatshirt, which was scarlet and had the insignia of a dolphin embroidered just below one shoulder and disguised the luscious curve of breasts he knew lay beneath. Suddenly he couldn't hold back the flashback memory of her nipples—rose-tipped and tasting of coconut sunscreen—which had been positioned so tantalisingly beneath his questing lips as he had licked them into cresting peaks. He felt the hard rush of blood to his groin and thought just how much he would like to lose himself in her again.

Until a rush of shame made him wonder why the hell he was thinking about sex at a time like this.

Ever-present guilt washed over him and Drakon shook his head to clear it. Focus, he told himself fiercely. Focus. Think about the reason you're here. The only reason you're here. He looked around, realising that the cramped dimensions and obvious lack of investment in the property she had inherited from her mother was playing right into his hands. But before he put his proposition to her, he had to get her to relax and to lose that tight look from her face. Which wasn't going to be easy, judging from the way she was staring at him as warily as if a snake had just wriggled its way from the nearby riverbank into her tiny sitting room.

Stepping over the row of shoes lined up neatly beside the front door, he glanced around, at a jug of holly on a table and the way the scarlet berries echoed the colourful flash of cushions which were scattered along the sofa. A flickering fire was burning in the grate—scenting the small room with applewood. Everything was polished and shining and all the contents of the room seemed old and lovingly preserved. In pride of place on the wall were two photographs of different men, both in uniform, and Drakon felt a clench of pain and an unwanted sense of identification. But he forced himself to concentrate on the positive. On the future, not the past. Because that was what was important, he reminded himself fiercely. The only thing which was important.

'Nice place,' he commented, making the kind of benign social observation which wasn't usually part of his vocabulary.

Her blue eyes narrowed suspiciously, as if she didn't believe him. As if he was secretly making fun of her by comparing this matchbox of a dwelling to the sprawling square footage of his many homes. But he *did* mean it. He'd never been inside this riverside cottage before but he'd passed it often enough when he was rowing for the prestigious English boarding school he'd attended, where Lucy's mother had been matron. The little house used to symbolise home for all the boys who were so far away from their own. He remembered seeing fairy lights in the window and a wreath on the door every Christmas. He remembered hearing laughter coming through an open door in the lush months of summer when the green reeds grew tall and the riverbank was bosky. But there was no Christmas wreath today, he noted.

'It suits my needs perfectly,' she said, rather primly.

Her words sounded defensive and Drakon found himself staring at her left hand, registering each ringless finger before lifting his gaze to her eyes. It was unlikely that her situation had changed since the summer but you never knew… 'You live here alone?'

A faint frown appeared on her brow. 'I do.'

'So…there's no man in your life?'

Hot colour rushed into her cheeks. 'I believe that's what's known as a rather impertinent question.'

'Is there?' he persisted.

Her blush deepened. 'No. Actually, there isn't. Not that it's any of your business,' she said crossly, before fixing him with an enquiring look. 'Look, what can I do for you, Drakon? You turn up without any kind of warning and then start interrogating me about my personal life, yet I've heard nothing from you for months. Forgive me if I'm confused. Is this just a random visit?'

Drakon shook his head. He had planned how he was going to present this. To somehow build it up and carefully cushion the impact. To make it sound as if it was just part of life and he was dealing with it. He hadn't been expecting to just come out and say it—or for the words to taste like bitter poison when he spoke them.

'No. This wasn't a chance visit. I intended to come here today. It's Niko,' he grated. 'He's dead.'

Lucy blinked in confusion for his words made no sense. Because Niko was Drakon's twin brother. The wilder version of Drakon. Niko was the unpredictable twin—always had been. The volatile twin. The one who made headlines for all the wrong reasons and had almost been expelled from school an unbelievable three times. But although Niko was reckless he was also full of life. Why, she remembered him as the kind of man who was positively *bursting* with life.

'What are you talking about?' she said and afterwards wondered how she could have asked such a naïve question, in view of her own experience. 'How can he possibly be dead?'

Drakon's face contorted with darkness and pain and that was when she knew he was speaking the truth.

'He died of a drug overdose,' he bit out. 'Last month.'

Lucy gasped, her fingertips flying to her lips, her heart crashing wildly against her ribcage as she wondered how she could have been so stupid. Didn't she of all people know that young lives could be cut down like a blade of grass being sliced by a tractor at harvest time? Had she thought Drakon Konstantinou was immune to pain and loss, just because he was one of the world's richest men and was always flying around the globe on his private jet, brokering deals to add even more dollars to his already massive fortune?

She wanted to rush over to him. To fling her arms around his tense body and comfort him, as she had comforted innumerable grieving relatives on hospital wards in the past. But that was the trouble with sex. It changed things. You could never touch a former lover and pretend it was impartial, even if it was. 'Oh, Drakon,' she said, in a low voice, and could see from his blanched features and haunted eyes that he was in deep shock. 'I'm so sorry. I had no idea. Please. Won't you sit down? Let me get you something.' She looked around rather distractedly, trying to remember what was in the ancient drinks cabinet. 'I think I have some whisky somewhere—'

'I don't want whisky,' he said harshly.

She nodded. 'Okay. Then I'll make you some tea. Strong tea with lots of sugar. That's what you need.'

To her surprise he didn't object, just sank into one of the fireside armchairs, which looked too flimsy to be able to deal with his powerful frame, and Lucy sped into the kitchen, glad to have something to occupy herself with. Something to distract herself from her racing thoughts. But her hands were shaking so much that the china was chinking madly as she pulled cups and saucers down from one of the cupboards.

Sucking in a deep breath, she waited for the kettle to boil, wondering why she hadn't realised right from the beginning that something was wrong. Hadn't she been taught to read the telltale signs of body language which might have suggested that here was a man mourning the loss of his only sibling? While instead she had been selfishly preoccupied with her own battered ego, reflecting on the fact that he'd dumped her after a long weekend of wild and totally unexpected sex. What did something like that matter in the light of what he'd just told her?

She made the tea and frowned as she picked up the tray, because a nagging question still remained.

Why *had* he told her?

Slowly she went back into the tiny sitting room, her head still full of confusion. He turned to look at her and suddenly Lucy was scared by the expression on his rugged features. By the stony look which made his black eyes look so hard and bleak and cold—eyes which said quite clearly *you can't get close to me*. Scared too by another instinctive urge to run over and hug him, wondering if she was using his heartache as an excuse to touch him again. Because hadn't she yearned to stroke his silken flesh ever since he'd set her body on fire and made her realise what physical pleasure really meant?

She poured tea, dropping four sugar cubes into his cup and giving it a quick stir, before placing it on a small table beside the fire. Then she sat down in a chair opposite him, her knees pressed tightly together. 'Do you want to tell me about it?' she questioned softly. 'About what happened to Niko?'

Talking about it was the last thing Drakon wanted, but if he was to get Lucy to agree to his demands it was unavoidable. And how hard could it be to do that? He was a master of negotiation in the business world— surely he was able to employ the same tools of demand, cooperation and compromise in his personal life if he were to achieve what it was he wanted.

'How much do you know about my brother?' he questioned.

She hesitated, shrugging her shoulders a little awkwardly. 'Not a lot. Once he left school he seemed to disappear off the radar.'

'*Neh.* That's a good way to describe what happened. He disappeared off the radar.' Drakon's voice grew distant and sounded as if it were coming from a long way off. But it was, he realised, with a jolt. It was coming from the past—and didn't they say that the past was like a different country? The Konstantinou twins, two black-eyed little boys, pampered like princes by a battery of servants yet overlooked by the wealthy parents who had employed those servants. They shared almost identical DNA and, for many years, few people could tell them apart, until they heard them speak. So similar in looks and yet so different in character. Sometimes they'd even been able to trick their own parents—but then, they'd lived such separate lives from their mother and father maybe that wasn't so surprising.

'Niko was the older of us—by just one and a half minutes—but those vital ninety seconds were all that were needed for him to be in line to inherit the family business. He thought he was going to be a very wealthy man—until the will was read and he discovered there was nothing left. All the money had gone.'

'How come?'

Drakon stared at her. Her bluebell eyes were a compassionate blur and for a moment he almost confided in her, until he drew himself short, reminding himself that certain segments of the past were irrelevant. He'd come here to talk about the future. 'The reasons don't matter,' he said, the words acrid on his lips. 'What is relevant is the way Niko coped with finding out the news, and the way he coped with it was with drugs. First it was a puff or two of dope at a party and then he started snorting cocaine, like so many of his buddies. But sooner or later, every addiction needs an additional boost because it isn't working any more.' His face twisted. 'And that's when he started on heroin.'

She didn't say anything. Had he expected her to? Had he secretly wanted her to come out with something trite and predictable so he could lash out as he had been wanting to lash out at someone for days now? He felt his jaw tighten as he continued with his story and yet somehow it was an unspeakable relief to unburden himself, because he hadn't really talked about this with anyone. Not even Amy. He hadn't dared. Had he been afraid that describing his twin's fatal weakness might somehow reflect poorly on *him*? Might hold up a mirror to the cold darkness in his own soul and the guilt which gnawed away at him because he hadn't been there for his brother when he'd most needed him?

'I didn't find this out until afterwards,' he ground out. 'Because he left Greece and kept his distance from me—from everyone, really—and resisted every attempt I made to meet up. I only realised afterwards that he wanted to hide the true extent of his drug habit from me. If I'd known I might have been able to do something, but I didn't know. I guess I was too busy trying to make my fortune. Trying to recover something of the Konstantinou name and reputation.' He sighed. 'But eventually, I heard that Niko was living in Goa and was in a steady relationship and I can remember thinking that maybe things might be different. Personally, I've never believed in the transformative power of love—but that didn't mean I wasn't hopeful it might work for Niko.' His mouth twisted cynically and there was a pause. 'Apparently they had a beachside wedding and then I heard that she'd had a baby.'

'B-baby?' she echoed.

Drakon saw the colour drain from her face but still he didn't say it. It was as if he needed to mould the facts into some sort of recognisable structure before he hit her with the big one. Was he hoping to build up an element of sympathy, so she would find it impossible to say no to him? 'He got in touch with me just after the birth, to tell me I was now an uncle. He…he asked me if I wanted to go and meet Xander for myself and I told him I would. So I scheduled in a trip to go and see them the following week and was hopeful that the birth of a healthy child might bring him the kind of fulfilment he'd been unable to find elsewhere. Maybe it would have done if he and his wife hadn't decided to celebrate in their own time-honoured way. Not with a bottle of champagne or a candlelit dinner, but a lethal cocktail of narcotics.'

Her face blanched even more. 'Oh, no.'

'Oh, *neh*,' he agreed grimly. 'My partner was on a business trip nearby and some instinct made me ask her to check on them unannounced.' He paused, suddenly finding the words very difficult to say. 'Their bodies were still warm by the time she got there. I got a local investigator to find out what he could, and a little searching revealed that Niko's wife was as hooked on illegal substances as he was.'

'Oh, Drakon. I'm so sorry.'

He shook his head. 'We spoke to the doula who'd been attending her throughout the pregnancy and the only thing I'm grateful for is that she must have retained some vestige of common sense, and was able to give up drugs for the whole nine months.'

She flinched, the words spilling urgently from her mouth. 'And the baby?' she demanded. 'What about the baby?'

'Is unharmed,' he supplied grimly. 'The life force is powerful. He is lusty and strong and with his Greek nanny now—safe and warm not far from here, in London.' He felt his mouth twist, as if recounting words he didn't particularly want to say. 'You see, Niko and his wife had named me as the child's official guardian and so he is living with me.'

She leaned forward, clasping her hands together

as if in prayer, an expression of earnestness on her face. But he could see indecision there, too, and she seemed to be choosing her words carefully. 'This is a heartbreaking story, Drakon—and I'm so sorry for your loss,' she breathed. 'But I'm still not quite sure why you're telling me all this.'

He stared at her. Was she really so naïve? Maybe she was. She'd certainly been *innocent* when he'd parted her thighs that hot summer evening and slid inside the unexpected tightness of her body. Though maybe he'd been the naïve one not to have realised that the wholesome Lucy Phillips had been untouched by another man. When he'd bumped into her in England she'd appeared almost invisible and the thought of seducing her couldn't have been further from his mind. And yet things had inexplicably turned sexual when he'd dropped in on her when she'd been staying on his island.

He remembered seeing her swimming in his pool, her strong arms arcing through the turquoise water in a graceful display of strength and power. Length after length he had watched her swim and when she'd eventually surfaced and blinked droplets of water from her eyes, she had looked genuinely surprised—and pleased—to see him. He shouldn't have been turned on by her plain and practical swimsuit but he had been, though maybe because he'd never seen someone of her age wearing something so old-fashioned. Just as he shouldn't have been unexpectedly charmed by the way she made him laugh—which was rare enough to be noteworthy. He'd found himself staying on for dinner, even though he hadn't planned to—and even though he'd told himself that her dress was cheap, that hadn't stopped him from being unable to tear his eyes away from the way the dark material had clung to her fleshy curves, had it?

Maybe it was inevitable that they had started kissing—and just as inevitable that they'd ended up having sex. The unexpected and unwanted factor had been encountering her intact hymen and realising he was the first man she'd ever been intimate with. At the time he'd been irritated by the fact she hadn't told him because, according to friends who knew about such things, taking a woman's virginity brought with it all kinds of problems—not least the kind of mindless devotion which was the last thing he needed. In fact, he despised it, for reasons which still made him shudder. His mouth hardened. He had enough difficulty keeping women at arm's length as it was, without some idealistic innocent longing for rose petals and wedding bells.

But his irritation had lasted no longer than it took to resume his powerful rhythm inside her. And she had surprised him. Not just because she had proved to be an energetic and enthusiastic lover who had kissed more sweetly than any other woman he'd ever known. No. Because she seemed to have realised herself the limitations of their brief affair and to have accepted the fact that he had ghosted her from his life afterwards. She hadn't made any awkward phone calls or sent texts carefully constructed in order to appear 'casual'. And if his abundantly healthy ego had been fleetingly dented by her apparent eagerness to put what had happened behind her, the feeling had soon left him, because it was entirely mutual. But it made him realise that in many ways Lucy Phillips was exceptional. Emotionally independent, a trained midwife and, thus, the perfect candidate for what he needed…

He felt his mouth dry as he studied her earnest face and the clothes which failed to flatter her curvy shape. It was hard now to believe that she had choked out her fulfilment as he had driven into her firm body or to imagine the way he had fingered her nipples in the blazing Greek sunshine so that they had puckered into tight little nubs just ripe for sucking. But when you stopped to think about it, *all* of this was hard to believe and he needed to present his case so that she would receive it sympathetically. Rising to his feet, he addressed her stumbled question as he slowly approached her fireside chair. 'I'm telling you because I need your help, Lucy.'

'*My* help?' she echoed, her bright eyes looking up at him in surprise as his shadow enveloped her in darkness. 'Are you kidding? How on earth can I help someone like you when you're one of the richest men in the world and I have practically nothing?'

'No, I'm not kidding,' he negated firmly. 'And, far from having nothing, you have something I need very badly. Niko's baby needs security and continuity. He needs a home and I'm in a position to offer him one. But not on my own. Not as a single man whose work takes him to opposite sides of the world and who has no experience of babies, or children. And that's why I'm asking you to marry me, Lucy. To be my wife and the mother of my orphaned nephew.'

CHAPTER TWO

LUCY'S MOUTH FELL open as she stared into the face of the powerful Greek billionaire, the flickering firelight illuminating the ebony and gold of his rugged features. She couldn't believe what Drakon had just asked her and his question made her feel as if she was taking part in a dream. An extra-surreal dream. But surely he wouldn't be looking so serious if he hadn't meant it. 'You want *me* to marry you?' she verified slowly.

He nodded—though his brief frown suggested he didn't quite agree with her choice of words. 'I do.'

Lucy shook her hair and her heavy ponytail slithered like a thick rope against her back. Wasn't it crazy—and sad—how, in life, timing was everything? If her brother hadn't been in the wrong place at the wrong time, he would still be here. And if Drakon Konstantinou had asked her this very question a few months earlier, her reaction to it would have been totally different. Because when she'd returned home after her brief excursion to his island home—high on a mixture of raging hormones and a heady introduction to multiple orgasms—she had prayed for a scenario just like this. She'd nursed the unrealistic fantasy that what she and Drakon had shared had been special. Super-special. She had longed for him to suddenly decide his life was empty without her and that he wanted them to make a go of things. Why wouldn't she, when he was like every woman's dream man—despite his undeniable arrogance and detachment? When she'd always had a secret crush on him…

Of course that had never happened. He had cut her out of his life as abruptly as he had blazed into it again—at a school reunion where she'd been employed by Caro's Canapés, the local catering firm for which she worked. In her plain green dress, she'd been serving sandwiches just before the pin-drop silence which had followed Drakon Konstantinou's entrance into Milton school's famous and historic hall. She remembered the way all the other men had consciously or unconsciously pulled back their shoulders and sucked in their stomachs, as if to big themselves up or look taller. But it had been to no avail because the Greek tycoon had still dominated the vast room without even trying. Like a black star, dark brilliance had radiated from his powerful body and drawn every single eye to him. Yet for some crazy and inexplicable reason, he had been looking at *her*.

Lucy remembered blushing deeply as she'd offered him an egg and cress sandwich because she'd been acutely aware of the time, years ago, when he'd gashed his leg while rowing for the first team and, eager to be a nurse herself, she had been helping her mother, the school matron, in the school sanitorium. Drakon had been lying on a narrow trolley, with blood seeping from his gaping wound, and Lucy had thought how much it must hurt as her mother had dabbed at it with antiseptic. But he hadn't shown it. He hadn't even winced, not once. She'd given him her fingers to grip and he had opened his eyes and stared at her. Stared at her with eyes as black as the night. A ripple of something unfamiliar and exciting had whispered its way down her spine and she had never forgotten that feeling. She had been only fourteen at the time, and Drakon a crucial three years older—it had been Lucy's first experience of physical attraction towards a member of the opposite sex and it had stayed with her, all those years. Why, it had fired straight back into life when she had extended the silver platter of sandwiches towards him and met the velvety blackness of his eyes.

Was it her corresponding blush which had amused him—which had deepened when he'd pointed out, in his drawling Greek accent, that it was a rare thing to see a woman blush these days? Or was it simply curiosity which had made him hang around as the reunion was coming to an end, and the headmaster was imploring him to join him and his wife for supper? But Drakon hadn't stayed. Amid a torrent of thundering rain, he had insisted on giving her a lift home in his fancy car and naturally Lucy had been tongue-tied by all that opulence.

It had been pretty scary to discover that her crush on him was as powerful as ever, and slightly unsettling that she couldn't seem to keep her gaze from straying to the muscular thrust of his thighs. She remembered the potent rush of warmth deep at her core, which had made her feel both excited and a little bit embarrassed, because she wasn't the type of person who usually thought about stuff like that. She never really came across eligible men and certainly nobody of Drakon's calibre ever entered her life. Even the ones who were more her type tended to glance over her shoulder whilst chatting at parties, as if searching the room for someone more interesting to talk to.

Yet after the reunion, when the throaty car had slid to a halt outside her tiny riverside cottage, Drakon had turned to her and said, 'So how are you, Lucy? I mean, *really*?'

Was it the sense of what had sounded like genuine interest—something she suspected was rare for a man like him—which had made her blurt out everything which had been on her mind? Well, not *everything*. She'd missed out the part which explained why she'd given up her beloved job in midwifery—because the reasons for that made her feel even less of a woman, and who in their right mind would wish to do that in the presence of such a gorgeous man? Instead Lucy had found herself telling him about her brother in the army, who had lost his life in that awful conflict, just as her father had done in a different war before that. And how afterwards her mother had seemed to lose the will to live and had just faded away—like one of those dusky pink roses which bloomed in the lavish walled gardens of Milton school.

She remembered the deep frown which had crossed the tycoon's face as he'd studied her admittedly pale skin and told her that what she needed was a holiday in the sun. Had she explained that such luxuries were far beyond her grasp on her wages as a waitress, or had he just guessed? She wasn't sure. All she knew was that he had extended a careless invitation for her to holiday on his own personal Greek island.

'You actually own an island?' she remembered querying in disbelief.

'Sure.' He had glittered her a smile. 'And my house is empty a lot of the time. It's yours any time you want to use it.'

So she had gone. It had been an uncharacteristic response to what had probably just been a throwaway gesture on his part, but it had been too good an opportunity to miss. Although he had casually mentioned that his private jet was available, Lucy had scraped together enough money to fund a cheap flight to Athens instead and then caught the staff ferry to his private island of Prasinisos, with a pile of engrossing books to read. It had been the most impetuous thing she'd ever done and she wasn't sure what she had expected. She certainly hadn't expected Drakon to suddenly arrive on a glittering super-yacht the size of Jupiter later that day, when she was emerging from the swimming pool looking like a drowned rat. Nor for him to join her beside the aqua glitter of the infinity pool once she'd showered all the chlorine out of her hair and the fierce beat of the sun had made her feel all lazy and laid-back.

For a while she'd said nothing, because instinct had told her he was a man who valued silence, and gradually she had seen Drakon relax—something she'd suspected he didn't do very often. He'd shown her the faint scar from the gash on his leg which she'd helped her mother to suture all those years ago, and something about that distant memory had made them both laugh. She remembered their eyes meeting and something intangible shimmering in the air around them. Lucy had been inexperienced, innocent and slightly out of her depth—all those things, yes. But she had also been excited and eager for what had happened later, after a delicious dinner on the terrace once his housekeeper had gone home. For Drakon to fold her into his arms and kiss her and then kiss her some more. It had been as if her every dream had come true in that moment. As if her body had been poised on the brink of something very beautiful.

She'd thought he would quickly get bored with someone who wasn't at all experienced but her tongue's tentative exploration of his mouth had caused a low growl of pleasure to rumble up from his throat. He'd held her so tight that her soft body had moulded into the muscular hardness of his, so that when he had carried her off to his bedroom it had felt nothing but right. Even that slight awkwardness when he had stilled inside her and momentarily glared at her hadn't lasted longer than a couple of seconds.

The following morning she had woken naked in his bed and he had brought her dark coffee, which was thick and sweet, before taking her in his arms again, and the next few days had passed by in a sensual blur. He'd made love to her on the terrace, and in the cabin of his yacht as he'd sailed her round his island and showed her all the little bays and coves. He'd fed her grapes and trickled Greek honey onto a belly which had quivered as he'd licked it off.

And three days later it had all been over, without anything actually being said. There had been no awkward conversation or protracted farewells. He hadn't insulted her by telling her that his diary was too jam-packed for him to be able to see her again. He'd just given her a deep kiss, said goodbye and dropped her off at the airport by helicopter so at least she hadn't had to endure that rather bumpy ferry ride back to Athens. She hadn't heard a squeak from him since and, once she'd realised it wasn't going to happen, her hurt and disappointment had gradually faded into the recesses of her mind, because Lucy was nothing if not practical. She'd told herself to remember all the good bits and she'd tried not to have unrealistic expectations, because that way you could avoid hurt and disappointment as much as possible. She had been getting on with her life—her rather ordinary and predictable life—until the Greek tycoon had blazed back into it with the most implausible suggestion she'd ever heard!

'I can't believe you're asking me to marry you,' she breathed.

'Well, believe it,' he returned softly. 'Because it's true.'

'But why me?' she questioned, wishing that her heart would stop thundering. 'There must be a million women who would make a more suitable wife for a man like you.'

He didn't even pay her the compliment of pretending to consider her remark and certainly didn't bother to deny it, just answered with a bluntness which somehow managed to be supremely insulting.

'There are indeed,' he agreed. 'In fact, if I were to measure suitability in terms of sophistication and familiarity with my world, you would be right at the back of the queue, Lucy.'

She swallowed. 'You don't pull your punches, do you, Drakon?'

'Do you think I should?' he mused. 'I've always been of the mindset that life is too short for prevarication and Niko's death has only confirmed that.'

He paused and as his night-dark gaze shimmered over her, Lucy wanted to tell him not to look at her like that—yet the craziest thing of all was that she wanted him to carry on doing it and never stop.

'I've never wanted to marry anyone nor have children of my own,' he said. 'Despite the fact that I have a vast fortune just waiting for someone to inherit.'

'Why not?' she asked quietly.

His black gaze seared into her, as if he was deciding how much to tell her. 'Because I don't believe in love. It's something I've never felt nor wanted to feel. To my mind, love is nothing but an invention which seems designed to excuse the most outrageous forms of behaviour.' His black eyes narrowed. 'But now I have an heir whether I like it or not and, because I am a twin, this child almost completely carries half my genes. So in a way, I have a ready-made family. I may not have wanted or planned it but now that I have it, I will make the best of it because that is how I operate. Providing Xander with a suitable mother and giving him some sort of grounding is the least I can do to try to compensate for such a horrible start to his young life. And while you may not have much money or be familiar with the world's high spots, you have something which makes you extra-special, Lucy.'

'Really? And what might that be?' Lucy's heart quickened, though afterwards she would be ashamed of her needy desire to have him shower praise on her, because it didn't happen. Instead, he listed her credentials like an employer telling her why she had surprisingly beaten the other candidates.

'You're a trained nurse for a start,' he drawled, his Greek accent deep and velvety. 'A midwife as I recall, which makes you extra-suitable. And you are both pure and respectable, if what I discovered about you back in the summer was anything to go by. Once I started considering you for the role, I realised that your virginity was actually a great asset.'

He didn't seem to notice that his last remark had made her cheeks grow heated. Of course he didn't. He was talking *at* her instead of *to* her, wasn't he? He didn't really care about her thoughts and reactions—nor about the fact that he was making her sound like an upmarket brand of soap. To Drakon Konstantinou she was nothing more than a commodity.

'Rather than being a bit of a bore, which was how you seemed to regard it at the time?' she questioned rather snappily.

'Yes, you could put it like that,' he said, without missing a beat. 'Your purity now takes on an entirely different aspect, Lucy, and it has become important to me. It's an indication of the way you've lived your life. You haven't had a vast number of lovers before me, and such reserve is rare among women.'

'But what difference does my lifestyle make to what you have in mind?' she questioned. 'Why does it matter that I was a virgin?'

His mouth had hardened so that suddenly it resembled a savage slash across the lower part of his face and she could see coldness and calculation enter his black eyes.

'Because you will be able to lead by example. I want an old-fashioned woman with old-fashioned values and you are the perfect fit. This baby carries the genes of two addicts who were willing to put their own pleasure before his welfare,' he continued bitterly. 'Not only do I need to ensure that never happens again, I also need to stack the odds in Xander's favour from now on.'

Lucy didn't say anything. Not straight away. Not when he was looking so forbidding and so...*angry*— though she realised he was angry with his brother and not with her. She rose to her feet from the fireside chair because she felt at a psychological disadvantage having to stare up at him like that and it was making her neck ache. And she needed to put some distance between them. Some very necessary distance to get her thoughts in order. Away from the spell of his proximity and coercive weave of his words.

She walked over to the opposite side of the small room and stared out of the window at the river. The moon was beginning to rise and was forming a dappled silvery path on the darkening water and she could see that a cottage on the opposite bank must have put up their Christmas tree. She blinked as she stared at the glittering lights—rose and gold and green and blue— but felt none of the prescribed magic as she turned to meet Drakon's hooded gaze. 'Isn't the normal thing in these kind of circumstances to employ a nanny?' she questioned. 'Which you already have done, by the sound of it. You can afford to engage a whole battery of staff, Drakon. Why do you need a wife?'

He shook his head, like a man who had all the answers—but hadn't he always seemed like a man with all the answers? 'Obviously the child will need a full-time nanny and Sofia is eager to continue in that role,' he said, and paused. 'But that isn't the point, Lucy.'

'Isn't it?' she asked quietly.

'No.'

He shook his head and Lucy could see the bleakness in his eyes. She thought how *empty* his face looked. As if he'd been drained of all emotion so that he resembled some dark and forbidding statue. As if his body were composed of cold marble instead of flesh and blood, and a sudden trepidation whispered over her skin as she realised there was no real warmth in this man. 'I don't understand,' she breathed.

'Then let me make it clearer for you. I don't want this child to grow up in that kind of world—the adopted child of a single billionaire,' he bit out. 'I don't want him looked after by a series of employees with no emotional investment in his future, like I was. I don't want him sent away to school like I was. Xander needs a family. A real family.'

Lucy swallowed, wondering which of them was being naïve now. Did anyone truly know what a *real* family was—or did they all just rely on the slushy default version you saw in films, or read about in books, with people clustered round a fire, throwing their heads back in mutual laughter? Yet having a family was the bedrock of society, wasn't it? It was the dream which the majority of people aspired to, even if the reality was often so different. Was he really suggesting that the legal union of two people who had briefly been lovers could magically create some sort of fairy-tale household?

But then her mind began to focus on something else. On a single word the Greek tycoon had just uttered and which now lodged itself deep in her mind.

Xander.

Xander, his nephew and innocent little baby.

A motherless baby.

Lucy's heart clenched with a pain she should have anticipated because unwittingly Drakon had stumbled across her Achilles heel. The reason why she always felt as if something inside her was missing and incomplete. The one part of her life which could never be fulfilled, unless...

Her mouth dried.

Unless she was brave enough—or crazy enough—to accept the billionaire's bizarre offer. Because wasn't he offering her the magic-wand solution she had once yearned for in the form of instant motherhood? Her mind began to race. Could it work? Could she provide what little Xander needed—and in so doing gain for herself what she thought had been lost for ever?

Take it slowly, she told herself firmly.

Slowly.

'This sounds like a very long-term plan,' she suggested carefully.

'It is.' Some of the coldness had left his face and in its place she could see conviction. And persuasion. 'I'm talking endurance, Lucy. About putting a child's needs first and making a promise to each other that neither of us intends to break. About commitment and stability.'

'How can you be so sure you could find that with

me?' She stared at him. 'When you don't really *know* me. At school you were years ahead of me. I was just the school nurse's daughter who was allowed to take certain classes with the boys. Apart from those times when you were having the wound on your leg attended to, you didn't even notice me. We were just ships which passed in the night and, apart from that, we've only spent a few days together.'

'You think that time we spent on Prasinisos didn't provide me with the opportunity to discover something of what makes Lucy Phillips tick?' he enquired softly.

Lucy wanted to turn away from the mocking look in his eyes but that would be an immature response to a perfectly reasonable question. Because they *had* been intimate—and it would be hypocritical to pretend they hadn't.

'I can't deny we were lovers,' she husked. 'But physical intimacy during a mini-break on a Greek island is one thing. Real life is another. We're strangers, Drakon. How do you know I wouldn't drive you crackers before the first month was up?'

His eyes narrowed but Lucy couldn't mistake the brief flash of surprise which had gleamed there. As if he couldn't quite believe that she was prevaricating instead of instantly accepting his offer.

And wasn't there a part of her which couldn't quite believe it herself? Making out as if there were men lining up and asking her to marry them every day of the week!

'We would have to work at it, in the way that people with arranged marriages have always done,' he said. 'And we will be walking into it with our eyes open—

without any of the myths of love and romance which set people up for disappointment, and failure. If we refuse to have unrealistic expectations about each other, then we should succeed.' He slanted her a smile. 'Does that reassure you?'

Lucy thought how clever he was. And how controlling, too. That slow smile—she was certain—had been angled at her deliberately in order to pump up her heart rate and it had worked, hadn't it? Was that the main reason he was here—because he thought of her as passive? Wasn't it time to demonstrate that while she might be poor and unglamorous, that didn't necessarily mean she was a complete pushover? 'So what's in it for me, Drakon?' she questioned. 'What made you think you could turn up without warning and ask me to become your wife? Were you so certain I'd say yes?'

Drakon's eyes narrowed. He felt a certain responsibility towards her because he had unwittingly taken her virginity and had quashed his desire to see her again because he'd known he was capable of hurting her. He'd suspected that someone like her would be unable to cope with a commitment-phobe like him, even though he'd been sorely tempted to have sex with her again. But that had been back then—when his life had been free and unfettered. This was now, when he had an unexpected burden of responsibility to shoulder.

His mouth hardened. 'I had an idea you might be tempted.'

'Because?'

Would it be cruel to point out that without him a limited future inevitably beckoned for someone like her? But wouldn't any future be limited compared with the one he was offering her with all the money she could ever desire? He looked once again at her bare fingers. 'You don't show any signs of settling down,' he observed.

'Not at the moment, no.'

'So do you see yourself continuing to make ends meet as a relatively hard-up waitress?' he mused. 'Is that how you want the rest of your life to pan out?'

There was anger on her face now. And something which looked like pride. 'I don't just waitress. I actually help Caroline with all the cooking,' she declared icily. 'And she's indicated that she'd be prepared to let me buy the business when she eventually retires, which is what I've been saving up for. The waitressing is just a means to an end.'

'And that's what you really want, is it, Lucy? Resigning yourself to a life of relative poverty. Of a futile wait for Mr Right, perhaps—'

'Excuse me?' She pulled back her shoulders and glared at him. 'You think all women are just waiting around for a would-be husband to leap into their life?'

He gave a careless shrug. 'I'm saying that plenty of them are, yes—at least, in my experience. But if that's what you're hoping for, let me enlighten you. That man is just fantasy. He's someone who may or may not materialise,' he said softly. 'Whereas a rich man with whom you're sexually compatible—a man who really needs you—he's here. Right here.'

His words had got through to her, he could see that. Just as he could see the temptation which flickered in her blue eyes.

'And if I were to agree…' Her voice tailed off. 'What kind of marriage would you expect?'

Drakon heard the uncertain note in her voice but her darkening eyes told a different story. And suddenly he found himself being sucked into a vortex of erotic recall. He remembered the softness of her thighs and the untamed bush of hair which concealed her untouched treasure. For perhaps the only time in his adult sexual life, he had been momentarily astonished—and not just because she hadn't waxed—because what woman of twenty-eight was a virgin in this day and age? He remembered the soft gasp she'd given when he had entered her, the faint pain of her initial response quickly giving way to breathless murmurs of encouragement and then, to her first sweetly sobbing orgasm. And hadn't that felt sublime? Hadn't he experienced a deep satisfaction as she had choked out her pleasure against his bare shoulder, her ecstatic response filling him with a rush of primeval pleasure?

He'd made love to her countless times during those few short days—justifying his seemingly insatiable appetite with the assurance that he was simply enjoying introducing her to sex. But it had been more than that, even though he'd been loath to admit it then and was even less inclined to do so now. Her untutored eagerness had lit a strange yearning inside him—one which was being ignited right now.

He felt the exquisite throb of desire at his groin and heard the powerful thunder of his own heart. Maybe it was wrong to be thinking about sex at a time like this, but didn't they say the life force was at its most powerful during periods of grief and loss? Wasn't it nature's way of sustaining the human race, as well as reinforcing that, while his twin brother might be lying cold and dead beneath the hard earth, he, Drakon, was very much alive and at the mercy of his senses?

He began to walk towards her, noticing the instinctive tremble of her lips as he grew closer, but she didn't stop him, nor show any signs of wanting to. She just stood there, her blue eyes bright and questioning, her thick dark hair spilling out of the untidy plait which snaked down her back.

'I would expect the usual things which marriage entails,' he said huskily. 'Physical intimacy, for a start. I think that's one thing we both know we really do have in common.'

Distractedly, Lucy rubbed her toe against the rug, scarcely able to believe they were having this kind of conversation. Normally she didn't have to deal with anything more taxing than someone asking whether there were any gluten-free sandwiches available. Yet Drakon Konstantinou had just come right out and told her they were sexually compatible—him with a vast cast of ex-lovers and her with only one! She had no experience of such things but instinct told her that his words were true.

But was it *enough* for her to accept his offer of marriage? Enough for her to turn her back on her old life and enter a new one, which might be exciting but was tinged with uncertainty? With a father and a brother in the military she had grown up surrounded by uncertainty and she'd hated it. She'd longed for a safer world. A more predictable world. It was one of the reasons why she'd never really made waves in her own adult life. Why she'd always followed the rules and played safe.

Until she'd bumped into Drakon Konstantinou one balmy summer evening and the world had spun on its axis.

She knew she should say no. She should retreat back into her comfortable little world and try to forget the sexy billionaire and his bizarre offer.

But Lucy had been badly affected by what had happened to her family. In a few short years it had been wiped out as if it had never existed. Her father, brother and mother had all died in relatively quick succession. Orphaned and alone, she'd felt as if she had no real place anywhere. Sometimes she'd felt invisible. She still did. As if people were looking right through her. And all these feelings were compounded by the fact that she could never have children and be able to create a family of her own.

She stared into Drakon's rugged face, hope flaring inside her despite all her misgivings. Because the Greek tycoon was offering her exactly that. Something she'd once thought impossible but which, unlike him, she *had* wanted. An instant family. A baby to love and to care for. Her mouth dried. Could it work? Could she *make* it work? And by doing that give them both what they needed—he a wife and she a child?

She licked her lips. 'When do you need an answer by?'

'I don't see any point in waiting. I am a man who likes to settle a deal as quickly as possible. Now would be ideal.'

She shook her head. 'Now is too soon, Drakon. I

need a few days to process this. To mull over everything you've said and decide whether or not it could work. It's too big a consideration to just toss you an answer.'

His black eyes narrowed and in them Lucy could see speculation.

'Of course, there's another factor which needs to be considered. I'd hate you to overlook that, Lucy.'

She asked the question without really thinking about it. 'Which is what?'

He gave a slow smile. 'Use your imagination.'

The dip in his voice and the suddenly smoky light in his eyes made Lucy realise he was going to touch her and on one level she recognised that it was studied and manipulative. But it still worked, because Drakon knew how to press all her buttons. Even though an inner voice was urging caution, Lucy let him pull her in his arms to kiss her and, oh, she was hungry for that kiss.

So hungry.

Her fingers coiled around his broad shoulders as the voice of reason tried to warn her this was only going to confuse matters. But her body was refusing to listen to reason—its hungry demands silencing every sensible objection. Because this was amazing. Sweet sensations were flooding her body and her newly awoken sexual appetite—honed by five months of aching absence—made her think she might faint if Drakon didn't quell this sudden urgent need inside her.

His hand drifted up underneath her baggy sweater, his fingers encountering the shivering flesh of her torso before moving upwards to cup the straining mound of her breast. It was exquisite torture to feel her nipple pushing greedily against the lace of her bra, and all the while his lips were gently prising hers open. Exploring. Probing. Making her melt with the sensual flicker of his tongue. Making her writhe her hips in wordless appeal. She could feel the tension in his powerful body as he levered one powerful thigh between hers and it eased some of the pressure, even as it managed to build some more. She could feel the hardness at his groin. A hard ridge pressing urgently against the immaculate cut of his trousers, which told her graphically just how much he wanted her. She should have felt shy but that was the last thing she was feeling and Lucy knew that if the Greek had ripped off her jeans and panties before positioning himself where she was aching most, she would have taken him deep inside her.

'Drakon,' she choked out.

But her words seemed to shatter the spell as, abruptly, the kissing stopped. Moving his head away, he rocked back on his heels, inscrutable black eyes searching her face intently, and Lucy could see a nerve flickering at his temple. Had he decided he didn't want her after all? she wondered wildly. Had that rapid near-seduction been a demonstration of his power over her, rather than real desire? And did that mean he was about to withdraw his offer of marriage?

'Yes, I want you very much,' he said, scarily answering her unspoken question before directing a rueful glance at his watch. 'But now is not the time. Nor the place. Not when my car is waiting and I have a raft of meetings I need to attend. But it will keep.'

'K-keep?' she echoed.

'Neh,' he agreed, glittering her a sudden smile. 'I've

never been married before, Lucy. I've never wanted to be part of such a flawed institution, if the truth were known. But if I am to be your husband—which I fully intend to be—then there will be plenty of opportunity for lovemaking. And don't they say that hunger is the best aphrodisiac of all?'

All the time he was speaking, his fingertip was tracing a line along the edges of her lips and Lucy hated the way her mouth quivered in response. Just as she hated his arrogant assumption that she would be his wife when she hadn't given him her decision. 'But I haven't said I'll marry you yet. And I can't do that until I've met baby Xander,' she added firmly.

A look of calculation entered his black eyes. 'The key word is *"yet"*,' he observed silkily. 'For it indicates that your acceptance is simply a matter of time. We both know that.' His black eyes glittered. 'Because you will marry me, Lucy. Not just because I can reward you with the things most people spend their lives craving, but because you are in a position to help a vulnerable little baby as no other person could do right now. But that's not all. You will marry me because you want me and the only way you're going to have me is by agreeing to become my wife.'

CHAPTER THREE

THERE WAS BARELY any room for the limousine to make its way down the icy lane and Lucy's heart was hammering as she locked the door of her cottage and made her way towards the luxury car. She looked around at the leafless trees and frosty bushes as if committing them to memory one last time—because who knew when she would be back?

Inadvertently she cracked through an icy puddle and mud sloshed onto her newly polished boots as Drakon's chauffeur opened the door of the car, her tentative smile being met with nothing more than a deferential nod. As she slid onto the back seat she could feel her anxiety grow and the doubts which had been bugging her for days threatened to overwhelm her. She thought about the way Drakon had kissed her and the way her body had responded so hungrily. She thought about his track record with women and her own miserable tally of just one lover. She thought about how detached and indifferent he could seem, except when engaged in some form of sensual contact and a very real fear washed over her as she realised she was entering territory which was completely alien to her.

You don't have to do this, she told herself. *It's not too late to pull out. Nobody's forcing you to become the Greek tycoon's wife. If he can't get you to look after his orphaned nephew then his money will buy him the best care in the world. It isn't your responsibility.*

For a split second she thought about jumping out of the car. About rushing back to the sanctuary of her cottage and emailing Drakon to tell him she couldn't go through with it. But then the limousine's powerful engine fired into life and they were on their way to London and suddenly it was too late for Lucy to change her mind. And wasn't the truth of it that deep down she didn't want to, for all kinds of reasons? It certainly wasn't the lure of the Greek tycoon's glamorous lifestyle which was calling to her. She'd seen enough rich boys at the boarding school where her mother had worked to know that money certainly didn't come with a guarantee of happiness. The thought of having a baby and a family of her own was the most powerful motivator, of course it was—but there was something else, too. Something which was much more intangible, and that was the way Drakon made her feel whenever he touched her. As if she were real. As if she were capable of things she'd never imagined she could do. It was a heady feeling but it was tinged with a danger she didn't quite yet understand.

All through the journey to the capital, she tried to relax, trying her best to keep her boots from smearing mud on the pristine leather interior. Not for the first time she wondered what had happened to one of her suede moccasins, which had mysteriously gone missing—and it was something of a relief to be able to think about something unconnected to Drakon as she tried to work out exactly what had happened to it. Once she had exhausted all possibilities she tried to concentrate on the landscape which was rushing past the tinted windows, but her busy thoughts ensured that most of what she saw remained a blur until they reached the centre of London. And that was when Lucy blinked in surprise, feeling as if she'd emerged from her countryside bubble to arrive in a city she scarcely recognised.

Because Christmas was all around and it was as if the entire city had been taken over by Disney. The big stores were shiny with tinsel and glitter and fake snow. Red-clothed Santas with fluffy white beards rocked manically as little children pressed their noses against the plate-glass windows. Past the giant tree on Trafalgar Square the luxury car purred and when they stopped at some traffic lights, Lucy opened one of the windows slightly so she could hear the carol singers who were collecting money for the homeless. Her heart clenched as she registered the first notes of 'Silent Night' because it always reminded her of her brother, and quickly she pressed the button so that the electric window floated up to blot out the nostalgic carol. Instead she focussed on the crowds of people who all seemed to be on a mission, hell-bent on buying gifts even though there were several weeks left until the big day.

There were plenty of things Lucy liked about Christmas. The lights. The colours. The music. The way usually inhibited people went out of their way to smile and say hello. She just didn't like the way it made her *feel*, because it seemed to emphasise all the things she didn't have. It was a time when you could feel extra-lonely if you lived on your own because most people seemed to have somebody, while she had nobody. It was when she most missed having a family. When she found herself feeling emotionally vulnerable—which wasn't a particularly nice sensation. Usually she tucked herself away with a large supply of chocolate and sobbed her way through just about every corny film which was showing on TV.

But this year was going to be different. Her teeth pressed down hard on her bottom lip and she gnawed away at it. And how. She had a wedding to organise and—this was the bit she still couldn't get her head around—she was going to be a Christmas bride. At least, that was the plan—although nothing had been arranged just yet, which was making the thought of marrying Drakon seem even more surreal than it already was. Excitement and dread flooded through her, yet the truth was that, despite her misgivings about becoming the Greek tycoon's wife, she had stumbled at the first hurdle. She had fallen in love with his orphaned nephew.

Her throat thickened as she remembered meeting the tiny baby—a meeting on which everything had hinged. She had insisted on Drakon being absent. Had she been afraid he would influence her? That he would distract her with his powerful presence and remind her of how much she still wanted *him*? She had expected objections from the powerful tycoon. She'd imagined he might wish to observe her first contact with his tiny nephew as a kind of interactive job interview, but to her surprise he had agreed to stay away. She'd been jittery with nerves—because the thought of holding a baby again after so long had thrown up all kinds of complicated emotions. Alone, she had waited in one of the reception rooms of Drakon's vast London apartment until the nanny had appeared with a snowy white bundle in her arms. Greek-born Sofia must have been in her fifties, though her step was spritely as she carried the baby towards Lucy.

And Lucy remembered the compassion which had washed over her as she'd stared down at Xander's tiny head and it had been pure instinct which had made her extend her arms so that she could cradle the infant close to her racing heart. She had been prepared for the pain which had speared through her at the thought that she would never hold a child of her own like this, but not for the instant bonding which had followed. Had it been provoked by tenderness for one who had lost so much at such an early age, or by the tiny starfish hand which had clutched her extended finger and melted her heart?

She had asked if she could give the baby his bottle and then cuddled him until he had fallen asleep. And soon after Sofia had taken Xander back to the nursery, Lucy's telephone had rung, as if it had been programmed to do so.

'Well?'

Drakon's question had been terse and to the point and there had seemed little point in prevaricating. Why pretend that this was anything other than a cold-blooded business arrangement?

'Yes.' Lucy's voice had been low but unfaltering. 'I will be your wife.'

'Good.' There was a pause. 'In which case, you need to pack a case and I'll send a car to collect you. Be ready tomorrow morning.'

'So soon?'

'What's the point of waiting, Lucy? Delay will serve little purpose.'

'But I've got three cocktail parties next week for Caro's Canapés which I'm booked to work at.'

'Leave that to me. I will arrange a suitable replacement.' His voice had dipped to become a murmured caress. 'I intend for you to become my wife as quickly as possible and I think we both know the reason for that.'

Lucy had opened her mouth to say something and then shut it again. Because didn't she want that too? Wasn't there a tiny part of her which worried that if they left it too long, Drakon might suddenly change his mind and realise that it was a completely preposterous idea to marry someone like her? And wasn't it crazy to realise how gutted she would be if that were the case? 'No, tomorrow sounds absolutely fine,' she said compliantly.

Which was why she was now on her way to Drakon's Mayfair apartment and her brand-new life. Trying not to feel like Cinderella as she perched on the edge of the limousine's soft leather seat and attempted to keep her muddy boots elevated.

Her heart was pounding as they skirted Hyde Park and drove towards the imposing modern block in Mayfair, which commanded a prime view of the city's largest park. Lucy peered out of the window, her heart missing a beat as she saw Drakon's imposing figure imprinted darkly against the glittering windows of the block. She blinked in surprise. He was waiting, she realised. Waiting for *her*?

He seemed lost in thought and hadn't noticed the car, giving Lucy the opportunity to study him unobserved. She thought that seeing him standing on the street made him seem even more of a stranger than he already was. She noticed a blonde wearing dark glasses and a fur coat do a double-take as she walked past him with a tiny white dog trotting on a red lead, though unfortunately the dog chose that precise moment to cock its little leg against a lamppost. Yet wasn't that the type of sleek woman he *should* have selected as his wife? Lucy wondered painfully, trying and failing not to drink him in with her hungry gaze.

On the cold winter day, he was dressed entirely in black and the effect was to make him dominate his surroundings even more than usual. The inky overcoat echoed the dark gleam of his eyes but his mouth was hard and unsmiling. He'd had his hair cut and the rockstar strands were now neatly trimmed in a style which seemed to emphasise all his olive-skinned beauty. Suddenly she realised he could make her blood sing even from this distance away, although the day was so cold and wintry. Being around him was like having a *fever*, she thought, clasping her fingers together so tightly that the knuckles cracked.

Some sort of notification must have gone off, for he slid his phone from his inside pocket and glanced down at it, then narrowed his black eyes to focus on the approaching limousine. Had he been forewarned that she was on her way, perhaps by his taciturn driver? In desperation, Lucy glanced down to see that her hands were shaking and a sudden shiver of trepidation whispered over her skin before she dared lift her head to meet his gaze. Was she imagining the faint flash of disapproval in his eyes as the car purred to a halt and he moved forward to open the door for her?

A cold gust of wind whipped through her as she stepped onto the pavement, acutely aware of the fact that her best coat was looking decidedly threadbare and that, although she'd spent an hour last night buffing up her boots, their newfound shine didn't hide the fact that they were old. She'd tried to do her best with her appearance but her resources were limited and even if they hadn't been—what *did* a poor girl wear when she was about to move in with her billionaire fiancé? She felt like diving back into the car and begging the driver to take her home, but somehow she managed to scrabble together a memory—an important thing she'd learnt on her very first day on the wards as a student nurse. And afterwards, whenever her mother had sunk into one of her deep depressions and Lucy had attempted to help her spirits up. *Keep it positive. Look on the bright side.*

'So,' she said brightly, tilting her chin upwards and managing a faint reproduction of a smile. 'Here I am.'

Yes. Here she was. Drakon tensed as he felt a rush of something he didn't recognise. Was it incredulity that he'd selected this woman to be his bride when she couldn't have looked like a more unlikely candidate if she'd tried? But he'd had no choice. And wasn't that the story of his life? he reminded himself grimly. That unwanted responsibilities were always waiting in the shadows to grab at him and to direct his life onto a path he had never intended...

Her big blue eyes were looking at him uncertainly and something made him dip his head to brush his lips over hers in a fleeting kiss, amused by her instinctive intake of breath and the sudden confusion of her expression, as if she hadn't been expecting him to embrace her so publicly. In truth, he hadn't been expecting it himself, but he found himself turned on by the fact she wasn't wearing any make-up and by the provocative tremble of her lips. Maybe he should take her inside and kiss her a little more thoroughly, so that she would lose that rather unflattering look of apprehension and replace it with one of passion instead.

'Let's go inside,' he said abruptly. Drawing away, he ushered her into the luxury complex, past the security guard who was regarding her with open curiosity.

'What about my suitcase?' she was saying as they reached the elevator and the doors slid open.

'What about it?'

'I've left it in the car.'

'The driver will bring it inside shortly. You don't have to worry about things like that any more, Lucy.' Rather impatiently, he pressed the button. 'You'll find my staff will deal with the more humdrum elements of your life from now on and you won't have to bother with logistics. So why don't you just concentrate on getting to know one of your new homes?'

'One of them?' she affirmed breathlessly.

The wave of his hand was careless. Sometimes he forgot that the extent of his wealth was remarkable to most people and he supposed he should be grateful that his new fiancée hadn't already tallied up all his properties with greedy anticipation. 'I have homes in New York and Athens as well as this one,' he drawled. My Greek island villa you have already seen, of course.'

'Of course,' she said.

He watched as she fixed her eyes imploringly on the bright red arrow indicating their progress towards his penthouse apartment, as if she was finding the confined space in the elevator claustrophobic. *You and me both,* he thought unwillingly, his attention drawn to the curves of her body, which her thin grey coat couldn't quite disguise. He could feel the pump of his heart and the throb at his groin and wondered whether he should rid himself of some of the frustration which had been building up inside him for days now. But thoughts of seduction were vanquished by the words which burst from her lips almost as if she hadn't planned to say them, her blue eyes suddenly darkening so that they looked as blue as a Grecian sea.

'I wasn't...' She drew in a deep breath. 'To be honest I wasn't expecting to see you until this evening. I thought you'd be working.'

Surely that wasn't disappointment he could hear in her soft English voice? A flicker of a smile touched the edges of Drakon's lips. Maybe there was more fire to Lucy Phillips than he had initially given her credit for. 'I had a rare window in my diary and I thought it might be less daunting if I was here to greet you myself,' he explained as the elevator reached the penthouse and the doors slid open.

'That's very kind of you.'

'Make the most of it. I'm not usually known for my kindness,' he informed her drily. 'Come on in.'

Obediently, she followed him into the reception room, and he thought how much she resembled a new member of staff as she stood nervously in the centre of his modern London apartment with its bird's-eye view over the park. But in a way, that was exactly what she was. As his wife, she would be fulfilling her prescribed role just as adequately as one of his chefs, or drivers, or housekeepers. And wasn't her trepidation one of the reasons he had chosen to marry her? She was both compliant and inexperienced and because of that he could mould her into the kind of spouse he wanted her to be, just as he would train up a new assistant.

'It's huge,' she commented.

'But you've been here before. When you met Xander.'

'Yes. That's right. But I only saw the nursery areas. I had no idea there was this other huge section.' She looked around, cocking her head to one side as if listening for something. 'Where *is* Xander?'

Drakon still wasn't used to having the baby around and he frowned, trying to remember. 'Sofia has taken him to the doctor for some sort of routine check. At least, I think that's what she said.'

She sucked in a deep breath. 'You didn't consider it might be better if I could have gone along as well? If I'm to be his, well, his...mother.'

Something unknown clutched at Drakon's heart like a vice. Was it anger that his brother should have treated his son with such a failure of care and cast him into the unwanted role of father? Or fear that he would be incapable of giving this child any true affection, as his own father had been unable to give him? With an effort, he pushed the bitter memories away—for what good would they serve him now?

'There will be plenty of time for you to play happy families, Lucy. First things first. Let me show you around properly and then I have a surprise for you.'

'I'm not crazy about surprises,' she warned him lightly.

'I think you'll like this one,' he promised.

Lucy thought how arrogant he sounded. Did that mean she was going to have to *pretend*? To smooth the way for their future marriage by showing him gratitude at all times? Would that be the grown-up way to proceed?

She began to follow him through the huge apartment, trying and failing to remember the precise configuration of the rooms. But she would quickly learn where everything was, she reassured herself—despite the fact that the entire ground floor of her riverside cottage would have fitted into one of the en suite bathrooms! One of the vast reception rooms led into a book-lined study, which looked more like a public library and contained leather-bound volumes in both English and Greek. There was an enormous kitchen with an adjoining dining room, three big en suite bedrooms on one side of the wide corridor, as well as the nursery suite on the other, which was completely self-contained.

'I've given you your own bedroom,' he said as his footsteps halted. 'I decided it would be more appropriate if we slept apart until the wedding. Something

befitting the status of my relatively innocent fiancée.'
His black eyes gleamed. 'That doesn't mean we cannot be intimate or imaginative, of course.'

'Oh?'

'I'll be right next door,' he informed her. 'It will be like a throwback to a different age. I cannot tell you how much the novelty of that appeals to me, Lucy.'

Lucy's breasts had grown heavy at his provocative words but her erotic recall was forgotten the moment he pushed open the bedroom door. Her lips fell open but she barely noticed the amazing view or huge bed, or the superb painting of a tiny fishing village which looked suspiciously like the one on his private island. All she could see were the piles of clothes which were *everywhere*, making the room look more like the changing room of an upmarket department store than a bedroom. There were sleek dresses hanging in front of the built-in cupboards and a gorgeous plum-coloured coat with a velvet collar. One of the cupboards was open and inside she could see colour-coordinated lines of beautiful silky shirts, and skirts which varied from pencil to flounce. Further along the rail were more casual clothes—cashmere sweaters which bore little resemblance to her own hand-knits and denim jeans which she was doubtful she'd be able to slide over her curvy hips. This must be the surprise he'd been talking about.

'I hope you like them,' Drakon said as she continued to stare at it all in silence.

Lucy forced herself to say something dutiful which wouldn't sound ungrateful, because there was no denying he must have gone to a lot of trouble. 'They're gorgeous. Did you—?'

'Actually, my partner chose them.'

'Your partner?' she questioned blankly and, although it was unconscious sexism on her part, she instantly imagined some strapping Greek male walking into a store waving a charge card.

'Amy,' he supplied, clearly oblivious to the sudden uncertainty in her voice. 'We've worked together for years.'

She wondered if he was aware of the emotional impact of his words, or of the exact way he'd phrased them—because didn't his relationship with his partner sound way more intimate and close than the one he had with *her*? Lucy could feel her heart punching against her chest in a way which was making her feel almost dizzy. 'I see. And does... Amy choose all your girlfriends' clothes for you?'

'Never. But then I've never been in a situation like this before. I knew your wardrobe was insufficiently versatile to be able to cope with your new role as my wife,' he said, clearly seeking diplomatic words to take the sting out of his statement. 'And I thought you'd be too busy packing to have the time to hit the shops.'

Was that so? Or just that he thought she would fail miserably at the task? That her lack of experience—and money—meant she'd be incapable of selecting her own clothes? But Lucy tried to be positive and take Drakon at his word. She had to be, or this simply wasn't going to work. And she would never have chosen any of these exquisite clothes—not in a million years. She wouldn't have dared purchase items which individually probably cost more than she earned in a month. The question was whether she'd be able to change or return any without embarrassment if they turned out not to fit.

On a nearby chest she could see a deep drawer which was partially open and, sucking in a breath, she walked over and pulled it wide open to find it filled with the most provocative lingerie imaginable. Sexy thong panties were lined up beside balcony bras. Silk stockings and lacy suspender belts lay side by side and Lucy blinked at them in disbelief, sudden ice rippling down her spine. 'Please don't tell me your partner choose *these*?'

He shook his head and laughed. 'Of course not. I bought these myself. It happens to be the most enjoyable shopping trip I've done in years, if you must know. Do you like them?'

Lucy continued to stare at them as she considered his question. On the one hand, of course she did. This was the kind of underwear she'd never imagined herself wearing, not in her wildest dreams. It was impossible not to like such exquisitely made garments, nor to imagine the amount of work which must have gone into making them, but... She turned to him, blinking her eyes rapidly. 'How on earth did you know my size?'

He shrugged. 'I guessed.'

'You guessed,' she repeated slowly. 'Because you have such a comprehensive knowledge of a woman's body that you instinctively know what size bra she wears?'

'I'm in the ship-building industry, Lucy. Learning about dimensions comes with the territory.' A smile curved the edges of his sensual mouth. 'The shoes were a little more difficult.'

'The shoes?' she questioned blankly as the expansive wave of his hand indicated rows of high-heeled shoes and butter-soft leather boots she hadn't even noticed before. She wondered what on earth he was doing as he bent down to retrieve something from underneath the bed, and was momentarily taken aback when he produced a suede moccasin and waved it in the air—like a magician plucking a rabbit from a top hat. 'That's my shoe!' she declared.

'I know.' He gave slow smile. 'I picked it up from that pile by your front door so I could get your size right, on the day I asked you to marry me. It isn't really a winter shoe, so I didn't think you'd notice it had gone.'

It took a couple of seconds before Lucy could bring herself to speak and when she did her words came spitting out like bullets. 'I *did* notice, as it happens. I don't actually own enough pairs of shoes not to realise when one goes missing.' She glared at him, still not quite believing what he'd just told her. 'So let me get this straight. You thought you'd go ahead with some modern-day enactment of Cinderella's slipper and I'm supposed to coo with delight in response?'

'I certainly had hoped for something a little more enthusiastic than your current reaction,' he offered drily.

'Well, please don't bother in future. Like I said, I'm not the biggest fan of surprises. In fact, don't bother with—'

But her sentence was destined never to be completed because Drakon had pulled her into his arms and was kissing her. Kissing her so thoroughly that all the breath left her lungs. And Lucy let him. No, that wasn't quite true. She actively encouraged him. Was it lack of oxygen which made her so instantly yielding? Which made her gasp out a note of breathless approval as his mouth roved hungrily over hers, before darting her tongue into his mouth as if it were a weapon? Or was it simply that she was so *incensed* by what he'd done—by his arrogance and control—that she felt as if she'd been taken over by a different kind of desire? So that very quickly the kiss became something it had never been on Prasinisos. This wasn't soft and searching but punishing, and hard. It was driven by frustration—that he had been so high-handed about overhauling her appearance and given someone she'd never met *carte blanche* to play such a key role in changing it. But there was physical frustration, too, gnawing away inside her like some alien creature she had no idea how to handle. She wondered if sex would release some of the tight frustration which was coiling inside her like a compressed spring. Whether now was the time to tell him she didn't want his *partner* buying her clothes for her. That she wasn't just some kind of doll who could be dressed up for his approval before she was permitted to be seen in public.

'I don't know why we're fighting about clothes, Lucy,' he said unevenly as they broke away to drag oxygen into their air-starved lungs. 'Since my expressed preference is to see you not wearing anything at all.'

And wasn't it pathetic how thrilled she was to hear that husky compliment? As if she was only just beginning to realise that, despite her somewhat homely appearance and complete lack of fashion sense, Drakon

Konstantinou really *did* fancy her. But that was one of the reasons she was here, Lucy reminded herself. Her midwifery training wouldn't mean a thing without the white-hot chemistry which seemed to combust whenever they touched.

She felt blindsided by the sense of something which, having been awoken, now needed urgently to be fed. Was that why she let him kiss her again and to deepen it with provocative intimacy, so that she moaned softly into his mouth? And something about that moan made him lever her up against the wall, his face dark and inscrutable as he looked down at her. She could sense the tension which was making his powerful body seem as tight as a strung bow and, where they were touching, her skin felt as if it were on fire.

His fingers were unbuttoning her grey coat and unashamedly roving beneath her sweater and when he jutted his hips forward like that, she could feel the hard column of his erection pressing against her. Beneath her thick denim jeans the molten slick of desire made itself known and Lucy longed for him to touch her there. His fingers were whispering over the cool skin of her torso, moving down towards the top button of her jeans, and she shivered as he popped it open then slid her zip down with a dexterity which suggested he must have undressed millions of women before.

But suddenly Lucy saw herself as an outside observer might see her—all windswept and rumpled with the Greek tycoon's fingers burrowing their way inexorably towards her panties. Why, she hadn't even taken her coat off! She'd only been in his apartment for ten minutes and all they'd done was to fight and kiss and now he was about to take it one step further. If she didn't put a halt to this then before she knew it, she would be pressed up against that wall with Drakon thrusting deep inside her.

She pressed her hand against his chest, feeling the powerful pound of his heart beneath her palm. 'We need to stop this right now.'

'Oh, Lucy. That's not the message I was getting a moment ago,' he drawled.

Well, it's the m-message you're getting now,' she said, unable to iron the tremble from her voice. 'I need to freshen up before Sofia comes back with the baby and to…'

'To what?' he questioned mockingly as her words tailed off.

Lips pressed together, she gave him a determined smile. 'To unpack my case and settle in. And to be honest, Drakon…' She hesitated. 'I think you're right about having separate rooms, but let's do it properly, shall we—with no sneaking around the corridors at midnight? Maybe we *should* wait until we're married until we have…"

'Sex?' he supplied, his eyebrows arching in disbelief. 'Is that what you're trying to say?'

She could feel hot colour flooding her cheeks and, although she realised she could be accused of having double standards, wasn't it better this way? Because what if her earlier doubts came true and she drove him crazy—wouldn't it be easier to draw a line under the whole thing if they *hadn't* become lovers? Easier to walk away if she hadn't had a second distracting taste of physical intimacy? And it would do Drakon good to demonstrate that he wasn't the one making all the rules, and she wasn't going to be totally submissive. To show him that she might have agreed to this marriage of convenience but that didn't make her into some sort of *puppet*.

'That's exactly what I'm trying to say,' she agreed primly.

Still he waited, as if she was going to suddenly turn around and tell him she was joking—as if no woman in her right mind would refuse the opportunity to fall into bed with him at the earliest opportunity.

And Lucy wouldn't have been human if she hadn't enjoyed the brief look of disbelief which flashed from Drakon's ebony eyes when he realised she meant every word she said.

CHAPTER FOUR

LUCY AWOKE TO the sound of a baby's cry and instinct made her sit bolt upright in bed, her heart clenching with painful recognition. Hunger, she thought, as she listened some more. Funny how you could still recognise the different nuances of an infant's cry even though it had been so long since that sound had been part of her daily routine.

Heavy-eyed after a restless night, she got out of bed and it took a few seconds for her befuddled brain to realise she wasn't tucked up in her cosy riverside cottage, but in the fanciest bedroom she'd ever seen. Her new home. The vast Mayfair apartment where she would live as wife to one of the world's most powerful men. Above her head, a chandelier glittered like a shoal of falling diamonds and silk rugs lay strewn over a pale wooden floor, which felt deliciously silky against her bare feet. Grabbing her dressing gown, she knotted it tightly around her waist. It was actually her old dressing gown which she'd brought with her from home because it seemed that her luxury replacement wardrobe didn't cater for a sensible garment you could throw on first thing in the morning to cover up your pyjamas and feed a baby in. *Presumably because once she was married she would no longer be wearing pyjamas.* Running her fingers through her hair to tame its tousled wildness, she set off towards the nursery.

The crying had stopped by the time Lucy got there and she was greeted by a scene of perfect domesticity. Sofia was sitting on a yellow sofa giving Xander a bottle while soft nursery rhymes played gently in the background. It felt a little strange for Lucy to be standing in her nightclothes in front of someone she'd only met a couple of times but the middle-aged nanny merely looked up and gave her a friendly smile as she entered the room.

'Good morning, Lucy,' she said. 'Did you sleep well?'

'Very well, thank you,' said Lucy with more politeness than truth—because nothing was more boring than hearing someone relate the story of what a bad night they'd had. She certainly didn't want Sofia quizzing her about the reasons for her restlessness. *Reason,* she corrected herself silently. One reason alone—all six feet three of him. 'You should have woken me.'

Sofia shook her head. 'Drakon said you were to be left undisturbed.'

Drakon. Lucy started at the mention of his name and she thought—how pathetic is *that*? Had her heart missed a beat because she'd resisted his sexual overtures when she'd arrived yesterday and been haunted by tantalising dreams about him ever since? Or because it was still difficult to believe that the gorgeous billionaire would soon be her husband and that this was now her reality? A reality brought home by the stilted dinner they'd shared last evening, presided over by his stern-faced housekeeper, Zena—a meal which had kept being interrupted while Drakon had dealt with one international phone call after another. He'd been talking to someone in New York when eventually Lucy had excused herself and his absent wave of farewell as she'd headed off to her bedroom had spoken volumes. He hadn't followed her and she hadn't really expected him to, because instinct told her that a man like Drakon would never beg a woman for intimacy when she had told him it wasn't going to happen. She'd lain there listening until eventually she'd heard him heading for bed, freezing with hope and expectation as his footsteps had paused outside her door, before moving on. As an introduction to life in the fast lane, it hadn't exactly felt welcoming. Or maybe he had just been making a point…

She stood in the doorway watching as Sofia fed the baby and suddenly felt almost redundant. With a touch of anxiety she licked her lips and looked around, but the room was pristinely tidy. 'Is there anything I can do? Some dusting, or tidying up?'

'No, honestly, I'm fine. It's all under control. Drakon employs an army of people to do the housework for him. He's going down for a nap shortly but you could do the midday feed if you like. But only if you have time before you go out for lunch,' Sofia amended hastily.

Lucy maintained her bright smile even though she was aware that her voice sounded brittle. 'I wasn't aware that I *was* going out for lunch.'

Sofia's eyes crinkled in a smile. 'Apparently. Zena

told me. The car has been ordered for you. Lucky you,' she added, in her perfect but heavily accented English. 'It will inevitably be somewhere grand.'

Lucy hoped her expression didn't give away her feelings as she returned to her bedroom and tugged off her dressing gown. Whether or not the restaurant was grand was completely beside the point. It was one thing to agree to a marriage of convenience, she thought furiously as she stood beneath the fierce blast of the shower. But quite another when she was being treated a convenience. Did Drakon think he could just move her around like a vacuum cleaner? How come the housekeeper and the nanny knew she was going out for lunch, when it was a mystery to her?

She dried her hair and, for the first time, tried on some of the new clothes which had been chosen by his business partner, Amy. Last night at dinner she'd stubbornly insisted on wearing one of her own dresses, still needled by the fact that Drakon had asked someone else to kit her out for her new role in his life. Yet hadn't her defiance backfired on her, so that she'd been left having to endure the entire meal feeling somewhat *less than*? Her navy shirt-dress dress was her go-to favourite but there was no doubt that the fabric looked cheap against all the unrestrained luxury of Drakon's home and Lucy was certain his housekeeper had been looking down her nose at her, as if wondering why someone like her was associating with the impeccably clad tycoon. Hadn't the same question crossed her own mind more than once as the evening had progressed?

So just go with the flow, she told herself as she rifled through the colour-coordinated rows of garments before pulling out a long-sleeved dress in silk chiffon. The soft violet hue was the colour which sometimes tinged a late sunset and, admittedly, a shade she would never have thought of choosing for herself. The delicate fabric floated to just above the knee and made her waist look positively *tiny*, and she teamed it with a pair of shoes higher than anything she'd ever worn before. Did the added height make her assume a rather awkward gait? Was that why the middle-aged housekeeper did a double-take as Lucy cautiously picked her way into the dining room for breakfast?

'Good morning, Dhespinis Phillips,' said Zena.

'Good morning, Zena.' Lucy sat down at the table and gave the housekeeper a nervous smile. 'Um…is Drakon…?'

'The master went to the office at seven this morning, but he left you a note,' said Zena, indicating an envelope which was propped up in front of a vase of flame-coloured roses. 'I will bring you some breakfast.'

'Thank you.'

Lucy thought about the housekeeper's words as she picked up the envelope. The master. It was an oddly archaic term of address yet it seemed scarily suitable. Because Drakon *was* the master, wasn't he? The master of all he surveyed. At least that was the impression he gave, with his cabal of loyal staff, his enormous wealth and his different homes dotted around the world. Was he expecting to become *her* master once they were wed— was she to obey him in all things, as the marriage ceremony used to demand but which most modern couples now rejected? And shouldn't this be something they discussed before she allowed him to slide that gold ring on her finger?

Slitting open the envelope, she pulled out a single sheet of paper, realising that this was the first time she'd ever seen Drakon's writing. It was exactly as she would have imagined it to be. Angular black lines slashed over the thick writing paper. Succinct, forceful and strong. A reluctant smile curved the edges of her lips. Just like him.

My car will pick you up at 12.25. We'll eat lunch at the Granchester for reasons which will quickly become evident.

Mysterious as well as autocratic, she thought as she drank some inky Greek coffee and picked at a bowl of iced mango, before getting up to leave.

She spent the next hour exploring the sprawling apartment and studying some of the books she found in the library, before going to the nursery to give the baby his feed. But at least her interaction with Xander cheered her, and as he glugged greedily on the teat she buried her nose in his silky hair, remembering how much she loved tiny babies and how much she'd missed them. And this baby would soon be her *son*. The child she had always longed for and never thought she'd have.

But she couldn't stem the dark doubts which began to crowd into her mind as she winded the infant and laid him in his crib. He was so cute, with his black eyes and matching hair—a miniature version of his father's identical twin brother. What if she fell hopelessly in love with this little infant and her marriage failed, as so many marriages did, despite Drakon's determination for that not to happen? Because he couldn't control everything, could he, no matter how much he tried?

He'd told her he didn't believe in love and that he'd never been in love—but who was to say that the thunderbolt wouldn't one day hit him, as it had hit so many cynical disbelievers in the past? In that scenario, wouldn't she become an also-ran in Xander's life? The woman with no blood ties with no real claim on the child who could be dispensed of as carelessly as you would yesterday's newspapers. Lucy sighed, knowing she mustn't think like that because nobody was ever given any guarantees in this life—you just had to do the best you could in the circumstances.

She was nervous as she snuggled herself into the cashmere coat with the velvet collar and slid into the back of the waiting limousine, and even more nervous when the car drew up outside the landmark Granchester Hotel after a ridiculously short journey from the apartment. Outside the impressive building, she could see an enormous Christmas tree, topped with a huge golden star and smaller gold and silver stars which dangled from the abundant branches. The doorman hurried forward to open the door for her and Lucy gingerly made her way into the gilded foyer in her new shoes, her heart missing a beat when she spotted Drakon, with his back to her, standing beside another decorated fir tree—almost as big as the one at the front of the hotel.

Dark, broad-shouldered and powerful, he seemed oblivious to the stares he was attracting from the other guests and she wondered whether something must have alerted him to her approach. Why else did he suddenly turn around? He was mid-conversation on his phone but his eyes narrowed and his words seemed to die away as she approached and, abruptly, he cut the call. Something about the way he was looking at her was making her feel breathless and excited and scared all at the same time and Lucy found herself resenting his effortless power over her.

'Lucy,' he murmured as he helped her slide the coat from her shoulders. 'You're here.'

'Yes, I'm here. Though I could have walked in less time than it took to drive!'

'I don't think so. Not in those shoes,' he commented wryly, his gaze travelling down to her feet and lingering on them for longer than was strictly necessary.

'You don't like them?' she asked, berating herself for needing reassurance but asking for it all the same.

Drakon heard the genuine doubt in her voice and, unusually, he was surprised—searching her face for signs of disingenuousness and finding none. Was she out of her mind? Didn't she realise that every man in the place was staring at her as if she'd just tumbled down from the heavens? Of course, she didn't. Because she was totally without guile, he realised. An innocent who stood out from the women he usually mixed with. But she looked *incredible*. Having slipped the coat from her shoulders, he saw the filmy dress, which hinted at the firm flesh which lay beneath, and in those spike-heeled shoes… He swallowed. Didn't her calves look ripe for stroking and her ankles made for wrapping around a man's neck?

'I like them very much,' he said unevenly. 'In fact,

there's a term which is commonly used to describe shoes like those but I don't think that now is the right time to introduce it into the conversation.'

Predictably, she blushed and Drakon felt a powerful beat of lust, which made him wonder why he'd arranged to meet her here, in one of the most public venues in the city, rather than exploiting the intimacy of his nearby apartment. *You know why,* he thought grimly. Because she had firmly stated that they weren't going to have sex until they were married and he was in no doubt that she meant it. Just as he was aware that he was in part responsible for her old-fashioned stance.

He frowned. He'd thought he'd tantalise her by offering her a separate room, thinking that *interludes* of pleasure would keep her on her toes. More than that, he liked his own space and was used to it because he'd never shared a bedroom full-time with a woman before. He'd thought he would use the opportunity for some extended personal space before things changed once they were married.

Yet Lucy had neatly turned the tables on him by telling him she thought they should wait until after the wedding before being intimate again. He sighed with frustration and anticipation—tinged with a grudging sense of admiration, because he couldn't think of another woman who would have refused to have sex with him.

And if that was the way she wanted to play it, why not go along with it? He had chosen her because of her pliability but the fact that she was now showing some token resistance made this arranged marriage of theirs seem a little less predictable. In a way, it amused him to let Lucy Phillips think she was calling the shots, because he could have broken her self-imposed sexual embargo any time he wanted. He knew that and he suspected she knew it, too.

The pupils of her eyes were huge and dark and he could sense the sudden tension in her body as she met his gaze, as if silently acknowledging the inexplicable chemistry which was sparking between them. He'd never seen her looking so sleek and so sexy. He'd never imagined she would scrub up this well. The tremble of her lips kick-started something indefinable inside him and a lump rose in his throat. Drakon swallowed, certain that if he reached out to whisper his fingertips over the pulse which fluttered so wildly at the base of her neck, or snaked his hand around her impossibly slender waist, she would do the predictable thing, and melt against him with a hunger which matched his.

But leaving aside the fact they were in a public space, it would be wrong to act on hormonal impulse. He would use restraint because this was too important a deal to jeopardise with sexual impatience. And if he was being honest, wasn't it turning him on to an unbearable pitch at the thought of being made to wait—he who'd never had to wait for a woman in his life? True, she might be playing games with him—possibly in an attempt to make him fall in love with her—but that certainly wasn't going to give him any sleepless nights. She would soon discover he was immune to the ruses women employed and was not in the market for 'love'. All he cared about was that Lucy Phillips was going to make the perfect mother to his adopted son and the exquisite sharpening of his sexual appetite in the meantime was simply a bonus.

Touching his fingers to her back, he guided her towards the Garden Room restaurant. 'Come on. Let's go and have lunch.'

They walked along a long corridor, where golden baubles and scarlet ribbons were woven into the seasonal greenery which festooned the walls, and he watched as she looked around and drank it all in.

'What an amazing hotel,' she exclaimed. 'It's enormous!'

'You've never been here before?'

'Funny you should say that, but no,' she answered, dead-pan. 'Five-star hotels aren't my usual stomping ground on one of my rare visits to the capital. I've seen photos of it, obviously.'

'I thought we could get married here,' he offered casually.

'Here?' she said, coming to an abrupt halt just before they reached the restaurant entrance and nearly losing her balance on the spike-heeled shoes.

'You really don't like surprises, do you?' He put out an arm to steady her. 'Why shouldn't we? It's a very famous wedding venue.'

'I know it is! Don't film stars and princes choose it for their nuptials?'

'I don't keep tabs on celebrity weddings unless I happen to be a guest at them,' he drawled. 'But Zac Constantinides, the owner, is a friend of mine, so he's given us a date when it was supposed to be shut. As a favour, you understand.'

'Of course,' she said faintly.

'It's a perfect solution, especially this close to Christmas. So what do you say, Lucy? Apparently, there's an in-house wedding planner who'll do most of the donkey work for you.'

Lucy registered his puzzled expression as she hesitated. Was he expecting her to gush her thanks, or swoon about the sumptuousness of the venue, instead of standing there chewing her lip in a state of nervous anxiety? But she was having difficulty getting her head round the idea of someone like her standing up in a place this grand and making her wedding vows.

But what was the alternative? Surely she could overcome her nerves enough to get married in one of the world's most glamorous venues—especially if she was marrying such a high-profile man. And wouldn't the wedding co-ordinator take away some of the stress?

'You had something else in mind?' he prompted, when still she said nothing.

Lucy shook her head. 'You don't mind the fact that it will be a very *public* wedding?'

'You think I want to hide the fact away? I'm Greek, Lucy,' he said simply. 'And we Greeks like a good party.'

'Okay,' she said, speaking as quietly as possible in order to eliminate any telltale tremble of nerves. 'In that case—why not?'

'Not the most rapturous reaction I might have hoped for,' he observed drily. 'But I suppose it will have to do. Come on. Let's eat.'

The maître d' greeted him with easy familiarity as he showed them to a table which offered a perfect view of the winter garden, with its icy fountain and dark red branches of dogwood.

'Are we celebrating anything in particular today, Mr Konstantinou?'

'We certainly are. Ask the sommelier to bring my fiancée a glass of Dom Perignon rosé, would you, please, Carlos?'

There was a split-second pause and, when he spoke, Carlos's voice sounded faintly strangulated. 'Certainly, sir. And for yourself?'

'Just water, thanks.'

Lucy waited until they were alone before she spoke. 'That man looked as if he'd just been hit by a sledge-hammer when you described me as your fiancée.'

'He was probably surprised, *neh*. I have a reputation which precedes me.'

'What kind of reputation?'

He gave a wolfish smile. 'As a man who has never wanted to settle down. A man who was fundamentally opposed to marriage. Maybe I was unconsciously drawing a line in the sand, to demonstrate that, from now on, things are going to be very different.'

Were they? Lucy wondered distractedly. But how different? A glass of champagne was placed in front of her but she stared uninterestedly at the fizzing pink bubbles before lifting her eyes to Drakon. 'I suppose you've brought loads of women to this hotel in the past? Probably to have lunch in this very restaurant before taking them to bed?'

His black gaze was very steady. 'I'm not going to lie to you, Lucy. I was never promiscuous or indiscriminate but I'm thirty-one, single and, yes, of course I've slept with women during that time. Why wouldn't I? The evidence is everywhere if you care to look for it—because you can find out pretty much anything online.' He leaned forward, across the starched linen of the tablecloth. 'But I'm hoping you won't bother because I'm being perfectly transparent with you. I see no point in pretending to you, or rewriting history. You may have been a virgin when we hooked up, but I most certainly was not.'

'So why announce our engagement to someone you don't really know? Was that really necessary?'

'I think so. Carlos is perfectly aware how these things work.' He gave a flicker of a smile. 'He'll mention it to someone, who'll mention it to someone else. The press will get to hear about it and there will be a diary piece—only by then it will be old news.' There was a brief pause. 'Like I said, it draws a line in the sand and discourages any hopeful overtures from ex-lovers.'

His statement was more matter-of-fact than arrogant and Lucy told herself it shouldn't have bothered her, but it did, and she was taken aback by the hot flash of jealousy which pulsed through her. But of *course* he would have plenty of exes eager to return into his life. Hadn't she been pretty keen to see him herself when she'd returned from Prasinisos, forever glancing at her mobile phone and wondering if he would ring? Which, of course, he hadn't.

And that was what she needed to remember. The one fact which should never be far from her mind. That she would never have seen Drakon Konstantinou again if his brother and sister-in-law hadn't decided to go on a narcotic-fuelled bender and leave their baby son with no parents.

'Did Xander have any other relatives?' she asked suddenly. 'Apart from his mother?'

He shook his head. 'I put an investigator on the case. Niko's wife was adopted as a baby, but had been estranged from her family for many years. There were no living blood relatives, so Xander will have no connection with the past.' His expression grew shuttered. 'And it will be better for him in the long run. Much better.'

'In your opinion.'

'It's my opinion which counts,' he said cuttingly. 'And what I say goes. And I'd rather my adoptive son wasn't in the grip of people I don't know. People who might influence him to follow the same sorry path as his parents.'

Feeling faint, Lucy gripped the stem of her champagne flute, but she didn't lift it to her lips. She was afraid that her hands would tremble too much and she would spill it all over the perfectly starched tablecloth. Because it wasn't just the things Drakon had said which freaked her out, but the way he'd said them. He'd sounded so...*ruthless*. As if you could take the parts of somebody's life which you didn't like and simply wipe them out—like airbrushing a photo or altering something on your camera phone. But if he'd sounded ruthless it was because he *was*, she reminded herself. She should forget that at her peril. Suddenly she was glad that she was going to be there for baby Xander. Glad she would be able to fight his corner, because surely he needed someone there for him when Drakon started being even more high-handed than usual.

Eventually she felt calm enough to take a sip of wine, which eased some of her tension, and beneath the table she stretched out her legs, her new pointy shoes touching what she thought was the leg of the table, but Drakon's mocking eyes informed her that she'd made direct contact with his calf. Hastily, she jerked her foot away and his gaze grew more thoughtful.

'So why don't you like surprises?' he asked suddenly.

It was a question she hadn't been expecting, and if she hadn't been so blindsided by everything which had happened in the last twenty-four hours Lucy might have glossed over it—because why revisit pain when you didn't have to? But Drakon seemed to have an uncanny knack of getting her to open up. He'd done it on the night of the school reunion and he was doing it again now. She wondered if it was because he'd known her so long ago, in those days when she'd had a mother and a brother and hadn't been such a lost soul. And surely if they were planning on spending the rest of their lives together, he needed to know some of the things which made her tick. Only some of them, mind. A twist of guilt seared her heart and she stared down at her fingernails before looking up to meet the searching gleam of his eyes. 'I guess I just associate surprises with unpleasant things.'

'What kind of things?'

'Oh, you know.' She shrugged her shoulders restlessly. 'All the stuff which comes with having family in the military. The heavy knock at the door, or the ring of the telephone late at night. The men in uniform who stand on your doorstep with grim faces as they prepare to give you the news.' News which rocked the foundations of your world and made you realise nothing was ever going to be the same again. Yet hadn't it been those experiences that had provided the lessons which had enabled Lucy to ring-fence her emotions and keep herself safe from pain? Which had forced her to build barriers around her heart so she could never be hurt like that again? She folded her lips together. Wasn't that one of the *good* things about agreeing to marry a man like Drakon—that he had spelt out he didn't do love either? He had his own emotional barriers in place and that made them equal in a totally unexpected way. He could never hurt her because she would never let him get that close.

And the bottom line was that he didn't want to get close.

'That must have been tough,' he observed.

'Life is tough, Drakon—as I'm sure Xander would tell us if he were able to speak.'

He nodded, his eyes still searching her face, as if he was seeing something he hadn't noticed before. 'I don't want any more children,' he said suddenly.

'I'm sorry?'

'More kids.' His voice was rough. 'One is my limit and if you want more—'

'I don't,' she said quickly, as relief washed over her. 'I think children should only ever be conceived in love and we've both agreed that isn't what is driving this marriage of ours.'

His nodded slowly, his eyes narrowing. 'There's something else we haven't addressed,' he said softly.

Her brow creased. 'Which is?'

'The ring.'

'The ring?' she repeated.

'An engagement ring. It's fairly traditional in most cultures, as far as I'm aware. Surely you must have been expecting one, Lucy? I thought all women had preferences about what kind of jewels they'd like in this situation.'

'No, Drakon, all women do not—at least, not those of us who live relatively normal lives. I have better things to do with my time than drool about diamonds.' Recklessly, she took another mouthful of champagne— a much bigger one this time—which really went to her head. *Serves you right,* she thought dazedly as she carefully replaced the glass on the table. 'I'm astonished you didn't ask your partner, Amy, to select one for me as she did my clothes,' she said, in an acid tone she'd never heard herself use before. 'Or maybe she already has?'

He shook his head. 'The answer is no on both counts. She couldn't have done even if I wanted her to because she's flown out to Singapore on business.'

'Gosh. How will you be able to manage without her?' she questioned, the lingering effects of the wine still evident in her unusually flippant tone.

'Amy's absence certainly makes me realise how hard she works.' Almost carelessly, he slid a small box across the table. 'I bought this for you myself, so if you don't like it you're at liberty to change it.' As Lucy continued to stare at it, he lowered his voice into a murmured command. 'Stop looking at it as though it were an unexploded bomb. Open it.'

With faltering fingers she did just that, and it was a

measure of just how glitzy the world in which she now found herself that Lucy realised she was expecting to see a whacking great diamond, or an emerald the size of a gull's egg. Because wasn't that what billionaires usually bought for their future brides, especially if it was an arranged marriage? Some huge chunk of glittering gemstone which would be way too big for her finger and look like paste on someone so unremittingly ordinary.

But as she flipped open the box to reveal a ring, it was to discover that Drakon had surprised her and in a way she almost wished he hadn't, because it made her feel quite breathless. Set in embellished gold was a square-cut sapphire the indefinable colour of a spot of ink dropped into a beaker of water, which glittered in the pale winter light that streamed in through the windows. It was delicate, unusual and beautiful. The most beautiful ring she had ever seen.

'What made you choose this?' she questioned shakily.

He shrugged. 'The jeweller asked me what colour your eyes were.'

Lucy's heart raced and a strange, restrictive dryness in her throat made it difficult for her to speak as for one split second she allowed herself to sink into a fantasy of longing. 'And you remembered?'

'It's hardly neuroscience, Lucy. I only saw you a couple of days ago.' His slightly impatient look was followed by a dismissive shake of his head as he picked up his menu. 'Come on. Let's order. I have a meeting this afternoon.'

CHAPTER FIVE

STANDING IN ALL her wedding finery and trying not to let her nerves get the better of her, Lucy waited in the anteroom of the grand ballroom where her marriage to Drakon was about to take place. Tightly, she gripped her bouquet, which contrasted so vividly with the snowy whiteness of her dress. Scarlet roses flared like beacons amid the lush greenery and a sprig of mistletoe had been playfully added at the last minute by the Granchester's in-house florist, as a nod towards the fact that it was almost Christmas.

Donna, the wedding planner, had arranged for carols to be piped through the hotel's sophisticated sound system because 'everyone loves Christmas carols'. But if the seasonal songs were supposed to be soothing or comforting then they had failed in their mission because Lucy's brow was clammy and her heart was racing beneath the heavily embellished dress which she'd been persuaded into against her better judgment. She'd wanted something simple. Something plain, in ivory—an outfit she didn't have to think about, rather than something which would wear *her*. But the dress designer had explained that a room as grand as the

Granchester ballroom needed a gown to stand out among all the lavish fixtures and fittings. Something which would fill the makeshift aisle rather than getting completely lost in it. Which was why she was wearing jewel-encrusted white silk satin, with an oversized veil cascading down her back, looking as if a tipper truck had just offloaded a ton of sequin-sprinkled meringue.

Her throat felt like dust and her lips were dry and she kept thinking, *Surely this isn't how a bride is supposed to feel?* Lost and displaced and alone. Wondering what she'd let herself in for and whether she'd been a fool to accept the Greek magnate's offer of marriage. But how did she *expect* to feel, when the hectic preparations for the imminent ceremony seemed to have done nothing but emphasise the huge differences between her and her billionaire bridegroom? Especially since, after citing a busy work schedule, Drakon had absented himself from all the arrangements—except for providing a list of guests he wished to be invited, which hugely outnumbered her own.

'So it's definitely just *five* guests on your side?' The wedding planner had clearly been puzzled as she'd looked at Lucy expectantly, as if waiting to be told there'd been an elemental mix-up in the numbers and she'd missed off a nought.

Lucy's smile had stayed firmly in place. 'That's right.'

'Okay… Well, if you're *quite* sure…'

She supposed it wasn't conventional for the bride to be so sparsely represented but Lucy had been strong in her determination only to have people there who meant something to her. Wasn't this wedding fake enough already without her shipping in a load of guests just for show? Her parents and brother were dead and her only other living relative was Auntie Alice, who lived in Australia and had been unable to make the wedding this close to the holidays. And it wasn't as if she and Drakon had already formed lots of friends between them as a couple, was it? They'd barely spent more than a couple of hours together at a time during the frantic run-up to the big day.

And whose fault was that?

Hers and hers alone. Her determination to keep their sleeping arrangements separate until after the ceremony had given Drakon free rein to throw himself into his work and he had been out at the office from dawn to dusk. Why, he hadn't even asked her a single question about what they'd be eating at the wedding breakfast!

Caroline, her boss from Caro's Canapés, was going to be in attendance—as well as two of the other waitresses, Judii and Jade. A heavily pregnant Patti, her best friend from midwifery days, was also going to be there—along with Tom, her new husband. And they all loved her, Lucy reminded herself fiercely. They would be rooting for her even if her sudden decision to marry a man they'd never heard her mention had perplexed them. She didn't even have anyone to give her away, but had been loath to go searching for someone suitable. Tom had kindly offered to step in but Lucy barely knew her best friend's husband. Which was why she would be walking towards Drakon completely on her own.

Donna stuck her head round the door and gave her a thumbs up. 'Ready?'

Lucy touched her fingers to the pale glittery veil which rippled down her back, and nodded. She just needed to remember the special Greek traditions she'd been taught and which were to be incorporated into the day. They would eat sugared almonds at some point and people would attempt to pin money to her dress. After their wedding rings had been blessed, they would be placed on their fingers three times—to symbolise the unity of their entwined lives.

And during all this she would try her best not to feel like a hypocrite.

'I'm ready,' she whispered.

The double doors were opened with a flourish and all Lucy could see was the long walk which lay ahead, decked on either side by chairs festooned with yet more greenery and slivers of golden ribbon. Everyone turned to look at her and she clutched her bouquet even tighter, aware that even in here Donna had gone over the top with the Christmas theme, but she hadn't wanted to come over as some sort of Grinch by telling her not to bother. Yet somehow the gloriousness of the occasion was starting to feel overwhelmingly poignant. Tall candles of scarlet flickered patterns of transparent gold onto the gilded walls and silver stars dangled on span-gled strings which hung from the vaulted ceiling. The sound of a carol being sung by a single boy's voice in Greek was making Lucy want to blink her eyes against the unwanted threat of tears and she hoped she didn't need to blow her nose during the service because she didn't have a handkerchief.

And there was Xander, fast asleep in the arms of his nanny, Sofia. Darling little Xander, whom she'd fed and played with that morning before she'd left for the hotel, wondering if Drakon ever intended to be anything other than a father in name. Because the man who was supremely confident in all things seemed wary of the innocent child he had adopted. She could count on the fingers of one hand the times she'd seen him hold the baby and she'd found herself wondering if she should try to bridge the distance he seemed to have constructed between himself and Xander. Was it her place to even try?

She began to walk with small steps—partly because she was terrified of toppling over in her spiky heels, but also in an attempt to quell her spiralling nerves as she saw her Greek bridegroom standing beneath an arch of Christmas roses.

As the music heralded her arrival, he didn't turn to look at her and although Lucy told herself it was easier not to have to face the enigmatic glitter of his eyes, it was also daunting to be confronted by his imposing back view. She gazed at his powerful body, clad in a dark suit which accentuated his broad shoulders and muscular limbs. A body which very soon…

No. She wasn't going to fret about her wedding night or give into the nebulous fears which had been bugging her. She wasn't going to start worrying that their time on Prasinisos had been an aberration—a peculiar one-off, fuelled by sunshine and novelty.

Because what if she disappointed her new husband on the first night of their honeymoon? What if the reality of an arranged marriage had somehow extinguished the passion they'd shared before? Wasn't that another reason why she had been secretly relieved to maintain separate rooms until the wedding—because she'd been afraid of being put to the test, and failing?

At long last she reached the fragrant green arch and Drakon turned around and stared down at her. He took her trembling hand in his and suddenly this became about much more than whether this was the craziest thing she had ever done. Suddenly Lucy felt breathless with longing as Drakon's strength seemed to radiate from his powerful frame, his black eyes crinkling in a way which reminded her how long she'd known him. Surely that counted for something. Surely they could make this work if they worked at it.

'Okay?' he mouthed.

She gave a quick nod. 'I think so.'

'You look beautiful.'

'Th-thank you.'

Her voice sounded tremulous, Drakon thought as the celebrant began to intone the words. And her face was as white as her dress. He stole another glance at her, aware that his compliment had been dutiful rather than genuine because this dazzling creature didn't look a bit like Lucy. The huge dress swamped her and the sequin-spattered veil did not seem to sit well with the simple country image she'd always projected. And her fingers were cold. As cold as the gold band which, moments later, he slid onto her finger. He looked down at a similar band which now gleamed unfamiliarly against his own olive skin. He'd never worn a ring before and it felt heavy and alien.

'I now pronounce you man and wife.'

The finality of the words shattered his thoughts like a spray gun and Lucy's blue eyes were blank as she looked up at him, almost as if the whole ceremony had happened without her realising it. *You and me both,* agape mou, he thought with a black-humoured sense of identity.

'You may now kiss the bride.'

Drakon slid his arms around her waist and bent towards her, aware that the kiss was mainly for the benefit of the watching congregation. He hadn't kissed her since that afternoon when she'd arrived at his apartment and, as a consequence, his desire for her had reached a level of intensity he'd never experienced before. For days it had been heating his blood and gnawing at his senses with a remorselessness which had left him barely able to think straight. It had tortured him. Tormented him. But hadn't he almost *enjoyed* the boundaries she'd primly put in place, which had heightened his exquisite anticipation of tonight's consummation? Strange to think that this most unlikely candidate was the first woman who had ever denied him anything. Which was why he didn't make this a real kiss. He didn't dare. He was afraid that once he'd started he wouldn't be able to stop. That he would pin her down to the ground and rip that monstrous dress from her body—contemptuously tossing aside the tattered satin to touch the soft flesh beneath. He gave a brief nod as he brushed his lips over hers, in nothing more than a swift acknowledgement that the deal was done and dusted.

But he was aware of the disappointment which flashed through her eyes as he pulled away from her.

And something else, too. Something which looked almost like *fear*, as the applause of the assembled guests echoed up into the gilded arches and they walked into an adjoining room to sign the register. Was it the sudden inexplicable need to quell that fear which made him whisper his fingertips against her waist, so that she relaxed a little?

'All done,' he said.

She nodded. 'I guess so.'

'So how does it feel to be Mrs Konstantinou? Kyria Konstantinou,' he amended as they made their way towards the desk, where the registrar was waiting.

'Slightly weird,' she admitted. 'Probably about as weird as it feels for you to have taken a wife, but no doubt we'll get used to it.'

Her brisk words were reassuring. Drakon had wondered if she would expect him to recite affectionate words he didn't really mean—saccharine statements which would leave him with a bad taste in his mouth. But if she was prepared to treat this marriage as nothing more than a business merger with benefits—what could possibly go wrong?

'I suggest the best way of getting used to it is by having as early a night as possible,' he said smoothly, scrawling his signature on the wedding licence and strangely pleased by the blush which flared in her cheeks. 'Since tomorrow I'm taking you on honeymoon.'

She blinked at him—unaccustomed mascara making her eyes look huge and smoky. 'We're having a honeymoon?'

'Isn't that traditional?' he murmured as his finger

trailed over her pearl-encrusted sleeve. 'As traditional as your white gown and veil? You'll enjoy it, Lucy. I thought we'd fly to my island for the Christmas Eve celebrations.'

'You mean Prasinisos?

He smiled. 'At the last count, Prasinisos was the only island I owned.'

She pushed the waterfall of white veil back over her shoulder. 'I never really thought about going to Greece at Christmas time.'

'You thought my homeland neglected the winter holiday entirely?' he challenged mockingly. 'Or that it only comes to life when you can dip your sun-baked body into the wine-dark sea?' He gave a soft laugh. 'Then you must be prepared to have your mind changed.'

'And what about Xander?' she asked tentatively. 'What's going to happen to our…son?'

Drakon frowned. His son. It was a word he had so far avoided using because it had been strange to think of himself as a parent. It still was. Every time he looked at the helpless infant, he could feel a cold fear clench at his heart, which made him turn away. But while nobody could accuse him of being falsely demonstrative, surely she didn't think him uncaring enough to drag the infant halfway across the world and back for a couple of days? He narrowed his eyes. 'The child's presence is unnecessary,' he said. 'And the journey will be too much.'

'But it's Christmas!'

'And you think a baby of less than three months will miss out on opening his presents?' he demanded.

'Please don't put words in my mouth, Drakon!'

'Then stop being so emotional. We will be gone for just three nights and then we will be back home in Mayfair.'

'It just feels… I don't know… It feels weird to leave him behind.'

'You'll get used to it. That's why we employ a loyal and caring nanny. Now, wipe that frown from your face and let's go and greet our guests. My godfather has travelled here from Honolulu and I really want you to meet him.'

With a heart which felt suddenly heavy, Lucy followed Drakon back into the ballroom to the sound of loud clapping and people crying, *'Opa!'*

Smiling at the guests, she tried to shake off her worries about guilt she'd felt when the celebrant had talked about them extending their family and her gaze had dropped to stare at the gleaming marble floor. But she'd told herself that none of his words were relevant, not in their case—and there was no need to feel guilty. Drakon didn't want any more children, so the fact she was unable to give him any was neither here nor there.

Her heavy train slithering like a giant white snake behind her, she accompanied her new husband to the far end of the crowded ballroom, where his godfather was holding court. A handsome, silver-haired property magnate in his early sixties, Milo Lazopoulos was charming as he bent to kiss her on each cheek. The adoring crowd around him instantly dispersed, leaving the two men to speak briefly in Greek before Drakon excused himself and disappeared. Putting her bouquet down on a nearby table and finding herself alone with his godfather, Lucy was forced to address Milo's probing line of conversation once the traditional pleasantries had been dispensed with.

'I thank heaven that Drakon has stepped up to the plate and taken on the responsibilities left behind by his brother.' Milo shook his head. 'It was a terrible business. A terrible end to all that golden promise Niko was born with. To lose everything because you want to stick a needle in your arm. I just can't understand it.'

'They say that addiction is an illness,' said Lucy quietly. 'So perhaps we should feel compassion for him.'

Milo's gaze was piercing. 'Drakon tells me you used to be a nurse.'

'That's right.' Lucy nodded. 'A midwife, actually.'

'Which means you are well equipped to take on a young baby,' he observed.

'I'm going to do my very best.' She wondered what else Drakon had told his godfather. That they had agreed to a loveless marriage which was more of a business arrangement than anything else?

'But you left midwifery?' Milo continued.

'Not everyone stays in the job for life,' she commented gently.

'Because it was too distressing?'

There was a pause and Lucy could hear the loud beat of her heart hammering beneath the embellished bodice of her wedding dress. He was insightful, she thought, as well as being blunt. There were distressing aspects in every field of nursing, of course there were. But she wouldn't be telling Milo about her real reason for leaving the profession. Or Drakon, come to think about it. There was no need to, she reminded herself painfully. 'Something like that,' she agreed.

Something about her guarded reply made Milo's eyes narrow. Was he aware of her misgivings and did this make him decide that his interrogation had been a little on the harsh side? 'You seem the perfect choice of wife for my godson, Lucy. Someone calm and solid. A safe harbour after all those years of him resisting all forms of commitment. Funny, we always thought he'd...' His words came to an abrupt halt as he plucked two glasses of champagne from a passing waitress and handed one to Lucy. 'Let me be the first to toast the beautiful bride,' he said, the fine lines which edged his black eyes crinkling into a smile as he held his goblet aloft. *Na zisoun!'*

But Lucy could be insightful too and as she chinked her glass to his she wondered what he wasn't telling her. 'Always thought he'd, what...?'

She could see speculation flashing in Milo's eyes, as if working out what she would or wouldn't be able to tolerate. But she kept her gaze firm and steady, willing him to tell her the truth. Because this was a marriage based on truth, wasn't it? Not fairy tales or fantasy.

He shrugged. 'We always thought he might marry Amy.'

Lucy nodded, recognising the name immediately. Of course. Amy. Drakon's business partner—and the woman who had bought his prospective bride a wardrobe of beautiful new clothes. The elusive Amy who was currently in Singapore wheeling and dealing and had apparently been unable to make the ceremony. She'd wondered if Amy's explanation of back-to-back meetings had been true, or whether it had been too painful for her to watch Drakon take another woman as his bride. Lucy hoped her expression didn't give her feelings away as insecurity began to pump through her veins. Instead, she aimed for the calmness she'd always been able to project even in the most trying circumstances—and this was hardly up there with those, was it?

'We haven't actually met,' she said, managing to produce a smile from somewhere.

Milo turned his head as there was some sort of commotion over by the double set of gilded doors and a murmur went up around the ballroom. 'Well, I think that's just about to change,' he said.

Lucy followed the direction of his gaze in time to witness the entrance of the most beautiful woman she had ever seen. The rich emerald material of her slinky dress provided a luscious backdrop for the shiny hair which spilled over her narrow shoulders like melted dark chocolate. Her lips were as red as the berries in the garlands of holly and people were crowding around her making spontaneous whoops of joy—their behaviour in marked contrast to the wariness they'd displayed when introduced to Lucy.

Amy's dark eyes were searching the room until they alighted on the bride and Lucy felt her heart give a great lurch as Milo spoke.

'Here's Amy,' he said quietly. 'And she's heading this way.'

CHAPTER SIX

'DON'T LOOK LIKE THAT,' Drakon instructed softly.

'Like what?'

'Like a sacrificial lamb all poised and ready for slaughter. Close the bathroom door, *agape mou*, and come over here so that I can take off your wedding dress as quickly as possible and make love to you, as I have been badly longing to do for so long.'

But Lucy felt paralysed and unable to move. Struck by unwanted fears and an apprehension which was making her limbs feel awkward and heavy. She was trying to blame it on the long day—on the tension leading up to the ceremony itself and the supreme weight of her heavy gown—but deep inside she knew the real cause of her anxiety.

She licked lips which had grown as dry as bone. Because she'd met Amy. She hadn't wanted to, but she'd liked Amy. She'd liked her very much. Her warm American voice had sounded both friendly and genuine. She'd found herself wishing that Amy had chosen her wedding dress because she was a damned sight sure it would have been more flattering than the one she'd ended up wearing. Remembering Milo's words,

Lucy had even found herself wondering why Drakon hadn't married the stunning partner who'd been with him for years—when she seemed so beautiful and confident and fitted into his world much better than Lucy ever could.

Her confidence had been battered by the meeting but somehow she had managed to survive the toasts and the dancing before Drakon had whispered that it was time for them to slip away. And now she was standing nervously in the honeymoon suite of the Granchester Hotel, about to begin her married life with a man she didn't really know.

She swallowed, removing the fragrant garland of roses and the attached veil from her head and placing both on a nearby table. Should she ask if he still wanted to go through with this? If seeing Amy had made him realise what a dumb thing he'd done by marrying someone like Lucy Phillips? Because if he *had* changed his mind then perhaps they could still get the marriage annulled before they actually consummated it. She was certain that was legally possible and it would certainly be a mature thing to suggest. She opened her mouth to speak, but no words came. All she could feel was the rush of hot colour to her cheeks.

'Still she stands there like a frightened lamb, which makes me realise I shall have to come to you instead, my blushing bride.' Drakon's words were cajoling as he began to walk across the marbled floor towards her, but he moved with the stealthy intent of a dark panther who had just spotted its helpless prey. He had removed his jacket and tie and undone the top buttons of his dress shirt and, with his olive skin glowing and black hair ruffled, he looked relaxed and supremely poised. Unlike her, who was feeling completely over-dressed and had started trembling violently, despite the warmth of the room.

He reached her at last and touched his fingertips to her cheek, slowly trailing their tips downwards until they reached the quivering outline of her lips. He bent to brush his mouth over hers in a slow kiss, before raising his head to look at her, his eyes still narrowed speculatively. 'Don't look so scared, Lucy,' he murmured. 'There's no reason to be. I mean, it isn't as if we've never done this before, is it?'

But never as man and wife, thought Lucy desperately—the sweet magic of his kiss fading as the enormity of her actions hit her. People said getting married needn't change anything but of course it did—other-wise, why would anyone bother? Because she wasn't just starry-eyed Lucy Phillips any more—the virgin who'd had a crush on him since for ever. Now she was the billionaire's wife and mother to his son—and suddenly she felt like an imposter. 'It just feels…different.'

'Then maybe we should stop overthinking it and just rely on our senses to do the work for us. What do you think? Turn around,' he said softly, without waiting for an answer.

She'd actually thought he couldn't bear to look at her anxious face but realised he wanted to undo each tiny hook of her wedding gown, his fingertips tiptoe-ing enticingly over her sensitive flesh. As the corseted bodice came apart and the cool air hit her skin, Lucy closed her eyes and silently practised different ways of asking the questions which had been plaguing her throughout the reception.

Tell me about Amy. How long have you known her? Have you ever made love to her? Or wanted to?

But Drakon's lips were following in the wake of his fingers. They were whispering over her back and trailing over her quivering flesh as he formed a featherlight path of kisses from neck to waist. Her skin flowered into goosepimples wherever he touched her and against her lacy bra, she could feel the insistent pushing of her nipples. Lucy sucked in a shuddering breath as he turned her around to face him again. The gleam of desire in his black eyes made something clench deep inside her and she wondered if she had taken complete leave of her senses. How could she possibly shatter the mood by asking him about another woman at a time like this?

'Now,' he murmured. 'Why don't we get rid of this dress completely?'

She heard the rueful note in his voice and was instantly on the defensive. 'You don't like it?'

He smiled as he traced a slow finger along the modest neckline of her very traditional gown. 'I thought it was perfectly appropriate for the entrance of my beautiful bride, but looser and freer is what I have in mind for what happens next.'

He slid the embossed satin of her gown over each shoulder and let the entire confection fall to the ground before effortlessly lifting her from the vast canopy of stiffened petticoats, until she was standing before him in just her white lacy underwear, hold-up stockings and spiky white high-heeled shoes. Slowly, he studied her and his black gaze felt as if it were scorching her skin where it lingered. 'Much better,' he said, and his voice was unsteady. 'Though I'm now feeling a little overdressed. Any ideas how we might redress the balance, Lucy?'

Lucy felt suddenly stricken with shyness as she lifted her fingers to his chest. Was he wondering what had happened to the uninhibited person she'd been back in the summer when he had awoken her sexuality and her appetite for him had been wild and untamed? She was wondering the same thing herself. But back then it had felt as if she had nothing to lose, while now the stakes seemed significantly higher. Yet wasn't she in danger of sabotaging their union before it had even started if she wasn't careful?

So snap out of it. Enjoy your wedding night with your gorgeous new husband. Make this so good he'll never want to look elsewhere for his pleasure.

'I have some idea,' she murmured. 'Let me help you out of this shirt.'

She was so nervous she could barely undo the first button, but as soon as she made contact with his skin all her reservations melted away like honey left out in the midday sun. How could she have forgotten just how beautiful he was? His olive skin gleamed with health and vitality and hungrily she ran her gaze over all that hard, honed muscle. Her fingers drifted over his hair-roughened chest and Lucy heard him expel a shuddered sigh as she slipped the shirt from his shoulders and it slid to the ground. Which just left his trousers. She swallowed. It was easy to see how huge and taut his erection was, straining against the fine material, and her cheeks grew hot as she dropped her head to his shoulder.

'Oh,' she whispered against his neck, shy once more.

'Anyone would think you'd never seen me in such an intimate state before.'

She swallowed. 'It seems like a long time ago.'

'It seems like that to me, too,' he agreed raggedly as he tugged at the belt of his trousers and swiftly bent to remove the rest of his clothes, his black eyes opaque with lust as he straightened up again. 'I've never had to wait for a woman like I've waited for you, Lucy. And it has been an exquisite kind of torture, do you realise that?'

Was it the thrill of the unknown which was making his voice dip with such husky intent as he unclipped her bra, so that her breasts sprang free against his bare chest? Did novelty alone account for the tense shudder which ran through his big body as he tugged her panties down over her thighs and kicked them impatiently away, before dextrously disposing of her high heels and filmy stockings so that they ended up in a white heap on the floor? Lucy didn't know and, right then, she didn't particularly care because he was lifting her into his arms and carrying her over to the bed, laying her down in the centre of the vast mattress like a willing sacrifice. His gaze moved down over her body. He stroked his fingers over her breasts, her belly, her hips, his narrowing eyes noting the restless wriggle of her bare bottom against the duvet. And then he smiled.

'Want me?' he questioned softly.

'You know I do,' she whispered.

He lay down on top of her, pushing her hair back from her flushed face before bending his head to kiss her. And as Lucy opened her eager lips to meet his, she felt a powerful wave of emotion rushing through her. Because *this* was the bit she remembered best. The sensation of his flesh pressing against hers. The long, drugging kisses and entwining of limbs and the feeling that this was somehow *meant* to be. Eagerly, she touched him back, and he moaned softly as she stroked him, and for a while they both seemed content with a rapt and silent rediscovery of each other's bodies. And then suddenly the tempo seemed to change. Drakon's body became taut as he captured her arms above her head and held them against the pillow, before pressing his mouth to her nipple so that she could feel the warmth of his breath against the erect skin.

'Oh,' she gasped softly.

'I love your breasts, Lucy,' he said huskily. 'They're so damned…big.'

As if to illustrate his pleasure, he began licking what felt like every inch of her, making her squirm with helpless delight. And meantime his hand had slipped between her legs and was spreading open her thighs, one finger thrumming urgently against her creamy heat so that Lucy's head fell back against the pillow. His rhythm was blissful and relentless—it rocketed her straight up to the stars and she came very quickly, her body arching beneath his hand as the spasms clenched low in her belly and then reverberated through her body like a sweet, spent storm. And when at last her eyelids fluttered open, it was to meet the black gleam of his penetrating gaze.

'And I like watching you come,' he observed throatily. 'I like it when your body goes rigid and you make those gasping little sounds at the back of your throat.'

These were starkly sensual statements which only an hour ago might have had her blushing like a schoolgirl, but not now—not when satisfaction was flooding through her still-pulsing body. Yet despite the intense pleasure which had transformed her, it wasn't enough, Lucy decided. Not nearly enough. Because she was no longer just some random woman he'd ended up having unexpected sex with on his private Greek island. She was now his wife and she wanted him to make love to her properly. She wanted him inside her. Badly. Reaching her arms up around his neck, she pulled his head down, and as his lips met hers a restless heat begin to rise inside her once more. She heard him give a low laugh as his tongue slipped inside her mouth and he began to circle his hips in a provocative demonstration of his arousal, until she thought she would go crazy with longing.

She realised he was rolling away from her and, for one illogical moment, wondered if her earlier fears had materialised and he was actually having second thoughts about consummating the marriage. But his reasoning was far more pragmatic than that. He was reaching for something on the bedside locker and Lucy swallowed when she saw what it was. A condom. Of *course* he would wear a condom. She could feel faint hysteria—and fear—spiral up inside her, because he'd told her he didn't want any more children and he was just making sure that wouldn't happen. He wasn't to know that protection was completely unnecessary in her case, was he?

'Drakon?'

His eyes were smoky with lust as he turned round. *'Ti?'*

'I'm… I'm on the pill.'

He smiled approvingly as he dropped the condom back on the nightstand. 'What excellent planning, my clever wife,' he murmured. 'That's exactly as it should be.'

Hysteria began to build again. Should she tell him she'd been on the pill for years because of her endometriosis? But by then he was rolling back towards her, pulling her into his arms with a groan of feral hunger, and Lucy could feel his naked hardness touching against her moist heat. He bent his dark head and was kissing her with a thoroughness which was making her heart want to burst out of her chest, because when he kissed her like that it felt like a fairy tale. And why would she risk destroying that by talking about her tragic gynaecological history at a time like this, when none of it related to their marriage plans?

'Now,' he breathed as he eased himself inside her. *'Evge!* You are so tight, Lucy. So very tight, my sweet little virgin.'

'But I'm not…' She gasped as he began to drive up deep inside her. 'I'm not a virgin any more.'

'Always,' he contradicted as his body took on an exquisite rhythm. 'Always to me.'

Did his raw words intensify her pleasure? Possibly. Again, Lucy came very quickly and so did he—and all her fears about the amazing chemistry they shared being some sort of fluke were banished. Afterwards she lay sleepy and sated in his arms but she felt him stir almost immediately and they did it all over again. And again. They did it so many times that she lost count and she must have dozed off, because the next thing she knew she was being woken by the sound of Big Ben chiming out midnight. But as the last chime faded into the night, Lucy knew she had to ask him the question which was still gnawing away at her—because otherwise wouldn't she just keep torturing herself with fevered imaginings?

She waited until he had poured two glasses of champagne and brought them back to bed, but her own drink lay untouched on the nightstand as she glanced over at Drakon's autocratic profile. He had picked up his phone and was reading something off the screen and Lucy cleared her throat, trying to make her words sound as nonchalant as possible. 'You seem very close to Amy,' she observed.

'Mmm...' he said absently as he put the phone back on the locker, screen side down. 'We've known each other a long time.'

Make it casual. All you're doing is finding out a bit more about him and the people in his life.

She tried to keep her voice bright but her words sounded as forced as the last bit of toothpaste you tried to squeeze from the tube. 'So how did you first get into partnership with her?'

There was a pause as he turned to look at her, his black gaze mocking. 'You really want to talk about this right now?'

Of course she didn't. She wanted him to put his

glass down and pull her into his arms and tell her he was starting to fall in love with her, but that was never going to happen, not in a million years. And in the meantime she had to face down her nameless fears or allow them to grow. To grow and run the risk of dominating her thoughts and ruining her relationship, even if it was a relationship which fell short of her dreams. 'I'm just interested,' she said blandly. 'And as your wife, it's useful if I find out as much as I can about you. There's loads about your past which is a mystery to me.'

Drakon took a sip of champagne and leaned back against the bank of feathered pillows. He didn't particularly feel like talking—but the sex had been so damned hot that he was feeling unusually accommodating towards his new bride. 'Me and Amy,' he mused. 'I guess it was one of those lucky meetings.'

'Sort of…star-crossed?' she ventured casually.

He shrugged, wondering why women always complicated things—or was she just trying to impress him with overblown quotes from Shakespeare? 'I don't know about that,' he said, a little impatiently. 'We were both working at the same office in Hong Kong and one night I decided to ask her out for dinner.'

'Because you fancied her?'

Drakon frowned. She might have been a virgin until very recently, but surely she wasn't *that* naïve? Because Lucy was practical. A practical and realistic woman who'd experienced her own share of bad stuff. Surely one thing which could come out of this unplanned marriage was the ability to be completely honest with her, because wasn't honesty the quality he valued above all else?

'Who wouldn't fancy her?' he questioned, barely registering the way she flinched, because by then his jaw had tightened with the memory of those turbulent days. 'I was in a bad place,' he admitted. 'My father's will had just been read to reveal that he'd basically blown the entire Konstantinou fortune during his lifetime. And my brother had gone ballistic when he'd discovered there was nothing left for him to inherit.'

'And you must have been disappointed to discover that you'd lost your own expected share of the family fortune?' she suggested.

He shook his head. 'That would never have been the case. The laws of primogeniture meant that, as the eldest son, Niko would have inherited everything.'

'And you never minded that?'

'Of course I minded! I'm not some sort of saint, Lucy.' His mouth twisted into a hard smile. 'But I'd resigned myself to my fate a long time earlier. And underneath it all, I discovered I was less like my father and more like my grandfather, who had worked his way up from the bottom to the very top. I knew I could make my own way in the world and that's exactly what I was doing. I'd been to university and got myself a decent degree and was a petrochemical engineer, working for a big company in the Far East.'

'But employees of big companies don't tend to make billions of dollars,' observed Lucy slowly. 'They don't own private jets or private islands or spend hundreds of thousands of pounds on last-minute weddings in luxury hotels.'

'No, they don't. And that's where Amy came in.' Drakon's voice became thoughtful. 'She was a geologist—the best geologist I've ever come across. After she'd explained she wasn't interested in me romantically, she told me that she'd seen the potential for oil on one of the Indonesian islands, but didn't have the wherewithal to explore it. And that's where *I* came in.' He paused. 'I believed in her passion and enthusiasm and my gut feeling told me she was onto something big. I'd just received a huge bonus from the company but I was growing bored and frustrated with working for someone else. I told Amy I was prepared to back her hunch but that we needed to really go for it. So we chartered a small company to do the drilling for us, and within six months we'd struck oil.' He took another sip of champagne and sighed. 'Best feeling in the world,' he reflected.

'I'm sure it was,' she said woodenly.

He turned to look at her. The rosy flush which had made her skin glow after a rapid succession of orgasms might never have happened, for her face was as pale as it had been just before she'd taken her wedding vows. He felt a flicker of irritation, because surely irrational mood swings had no place in what they had both agreed was to be a purely functional marriage. 'Is something wrong?' he questioned coolly.

Lucy wanted to jump up from the bed and rail at him for his insensitivity. To tell him that yes, of *course* there was something wrong. It was the first night of their honeymoon and not only had he confided that discovering oil was better than having sex with his new bride—he'd also confessed that the gorgeous Amy had once turned him down!

But one thing puzzled her more than her very natural feminine outrage at his reaction. Because Drakon was a determined and charismatic man who attracted women like ants to honey. Who was to say that Amy mightn't have lived to regret her impetuosity in refusing a relationship with someone like him—especially once he had decided to adopt Xander?

'So when Xander was orphaned, you weren't at all tempted to ask Amy to marry you, just in case she'd changed her mind?' she questioned slowly. 'Seeing as how you know each other so well and clearly get on.'

He narrowed his eyes and seemed to be running something over in his mind because it took a moment or two before he answered. 'That was never going to be on the cards, because I needed not just a mother, but a wife in the fullest sense of the word.' There was another pause. 'Amy's gay, Lucy,' he said eventually. 'She explained that at the time. She just hadn't come out to her family about it yet. She still hasn't. Like I said, you were my first choice. My only choice, really.'

Lucy supposed he must be paying her a compliment but somehow it didn't feel like one. Somehow it felt like being second-best and that wasn't such a great way to start married life. She turned to pick up her champagne glass but the fizzing bubbles only seemed to emphasise the flatness of her mood, when she realised that Drakon was sitting up in bed and pointing out of the enormous picture windows opposite.

'Will you take a look at that?' he exclaimed softly, his Greek accent velvety and pronounced.

She turned to follow the direction of his gaze, where the dazzle of the city was just visible through the bare branches of the trees—but that wasn't what had caught the tycoon's attention. It was the giant snowflakes which were tumbling from the sky like acrobats, turning golden in the bright light which streamed from the hotel windows.

'It's snowing,' said Lucy dutifully, trying to replicate his wonder since she supposed it was rare to see snow in Greece. But the irony of this final fairy-tale aspect to her Christmas wedding didn't escape her.

She was lying in a rumpled bed, having had mind-blowing sex with her stunning bridegroom, while outside the world was magically turning white. It was like something out of a movie.

But just like a movie—none of it was real.

CHAPTER SEVEN

THE PRESS WERE out in force next morning when the newly-weds left the Granchester Hotel in a flurry of flashbulbs. Drakon's hand was pressed lightly against Lucy's back as he guided her through the scrum of photographers and she looked up at him in gratitude just as the flash went off. And that was the photo which made the online edition of Britain's biggest tabloid. Lucy Konstantinou, standing by the giant hotel Christmas tree with shining eyes and snowflakes on her nose, while Drakon looked down at her with something indeterminate written on his hard and handsome face.

On the way to the airfield Lucy insisted on stopping by the apartment to check on Xander, but the baby was fast asleep and Sofia was assembling a new interactive baby mat with bells and squeaky cushions, for when he awoke. The nanny had looked up when they'd walked in, a question creasing her eyes, as if surprised to see them. Almost as if this unscheduled stop was as unwelcome to her as it had been to Drakon.

'Satisfied?' her new husband had demanded as the limousine had pulled away from the kerb and Lucy had nodded before staring out of the window at the falling snow, feeling kind of *extraneous*. Not a real wife, nor a real mother either, it seemed.

There were photos of them boarding the plane at Northolt, where the fields surrounding the airstrip were soft and white and more clouds of snowflakes swirled from the sky. There was even a shot from inside the wedding reception—though it was a mystery who had taken it—in which she and Drakon had been feeding each other hunks of creamy wedding cake.

Nobody would have guessed from that laughing image that at that precise moment Lucy had been in an agony of self-doubt about Amy and her place in Drakon's life. Yet now that fear had been banished and they were just about to begin their married life together and everything should be just fine and dandy, shouldn't it?

Shouldn't it?

Cosseted in the luxury of Drakon's plane, Lucy scrolled down the newspaper website past all the pictures. *English Nurse Marries Greek Billionaire!* ran the headline, and she found herself wondering why newspapers seemed obsessed with stereotypes.

Her smile was wry. Or maybe they were simply more perceptive than she gave them credit for. Perhaps they had homed into her dreamlike state before, during and after the ceremony—and managed to work out for themselves that this all felt as if it were happening to someone else, not her.

The jet flew them straight to Prasinisos and once Drakon had dismissed the flight attendants, he pulled her into his arms and started to kiss her. And wasn't it strange how sex could melt away your misgivings? Because the only thing she seemed able to rely on was her body's reaction whenever Drakon touched her. It had only been a few hours since they'd last made love but already she was hungry to feel him inside her again. To feel him and taste him and shudder out her pleasure as he filled her with his thrusting hardness. Inside the plane's master bedroom, he peeled off her clothes with care, as if he were slowly unwrapping a Christmas present, and he laughed when she tugged at his clothes with more eagerness than finesse.

'Are you going to rip my shirt off, Lucy?'

'If you could be bothered to help me with the buttons that wouldn't be an option.'

'Or maybe I'm enjoying being the passive object of your desire?'

'You? Passive? I don't think so.'

'I don't think so either,' he growled, pushing her back on the bed to bury his dark head beneath her thighs, so that she had to bite at the knuckles of one hand to prevent herself from shouting out her pleasure. Eventually he moved back up her body and thrust deep inside her and she could feel the shimmering of another intense orgasm waiting in the wings. Afterwards she repaired her hair as best she could but her cheeks still had a fiery glow as the plane touched down on his private island.

It felt strange to be back. Last time Lucy had visited Prasinisos had been for an unexpected freebie weekend when it had been impossible not to be overawed by the beauty of Drakon's exclusive home. But she'd also been aware of how broke she was in comparison to her wealthy host—a difference which had been brought home when his driver had been sent to meet her, widening his eyes before quickly composing himself.

That same driver was here today—Stavros, his name was—but there was no such look of bewilderment on his face. Maybe he didn't even recognise her as the same woman. Why, when she'd looked into the mirror this morning Lucy had barely recognised herself! Her designer clothes were exquisitely cut and hugely flattering and she knew that the cost of her shoes and handbag had been eye-wateringly high. She *looked* expensive and felt expensive—as if she had every right to be married to one of the world's wealthiest men. But inside she was the same Lucy, wasn't she? The woman who was not really a complete woman, married to a man who seemed indifferent to love and emotion.

But unless she wanted to ruin this honeymoon, she was going to have to put a lid on her insecurities. To learn how to manage and adjust them. She had just married the most amazing man and was about to experience the holiday of a lifetime and she owed it to them both to make the very best of it.

Drakon was quiet as they drove up the rugged path towards his cliff-top villa past the dramatic outcrop of rock which some people said resembled a man's face. He could feel the tension of the last few weeks leeching from his body, and not simply because of the post-sex endorphins which were lingering after that amazing mid-flight encounter with his new wife. No. It was a sense of achievement which now prevailed because it had all worked out exactly as he'd planned. He'd pulled it off. He had gained a suitable mother for his baby nephew and all he needed to do now was to play the part of contented newly-wed with conviction. Still, if the first twenty-four hours of married life were anything to go by, that shouldn't be too difficult. Leaning back against the leather seat, he gave a small smile as Lucy's excited voice broke into his reflection.

'Look! Over there. What's that, Drakon?'

He narrowed his eyes in the direction of her pointing finger. 'It's a peregrine falcon. Never seen one before?'

'I'm not sure. And if I did I wouldn't know what to call it.'

'Call yourself a country girl?' he teased.

'As you know, I only live an hour outside London, which is hardly rural isolation,' she protested as she leaned forward to get a better look at the falcon. 'Wow. That's amazing. So fast and so graceful.'

'And so deadly,' he commented, deadpan. 'To small mammals, at any rate.'

'I suppose so.' She turned to look at him. 'And the sea is very blue. Do you suppose there's any chance of going swimming?'

Drakon thought how wistful her voice sounded and was reminded of the first time he'd seen her here— with her body ploughing through the azure waters of his pool. 'It's December, Lucy,' he reminded her gently.

'And people in the UK swim in all weathers,' she informed him. 'In the newspapers recently was a photo of a woman in Scotland who had to smash her way through the ice with a pickaxe before she could go for her daily swim.'

He laughed. 'I'm not sure I'd trust you with a pickaxe. We'll see. But not today. Today I have only one thing in mind and that's to take my beautiful wife to bed as quickly as possible.'

Lucy wanted to object. To tell him not to say things like that because she wasn't beautiful and they sounded dangerously romantic and she was afraid of getting sucked into a vortex of false promise, which would make her long for things which were never going to happen. Because flattering words didn't really mean anything, did they? They were just words.

They reached the palatial villa where all the staff were lined up to greet them and it was only after she had shaken everyone's hands that Lucy noticed the giant decorated tree which was glittering in one corner of the vast sitting room which led off the marbled foyer.

'I didn't know you had Christmas trees in Greece,' she said wonderingly as she gazed at lush branches strewn with stars and fairy lights.

'On the contrary, we love them. Sub-zero temperatures aren't obligatory,' answered Drakon with soft mockery in his voice. 'On Christmas Eve the children sing carols and carry model boats painted gold and decorated with nuts. And we give presents, of course.'

Lucy thought about the modest gift she had tucked away for him in her suitcase and realised how humble it would appear in this lavish setting, as Drakon led her upstairs to the vast bedroom which overlooked the Mediterranean. The room was full of bright light and winter sunshine but she found herself glancing around nervously, and her voice was diffident when she spoke. 'It looks...*different* in here.'

'It is.' The sweeping movement of his hand indicated the pristine linen adorning the king-size bed, as well as a soft new shade of grey on the walls. 'I decided to have the room redecorated before you got here.'

She was silent for a moment. 'Oh? And why was that?'

'Does it matter why?'

Lucy tried to stem the question but she couldn't. Afterwards she would try to justify it by reasoning that she needed to know exactly where she stood, but perhaps it was more like worrying a healing cut on your finger and inadvertently making it bleed again. 'I think so,' she said lightly. 'Aren't we supposed to be honest with each other now we're married?'

There was a pause. 'I just thought it would be good to start afresh, with a completely clean slate.'

'You mean, we'll be using sheets which haven't been slept in by any other woman?'

He winced. 'If you like.'

She nodded, hating the completely unreasonable urge to cry which was making her eyes prickle. She knew the reality because he'd painstakingly spelt it out for her in London, just so there could be no mistake. He'd explained that he hadn't been sexually indiscriminate but, even so, of *course* he'd had plenty of lovers before her. And why *shouldn't* he? *She* was the freak, not Drakon. She was the woman approaching thirty who'd never been intimate with anyone until she'd melted into the arms of her Greek lover.

'But won't you miss it, Drakon?' she forced herself to question huskily. 'The variety of having all those different lovers? Though maybe I'm being presumptuous in assuming there won't be any in the future.

We've never discussed whether this is going to be an open marriage before now, have we?'

Drakon could hear the bravado in her voice and admired her outspokenness, knowing that few women would have been so matter-of-fact about such a tricky subject. Until he reminded himself that her candour was only possible because neither of them had any real emotion invested in the relationship. And that was why this marriage had a chance of succeeding—*because* there were no unrealistic expectations of love. And if she wanted honesty, didn't he owe her that? His mouth hardened. Of course he did. Especially when he found lies so detestable.

'I thought I'd made it clear that I would pledge to you my sexual loyalty,' he said coolly. 'Because I know how destructive infidelity can be. I'm not planning on having anyone other than you as my lover, Lucy, because sexually you thrill me in every way.' He sucked in a deep breath. 'But right now I'm having difficulty talking because the desire to pin you down on that bed and lose myself deep inside your body is pushing everything else from my mind.'

'Then what are you waiting for?' she questioned shakily.

He could hear the relief in her voice as he walked towards her, enjoying the instinctive darkening of her eyes as he unbuttoned her coat and hung it over the back of a chair. 'You seem to be wearing rather a lot of clothes,' he complained as he bent to unzip her knee-high boots.

'It was s-snowing when we left the Granchester, if you remember,' she breathed, perching on the edge of the bed as he slid the soft leather over each calf.

'Well, it isn't snowing here.'

She lifted her hips accommodatingly to allow him to slither her skirt over them. 'Does it ever snow on the island?' she queried conversationally.

'I didn't bring you here to discuss the damned weather,' he growled. 'We're not in England now.'

He undressed her efficiently and though on some level he registered the fine fabric and cut of her new clothes, it was the naked Lucy which made his senses soar like the peregrine falcon which had swooped through the sky on the journey here. His fingers skated over her big, pale breasts and traced featherlight paths over her arching ribcage and although he was rock-hard and eager to thrust deep inside her, he made himself wait. As he slowly kissed her belly and licked a teasing line downwards, he lifted his head to look at her.

'You've waxed,' he observed, one demonstrative finger circling the satin-smooth skin of her inner thigh. 'I noticed it last night but was a little too...*preoccupied* to mention it.'

'Drakon!'

'You want to be intimate in all ways?' he mused. 'Or do you want always to behave like a virgin and talk like a virgin?'

She shook her head. 'The...the wedding dress designer advised I get it done.' She gasped as his finger dipped lower. 'She said she thought...less is more—'

'Except concerning the application of sequins, of course,' he commented drily as he moved over her.

He made it last as long as he could—which was precisely long enough to allow them both to choke out their almost simultaneous pleasure. The second time he took it more slowly, enjoying Lucy's cries of wonder as her nails dug into his shoulder. When eventually they fell asleep, the setting sun was blazing through the huge windows so that the interior of the bedroom resembled a coral furnace. And when they woke, diamond-bright stars had been dusted over the clear, night sky. Drakon clicked on a lamp to see Lucy struggling to open her eyes, her nut-brown hair spread like satin over the pillow.

'What time is it?' she enquired sleepily.

'Dinner time.' He glanced over at his wristwatch. 'At least, it will be soon. Spiro was in the process of preparing a wedding feast and if you want to shower—'

'I do. I won't take long.'

'Take as long as you like. This room has two bathrooms.'

She nodded and rose from the bed but she didn't lean over and kiss him and, for Drakon, it felt as if all the intimacies of the previous few hours hadn't happened. As if she'd filed them all away under Sexy Lucy and gone back to being Sensible Lucy. He told himself he liked it that way. That it would be easier if they compartmentalised their lives like that all the time. But then she went and spoilt it all.

'Drakon?'

Something in the way she said his name warned him, for it contained that curious note of emphasis which women made whenever they were about to start prying. Perhaps hoping to distract her with the sight of his ever-present desire, he pushed back the rumpled duvet and got out of bed. 'What?'

But she deliberately kept her gaze fixed on his face,

not his groin. 'Earlier on, when you said…when you said you knew how destructive infidelity can be… Were you talking about your own experiences?'

He made no attempt to hide his displeasure. 'Does it really matter?'

'I think it does, yes. Did someone cheat on you?'

In a way, yes, though not in the way he suspected she meant. 'Go and have your shower, Lucy.'

'But—'

'I said *go*.'

He went into the second bathroom and stood beneath the fierce jets of the shower before quickly shaving and dressing and hoping Lucy would have had the sense to forget it and move on. But when eventually she'd finished getting ready—standing in front of him in a velvet dress the colour of the night sky outside the window—he could see that look of stubborn determination still on her face.

'Are we going to talk about it?' she questioned.

'About what?' he said, deliberately misunderstanding.

'About the infidelity you were referring to earlier.'

'It's nothing.'

'Doesn't sound like nothing to me. And weren't you the one who suggested the necessity of intimacy in this relationship?'

It was a clever twisting of his own words and Drakon felt trapped—but he could hardly storm out of the room and tell her to go to hell, could he? Not on the second night of his honeymoon. 'Is this what they taught you to do at nursing school, Lucy?' he demanded. 'To keep digging and digging until you got your answer?'

Biting back an exclamation of impatience, he walked over to the dressing table and extracted a pair of golden cufflinks from one of the drawers. But he was aware that he was playing for time and he suspected Lucy was aware of it, too. He could sense her watching him, and waiting—but the overriding feeling he was getting from her was one of compassion rather than prurience. And suddenly Drakon found himself wondering why he was so intent on keeping his memories locked away, because it wasn't as if anything he told her was going to affect the practical nature of their relationship, was it?

Slowly, he slotted the second cufflink in place so that it lay flush and gleaming against the cream silk. Mightn't it be a relief to confide in her something he'd only ever discussed with his mother? His mouth twisted. His lying mother. He felt the knot of pain in his gut tighten as he turned back to face his new wife.

'Okay.' He watched as she sat down on the end of the bed, her eyes fixed unwaveringly on his face, and it was only then that he began to speak. 'You're probably aware that I grew up in extreme luxury?'

She gave a short laugh. 'There were no poor boys at Milton school, Drakon.'

He nodded. 'No. I guess there weren't,' he agreed thoughtfully. 'My father was the only child of an extremely wealthy man, but he didn't follow my grandfather into the business. In fact, he'd never worked—he just lived off the profits of the company which my grandfather had painstakingly built up from scratch. Maybe the fact that everything had always been handed to him on a plate and the lack of purpose in his life were what lay behind what I was to later discover were his fundamental lack of self-worth and low self-esteem. But from the outside, at least, things looked perfect. He married my mother, who worshipped the ground he walked on, which only made his sense of entitlement all the greater. Everything she did was for my father. It was my first experience of unconditional female adoration, though it certainly wasn't to be my last. She spent the majority of her time completely pre-occupied with her appearance. Trying to stay young. Trying to fight nature's natural progression with one surgical procedure after another. By the time she was in her forties, her face was so cosmetically altered that she could barely move her mouth to smile.'

'And what was she like towards you—and Niko?'

'We were superfluous to requirements. In short, we got in the way.' His mouth twisted. 'When Niko and I were seven they sent us away to school in England, and after that I felt as though I had two very different lives. My life in England and my life in Greece. But every time I went home on vacation, I could sense things weren't right. I remember the atmosphere as being incredibly *tense*. I knew the marriage wasn't happy, but since I had no idea what a happy marriage looked like, I just accepted it. But things seemed to be getting worse and every time I asked my mother if anything was wrong she would just fob me off and tell me everything was just fine. Tell me that my father was nothing less than a genius and it was none of my business.'

'But it wasn't fine?' she interjected, into the silence which followed.

He gave a bitter laugh. 'You could say that. Behind the scenes everything was breaking down at an un-believable speed. She knew that and she must have known how the outcome of the decline would impact on all our lives but she lied to me.' His voice grew silent for a moment. 'But it wasn't until my father's death that it came out just how comprehensively she'd lied. One sordid fact came spilling out after another—and the bubble which had been the perceived perfection of Konstantinou family life burst in the most spectacular way.'

'How?'

He didn't answer straight away and when he did, he winced, as if he had just bitten into something sour. 'I learned that for years my father had been entertaining a series of high-class hookers. Women who indulged him in whatever depravity was his current favourite and, from what I could gather, there were plenty of those. In turn he indulged them with whatever took their fancy—anything ranging from large diamonds to fancy apartments. He became a regular at the world's biggest casinos and high-rollers like him always attract a following of low-lifers. As a result, the business was in tatters and there was barely anything left. It wasn't what Niko had been led to believe would be his inheritance and that was the beginning of his descent into addiction. That was when he disappeared. I should have done something,' he added bitterly. 'I should have prevented it.'

'But what could you have done, Drakon?' she questioned urgently. 'Because I'm getting the feeling that you're shouldering most of the blame here.'

Drakon clenched his fists as familiar feelings of anger and frustration pulsed through him. 'Because by then I had some idea how commerce worked and could have helped,' he bit out. 'I could have found some sort of rescue package to have halted the decline of the company, or implored my father to seek help. If my mother had told me the truth instead of pretending nothing was wrong, then I could have done everything in my power to turn it around.'

She shook her head. 'But sometimes the best will in the world won't make people do what you want them to do!' she said, holding the palms of her hands towards him in silent appeal. 'Even if you'd known about it, your father might have blocked all your attempts to save the company—he might still have chosen his life of depravity. Sometimes you're powerless to do anything except sit back and watch while other people make their own mistakes, and there's absolutely nothing you can do about it.'

But Drakon shook his head, closing his heart and his ears to what she was saying. 'I don't do powerless, Lucy,' he said. 'Not any more. That's something you need to know about me. Maybe the only thing.'

His words tailed away as the bells from the village church began ringing out and he could hear the sound of the children beginning to sing the traditional *kalandra*, but Drakon found himself unable to feel any sense of joyful celebration as he glanced down at his watch.

It was Christmas Day.

CHAPTER EIGHT

PUSHING ASIDE THE festive wrapping paper, Lucy felt her eyes widen as she pulled a circlet of glittering diamonds from the dark leather box. 'Oh, Drakon,' she said.

'Do you like it?'

'How could anyone not like it?' she questioned shakily, slipping the bracelet over her wrist and holding it up in the air so that it sparkled like a ring of rainbows in the winter sunshine. But the truth was that it felt too expensive. Too impersonal—and nothing like the ink-spot sapphire which he'd picked out himself. She wanted to know who'd chosen it but she also didn't *want* to know, for fear that it might have been Amy or one of his assistants. And in the meantime— how humble was her own little present going to look in comparison to this?

A little awkwardly, she walked over to the Christmas tree and bent to retrieve the gift she'd placed there earlier. 'It's not very much,' she said as she handed it to him.

'I'm sure it will be perfect,' said her new husband, his voice carrying the bland reassurance of someone who was impossible to buy for.

But she saw his face change as he pulled out a small picture from within the neat folds of holly-strewn paper.

'You don't like it?' she questioned anxiously as he stared at it in silence.

'I... It's a line drawing of Prasinisos,' he said slowly, lifting his head to look at her. 'Where on earth did you get it?'

'I found it in London just before the wedding. There's a tiny shop in an arcade close to Leicester Square station which specialises in maps and drawings of small islands. I couldn't believe it when I saw it there. You haven't already got it, have you?'

He shook his head as he turned it over, his thumb caressing the worn leather frame, and an odd kind of smile touched the corners of his lips. 'No, I haven't got it.'

'I know it's only—'

'It's not *only* anything,' he corrected, almost fiercely. 'It's probably the most personal gift anyone has ever bought me. And now I think I'd better thank you properly, don't you?'

Lucy smiled and bit her lip. 'If you like.'

'I really did think you might have learned to stop blushing by now.' He gave a low laugh and she felt as if she'd just won the lottery. 'Come here.'

It was a Yuletide like no other Lucy had ever experienced, but then she'd spent so many of them on her own these past few years that maybe she had simply forgotten what it was like to celebrate. For lunch they sat down to a festive feast which had been prepared for them by Spiros, the chef. There were shiny crackers and napkins embroidered with stars on the table, and shiny *christopsomo* bread, which was traditionally eaten on Christmas Day. The delicious loaf was flavoured with cinnamon, oranges and cloves and Drakon told her that it translated literally as 'Christ's bread'. Afterwards, they ate lamb with salad and a delicious walnut-covered cake called *melomakarono*—which was also traditional.

After retiring to their bedroom for a sex-jammed siesta, Drakon drove her to his favourite cove, a curving crescent of deepest blue, and Lucy kicked off her shoes immediately, feeling the pale, soft sand between her toes as she gazed out at the glimmering horizon. 'I'd love to go for a swim,' she said, a little wistfully.

'It's way too cold.'

'I guess.' She sighed. 'Anyway, it's pointless wishing because I haven't brought my costume.'

'And because only a crazy person would swim on a day like this.'

Lucy stared out at the sapphire water on which the winter sunshine was dancing in undulating lines of liquid gold, telling herself that this might be Greece but it was still winter and Drakon was probably right—only a crazy person would want to swim on Christmas Day. Yet something was compelling her to take to the water and she couldn't work out if it was just a sense of feeling so intensely alive, or the powerful sense of hope which had been building up inside her since their plane had touched down on Prasinisos. Because despite her initial misgivings about the trip, this felt as if it was rapidly turning into a proper honeymoon. Not just the sex, which had been perfect as always—but because Drakon had revealed a chink in his steely armour and allowed her to look inside at the man beneath. He had confided stuff about his family which made her understand him a little better and didn't that spell only positive things for their future together?

He was standing silhouetted against the shoreline, his black hair ruffled and the light breeze blowing at his linen shirt, which was tucked into a pair of faded jeans, and he looked so utterly gorgeous that a thrill of pleasure ran through her. Was that what made her feel so uninhibited? Why she suddenly peeled her sweater over her head and dropped it on the sand, before starting to unbutton her jeans?

His black eyes narrowed as the denim slid to the sand. 'Now what are you doing?'

'What does it look like?'

'You're not planning on going *skinny-dipping* are you, Lucy?'

She registered his tone of mocking incredulity and forced herself to focus on her smile rather than the goosebumps which greeted the removal of her jeans. 'Why not?' she queried innocently as she unclipped her bra and wriggled out of her knickers. 'Didn't you say you owned this beach and nobody ever came near it?'

She relished the look in his eyes as she turned to pound across the beach and ran into the water. She was too intent on forcing herself to plunge straight beneath the icy depths to take any notice of what Drakon might be doing, but she was curving her arm into a powerful front crawl when she realised he was swimming right beside her, black hair plastered to his head like a seal, his naked body gleaming olive-gold underneath the water. In silent acknowledgement of his unspoken challenge, Lucy set off, racing in a line parallel to the shore, and gave it everything she had. She was the strongest female swimmer she knew, but it wasn't nearly enough to beat her powerhouse of a husband.

He made it look so effortless and was barely out of breath when eventually she swam into his waiting arms, and he laughed against her wet neck and kissed it over and over again as she wrapped her legs around his back. The exercise had given her immunity against the chilly sea and it felt perfectly natural for Drakon's hands to begin a sensual exploration of her body beneath the surface of the water. And perfectly natural for her to do the same to him. His mouth was on hers—it tasted salty and cold and her nipples were like bullets as they pressed into his chest. A small butterfly beat of awareness at her clitoris was making itself insistently known and he gave a small groan of pleasure when she curled her fingers around his hardness.

'I want to do it to you now,' he whispered.

'Then do it,' she whispered back.

He covered her mouth with his seeking lips and Lucy's brain just went to mush. His lips were on her neck and then her breasts. His hungry fingers were parting her aching folds and as he nudged his moist tip against her, she tightened the grip of her legs around the jut of his hips. She gasped with pleasure as he made that first thrust, tilting to accommodate the huge width of him, and the angle of his penetration made her gasp some more. She came very quickly, glad he was supporting her buttocks as he choked out his own fulfilment, and she could feel the rough rasp of his jaw as his head sank against her shoulder, his mouth pressing against her wet hair.

'I never thought I'd make love in the sea,' she said, once she could trust herself to speak again.

'And your verdict?'

'It was...*okay*,' she said, and he laughed.

'Just okay?'

She shrugged.

'Then maybe I'd better do it to you again,' he growled with soft intent and Lucy only pretended to run away from him.

Afterwards they swam back to shore and dressed with numb fingers, hastily pulling clothes onto their still-damp bodies. But any coldness was forgotten the moment they got back to the heated car where soft blankets were stashed on the back seat and Drakon must have arranged for Spiros to make a thermos of creamy hot chocolate, lightly laced with brandy, which they drank from a shared cup.

'Drakon?'

'Mmm?'

'Did you...did you *plan* this?' questioned Lucy suspiciously, surveying him across a cloud of steam.

'The outing?'

'The sex.'

There was a pause. 'Put it this way, I like to cover every eventuality.' The smile he gave her was automatic but suddenly Drakon found himself looking away from her searching blue gaze to stare at the horizon ahead. He swallowed, still reeling from the intensity of what had happened back there in the water. Not just because it had been outside—he certainly wasn't a secret exhibitionist craving to be observed *in flagrante*—and he'd meant what he said when he'd told Lucy that his beach was completely private.

No. It wasn't that. It had more to do with the closeness he'd felt when their bodies had been locked together in that urgent, underwater coupling. Almost as if they'd been part of the same body. It had felt... *unsettling*. Disturbing. It had brought with it echoes of the past. Of things happening which were outside his control—and that was a feeling he'd vowed never to replicate. More than that—hadn't he felt the twist of something unknown in his heart when she'd held her face up to his and he'd started to kiss her? There was something about her sweet enthusiasm which was difficult to resist and that wasn't the only thing about her which was dangerous. Somehow she'd manged to peel away some of the defensive layers which were such an intrinsic part of his make-up. He'd talked about stuff he usually kept locked away and in the process she'd made him feel as if she'd burrowed inside his head.

He felt his skin icing as he started up the engine and the four-by-four ascended the cliff road, past the rocky outline of the man's face. Well, it wasn't going to happen again. She wasn't going to get any closer than she already had and maybe he needed to show her that, once this honeymoon was over. Despite the thoughtfulness of her Christmas present, which had affected him in a way he hadn't been expecting, it didn't actually *mean* anything, did it? This was never intended to be anything more than a marriage of convenience and it was pretty *inconvenient* to have a wife who was always prying like that. He was silent on the drive back to the villa and glad when his phone started vibrating the moment they entered the complex and he could excuse himself to deal with a phone call from one of his brokers in New York.

'I'm not sure how long this will take,' he called to her, over his shoulder.

'No worries. Honestly, I'm fine.' The dreamy note in her voice hinted at inner satisfaction. 'Take as long as you need,' she called back.

Left alone while Drakon retreated to his glass office, Lucy wandered around, feeling deeply content. It felt almost as if she were *floating*. As if she were walking on air. She didn't even mind her new husband shoe-horning in a little work, despite his avowed intention to put business on the back burner during their honeymoon. Who cared if he'd succumbed to a call from his busy empire when this brief time together had exceeded all her expectations? When their interactions as a couple had filled her with the tentative hope that they shared a basic compatibility which could grow, if they nurtured it—and that maybe this marriage could become more than she'd ever dreamed it could be.

She texted Sofia, who informed her that Xander had discovered the use of his hands while they'd been away and had been trying to grab the soft toys attached to the sides of his cot.

Lucy texted back.

Sounds very advanced for a seven-weeker! Can't wait to see you both tomorrow. X

And it was true. She couldn't. Funny how you could bond with a tiny baby, even when you didn't realise it was happening. Even when it wasn't your baby. Couldn't they become a *real* family, she wondered hungrily, even if it was a somewhat unconventional family?

She glanced up as Drakon returned, his expression slightly preoccupied as he walked into the room. 'Is everything okay?' she questioned.

'Mmm?' He glanced across the room at her as if he had only just noticed she was there. 'I'm going to have to deal with a conference call a little later.'

'Oh? Must you?'

'Yes, I must,' he said smoothly. 'I'm afraid it can't be helped.'

It was disappointing. Of course it was—and part of her wanted to ask him to put whatever or whoever it was on hold, so they could enjoy every last second on the island. But Lucy was made of stronger stuff than that. She might have sometimes resented the military life in which she'd grown up, but being an army brat had taught her how to be strong and resilient. She needed to remind herself why Drakon had married her. Mostly because he wanted a mother substitute, but hand in hand with that went his own need for a supportive wife. She had to look on anything else as a bonus, rather than with any sense of entitlement.

'That's okay,' she said. 'I might do some packing so we aren't rushing in the morning.'

And that was how Lucy spent the last evening of her honeymoon. She took a long bath and washed all the sea water out of her hair. Then she packed her case and started reading a previously unopened novel she'd brought with her.

And though it was difficult to empathise with a woman who found herself marooned in a snowy cottage on Christmas Eve with a brooding stranger— *why on earth had she set out for the cottage when the weather forecast had been so atrocious?*—Lucy gave it her best shot.

At least Drakon made it down in time for dinner but he ate more perfunctorily than with any obvious signs of enjoyment and refused Spiro's home-made baklava, which made the chef go into a slight sulk. Only at bedtime did things settle into an agreeably familiar pattern, when her new husband took her to bed. He pulled the duvet over them like a private snowy tent and began to kiss her, and all the faint frustrations of the evening were forgotten. He made love to her very quickly, as if he were seeking some sort of release— but Lucy wasn't going to analyse that either. She just revelled in the elation which pulsed through her veins afterwards. Because this was bliss. Being in Drakon's arms was like finding her own tiny piece of heaven. Through heavy-lidded eyes she studied his profile, his skin silvered by the moonlight which flooded in from the windows, his indifferent expression giving nothing away.

'Did you sort all your business out?' she questioned.

He frowned. 'Are you really interested in talking about that right now?'

Was that censure which underpinned the hint of mockery in his voice? 'I thought you might want me to show some interest,' she said, a little defensively.

'Well, I don't. At least, not in that. Only in this.'

Lucy's head fell back against the pillow as he gave a featherlight flick of his tongue against her nipple and she squirmed when he licked some more and his hand crept down between her thighs. And although warm desire flooded through her, it was followed by a feeling of frustration which had nothing to do with the physical. Because this was a familiar pattern with Drakon, she recognised. He used his physicality to distract her from subjects he had no desire to pursue. And it worked. Every time. That was the magical yet ultimately infuriating thing about her husband. That he had the power to manipulate her. To use sex to quieten or console her—and there didn't seem to be a thing she could do about it.

They left the island at noon the following day and arrived in London just as dusk was falling and the Christmas lights in the city were starting to glow in the fading light. Inside the lobby of the luxury apartment block shone a glittering tree she'd barely noticed before the wedding—and this evening it seemed to symbolise a faded air of festivity which echoed her own increasingly flat mood. In the elevator she badly wanted Drakon to kiss her but he was busy looking at his phone and Lucy knew she needed to ruthlessly prune any romantic fantasies instead of allowing them to grow. They'd had a great honeymoon. So what? That didn't change anything, did it? That didn't mean he'd suddenly started to care for her, did it? Yet she had started to care for him even more than she'd done before. That was the truth of it.

Be careful, Lucy, she thought. *Be very careful.*

The elevator doors slid open and she walked straight into the apartment, where a smiling Sofia was waiting with Xander in her arms. The baby was dressed in a green sleepsuit covered with red-nosed reindeers and Lucy felt a welling up of something hard in her chest which took her breath away as she cradled the infant. He was so tiny and helpless and…she'd missed him, she realised with a wrench. Had Drakon missed him too? she wondered, turning her head to speak to her husband.

'Drakon? Look. See how he's…' But Lucy realised she was talking to an empty space. That Drakon had slipped from the room without a word and, from the fading sound of his conversation, it appeared he was already on the phone to somebody.

She tried not to let it bother her as she played with the baby. She bathed him and fed him and sang a crooning little song she remembered from those long hours of night duty when she'd worked in the neonatal unit at St Jude's hospital. She gave Sofia the evening off and, once Xander was asleep, Lucy changed into a dress she'd never worn before. Before she'd met Drakon, she would never have dared. Silky scarlet jersey clung to her hips and the slashing V neckline gave an uncharacteristic glimpse of shadowed cleavage. Spiky-heeled black shoes with scarlet soles completed the outfit and she styled her hair into a fashionably messy topknot which the Granchester hairdresser had showed her how to do.

Zena had prepared a meal which she'd left for them and Lucy was just lighting tall candles in the dining room, when Drakon walked into the room. The top two

buttons of his shirt were undone and she could see the
faint darkness of chest hair, which arrowed downward
in a beguiling path. He hadn't changed since they'd
arrived back from Prasinisos, she realised, narrowing her eyes. He must have been on the phone all this
time. He was looking around the room, taking in the
holly-strewn centrepiece with tall silver candles which
adorned the table and the bottle of champagne which
protruded from an ice bucket.

'This all looks very…festive,' he observed, with the
air of a man who had just been told that his dentist was
about to make an unscheduled visit.

'Doesn't it?' Lucy said brightly. 'Zena must have
gone to a lot of trouble and it's still…well, it's still
Christmas.'

He turned his attention to her outfit. 'Is that why
you're dressed like the personification of seasonal sex
in your Santa-red dress?' he questioned huskily. 'Because you want me to unwrap you?'

Lucy swallowed as her nipples tightened in time to
his slow scrutiny. 'I don't see why not,' she whispered.
'We might no longer be on honeymoon, but that doesn't
mean we can't still make love after dinner every night,
if you want to, which I'm rather hoping you do.'

'Who knows what either of us will want? This is still
all very new—to both of us.' He picked up the champagne bottle and began to tear the foil from its neck.
'Let's just take it one day at a time, shall we, Lucy?'

His voice was soft but entirely devoid of emotion,
and as she looked into the unfathomable darkness of
his eyes Lucy wondered whether he intended his words
to sound more like a threat than a promise.

CHAPTER NINE

DRAKON SAT BACK in his chair and twisted the stem of his wine glass between his fingers as he studied his wife who was sitting opposite him in the large dining room of his Mayfair apartment. Candlelight flickered over the polished table and over the dark, coiled gloss of her hair. 'Did I mention that I need to go to Singapore tomorrow?' he questioned.

Lucy looked up from her bowl of Greek lemon chicken soup, her spoon suspended in mid-air. 'No, you didn't.' A frown criss-crossed her brow. 'Tomorrow? Just like that? Without any kind of warning?'

'That's business, Lucy.'

'It seems to be a very demanding business.' She hesitated. 'When you always seem to be working.'

He shrugged. 'Billion-dollar empires don't just happen without someone putting in the legwork.'

'It would be nice...' her voice trailed off and, once again, she seemed to be picking her words carefully '...if you could spend a little more time with your son.'

Drakon felt a flicker of irritation because that felt almost like a criticism, and it was not in her remit to criticise him. But why not placate her when he was

going away tomorrow, by wiping that look of uncertainty from her face? 'That will happen,' he said.
'When things are a little quieter.'

She looked unconvinced and maybe he couldn't
blame her for that because, in truth, his heart was not
engaged in fatherhood. He could see her hesitating,
worrying her teeth into her bottom lip as if she was
trying not to say something, but she said it all the same.

'Do you *have* to go, Drakon?'

She tried to keep the question casual but in this she
failed because it was a refrain he'd heard from women
countless times over the years and Drakon tensed—
because didn't her words almost *justify* his intended
trip? Didn't they reinforce what he suspected was her
growing emotional dependence on him and make him
aware of the subtle ways she was trying to steer him
away from his work? But she had to understand that no
way was he going to take his eye off the ball, because
he'd seen what could happen if you did. He was still
his own boss and a man who answered to nobody—not
to his adopted baby and certainly not to his wife—and
the sooner she realised that, the better.

Steeling his heart against the reproach in her eyes,
he shrugged. 'I'm afraid I do,' he answered coolly. 'I
don't know if I mentioned that we're trying to extend
our oil refinery—'

Her voice sounded stiff. 'No, I don't believe you
did. You don't exactly encourage me to keep up with
what's going on in your empire, do you?'

Ignoring the underlying complaint in her question,
he picked up a piece of home-made pitta bread. 'Amy
hasn't been able to get anywhere with the government.

She keeps coming up against opposition—she suspects it's because she's a woman—and I really do need to be there.'

'Of course you do.' But Lucy put her soup spoon back down on the plate, her appetite suddenly deserting her. Was that because, although Drakon was going through the motions of *sounding* apologetic, the anticipation in his voice suggested he really wanted to go off on a last-minute trip to the Far East? And wasn't the truth of it that he probably felt trapped in a marriage he'd never really wanted?

Because the honeymoon was over. At least, that was how it seemed to her. Within twenty-four hours of returning to London from Prasinisos, life had picked up a new routine and Lucy realised just how much time she was expected to spend on her own. Drakon had resumed what she was to discover were his habitual twelve-hour days at the office, leaving her at home with Xander, Sofia and the rest of his large contingent of staff.

She took to rising deliberately early in order to eat breakfast with her husband before he left for the office, knowing he wouldn't return until dinner time. Because what was the point of being married if you never got to see the man you'd married? At least when she was pouring strong coffee and offering him a croissant—which he would invariably refuse—she felt as if she was going through the motions of being a married woman. But only at night did she feel like a real wife, when Drakon undressed her and took her into his arms. When he made her cry out with disbelieving pleasure as his lips and fingers and tongue opened up her senses. Her breasts would grow full and aching—her nipples pebbling into tight little bullets as he grazed at them hungrily with his teeth. She opened her legs and took him deep into her body, his hard heat filling her and making her feel, well... complete. Was it crazy to admit that was the effect he had on her? Suddenly she could understand all those things she'd read about successful sex—as if some kind of transformational magic had taken place between two people.

Afterwards she would lie in his arms, her ear pressed close to his chest, listening to the dying thunder of his heart. Their legs would still be entwined and she could feel the sticky trickle of his seed on her thigh as she longed for him to say something—*anything*—which would make her understand just how he really felt about her. But there was nothing—which made her conclude that he felt nothing. Inevitably, he would fall asleep straight away, leaving Lucy lying there, her eyes adjusting to the mysterious shadows which seemed to be lurking in the corners of the vast room. Was this how it was going to be from now on, or was there a possibility that their incredible physical closeness might eventually lead to some kind of emotional bond?

The signs weren't promising. At times, she still felt like something he had acquired—in the way he might acquire a new yacht. One morning he presented her with a credit card—a shiny platinum affair which glowed against the starched white linen tablecloth, as he slid it across the table towards her.

'What's this?' she questioned blankly.

'Surely you can work that out for yourself, Lucy.'

'A credit card?'

'I thought you'd be pleased. You need your own money,' he added, in response to her blank stare.

'But how can it possibly be my money when I haven't earned it?'

It was a naïve question and maybe she deserved the answering elevation of his brows.

'You could work a million hours a week and never earn a fraction of what I do,' he said, his gentle tone not quite taking the sting out of his words. 'You shouldn't have to come to me every time you want to buy something. What if you want to get yourself a new car? Or redecorate the apartment? Put your own stamp on it. That kind of thing.'

Her own stamp. Lucy gritted an automatic smile as she poured him a cup of the strong black coffee he seemed unable to function without. His statement would have been funny if it hadn't been so sad. Because how could she possibly make her presence felt when her brilliant billionaire husband dominated everything and everyone around him? She had no desire to change a beautifully decorated home just for the sake of it—because that would be a terrible waste of money and that wasn't the way she had been brought up. But she was certainly going to have to find something to do with her days, other than help Sofia look after Xander.

Xander.

A lump rose in her throat. The child she was loving more with every day which passed. Was it knowing that he was going to be her *only* child which made her feelings for him so fierce and fundamental? Sometimes when Drakon was at the office she found herself staring down at the infant lying sleeping in his crib. The infant still largely ignored by his adoptive father—unless you counted the perfunctory kiss Drakon sometimes planted on his head if ever his return from the office managed to coincide with Xander being awake, which wasn't often.

Sometimes Lucy found herself wondering if he timed his arrival home deliberately, to make it so. If he was determined to keep his distance. Why, even on Sundays—Sofia's and the rest of the staff's day off—the workaholic tycoon didn't go out of his way to bond with his baby son, did he? He still managed to absent himself for long periods of time, going out for a sprint around Hyde Park and returning covered in spatters of mud with his black hair clinging in damp tendrils to his neck. Or holing himself up in his home office to read through long contracts with horribly small print.

True to his word, Drakon went to Singapore the very next day and was gone for two weeks. Two whole weeks with phone calls his only method of communication. He blamed their sporadic nature on the time difference between London and Singapore and maybe that was true. But to Lucy it felt as if they were a million miles apart, rather than six and a half thousand. All he seemed to want to talk about was how brilliantly the talks about extending the oil refinery were going. He even sent a photograph of him and Amy sitting in some plush restaurant in the famous Botanic Gardens of the city, having dinner with a load of government ministers. Lucy felt as if he were standing on the deck of a ship which was moving further and further away from her. And all she could wonder was whether this was how it was going to be from now on.

'So, when are you coming back?' she asked.

'Tomorrow lunchtime. I've asked for the plane to be ready at midnight.'

Lucy spent the day trying to contain her state of excited expectation, but at the appointed hour she heard her phone ringing, rather than the welcome click of Drakon's key in the lock.

'Where are you?' she said as his name flashed up on the screen.

'*Agape*, forgive me.' He paused. 'A last-minute meeting was scheduled with the trade and industry minister.'

'And you had to be there?'

'Yes, of course I did,' he said coolly. 'Do you have a problem with that?'

Too right she did, but Lucy held back from saying so because the sensible side of her knew she was being unreasonable, while instinct told her she was only going to make matters worse if she turned this into a battle. Yet Drakon was worth fighting for, wasn't he? For Xander's sake mostly, but for hers too.

Because no matter how much she tried to tell herself it shouldn't be happening, her feelings towards the man she'd married were growing—feelings which had never been part of their marriage deal. Unstoppable emotions which had been nurtured during their brief honeymoon and taken on a life of their own. She tried blaming it on her lack of experience, convincing herself that a woman who'd reached the age of twenty-eight without ever having sex would be in danger of mistaking physical pleasure for something else. Something which felt uncomfortably like love. And she didn't want to love Drakon. The last thing she could afford to do was to waste her emotions on a man who'd told her right from the start that he didn't believe in love. Because that would be a self-destructive course and would detract from something she *could* do. Something positive and good—which was to strengthen the bond between father and son.

Because if Drakon wanted their marriage to endure, which was what he *said* he wanted—then he couldn't keep the baby at arm's length the whole time, as he'd been doing until now. She didn't think he was necessarily being unkind to Xander. It was just that he didn't know *how* to love him because he had no experience of parental love to fall back on. Maybe he had to learn to be a good father another way, and maybe she could help…

So just do *it,* Lucy thought to herself. *It's no good complaining about the state of your life if you don't do anything to try to improve it.*

She spun into action that same day, signing up for family membership at the local gym which she sometimes passed on her way to the park. Mayfair didn't run to budget gyms so the one she joined was eye-wateringly expensive, but it did have the benefit of a super-sized swimming pool. She tried it out a few times—in fact, her hair was still damp when Drakon arrived back from Singapore, his black eyes faintly bemused as he saw the drying locks of hair clouding around her shoulders.

'What's all this?' he questioned as she went into his arms to kiss him.

'I've joined a gym.'

'That's good,' he said absently as his phone began to trill in his pocket.

She made no further mention of it until the following Sunday morning, just as Drakon replaced his empty coffee cup and told her he was going to read through a new contract in his study, but Lucy shook her head, feeling her heart pounding nervously in her chest.

'I'd much rather you didn't.'

There was a split-second pause. 'I'm sorry?'

'Not today, Drakon. I wonder...' she licked her lips '...would you mind coming swimming with me and Xander instead?'

'Swimming?' he demanded. 'Don't be ridiculous. At his age?'

'They can start lessons as early as four weeks,' she informed him calmly. 'In fact, he's had a couple at the new gym already but they've got a class this morning and it would be nice to have some company.' She sucked in a deep breath. 'I think you might enjoy it. And before you trot out all the reasons why that's not possible—can I just ask what's the point of being one of the world's most successful men if you take less time off than the average factory worker?'

Drakon met her resolute expression and felt a flicker of mild irritation at the fact that she was so openly defying him. Yet he couldn't fault her logic, no matter how much he'd like to be able to. In fact, there was little about his new wife he could fault—and hadn't that been the biggest revelation of all? She was…

He studied her.

She was *surprising*. She was like the first soft shimmering of spring after the harshness of winter. Like a welcome sea breeze which whispered over your skin on the hottest day of the year. Her skills as a mother had never been in question because Drakon had known exactly what he *didn't* want from someone taking on that particular role. His mouth hardened. He'd wanted someone as unlike his own mother as possible—without her brittle exclusion of her own children, and her all-encompassing absorption in her philandering husband, and her preoccupation with her own appearance. He'd wanted someone soft and caring and honest and true. Someone with a heart and someone with a conscience—and Lucy had ticked all those boxes, and more.

He swallowed. Much more.

He hadn't been expecting her to keep surprising him as a lover, nor imagined he would find it difficult to drag himself away from the seductive sanctuary of her arms each morning. Sometimes he would even find himself glancing at his watch at the end of a working day and itch to get away, but he forced himself to work as late as he'd always done, because independence was key to his success. Wasn't that one of the reasons why his Singaporean trip had provided such a welcome relief and the space he needed? Because no way was he ever going to rely on another human being and open himself up to pain.

Yet Lucy wasn't asking for the world, was she? She

wasn't demanding emotional reassurance, or expecting him to bolster her unrealistic dreams about marriage. She simply wanted him to accompany her while she took the baby swimming. Not the biggest ask in the world.

'What time do you want to leave?' he growled.

'In about an hour.'

'I have a couple of calls I need to make first.'

'Of course you do,' she said, with a smile which somehow niggled him.

The gym was only a short walk away, reached through an oasis of a garden square which was new to him, but then, it was a long time since he'd taken a walk in London just for the sake of it. Feeling like a man who had just emerged from a long sleep, Drakon heard the unmistakable sounds of birdsong coming from the bare branches of a tree, before peering down at a carpet of snowy white flowers whose white tips were pushing their way through the grass.

'Snowdrops,' said Lucy as she followed the direction of his gaze.

'I know they're snowdrops,' he snapped.

He was slightly disconcerted to discover mixed changing rooms at the upmarket gym—he hadn't been in *any* kind of changing room since uni—and by the way Lucy thrust a pair of impossibly tiny armbands at him.

'Could you put these on Xander?'

He looked at them with a frown. 'Can't you do it?'

'Well, I *can*, of course—but I thought you might like to.'

What could he say in response? That he had no desire to do so? That the thought of touching the baby filled him with dread because he was so impossibly tiny? Especially as a nearby blonde was openly listening into their conversation, her eyes devouring him in a predatory way he hadn't come across in a while. Was that because he never really looked at other women any more, other than to compare them unfavourably to Lucy? He shot the blonde a glance before disdainfully averting his gaze. She was practically falling out of some skimpy bikini and he thought how much sexier his wife looked, clad in a sleek one-piece which hugged her toned curves.

He turned back to the task in hand and stared down at the tiny baby who was now cradled in the crook of his arm. It was a nerve-racking experience to slide on the armbands and he wanted to lash out at Lucy for making him do it, when he looked up and met the soft understanding shining from her blue eyes.

'You're doing just fine,' she said softly. 'Babies are stronger than they look and all dads feel funny at first. I've seen men the size of mountains looking completely lost when confronted with a newborn. You just need to do it more often. You know what they say. Practice makes perfect.'

But Drakon could hear his heart pounding. Pounding in a way he didn't recognise. Xander was wearing a hooded little towel which made him look like a miniature caped crusader, but nothing could detract from his vulnerability, despite the fact that he was over three months old now. Drakon stared into black eyes framed by impossibly long lashes. He had his father's eyes. Niko's eyes, he realised with a wrench. But they were *his* eyes too, for hadn't he and his twin brother been identical, sharing almost the same DNA? He stared down again at his adopted son and something inside him turned over and started to melt.

And that was how it started. Insidiously at first, but with gathering force—like the fierce Meltemi wind which blew through his homeland every summer—Drakon began an emotional connection with the child he had adopted.

He tried to deny it. To convince himself his life wouldn't change in any way because he didn't want it to change. He would play the part of husband and father, yes. That had always been part of the deal. But he would play it from a suitable distance, for that was how he operated. He was there to support Lucy in her role of mother, because that was her primary role. At times he'd started to wonder whether she truly understood and accepted the boundaries within their relationship, then something happened which made it clear he was going to have to spell it out for her.

The episode in question occurred when he was returning from a day trip of meetings in France and found his limousine waiting for him at the airfield. Unusually, the chauffeur remained in the driving seat and Drakon opened the rear door himself, to discover Lucy sitting on the back seat waiting for him—a vision in a silky dress which matched her eyes and suede high-heeled shoes in exactly the same colour.

'Hi,' she said.

'Hi,' he said, his eyes narrowing as some unknown fear clouded his heart. Something to do with Xander, perhaps? 'Is something wrong?' he demanded.

'No, nothing's wrong. I just thought it would be fun to come and meet you for a change.' She crossed one pale, stockinged leg over the other and tilted him a smile he'd never seen her use before. It was a slightly nervous smile but also kind of...*predatory*.

His senses were on instant alert as he got in beside her, noting the tense atmosphere inside the tinted interior of the car. He could see that she'd floated up the soundproofed and darkened screen which separated them from his chauffeur, so they were in a private world of their own. As the powerful vehicle pulled away she leaned forward to kiss him, guiding his hand up her skirt to illustrate the fact that she wasn't wearing panties. Before too long she had unzipped him and was straddling him, easing herself slowly down onto his rigid length and riding him as if they were in some kind of erotic rodeo. He felt compromised and manipulated but his desire for her was so intense that he had no choice other than to submit to her sexy ministrations. Even when inside her he tried to hold back—to make her wait for what he knew she wanted—but suddenly his seed was pumping out and he was moaning softly against her mouth.

It was undoubtedly the most stimulating homecoming he'd ever experienced—possibly because it was so unexpected. It was hard to believe this was the same blushing virgin he'd seduced on his Mediterranean island, and that disturbed him almost as much as this sudden reversal of control. He'd chosen her for her suitability and purity. Didn't she realise that he had chosen her because he had wanted a mother for his son? If he'd wanted a vamp, he would have married one.

'So what was all that about?' he demanded, once he'd got his breath back.

She paused in the act of smoothing down her rucked skirt before looking up, and he was caught in the teasing crossfire of her bluebell eyes. 'You didn't like it?'

He didn't respond to the feigned innocence in her voice. 'I didn't say that. I just wondered if there was any particular reason for such a mind-blowing home-coming and whether this is something I should expect every time I take a flight in future?'

Something in the repressive tone of his voice sent a shiver down Lucy's spine. He was looking at her with a stony expression in his black eyes, which somehow contradicted his passionate response, and she felt a worm of worry wriggling away inside her. Should she tell him the truth? Should she confess she'd been concerned he might find too much domesticity and fatherhood stultifying and she wanted to reassure him that she intended to remain as exciting a lover as possible? But that might let too much light into her occasionally paranoid thoughts and make what had just happened seem almost...*predictable*. Surely it would be better to allow a little mystique to prevail. To keep her gorgeous husband on his toes and ensure he'd never get bored and want to walk away from her, because that was something she couldn't bear to contemplate.

Still a relative novice to the game-playing of romance, she flicked him a smile. 'You'll just have to wait and see, won't you?'

'I guess.'

But her attempt to engage him again fell disappointingly flat for he picked up his briefcase and began rifling through it, effectively dismissing her. Quickly Lucy looked out of the window, terrified her gaze would betray her feelings, though he wasn't actually looking at her. But if he was...

She swallowed. If he was then mightn't he recognise that she was falling in love with her Greek husband, even though she knew there was no way he would ever return those feelings? Even though he now seemed to be in a strange kind of mood after she'd plucked up enough courage to travel to the airfield to seduce him. She never knew what was going on inside his head, because he rarely told her. Sometimes she felt as if they were growing further apart rather than closer, despite their cohabitation. Yet when he relaxed enough to let his guard slip...didn't she adore the man who existed behind the brittle exterior he'd formed to protect himself? The man who'd suffered such a loveless childhood, which meant he kept all his emotions locked away. And didn't she cherish a hope that his feelings for his son were growing—and would continue to grow if she could help facilitate that?

But it was hard to communicate with someone who was increasingly absent and Lucy's growing sense of insecurity was fuelled by Drakon jetting off again. This time he was travelling to Indonesia with Amy and communication filtered down into the usual snatched phone calls, squeezed in around the time difference. Lucy kept herself busy with Xander and that was always a pleasure. A growing pleasure. With every day which passed the baby was growing more and more aware and when she went in to him each morning, she was rewarded with the sunniest of smiles. Sometimes he nuzzled his silky little head against her neck, and Lucy felt a pure joy which was almost *painful* in its perfection. He was just gorgeous. The most gorgeous little baby in the world.

She had just put Xander to bed, sung him a small medley of lullabies and was standing beside the crib watching him when she heard an almost imperceptible sound by the door and glanced up to see Drakon standing silhouetted there. Lucy's heart leapt with instinctive longing but when he made no move to join her, she crept from the nursery to find him waiting for her in the corridor. After days of absence, his powerful body looked especially muscular and virile, though the expression on his dark face seemed much sterner than usual.

'How long have you been standing there?' she whispered.

'Long enough.'

'I wasn't expecting you back until Friday.'

'I know. I tried to ring a short while ago, but you didn't pick up.'

'I was bathing Xander.'

'So I see.' He smiled then. 'Your hair is damp.'

Self-consciously, she patted the dishevelled strands. 'I'd better go and tidy up. Don't you want…to say goodnight to Xander?'

He shook his head. 'I don't want to risk waking him. I'll see him in the morning.' There was a pause. 'Would you like to go out for dinner tonight, Lucy? Just the two of us. I thought we could try that new Italian restaurant in Knightsbridge.'

'I'd love to,' she said, a little breathlessly. 'I'll go and get changed.'

'Why don't you wear that green dress you had on the other night?' he suggested carelessly, his words fading away as he walked towards one of the dressing rooms.

Lucy hurried away to get ready, wondering if she was just imagining that Drakon's mood seemed...*different* tonight. Had something happened during his business trip to Indonesia? Had he met a woman and realised how constrained his life was by marriage to someone he was only with because it happened to be *convenient*? Was that why he had asked her to wear her admittedly on trend but least sexy dress, with its high ruffled neck and knee-length skirt?

She was silent in the car on the way to the restaurant but Drakon seemed too preoccupied with his own thoughts to notice. And it wasn't until they were seated at a table at the far end of the discreetly lit eatery in Knightsbridge, with two Bellini cocktails sitting in front of them, that she plucked up courage enough to ask him. Because hadn't he seemed more distant than usual, ever since that time when she'd surprised him at the airport in the back of the car? Moistening her lips with the tip of her tongue, she stared into the dark gleam of his eyes.

'Is something wrong, Drakon?'

He paused for long enough to magnify all her unspoken fears. Long enough for her heart to begin pounding painfully hard in her chest. But what he said next made Lucy's heart pound even louder.

CHAPTER TEN

'I WANT US to have another baby, Lucy.'

Lucy's fingers dug into the linen tablecloth as she struggled for words which wouldn't seem to come. 'What…what did you say?' she croaked.

He leaned forward. Close enough for her to reach out and touch his gorgeous face and on some instinctive level Lucy was tempted to do just that, knowing in her heart that in a few minutes' time such a move would inevitably repulse him. Because wasn't this the moment she'd been waiting for? The moment she had been secretly dreading?

'Another baby,' he repeated. 'A child of our own.'

'A child of our own,' she echoed dully.

'Neh.' His black eyes glittered. 'It makes sense.'

'Does it?'

He didn't seem to register the wobble in her voice and Lucy was grateful that her hair was successfully concealing the prickles of sweat which were beading her brow.

He nodded. 'Of course it does. Perfect sense.'

'B-because?'

He sucked in a deep breath before the words came

out in a rush, as if he'd prepared them before saying them. 'Because Xander needs a brother or a sister. I don't want him growing up in a world occupied solely by adults. I want him to have someone to play with. Someone to keep him company. Someone who is there for him, fighting his corner. I want us to be a real family. To give him the brothers and sisters he needs, which might help erase the terrible start he endured at the beginning of his young life.' He paused, and his black eyes had suddenly grown very intense. 'And you are such a good mother that I think you need a child of your own to love and care for, as you have loved and cared for little Xander. Don't you, Lucy?' His mouth quirked into a reflective smile. 'Something more worthwhile to keep you busy, rather than having to put on silk stockings to come and meet me at the airport.'

Lucy stared at him in dismay, and not just because he was making her sound like some kind of amateur hooker. Because this was the moment she'd dreaded. The moment she'd prayed would never come. But in the long run, mightn't it all be for the best? Couldn't admitting the bitter truth she'd nursed for so long provide some sort of catharsis for them all? Drakon had said he wanted a real family and she wanted that too. Couldn't she show him that what they already had could be enough, if they were prepared to work at it? With an effort she composed herself, acutely aware of the fact that they were in a public place.

'Perhaps we should order first,' she said.

He narrowed his eyes. 'Some men might be offended by your preoccupation with dinner,' he observed, with a flash of mockery. 'Are you so hungry that you can't wait a moment longer or do you just want to make me suffer by making me wait for your answer?'

It was more the fact that she could see the waiter hovering in the background and Lucy didn't want him coming over and disturbing them when she was in the middle of her story. The story she wished above all else she didn't have to tell. Just as she wished that Drakon had worded his proposal with more affection and that he wanted more children for reasons which had to do with love, rather than expediency. But it was pointless wishing for the impossible. She knew that better than anyone. With cold dread, she cast her eye over the menu and chose something which would take ages to prepare and then attempted to speak as if she actually cared about it. 'Why don't we have the chateaubriand, to share?'

'If that's what you want.'

If only he knew that the only thing she wanted could never be hers. Lucy spoke quickly to the waiter and, once the order had been given, clasped her hands together as if praying for a courage she wasn't sure she possessed.

'Drakon. There's something...' Her voice trembled. 'Something I haven't told you.'

His body tensed—as if her tone was warning him that what she was about to say wasn't just some undiscovered quirk of character. 'Oh?'

She sucked in a deep breath but the air which made its way to her lungs was scorching her airways. 'I can't give Xander the brothers and sisters you want for him,' she husked, 'because I'm…'

Go on. Say it. Say those two painful words which you've never quite been able to get your head around.

'I'm…infertile.'

There was total silence as he sat back in his seat and Lucy searched his face for some kind of reaction. But there was none. His enigmatic features were as unreadable as they'd ever been, and somehow that felt much worse than open pain, or anger.

'Have you known about this for long?'

The conversational tone of his voice gave Lucy the hope she needed and she nodded. 'I found out while I was nursing. It's one of the reasons which made me leave midwifery. I found it…' She swallowed as she tried to convey some of the pain she'd felt—not just the physical pain of endometriosis, but the emotional pain of knowing her womb was always going to be empty. 'I found it increasingly hard to be around pregnant women and babies. Every day when I went into work, I was reminded of what I could never have.' She searched his expression but still she could pick up nothing from his hard-featured stillness. 'It's one of the reasons I never really had any boyfriends before you, because most of the time I only felt like a shell of a woman.'

And now the cold words which began to fall like stones from his lips gave her a clue as to what he was feeling.

'But you didn't think it was pertinent to tell me all this before we were married?'

'I meant to. But we didn't really know each other

back then, did we? It's not the kind of thing you just casually drop into the conversation with a virtual stranger.' She licked her lips. 'And it didn't seem relevant, because you said you didn't ever want children of your own.'

'But things change, Lucy,' he ground out. 'We're both intelligent enough to realise that. People change their minds all the time. I would like to have been given the choice instead of having it taken away from me, without my knowledge.'

Lucy shook her head, but it didn't change the fact that her throat felt as if someone were pressing their fingers against it, making it almost impossible to breathe. But she needed to breathe. To try to explain how it had been. How it had felt. 'A couple of times I intended to tell you—but the right time never seemed to come up,' she said. 'The preparations for the wedding were so intense and all-consuming that I never found the opportunity to start a conversation about it.'

'You could have made the time,' he said repressively.

Her head was hurting and so was her heart. She could sense that he didn't understand and she wanted to make him understand. 'Did you ever see that film about Queen Elizabeth I—the one which won all the awards?' she questioned suddenly.

'What?' he demanded, his dark look of accusation momentarily morphing into one of perplexity.

'The English Queen was almost completely bald, and she hid her baldness beneath a lot of elaborate wigs,' she rushed on. 'But they said that anybody who had seen her in her true state could never look at her in quite the same way again. That she remained permanently ugly and scarred in the mind's eye of the beholder. And that's how *I* felt, Drakon. I didn't want you to look at me as less than a woman. As some barren creature only to be pitied. I wanted you to continue to desire me and want me.'

He gave a short and bitter laugh. 'So you lied to me?'

'I did *not* lie!' she protested. 'The subject never came up.'

'Oh, but you did. It was a lie by omission—and deep down you know that, Lucy.'

She stared at him, unable to deny his bitter allegation.

'It was a lie by omission,' he repeated with quiet force, his face a blur of rage. 'In fact, I don't think I've ever met a woman who *doesn't* lie. It seems to be stamped into their very DNA. I learnt it first from my own mother, almost as soon as I'd left the cradle, and I've been having it reinforced on a regular basis ever since.'

Lucy heard a note of *triumph* which edged the cynicism in his voice as their meal was brought to the table, and she watched in excruciatingly tense silence as the meat was carved into neat slices and heaped onto their plates.

'I guess in a way this has made you happy?' she ventured, once the waiter had gone.

'Happy?' he echoed. 'Are you out of your mind?'

'Not at all. This must be a self-fulfilling prophecy for you,' she said slowly. 'You don't like women and you don't trust them—you never have. And I've just given you yet another reason to hate us as a sex.' She sucked in a deep breath. 'The only thing I can say to you, Drakon, is that I'm sorry. And if I could have the time back, I would do it differently.' She could hear her voice starting to wobble. 'Except that then you might never have wanted me and I would never have become your wife and learned to love you as I do.'

'Love?' he queried disdainfully. 'You think I want your tainted love, Lucy? That I want to spend the rest of my life with a liar?'

Lucy recognised that their marriage was hanging precariously in the balance. That a delicate line as fine as a spider's web was all that lay between happiness and loneliness. One clumsy move and it would all be lost. Yet surely what they had discovered together was worth fighting for. Fighting with every single breath in her body. 'But we're all capable of lies by omission. Of fashioning reality to look like something quite different,' she pointed out quietly. 'Even you, Drakon.'

'What the hell are you talking about?'

'I'm talking about your close friendship with Amy. So close that even your godfather told me he thought the two of you would get married and so did everyone else. And before you remind me that Amy's gay— surely that's all part of it. She hasn't come out, for whatever reason—so it probably suits her very well to have people speculate on the true nature of her relationship with her business partner.' She took a sip of her cocktail and felt the champagne and peach juice foam against the dry interior of her mouth.

'That's different,' he snapped.

'Is it?' she questioned quietly. 'Oh, Drakon.' Her voice was filled with a deep sadness which she couldn't seem to hold back. 'Can't you ever forgive me? Can't we just put all this behind us and start over—now that everything's out in the open?'

But she got her answer instantly as he rose to his feet, towering over her and the table, his muscular shadow seeming to swallow her whole.

'I'll tell you exactly what's going to happen now,' he said quietly. 'I'm going to pay the bill and leave. And then I'm going outside to catch a cab. You can take the car.'

'I don't want your damned car!'

'Really? Then how are you proposing to get back to Milton tonight?'

'To Milton?' she repeated blankly, blinking her eyes at him in sudden confusion. 'You mean, back to my cottage?'

'Of course that's what I mean! Where else did you think you'd be spending the night, Lucy? Do you really think I want you in my home in the light of what I've just learned?'

'Drakon…' Lucy felt as if she had fallen down a deep well only to discover there were no footholds to allow her to get back up again. She had expected his censure, yes, and his condemnation, too. Deep down she'd felt as if she deserved both those things. But surely not such an instant and outright rejection, which felt so final and so *permanent*.

'What did you *think* was going to happen after this astonishing revelation, Lucy?' he demanded cruelly. 'That we would just go back to Mayfair and pretend nothing had happened? That we would make love and carry on as normal?'

She shook her head as a pair of dark eyes and a silky head swam into her mind. 'But what about Xander? What's going to happen to our son?'

'Xander has a nanny—and a father,' he said coldly. 'We don't need you, Lucy. Perhaps we never did. I will arrange to have your stuff sent to the cottage—'

'Please don't bother. Keep it!' she said furiously. 'I won't be able to wear those kinds of clothes in Milton, anyway!'

'That's entirely your decision. Oh, and I don't think I have any further use for this, do you?' he added contemptuously. She saw him twist his gold wedding band from his finger before letting it fall with a tiny clatter onto an unused side plate and fixing her with a final withering look. 'Obviously I will make sure your settlement is generous, provided you agree to a swift, no-claim divorce. I don't think there's anything else, do you? Other than to say goodbye.'

He turned and made his way through the restaurant, oblivious to the curious eyes which followed him, and Lucy wondered if she would be able to manage that same degree of insouciance. But most of all she wondered just how long she would be able to keep the hot flood of tears at bay.

CHAPTER ELEVEN

Don't forget Xander's check-up appointment at the clinic tomorrow. Sofia already knows but thought you might like to accompany them. L

DRAKON STARED AT the text message from his estranged wife which had just appeared on his phone and his brow creased in a frown. It wasn't the first he had received—all to do with the welfare of his son, he noted, and all signed off with Lucy's initial and not a single endearment.

Initially, he'd been surprised that she'd bothered contacting him, given the unceremonious way in which he had dumped her at the Italian restaurant. But wasn't that a mark of Lucy's soft and caring nature—that she wouldn't allow hurt pride to stand in the way of her concern for the baby she had mothered so beautifully? Another stab of the pain pierced relentlessly at his heart. The same damned pain which had been plaguing him since her departure. Fury and denial rose up inside him in a hot and potent mix. He kept telling himself it wasn't *her* he missed—it was her presence as Xander's mother which was making him feel so remorselessly uncomfortable.

And an inner voice mocked him every time that thought came into his head, because deep down he suspected it wasn't true. For a man so enamoured of the truth, wasn't he falling short of his own high standards? Because hadn't Lucy taught him how to relax around his son, so that now he felt completely confident whenever he cradled little Xander in his arms? Yet it hadn't always been that way. A lump rose in his throat and his heart began to pound. Before Lucy had come into their lives, the realisation that he must adopt his orphaned nephew had lain heavy on his heart. It had been a task he had been prepared to undertake—but Drakon's attitude had been reluctant. Not any more.

He stared down at the sleeping infant and his heart clenched. These days he embraced fatherhood with a sense of immense satisfaction and with something else, too. Something he'd never thought he'd feel towards Niko's baby—and that something was love.

Restlessly, he left the nursery and moved aimlessly through the Mayfair apartment which had felt so vast and so empty since his wife had moved out. He missed her in his bed at night—and the hard, physical ache which greeted him each morning bore testimony to that.

Just as he missed talking to her over breakfast and dinner and swimming with her in the Greek sea on a winter day when surely no sane person would have swum.

He had the services of the best nanny in the world

and the wherewithal to find another any time he wished. He had an address book practically overflowing with women who would be eager to provide him with whatever consolation he required.

He drew himself up short, reminding himself that he didn't *need* consolation—because that would imply that he was grieving for something and he wasn't.

Really, he wasn't.

Of course she missed him. That was only to be expected. But it was *Xander* she missed, Lucy convinced herself fiercely. She certainly didn't miss his pig-headed father. And of course it was weird being back in her tiny riverside cottage and waking up alone every morning, without the warm and muscular body of Drakon stirring beside her in more ways than one. But she would get over it. She had to. And all things passed eventually—some just took longer than others.

At least she'd got her job back. She had telephoned Caroline and had a brief and uncomfortable conversation. Her mentor and employer had diplomatically agreed not to quiz her about the reasons for the end of her brief marriage and Lucy had gone back to work as a waitress. The jobs were busy and distracting—which was probably a good thing—and she tried her best to pin on her brightest smile, hoping it would conceal the pain of missing the family life she'd so nearly become a part of.

One night she put on her pale green uniform and went to work at a large house outside the town, handing out canapés to the guests of a local landowner whose daughter had just got engaged. The whole affair seemed destined to mock Lucy, from the moment she was diverted to enter the house via the back door and told to tidy up her hair, to someone impatiently dismissing her and her tray, as if she were a large fly who had just landed on a piece of sushi and started laying eggs. She'd forgotten how patronising the rich could be, when you were in a position of domestic servitude. The newly engaged woman was flashing her massive and rather vulgar ring and, stupidly, Lucy found herself thinking about the discreet ink-spot sapphire which was tucked away at home with Drakon's discarded wedding band, which she had snatched up before leaving the restaurant, and wondering whether she ought to send both back to her estranged husband.

The moon was high in the sky by the time she left the party and, although transport home was included, Lucy had no desire to sit on a steamy and overcrowded minibus, especially as she was always the last one to be dropped off. Despite the ever-present drizzle, she set off to walk along the familiar roads and lanes, pausing briefly by a small footbridge, to watch the dark gleam of the water as it flowed beneath her. Because the river never changed, she thought gloomily. It had been the same all through her life and would be the same once she was dead and gone.

An unfamiliar sense of melancholy washed over her as she brushed past a low-hanging branch of wet leaves on the final approach to her cottage and tiny droplets of water showered over her. And then she nearly jumped out of her skin as a large figure loomed out of the darkness, her instinctive fear quickly replaced by an intense feeling of longing as she identified the late-night intruder.

Drakon.

Drakon Konstantinou, in all his towering and muscular beauty. Her heart twisted with pain and regret, but indignation was a far healthier reaction and that was the one she clung onto. 'What the hell do you think you're doing, jumping out of the shadows like that?' she demanded. 'You gave me a fright.'

'And what are you doing walking back alone at this time of night?' he returned furiously. 'Anything could have happened to you!'

'I can't think of any fate worse than my former husband turning up unannounced like this!' she retorted. 'What are you doing here, Drakon—have you come to gloat?'

Despite the darkness of the night, Drakon could see the fury spitting from his wife's eyes and his heart sank. Because this wasn't what he had planned. He'd thought she'd be home and he'd be able to talk his way into the cosy comfort of her small cottage within minutes. But the place had been in darkness and he'd been walking up and down this damned riverbank for hours, his tortured mind conjuring up pictures of where she might be, especially since her phone had been switched to silent and she hadn't bothered to return any of the calls he'd been making all evening.

Yet could he blame her for being so angry?

No, he could not.

Rarely in his life had he been forced to admit that someone else had the higher moral ground, but he did so now, repeating the same words he'd used when he'd turned up on this very same spot a few months back, asking her to marry him.

'Can I come in?'

'No, you can't. Contact me through my lawyer.'

He frowned. 'Have you got a lawyer?'

'Not yet. But I will. At least I suppose I will—isn't that what people do when they're going through a divorce?'

'I don't know, Lucy, because I've never been married before and I don't want a divorce.'

'Well, I do! I can't think of anything worse than—' She stopped abruptly, as if his words had only just sunk in, and eyed him suspiciously. 'What do you mean, you don't want a divorce?'

'There's no qualifier to that statement,' he said drily. 'I just don't.'

'Well, I do.'

He sucked in a deep breath as he read the defiance on her shadowed face. 'We can't have this conversation on the doorstep.'

'We seem to be managing perfectly well, so far.'

'Open the door and let's go inside, Lucy,' he said gently. 'Your hair's all wet.'

Lucy wanted to shout at him. To tell him not to adopt that silky tone which made her think of all the times he'd cradled her after they'd made love and made her feel so cherished and protected and wanted. Because all that stuff had been an illusion. It had withered and died at the first test, hadn't it?

Yet she recognised it would be immature to send him away when he had come all this way to see her. They needed to deal with this situation like adults.

He probably wanted her to promise not to give her side of the story to the press—as if she would dream of hanging out all her heartache for the world to see. And besides… She glanced nervously at the look of determination which was making his jutting jaw look so formidable. She swallowed. He didn't look anything like a man who would accept being turned away.

'Oh, very well,' she said crossly. 'But this had better not take long.'

She made him wait while she lit a couple of lamps and put a match to the fire because the temperature in the room was positively arctic. Then she took off her comfy black work shoes and shot him an acid look as she lined them up next to the others in the hallway. 'I'm assuming you won't be spiriting away any of my shoes this time?' she questioned sarcastically.

But he didn't rise to the bait. Instead he walked over to the window and stared outside, his head bent and shoulders suddenly hunched, like a worn-out fistfighter on the brink of defeat who was about to make one last stab at victory. 'I just want to say that I'm sorry, Lucy,' he said, and when he turned round Lucy was shocked by the ravaged expression she could read on his rugged features.

'It doesn't matter,' she said woodenly.

'Oh, but it does. It matters a lot. It matters more than anything else in the world that you realise how bitterly I regret the things I said to you that night.'

She shook her head, because hadn't her nurse training taught her always to see the other person's point of view? 'It doesn't,' she repeated, as generously as she could. 'We all say things we sometimes regret when we're angry. Or even when we're not angry. It's okay, Drakon. Honestly.'

'No, it's not okay,' he flared. 'It's anything but okay. Stop trying to be kind and reasonable, even though those are the very qualities which drew me to you in the first place.'

'Stop talking like that and just tell me why you're here, Drakon,' she demanded, her voice trembling with anger, because she didn't need to know these things. In fact, weren't they making the situation even worse?

'I'm here because I miss you, Lucy,' he bit out. 'I miss you more than words can ever say and in every way—physically, mentally and emotionally. And Xander misses you, too.' He shook his head. 'I can't believe I didn't even let you say goodbye to him.'

'But Xander has a nanny,' Lucy put in fiercely, because it wasn't fair for him to do this to her. To put her heart through the wringer all over again, only to leave her high and dry. 'As you told me on the night we parted. Just as you told me you couldn't tolerate a woman who had lied to you. And as for not saying goodbye to a baby of that age—what difference would it have made? Xander is too young to have realised what was going on and it would only have upset and confused the baby and Sofia.'

'But that wasn't why I did it,' he persisted. 'Why I wouldn't allow you to go to him.'

'No. I realise that. You did it to punish me because I had failed to live up to the image you'd created of me as your ideal woman.' She drew in a deep breath. 'Because that's the truth of it, isn't it, Drakon? You'd put me on a pedestal and that's where I was expected to stay. The nurse. The virgin. The mother. And you didn't like it when I blurred those roles, did you? When your good girl became a good-time girl and seduced you in the back of the limousine, you could hardly hide your dismay. You couldn't bear to accept that I had flaws, just like everyone else—or that I was a real person with real needs. Maybe if you hadn't been so intent on perfection, I might have had the courage to tell you I was infertile before. But I didn't want to risk you not marrying me,' she admitted huskily, because what did she have to lose now? 'I had an opportunity to do just that when we first discussed it, over lunch in the Granchester that day, when you presented me with my engagement ring.'

'But you didn't?' he questioned slowly.

'No, I didn't. You didn't ask why I didn't want children of my own and I was glad you hadn't, because in that moment I was living the dream and I didn't want to wake up from it. And like I said, we didn't really know each other—there was no expectation that we would ever care for each other—so why would I confide something so intensely personal?'

There was silence for a moment and when eventually he spoke, his voice was very low. 'What if I were to tell you again that I'm sorry for what I did and that I care very much? What if I were to tell you that my life has been empty without you and that I love you and want to spend the rest of my life with you and our son?'

Lucy couldn't prevent the surge of hope which flooded into her chest, but she quashed it and forced herself to ask the question which still hung between them, like a dark spectre. 'But you want more children, Drakon!' she declared, her voice shaking. 'That hasn't changed. You want more children and I can't give them to you.'

'I wanted more children with you,' he corrected sombrely. 'And if that isn't possible, then I will count my blessings and be content with the family I've already got. All I'm asking is for another chance, Lucy. To show you that I mean what I say. To love you in the way that you deserve to be loved.'

Lucy stared at him as those two words resonated more than any others. *Another chance.* How could she deny him that, even if she wanted to? Because how many people would give everything they owned for one more chance? Her brother would have liked the chance to have dodged that stray sniper's bullet—and if that had happened, her mother would never have faded away, like the blowsy roses which grew in the walled garden at Milton school.

She swallowed, knowing that this was the biggest and most important decision she'd ever had to make. If she accepted Drakon's offer, she would be taking a risk and she had never been a natural risk-taker. But what was the alternative? To turn him away and say goodbye? Yes, she might get hurt if she stayed with him—that was a very real possibility in every single relationship—but wasn't she being given the opportunity to spend the rest of her life with the only man she had ever loved? And wouldn't the hurt of turning him away transcend any other pain she'd ever known?

Because Lucy had glimpsed a world without Drakon in it and it was a bleak one. And maybe this place in which they now found themselves was the best place of all. One where all the barriers and fears with which they had surrounded themselves had crumbled away and all that was left were two people who loved each other and wanted to be together. She clasped her hands together as if in prayer and looked at him with all the tenderness she had never dared show before.

'Yes, Drakon,' she said softly. 'Yes, to everything you ask of me. Because I love you, too. I love the man I see beneath the hard layer you present to the world— and I'd like the world to see more of him.'

He nodded as he took a step towards her. 'Just know one thing, Lucy.' His voice was shaking as he pulled her into his arms and buried his face against her hair and she could feel his powerful body trembling. 'That I won't ever let you down. Not again.'

But Lucy knew that already, in the only place which mattered.

She knew it in her heart.

EPILOGUE

'YOU'RE NOT COLD?'

'Cold?' Lucy smiled up at Drakon. His arm was protectively clasped around her shoulders and she thought how handsome he looked in his dark dinner suit and black bow tie. 'Not at all. Mainly because I'm wearing thermal knickers.'

'Are you joking?'

'Of course I'm joking, darling. Do you really think I would have passed over all that deliciously decadent lingerie you bought me for Christmas in favour of a pair of sensible pants? And besides...' She snuck a glance at the jewel-studded wristwatch she'd also found nestling at the bottom of her stocking a week earlier. A delicate watch with ink-spot sapphires he'd had made specially. 'It's not long to wait until the fireworks.'

Her husband's black eyes gleamed as he studied her. 'Do you know how much I love you, Lucy Konstantinou?' he questioned softly.

'I think I've got a good idea. Just so long as you understand that the feeling is completely mutual, my darling. *S'agapo*.'

Noting Drakon's nod of contentment at her increasingly confident use of Greek, Lucy took the opportunity to look at the lavishly dressed guests who were milling around, drinking champagne beneath the fairy lights on the roof terrace of the Granchester Hotel as they waited for midnight.

'People seem to be having a good time,' she whispered. 'Don't you think?'

'Mmm,' he said, more concerned with dipping his head to brush his lips over the fall of her hair. 'The best time in the world, but of course—the moment I'm most looking forward to is when the fireworks are over and I can take you along to the penthouse suite to continue our own, very private party.'

'I'm looking forward to it, too,' said Lucy. 'Though I'm still not quite sure why we're staying the night here, when we only live down the road in Mayfair and have a car at our disposal.'

'I thought you might enjoy sleeping in the same bed we occupied on the first night of our honeymoon.' His mouth quirked. 'Or not sleeping, as the case may be.'

Lucy gave a contented sigh. 'You are a very romantic man, Drakon Konstantinou—as well as being an exceedingly sexy one.'

'I do my best. Because I gather that's what you like.' He whispered a fingertip over her waist. 'Am I right, *agape mou*?'

'Irrefutably,' she purred.

It was New Year's Eve and Drakon had thrown the party to end all parties to celebrate the discovery of a new oil field, which was being mooted as the biggest find in almost a century. And although Lucy sometimes mused that he really didn't need to earn any more money, the philanthropic arm of his empire had benefited in so many ways that she couldn't really complain. Her husband had taken over the entire hotel and the evening was—apparently—the hottest New Year ticket in town. Movers and shakers had flown in from pretty much every country in the world, as well as Hollywood actors and international sports stars, whose arrival was thrilling the growing crowds who had gathered outside behind the roped-off barriers.

Everyone who'd been at their wedding was here. Caro and her husband, as well as Lucy's two waitress friends, Judii and Jade. Patti and Tom were enjoying their first outing since the birth of their second child. And Amy was there too, with her not-so-new partner and proclaimed love of her life. Lucy smiled. When she and Drakon had decided to give their marriage another go, he had arranged a meeting with Amy. Gently, he'd explained to his business partner that the smokescreen of their close working relationship must necessarily end, because he intended travelling a lot less in future and spending more time with his family. Perhaps his words had galvanised her into action, for Amy had taken Michelle to meet her parents and told them she was in love. And in the end, perhaps her parents had recognised that their daughter's happiness was more important than a prejudice which they simply had to learn to let go of.

Lucy sighed as she stared up at a clear and starlit sky, which boded well for the eagerly awaited fireworks. What a long time ago their wedding seemed now, and how the years seemed to have flown by in the time it took to blink your eye. Three whole years—and back then she'd been so scared. A trembling mass of nerves in her too-fancy dress as she'd walked down the aisle towards a man she'd never stopped wanting. She'd never for a moment imagined she'd get love and devotion from someone who made no secret of having a heart of stone. But Drakon's heart wasn't made of stone, she'd realised. These days she would describe it as a heart of gold—for he had learnt to show his love, not just for her, but for their darling little Xander, who flourished with each day which passed.

'Something is different about you,' Drakon said, his velvety voice breaking into her thoughts.

Lucy turned her attention away from the star-spangled sky to study the ruggedly handsome face of her husband. 'What do you mean, *different*?'

He shrugged. 'You've been…thoughtful all day,' he said slowly. 'And your face has a kind of radiance about it which I've never seen before.'

How perceptive he was, Lucy thought, and savoured the moment before telling him what she still couldn't quite believe herself. 'I'm pregnant, my darling,' she said softly. 'I'm having your baby, Drakon.'

He stared at her without comprehension and it was several dazed moments before he could speak. 'But you said—'

'That I had endometriosis and because of that I was infertile, yes. That's what I was told. So when I started getting symptoms of pregnancy, I thought it must be something else. But when I saw the doctor this morning, she confirmed what I hardly dared dream. She told me that miracles do happen, and this is ours, Drakon—our very own miracle.'

Drakon felt a lump rise in his throat and the hot spring of tears at the backs of his eyes as he put his arms around her and held her tightly against his beating heart. Not for the first time, he wondered what he had done to deserve a wife like Lucy. A woman who had been prepared to take on an orphaned baby and to love the helpless tot without condition, just as she loved him. She had forgiven her sometimes irascible husband his many transgressions and taught him the things in life which were truly important, and the most important of these was love.

'I discovered that myself on the day I met you again, my love,' he said gruffly. 'Although it took me a long time to realise it.'

She pulled back from him. 'Realise what?'

'That miracles really do come true. Sometimes they are right in front of your eyes…you just have to let your vision clear for long enough to see them properly.'

'Oh, Drakon,' she said shakily.

The first chime of Big Ben rang out and the guests began counting down the seconds towards midnight. Trumpets sounded and streamers were popped and people started to sing as the final chime faded away. But as one year merged seamlessly into the next and a kaleidoscope of fireworks exploded on the London skyline, nothing came close to the burst of joy in Drakon's heart as he held Lucy tightly in his arms, and kissed her.

* * * * *

HER CHRISTMAS
WISH

SHERELLE GREEN

I would like to dedicate this to the Kimani readers who have given me so much book love and support over the past few years. Please accept this as a token of my gratitude and appreciation! I hope you continue to read the amazing stories myself and others are releasing and writing for your enjoyment. There are so many amazing novels out there waiting to be read by you!

Prologue

If there was one word to describe Kyra Reed, *ambitious* would be at the very top of the list. She went after what she wanted, and tonight, for her twenty-first birthday, she wanted Luke O'Connor. Preferably, naked.

It was bad enough that she'd spent most of her adolescence pining over someone who only seemed to look at her like a little sister, but then, she also had to compete against the flock of women parading around Chicagoland hoping to catch Luke's attention. She didn't have a claim on him. Had never dated him. Yet, that didn't stop her from feeling like Luke was hers, whether he realized it or not.

"Are you having fun?" her friend Cheyanne asked as she handed her a red Solo cup.

"Of course I'm having fun." Kyra's gaze traveled around the birthday party that her college friends had thrown her. "Have you seen my brothers and their friends?"

Cheyanne glanced around. "I think your brother Ajay went with Mike to get more ice. But Taheim should be here somewhere. He was with his guys. Jaleen and...?"

"Luke," Kyra said. "Those three are inseparable sometimes."

Cheyanne wiggled her eyebrows. "Right. How could I forget about your unhealthy crush?"

"It's not unhealthy," Kyra said.

"Oh, really? You've liked the man since you were ten. Probably before that. Are you telling me you don't think it's unhealthy for your state of mind to like him and still not say anything?"

Kyra shrugged, taking a sip of her drink. "I'm just waiting for the perfect moment."

Cheyanne rolled her eyes. "Girlfriend, he's known you most your life. How much more time do you need? The Kyra I know always goes after what she wants."

Kyra cringed at her words because it was true. She did go after what she wanted. "No need for the best-friend talk because I plan on telling him how I feel tonight."

Cheyanne's eyes widened as she asked, "Are you for real? You're finally admitting your feelings?"

"I'm very serious. It's long overdue."

Cheyanne squealed. "I'm so proud of you, and for telling me this, I'll tell you where he is."

Kyra carefully slapped her on the arm. "Are you saying you weren't going to tell me where he was unless I admitted I'd tell him my feelings?"

Cheyanne nodded. "That's exactly what I was going

to do." She motioned with her head to indicate the back door. "The boys are in the backyard."

Kyra gave her friend a quick hug and wasted no time heading to the backyard. It wasn't until she was almost out the door that she heard Cheyanne ask her what she'd planned on doing to get Luke alone. Kyra hadn't made it that far, but she was good at winging it.

The moment she stepped into the backyard, it felt like no one existed at the party except for Luke. People said "happy birthday" as she walked past, but the smile she gave them had less to do with the warm wishes and more to do with the sexy twenty-six-year-old man standing a few feet away from her.

Kyra had always wondered if the reason Luke often kept his distance was because of their age difference, and for that reason, she'd been anxious to become an adult to see if he paid her more attention. Much to her dismay, when she turned eighteen, he'd seemed to treat her like the same ol' Kyra. At nineteen, not much changed. At twenty, he got a little friendlier, but for the most part, he'd kept their relationship rated G, with a couple of PG-13 episodes thrown in the mix.

At twenty-one, she was tired of waiting for him to notice her, and tonight, she was laying out all her cards whether he liked it or not.

"Hey, guys," she said as she approached. "Enjoying my celebration?"

"Your friends know how to throw a party, sis," Taheim said.

Jaleen nodded. "Yeah, they weren't doing parties like this way back when I was in college."

Kyra rolled her eyes, slightly annoyed by the way Jaleen made it seem like he was so much older than her.

"Jay, you talk like y'all are old as hell, when you're only in your upper twenties."

"Wait until you start working in the real world," he said. "You'll start to feel the same way."

Taheim pulled her in for a hug and ruffled her hair. "Can't believe my baby sis is twenty-one now."

Kyra pushed him away. "Stop, Taheim. You'd think after all this time you'd learn to treat me like an adult. Didn't Mom ever teach you not to mess with a black woman's hair?"

He smirked in that annoying big-brother sort of way. "She did, but I chose to ignore that lesson when dealing with my little sis. A girlfriend maybe, but not you."

She crossed her arms over her chest. "Just my luck." Turning to Luke, she batted her eyes and asked, "How has life been treating you?" *In other words, please tell me you're still single.*

"Life is good," Luke said with a nod. "I can't complain. What about you? Excited to graduate soon?"

"Can't wait." She adjusted the strap of her blush-colored dress, enjoying the way Luke's eyes were slyly taking her in as he sipped his drink. *Progress.* A year ago, he never would have looked at her like that. Taheim started talking to Jaleen, giving her the chance to have a slightly more private conversation with Luke.

"I'll miss living down South during the school year," she said. "The weather here is beautiful." Kyra had chosen to go to an HBCU in Georgia, but planned on moving back to Chicago after graduation.

"I'll bet," Luke said. "I went to school in New York, so the weather wasn't much different than Chicago. Have you decided what you want to do after graduation?"

She shrugged. "My degree will be in business management, but no idea what I want to do. I love being a retail-store manager, so maybe I can find something in Chicago."

Luke laughed. "You're the only person I've ever met to say they love retail."

"I do love it," she replied with a laugh. "There's so much more to it than people think. For example, in some positions, you only use certain skill sets. I, on the other hand, must have an array of knowledge to tackle what goes on day in and day out at a store. Right now, I work at a chain shoe store, but I only got the job because the previous manager went on maternity leave and never came back. So I felt like I had a lot to prove. That was a year ago. Today, the district manager loves me and said I'm the youngest to ever hold my position and do so well."

Luke smiled. "That's impressive, but you've always been impressive. Nice to hear that your district manager thinks so, too." His eyes dipped to her lips and had Kyra not been glued to his every move, she wouldn't have caught his glance.

Not wanting to lose the spark, she turned as if she was surveying the backyard to give him a view of her firm, round butt, which was just the way she wanted it thanks to Cheyanne dragging her to the gym every day for squats and those machines that made her calves ache. "Looks like the crowd is dying down out here."

She turned back to Luke in time to see him raise his head as he looked nervously from her to Taheim, who wasn't even paying attention to what he was doing.

"Sis, we're about to meet up with Ajay and Mike," Taheim said, interrupting the moment. "The game is on at one of the bars down the street. Mind if we dip early and catch you at breakfast before we fly out?"

"Of course not," she said. "If you stayed, you'd just whine about missing the game, anyway." *Plus, I want to be with Luke without your prying eyes.*

"Yeah, you already know." Taheim nodded to Luke as he and Jaleen began to walk out the back gate. "Man, you coming?"

Luke glanced from Taheim back to Kyra. "Uh, yeah, I guess I am."

"Actually," Kyra said, lightly gripping Luke's arm, "I'm having some problems with the real-estate class I'm taking and Luke offered to help me."

Taheim lifted his eyebrow at the same time Luke asked, "You're taking a real-estate class?"

"Yes," she lied. "I want to be well versed in every aspect that I can. Who knows if I'll ever want to sell real estate on the side?"

"I don't remember you mentioning that class before," Taheim said while an amused Jaleen stifled a laugh. Kyra couldn't be sure, but she got the distinct feeling Jaleen knew exactly what she was up to.

"I don't have to tell you everything about my life," Kyra snapped at Taheim. "I rattle off classes I think interest you. But for this one, I am in way over my head. I should have dropped it at the beginning of the semester, but now, I'm stuck with it. This last homework assignment is really stumping me."

"I could take a look at it," Luke suggested. He turned to Taheim and Jaleen. "How about I take a look at Kyra's homework and then walk to the bar and meet you guys there?"

It wasn't unusual for Luke to help Kyra with her homework. When they were younger, she used to ask her brothers, but they always made it seem like she was annoying them when she asked. Luke wasn't like that. He stopped what he was doing every time she needed help.

Taheim looked skeptical for a moment, then shook it off and texted Luke the address. "If we change bars before you get there, I'll let you know."

Luke nodded his head. "Bet." Once they were alone, minus all the folks still at the party, Kyra wasted no time tugging Luke toward the house and up the stairs.

"Whoa, why are you walking so fast?" Luke asked, tripping up the stairs.

"I'm just really anxious for you to help me with this homework," she lied again as they entered the house. "It's been bugging me for years."

"Years?" Luke asked as they reached her bedroom. "You just said you started taking the class this semester."

Kyra groaned. She may have a huge crush on Luke, but perceptive, he was not. "I'm not really taking a real-estate course," she said, shutting and locking her bedroom door. "I just lied to get you in my bedroom." His eyes widened in surprise, so Kyra took the opportunity to push him down onto her bed while he was still surprised. "Why do you think I wanted to get you to my bedroom, Luke?"

Luke opened his mouth, but no words came out.

"I'll make it easier for you." Kyra reached for both her dress straps and let the material fall to the floor, leaving her in just her blush-colored lingerie. "Why do you think I wanted to get you to my bedroom, Luke?"

He visibly swallowed as his eyes roamed up and down her body, taking her in. "Uh, I don't want to assume you took me up here to have sex, but the way you just removed your dress, it's looking that way."

Kyra smiled. "Good job. That's exactly why I lied to get you up here. I'm tired of denying how attracted

I am to you and I'm pretty damn sure you're attracted to me, too."

Luke looked her up and down again. "Uh, although that may be the case…we can't have sex. That can't happen."

"Why not?" she asked.

"Because you're Taheim's little sister."

She shook her head. "Try again."

"Because you're five years younger than me."

"But still an adult," she countered. "Try again."

"Because your brother Ajay would kill me."

"Nope, not the right answer." Sticking with her plan, Kyra removed her bra next and was rewarded with a slow whistle of appreciation. And if that wasn't enough to prove he was interested, she noticed him growing harder by the second.

"I have a girlfriend," he spluttered. "So it's wrong for me to even be in here."

Kyra smirked. "What's her name?"

"Whose name?" he asked, eyes glued to her nipples.

"Your girlfriend, dummy."

"Her name is, um… It's, uh… Her name is Jaime."

Kyra frowned and looked toward her desk, which had a picture of herself with her childhood dog, Jaime. Stepping closer to Luke, she straddled him on her bed so that her breasts were almost level with his eyes. "Are you making up your girlfriend, Luke?"

He nodded his head.

"Did you make her up because you want to have sex with me tonight but are worried about the consequences?"

He nodded his head again. Dropping her mouth to his right ear, she whispered, "Screw the consequences."

She wasn't sure what made him grip the back of her head and bring her in for a kiss, but his mouth was on hers before she could say any more words. Just as she'd imagined, the kiss felt amazing, his lips bringing the perfect amount of pressure.

His hands were all over her backside, roaming up and down her thighs in fluid strokes. He smelled delicious. Even better than he had a couple of minutes ago because all of her senses were heightened with him so close.

"Kyra," he whispered in between kisses. Gone was the kid-sister voice he often used when talking to her. The way he'd said her name was the way a man spoke to a woman he was interested in, and the fact that she'd even gotten Luke to loosen some of his caution-when-approaching behavior was causing her insides to do a happy dance.

Unable to help herself, Kyra began twisting her hips, relishing the fact that he was getting even harder than before. "I always imagined it like this."

"Imagined what like what?" he asked.

"Imagined what kissing you would feel like. I've waited for this for so long, I can hardly believe we're finally about to have sex."

Luke froze, his hands gripping her hips to stop her from moving. Blame it on her big mouth. Or blame it on the tequila shots she'd had earlier in the night, but somehow, she'd managed to break the trance they'd been in a few moments ago.

Without warning, Luke hopped up from the bed, nearly knocking her over in the process. He caught her right before she hit the floor and helped her stand, then thrust one of her blankets at her.

"This was a huge mistake," he said. "We can't do

this." He ran his hands over his curly hair. "In fact, this never happened."

Kyra shook her head. "Of course it happened and you can't act like it didn't. I've been waiting to be with you my entire life."

He groaned. "Kyra, you can't say shit like that. We can't get together."

"Why not?" she yelled. "Don't bother telling me you aren't attracted to me because I know that's a lie."

"You're an attractive woman," he said. "But you're also off-limits."

"Says who? My brothers? Why do you care what my brother's think?"

"They're my best friends," Luke explained. "Had I known this is what you wanted me to stay behind for, I never would have agreed. Have you even had sex before?"

Kyra shrugged. "What does that matter?"

Luke shook his head. "I should go meet the guys. We can talk about this more in the morning."

As a last-ditch effort to get him to stay, Kyra pulled Luke down for a kiss. To her surprise, he actually kissed her back, until he pulled away from her again a few seconds later. "No, we can't do this. I'm sorry I let it get this far."

"I'm not," Kyra yelled. "Not even close. You want to be with me just as much as I want to be with you. No use denying it." She stepped closer to him. "Do you honestly think I haven't seen you watching me since I was sixteen? Admiring me even more at eighteen? Checking me out downstairs now, at twenty-one? You want me, too—you just don't want to admit it to yourself."

Luke shook his head. "You make me sound like a

creep. I'm way too old for you and this can't go further for reasons you're too young to understand. Find a boy your own age."

Kyra huffed. "I can't believe you're acting like this right now. If you think I won't try this again, you've got another thing coming."

Luke's eyes darkened in frustration. "Kyra, the truth is, although you're beautiful on the inside, I could never be with a woman like you. You and I don't mix, and as far as personalities go, I could never date someone who's so surface. Besides, you need to do some more maturing and growing right now. There's a man somewhere on this campus who would love a woman like you, but me? I'm looking for a woman with more substance right now."

Kyra stepped back, his words shooting at her like piercing bullets. Blame it on her I-don't-care attitude, but it wasn't the first time someone had assumed she didn't have much substance. She just never expected it to come from Luke.

"Get the hell out of my room," she spat. "Right. Now."

Luke shot her a look of sympathy, as if he wanted to take back his words. Kyra wanted to tell him it was no use. She'd already heard them and although she wished they hadn't hurt, they did.

He mumbled something when he neared the door, but she couldn't make out what he'd said. The minute he shut the door, she succumbed to the tears she'd been holding. She cried over his false assumptions about her character. She cried because her decade-long crush was now over. But even more upsetting, she cried for the amazing man who'd just broken her heart in two, because there was no way Luke could take back those words. They were tattooed on her brain and after she picked herself up from this heartbreak, she'd be smart to remind herself that this situation would be the last time she let a man make her feel as though she was unworthy of love.

Chapter 1

Ten years later...

"I don't care how many winters I spend here, this will never feel like Christmas," Kyra Reed huffed as she flicked her finger at the small Santa figurine that sat next to the register at Bare Sophistication Boutique and Boudoir Studio in Hollywood.

Kyra always thought it was crazy that right after Halloween, Christmas decorations were immediately put up. That was too soon in her book. However, since she worked in retail, she had to follow the wacky tradition.

"It doesn't seem much different to me," Aaliyah Bai-Burrstone, her pregnant ex-coworker, said. "Feels more like Christmas here than when I'm back home."

"That's because our husbands are our home," Nicole explained. "Plus, we're from Miami and I'm sure Kyra was talking about the fact that in Chicago, she's used to all that snow during this time of year."

When Nicole LeBlanc-Burrstone wasn't working at the production company she owned with her husband, Kendrick, she was at the boutique doing makeup and hair for the boudoir studio. Nicole and Aaliyah had originally worked at Bare Sophistication Miami. However, when the owners of the boutique chain decided to open an office in Hollywood, both of them, along with Kyra, who was working at the shop in Chicago, had decided to move to Cali.

Nicole and Aaliyah had also both married cousins and while Aaliyah still popped in every now and then to do boudoir photoshoots, she was now pursuing her dream as a professional photographer, traveling around the world with her husband, Bryant, whenever they got the chance.

"That's exactly what I mean," Kyra said, smiling at the way Aaliyah rubbed her protruding belly. "Personally, I can't stand the snow. But back in Chicago, the first snowfall was a clear indication that Christmas was right around the corner. I mean, I've seen more Santas dressed in swim trucks than I have in fluffy red suits."

"Yeah, that part is weird," Nicole said. "Cali seems to be infatuated with Surfboard Santa. It's not like that in Miami."

Aaliyah made a strained sound, causing Kyra and Nicole to turn her way.

"Are you okay?" Kyra asked.

Aaliyah nodded her head. "I'm good. Just wishing baby Burrstone would calm down today so I can help you both pack. He or she seems to want me sitting still with little movement."

"We got this," Nicole said. "You just rest."

"And let us do all the work?" Kyra laughed. "I honestly can't believe that after only a few years, we are switching locations, but I'm excited for this change."

Nicole glanced around at a couple half-filled boxes. "Are you sure we should be packing these up? We don't even have a new location for the shop yet."

Although Kyra loved the location of the current shop, when her sisters-in-law, Winter and Autumn, had visited her in Hollywood, she'd pitched her idea of expansion and, thankfully, they'd agreed that their quaint Hollywood shop had outgrown the space it was in.

"I've checked our inventory and I don't think we need to put out these items until spring. I plan on finding the perfect location before New Year's so we can jump-start the New Year with a bang!"

"What about your apartment?" Aaliyah asked. "Isn't your lease up soon, too?"

Kyra sighed as she continued to pack the box full of lingerie. "Yeah, which sucks because I should have started looking for a new place months ago."

"You can stay with us until you find somewhere," Nicole suggested.

"I'm good, but thanks, Nic."

"Or Bryant and I," Aaliyah offered.

Kyra glanced down at her friend's belly. "Ah, no. Definitely not. I love y'all, but you and Bryant need to enjoy the time you have before that baby pops out of your belly. Plus, you will not be using me as a babysitter if it takes me too long to find a place."

"Shoot," Aaliyah muttered, snapping her fingers.

"I'm sorry we can't be more involved in the move," Nicole said. "But I know a couple good Realtors in the area, so I could reach out to them and set up some more appointments."

Kyra shrugged. "It's no big deal. You're both newly married and, Nic, you have your beautiful baby girl, who is top priority. And that's not to mention your production company. And Aaliyah, you're a soon-to-be mom and have a ton of photography gigs lined up. I'm excited for more responsibility at Bare Sophistication and Taheim already said he knew a real-estate agent here who could help me. As a matter of fact—" she stumbled, removing her phone from the back pocket of her jeans "—he asked me to call him tonight since we're closing early. Leave it to me to forget. Do y'all mind?"

Aaliyah and Nicole both nodded their heads as Kyra began to dial her brother's number. He picked up on the third ring.

"Sis, I was hoping you remembered to call me."

"I almost forgot," she said with a laugh. "How are Winter and the kids?"

"Good, good. Everyone's good. But listen, I know you're in a time crunch to find a new location for the shop and are looking to buy a condo. You're trying to do this all before the New Year, right?"

"Yes, I am. I was aiming for before Christmas, but I haven't even started looking yet with less than two months to go."

"You know, Winter and Autumn will understand if you can't find a shop before then. These things usually take at least half a year."

"I know they'd understand, but I at least want to try and find something. I promised them I would manage this expansion and I want to keep my word."

Taheim laughed. "I figured you would say that. Which is why I called in a favor to have one of the top real-estate agents in the game to help you out."

Kyra perked up. "Okay, big brother, enough with the secrecy. Who is it?"

"Luke O'Connor," Taheim said proudly. "You remember Luke, right? One of my guys. Last you saw him was probably at my wedding."

Kyra frowned. *Luke O'Connor.* Did she remember Luke? Of course she did. All sexually frustrating wish-I-could-knee-him-in-the-balls-for-rejecting-me Luke. "Uh, yeah, I remember Luke. But I thought you mentioned last year that he'd moved to London?"

"He did, but he surprised us by coming back. In fact, he just moved to LA a couple months ago."

Kyra swallowed hard. "He—he lives here? In LA?"

"He does. What are the odds you'd both end up in the same city, right?"

"Yeah," she said, her voice cracking. "What are the odds?" She glanced at Nicole and Aaliyah in time to see them share a curious look.

"Yes, he's living there and from what he's told me, he just opened the new O'Connor Realty Group office with his younger brother."

Kyra shook her head. "Wait, Luke has a younger brother?"

"Sure does. His pops never told him. He only found out he existed a couple years ago. They've been building their relationship and his brother is from LA, so moving there felt right."

"Did his girlfriend move here, too?"

"What girlfriend?" Taheim asked. "If you're talking about the one he dated a few years ago, they broke up a while back."

Broke up? I really haven't been focused on his life

like I used to be. In other words, she hadn't done any social-media stalking in a while.

Kyra pinched the bridge of her nose. "Okay, so, Luke agreed to help me find two locations. Are you sure he even has time since he just opened his office?"

"Yeah, he has time. You know how we do in Chicago. We look out for each other. Living in Cali doesn't matter."

Kyra waved her hands. "Taheim, if you haven't talked to him yet, you don't have to. Nicole actually knows a couple of great real-estate agents."

"Sis, I said I called in a favor, remember? So there's no need," Taheim said. "As a matter of fact, that's him on the other line. I'll hit you up after, sis."

"No, wait. Taheim." She called his name, but it was too late. Kyra tossed her phone to the side and dropped her head into her hands. "This cannot be happening."

"Okay, who is Luke and why is he causing you to look so distraught?" Nicole asked.

"Yeah, I can't tell if you want to cry or throw up," Aaliyah added.

Kyra lifted her head. "Definitely throw up. Y'all know me. I'd never cry over a man."

Nicole nodded her head. "True. Then what gives?"

Kyra bit her bottom lip. "Back in the day, I used to have a crush on this guy, Luke. A part of me thought he even knew it, and at one point, it seemed like maybe he felt the same way. So I asked him, point-blank. And he told me he didn't. So I guess you can say that Luke is the man I always wanted to be with, but couldn't."

Aaliyah shot her a look of sympathy. "And knowing you, there's more to the story that you aren't telling us."

Instead of responding, Kyra just looked away.

"There's always more to every sad love story, isn't there?" And unfortunately, hers wasn't the type of self-reflection she wanted to have this close to the holidays.

"I'm sorry, what was the favor you needed again?" Luke had heard loud and clear what Taheim had asked him, but he needed to hear it again. Just for clarification.

"Man, your head must be in the clouds," Taheim said with a laugh. "I was just asking if you could help out Kyra. She's looking for a new location for the boutique and a condo for herself. She's short on time because she's trying to purchase both before the New Year."

Kyra Reed needs my help. Yeah, he'd heard him right. "I don't know, man. Are you sure she needs my help? Maybe she already has a real-estate agent to help her."

"She doesn't," he said. "I told her you would be the best man for the job. I know you already got a load of clients, but are any looking for large real estate? Finding a place for the new Bare Sophistication office could be good for you, right?"

Luke frowned, rubbing his forehead. Although he'd landed some great clients since opening a couple of weeks ago, he'd given most of them to his younger brother, Nash, so he could focus on other aspects of the business.

But there wasn't anything he wouldn't do for her. Even if that meant spending time with her when he'd made a promise to avoid her as much as he could since he'd just moved to LA.

"Okay, man. I'll hit her up so we can meet. Text me her number."

"Thanks, Luke," Taheim said. "This means a lot." They chatted for a few more minutes before ending the call.

"Damn," Luke muttered, leaning back in his desk chair. He shouldn't have been at the office so late, anyway, but he didn't quite feel at home at Nash's place yet. Nash had insisted that he stay with him when he learned he was living at a hotel until he found his own place. Reluctantly, Luke had agreed, but damn, he liked having his own place and his own space. Besides, he was only going to be in LA for the next six months or so. Luke had offices in his Chicago hometown as well as New York, but until he showed Nash the ropes of running the LA office, he'd be living here.

Standing up to finally gather his belongings and leave for the day, Luke wondered if Kyra was as cool with him helping her as Taheim had made it seem. The last time they'd truly spoken was at Taheim and Winter's wedding, and Kyra had made it very clear that he was the last person on earth she wanted to see.

When he reached his car, he called the number Taheim had sent him. Surprisingly, she answered on the second ring.

"Hello?" Her sexy voice filled the line, making him lose his train of thought. *Why does she always sound like that?* It was a mixture of sultry and breathless, making his thoughts anything but PG-13.

"Hello?" she repeated.

"Kyra, hi. It's… It's Luke."

"Hi, Luke," she responded with zero emotion. *Tough crowd.*

"Taheim mentioned that you need help finding a couple locations and since I just moved to LA, I was wondering if you wanted to meet sometime this week to discuss your needs."

"My needs?" she asked.

"Yeah, I want to help you get everything you want." Luke cringed at his words. *Could you sound more like a personal ad!*

"Right, well, I can meet tomorrow."

Damn. He didn't think she would say she could meet so soon. "I can meet tomorrow as well. How about noon?"

"That would work. I'll text you the address to a café near the boutique. Thanks for calling."

"Okay, sounds—" The call was cut short before he could even finish his sentence. "That's more like the Kyra I know," he muttered to himself. In the back of his mind, he knew he deserved her anger. Back in the day, he hadn't treated her well after learning that she had a crush on him. He'd tried to say enough to get her to understand that they could never be together, but it had backfired and resulted in them not talking for years.

Feeling so distant from Kyra was something he never thought would happen. Often, he'd told his mom that even if he and Taheim weren't friends anymore, he couldn't imagine not having Kyra in his life. Although he'd had a decent childhood, it wasn't all sunshine and roses. Kyra was a beacon of light for him. A reminder that there were good people in the world who cared about you even when you didn't care about yourself.

And what did you do, idiot? He'd pushed away one of the few people who meant a lot to him. That night she'd tricked him into going to her bedroom, he hadn't just lost one of his closest friends, he'd lost the woman whom he'd promised to always be there for. He'd apologized years ago, but she hadn't been willing to hear him out. At least now, he hoped helping her find a location for the boutique and a new home would show her that deep down, he was still the same Luke he used to be.

Chapter 2

There wasn't anything more nerve-racking than waiting for a meeting to take place that you were absolutely dreading. Kyra had arrived at the café ten minutes early to snag a table and calm her nerves since meeting with Luke today was probably on her list of things she'd be okay never doing again.

In retrospect, asking him to meet today had been a bad decision, but all she'd been thinking about was getting the meeting over with so that she wouldn't dread it all week. She hadn't planned to be rude and hang up on him, but just hearing his voice, all deep and husky, made her stomach drop. She hadn't heard it in so long after dreaming about it more times than she could count. It wasn't fair for him to sound that good and her only worry was that he looked better than he sounded.

She had an idea of how fine he still was, but she was

proud of herself for not stalking his social-media pages like she used to. In fact, she had even blocked him from a few platforms so she wouldn't be tempted to look.

It's okay, girl, she thought to herself. *You're a strong-ass woman and seeing the man who broke your heart all those years ago will not shake you.*

"Kyra?"

She closed her eyes at the voice, counting to three before looking upward. The minute her eyes landed on Luke in his dark gray suit and pearly white smile, she knew she should have at least counted to ten before setting eyes on him.

"Hi, Luke."

Even though she was sitting down, his eyes slowly looked her up and down in a way that surprised the hell out of her. "I almost didn't recognize you," he said. "You look nice with the copper highlights."

Kyra ran her fingers through her shoulder-length hair. "Thanks. I just got them, actually. I'm surprised you noticed."

He smiled as he took a seat across from her. "I've always noticed you."

Always noticed me? Kyra squinted, confused by this version of Luke. Instead of letting her thoughts wander, she decided to ask him about what he'd said. "What's wrong with you?"

He squinted. "What do you mean?"

"What do you mean, 'what do I mean'?" She leaned closer so that he could hear her without her voice carrying. "You said you've always noticed me? In my mind, that's the complete opposite of how you've always treated me."

Luke dropped his head a little. "In the past, I've

called you and apologized for how I treated you on your twenty-first birthday. After that, I texted you an apology. Then, at Taheim and Winter's wedding, I—"

"Let's not talk about my brother's wedding," Kyra said, cutting him off. "And while I appreciate your apologies, you've still never openly mentioned noticing me at all."

Luke shook his head. "Why are you always so difficult?"

Kyra shrugged. "It's in my DNA, but regardless, you don't have a right to say that about me anymore. So how about we just continue on with the meeting."

"Are we not even getting anything to eat?" Luke asked, glancing around.

"There is no time to eat. I have to get back to work soon," she lied. She took out the packet of info she'd put together with what she was looking for in regard to the location for the boutique, as well as a condo. "This packet has all the information you need to get started on setting up appointments."

Luke flipped through the pages, shooting her a look of surprise. "Uh, this is very thorough, but I sort of thought we would talk about everything in person. Hence the meeting."

Kyra leaned back in her chair. "Regarding the boutique, we're looking to stay within a mile of our current location. Unlike the current building, we need a storefront and would love a storage facility or something connected to it for us to stock additional merchandise. And we don't want to be on a run-down block. The current square footage of our boutique is listed in the packet and we now want at least one thousand square feet more.

Also preferably it would be two levels or sections for the boudoir studio."

Luke nodded his head. "Of course. I've been to the boutique in Chicago and I even checked out the one in Miami. I'll have to check out this location to make sure I find some options with the same vibe and energy as the others."

"You can stop by anytime this week," she said. "I'll be there every day during store hours and after hours prepping for the move."

Luke smiled. "Wow, you're already packing up? I'm glad you're confident that I will find you some great places."

"I'm not," she stated. "But I'm confident in me finding a real-estate agent capable of finding the perfect place if you don't show me some good options within the next two weeks."

Once again, Luke shook his head. "Different hairdo, same sassy Kyra." He flipped through several more pages. "The wish list for your condo is pretty long. Are you sure you're looking for three bedrooms?"

"Of course I'm sure," she said. "My bedroom, the guest bedroom and my activity room."

"Activity room?" Luke asked. "Like the type of room parents create for their kids."

Okay, clearly, he doesn't want to get in my good graces. "No, not like the type of room parents create for their kids. Mine is an adult activity room, not that it's any of your business why I want three rooms. You're just my real-estate agent. You aren't allowed to judge."

"But I am allowed to remind you that with the budget you listed, finding three bedrooms in LA is next to impossible. Especially since you're also asking for an outdoor space, walk-in closet and an in-unit washer and dryer."

"I have expensive tastes."

"And a shoestring budget," Luke huffed.

Kyra rolled her eyes. "See, this is why I didn't want your help finding a place, but Taheim insisted. I suppose having these places purchased before the New Year is asking too much, too, right?"

"A little bit, yeah. Finding the place is one thing. Finalizing all the documents, getting the lawyer and accountant involved, and working out your loan approval are other issues entirely."

Kyra frowned. "I thought you're supposed to be one of the best real-estate agents around? Are you saying you've failed before you've even started?"

"I'm just trying to be realistic," he explained. "That's all."

Kyra glanced at her phone before looking back to Luke. "Well, keep all that realism to yourself until you've actually tried to find what's on my list. Deal?" She started gathering her stuff, not caring about the fact that Luke was looking at her as if he wanted her to stay and finish their conversation.

"Deal," he finally said.

"Great. If you have any additional questions for me that aren't answered in the packet, then text me. Other than that, I'll see you when you drop by the shop."

Luke blew out a breath. "Okay, I'll see you then." Walking out of the café, Kyra made sure she held her head high and reminded herself to stay firm on her decisions. True, she knew her list was a little unrealistic, but didn't care. Apologies or not, she wasn't ready to let him back into her life easily.

* * *

"Wait, and who is this again?" Nash asked, following Luke into their new office building.

"Kyra is one of my closest friends' sister," he explained. "She needs help finding a couple locations, but she wants to nail this down by January."

"Did you tell her finding anything that soon is damn near impossible?" Nash asked.

"Of course I did. But if you knew Kyra, you'd know it's no use. I guess you can say she lives life on her own terms, and if you try and tell her any different, she's not trying to hear you."

Nash smiled as he settled into his office right across from Luke's. "Sounds like my kind of woman. Is she cute?"

Luke froze. "Uh, yeah. I guess."

Nash shook his head. "Ah, nah, she doesn't sound like it based off that look you're giving right now."

"No, trust me, she's attractive. *Very* attractive. And she doesn't even try to be. It just naturally pours out of her, inside and out. It's that type of beauty that slaps you in the face when you aren't looking. She tries to act all tough like she doesn't let much bother her, but deep down, she's a softy. I remember when she went through her tomboy phase. Even then, she was cute."

Luke wasn't sure how long he rambled on. However, when he noticed how quiet Nash was being, he looked across the hallway to see his brother wearing an amused grin. "What's that look for?"

"Bro, you could have saved a lot of breath complaining about Kyra on the way to the office if you'd just told me up front how much you're feeling her." For more emphasis, Nash wiggled his eyebrows.

"Yeah, we used to be close when we were younger, but I'm not feeling her the way you're implying. I just know a lot about her."

Nash lifted an eyebrow. "Right. Keep telling yourself that."

"I'm serious. Didn't you hear the part where I said she's my best friend's sister?"

"Nope. I heard the part where you called Taheim a close friend. I figured it was strange considering you've told me so much about Taheim and Ajay. So I know they are a couple of your best friends. I also have eyes just like you do. Taheim's always posting pictures of his family on Instagram and I think I've seen his sister in a few. She's bad, though. Got that Zoe Saldana vibe going on. I understand why she'd get you all hot and bothered."

Luke waved off his comment. "Man, you don't know what you're talking about. Kyra doesn't make me hot or bothered. She's like a little sister to me."

"In that case, thank God we don't have a little sister. Unless we don't know she exists yet, just like we didn't know about each other. Oh, wait..." Nash snapped his fingers. "Have you had a DNA test done on Kyra to make sure she's not our sister?"

"No, fool. I didn't do that. Trust me, Kyra Reed is not related to us. I've known the Reed family most of my life. She's definitely not our sister."

"Great, then you can ask her out on a date and stop tripping."

Luke put his hands in the air. "I can't ask her out. Have you not been listening to anything I've been saying? She's Taheim and Ajay's younger sister. That's like, asking to fuck up two decades of friendship."

Nash squinted his eyes. "Taheim and Ajay don't

strike me as the type to give the you-can't-date-my-sister speech. Especially when it was Taheim's idea for you to help her out in the first place."

"Well, they did," Luke said, thinking back to the conversation he'd had with Ajay all those years ago. "Kyra had a crush on me and everybody but me knew it."

"Because you were too busy denying your own feelings for her," Nash said.

"Exactly!" Luke's face dropped. "Wait, that's not what I meant. What I meant to say is I was too busy dealing with my own shit to recognize anything else going on back then."

Nash smirked. "Right. I get it." However, his look was saying that he absolutely didn't buy it.

"I'm serious, but you look like you don't believe me."

"How long have we known each other?" Nash asked.

Luke shrugged. "About a year, I guess."

"And how long does it feel like we've known each other?"

Luke thought about the quick friendship he'd built with his brother. "Feels like we've always been in each other's lives."

"My point exactly. I may not have been in your life back then, but I know you better than you think I do. My guess is you suspected she had a crush, but you were too busy denying your own feelings for her. Don't you get it, bro? You're living in your own romance movie right now. Boy meets friend. Friend introduces boy to little sister. Boy adores little sister. Sister begins to have crush on boy. Feelings continue as boy and girl get older. Boy messes up. Girl gets pissed. Years later, boy has chance to make it up to girl. Girl makes boy pay for breaking her heart. Boy and girl have revelation. They fall in love and live happily ever after."

Luke blinked. "What makes you think I messed up with her?"

Nash snorted. "Man, please. Men always mess up. Now is the part of the movie when you try to win back her love in case you weren't following."

Luke shook his head. "Uh, you have quite the imagination."

"All I'm saying is now is your chance to finally see what could have been. And although Taheim will probably be the best man, you betta make me a groomsman."

"For my imaginary wedding?"

"Yeah, fool. Have you not been listening? We already know how this story ends. At least, that's how you want it to end. There's also the possibility that you will mess this up again and girl will run off with another guy, but I'm going to help you out so that you don't lose her before your relationship even starts."

Luke laughed. "I don't know whether to listen to your crazy advice or just forget we had this conversation."

Nash walked across the hall and leaned against the doorjamb of Luke's office. "Were you listening to anything I just said? Bruh, you were already taking my advice before I even finished giving it. Man, are you sure you're not the younger brother here?"

"I have three and a half years on you," Luke said. "So, yeah, you're the youngest."

Nash popped his collar. "But clearly, I'm the intelligent one."

"Nah, I'm just entertaining you this morning because I figured your ego needed a boost since you're talking all this romance mess."

"My ego never needs a boost," he said. "I stay ready. Don't hate because I'm spitting that knowledge."

Their banter continued for a few more minutes and Luke had to admit, he'd wished he'd had Nash in his life growing up. There wasn't a day in his adolescence when he didn't wish he had a brother, but he'd also known it wasn't going to happen. His parents were the type that never should have had kids together in the first place.

Now that he had Nash in his life, he tried not to think about all the parts of his childhood that he wished he could change, but rather, he was focused on building his relationship with his brother. Already, dude was saying things that got under his skin, but then again, what younger brother didn't say things to annoy their older brother? Regardless, Luke couldn't deny that Nash had his mind racing with how he needed to proceed with Kyra.

Chapter 3

"Um, I don't like this place, either," Kyra said for the third time that morning.

"Let me guess," Luke said. "The view from the front balcony isn't good enough?"

"No, the view is great. But this is only one and a half bedrooms and no washer and dryer in the unit."

Luke shook his head. "This is a two-bedroom unit and I already told you that it could be installed for a little extra."

"You call this closet a second bedroom?" Kyra asked, nodding her head to the bedroom on the left. "You could maybe fit a twin-size bed in there, but not much else. They should just call it a closet."

"They already have a master closet in the other bedroom," Luke reminded her. "This is definitely a second room."

Kyra shrugged. "It's still a closet."

"This is LA. Some rooms are small."

"Well, then I need you to do better and find me something that's not a closet."

Kyra wasn't really surprised that she and Luke had been disagreeing for most the morning. She was surprised when he'd called her last night and asked if she could check out three condos with him. She'd only just met with him two days ago.

Luke sighed. "Please tell me you're not going to be this difficult the entire time."

Kyra shook her head, ready to tell him that she wasn't being difficult, when a thought came to mind. Luke may have given her a half-assed apology back when he'd made her feel like she was absurd for flirting with him, but he hadn't felt her full wrath yet. She'd been too busy nursing a broken heart and avoiding him at all costs—which had been pretty difficult considering her brothers seemed so intent on inviting him to everything.

Turning on her heels, she crossed her arms over her chest and told him, "I can be difficult if I want because this is a big purchase for me. My first big purchase, in fact. Would you talk to your other clients this way?"

"When they are being unreasonably rude, yes."

"So now I'm unreasonable, too?" she huffed. "And you really think it's for no reason?" Kyra walked toward the front door. "This was the last place we had to see today, right? How about we just meet up when you find more places."

"Kyra, wait," Luke said, approaching her as she neared the door. "I think we knew early this morning that today wasn't going how either of us planned. So how about we have lunch—and I mean actually have lunch—at the café near the boutique. I really do want to find you a condo you will love and I want to have at least a couple store-fronts for you to check out this week, so I need to see the place."

Kyra bit the side of her cheek and observed Luke, taking note of the sincerity in his voice. Oh, she still wanted to make him pay for how he'd treated her, but she also wanted to hit. She'd skipped breakfast because her nerves were so bad. "Okay," she finally said, sticking out her hand. "For the sake of a tasty turkey-and-cheese sandwich, let's call a truce so we can eat lunch."

Smirking, he slipped her hand in his, the warmth immediately giving her those tingles she hadn't felt in far too long. "It's a deal."

Luckily, when they arrived at the café, the lunch crowd wasn't too bad. They both ordered sandwiches and took a seat in a booth by the front windows.

"This is my favorite place to sit," Kyra said, doing her best to refrain from soaking in how delicious Luke looked now that she'd called a truce for the next half hour. "I do the best people-watching here."

"You still people-watch, huh?"

"Always! I also still play the people-watching game I used to play when I was a kid. The one where you decide a person's occupation, age and main personality traits based off how they dress and walk."

"I remember," Luke said with a laugh. "Didn't your mom tell you to quit being so nosy when Mr. Henderson who lived next door complained about you?"

"He only complained because I caught him cheating on his wife," Kyra explained. "I may have only been eight at the time, but even then, I knew he shouldn't be kissing that woman who used to sneak into his house after his wife went to work."

Luke laughed. "Detective Kyra, blowing up marriages even at a young age."

She lifted an eyebrow. "The way you're saying it makes it seem like I've blown up other marriages."

"You have."

"Whose marriage?"

"Remember Mr. Roscoe who drove the ice-cream truck? One day, he didn't give you the ice-cream bar you wanted because he said he didn't like your attitude."

"My attitude? You know how Mr. Roscoe was. He had an attitude every day, but had the nerve to try and cheat little kids out of money by serving those off-brand Popsicles and ice-cream bars."

Luke nodded his head. "That may be true, but you didn't have to walk all the way to his house and tell his wife that he spent a little too much time with Shirley from down the street. All it took was one accusation for his wife to follow him the next day and find him at Shirley's house stepping out on his marriage."

Kyra shrugged. "Not my fault. He should never have tried me in the first place. Had he treated us kids better, I never would have said anything."

Luke laughed, the sound causing her to laugh right along with him. It was always that way with Luke. One minute he'd be saying something to annoy her, and the next they'd be laughing over something one of them said.

"I've missed this," he admitted after he took a bite of his sandwich. "I understand why we grew apart, but I've missed laughing with you over stupid stuff."

Kyra smiled. Luke's dark-honey complexion and deep brown eyes almost made her choke on her water as she watched him. Observed him. Wondered when he'd chosen to cut off his curls and trade them in for a low fade. He was the same Luke, yet he was far from the boy she used to know. However, there was a part of her that also felt like not much had changed. His core was still the same. Despite how pissed he'd made her when he'd broken her heart, he really was a good guy. Still cared about doing charity work and giving back to his community, unlike some other guys she knew. Social media couldn't tell her everything, but it told her enough to paint a picture of the type of man Luke had turned out to be.

"I know what you mean," she finally replied. Her eyes held his as she took a bite of her own sandwich. Back in the day, she felt like she always knew what Luke was thinking. However, the man sitting across from her was harder to read. His feelings were more guarded than she'd remembered.

Understanding teenage Luke and young-adult Luke was a quality she'd perfected. But grown-up Luke, who was looking at her with low-lidded eyes? Yeah, she needed more practice with this one.

"Here's the shop," Kyra announced as they walked through the door. As Luke had predicted, the shop was buzzing with customers on their lunch break. "The main level is our boutique and the top level is our boudoir studio."

Luke glanced around, admiring the shop. "I really like the decor," he said. "Seems to fit the flow of the Chicago and Miami boutiques, but it has a certain Cali flair."

Kyra smiled. "That's what we were going for." She spoke to a couple of the associates who greeted them when they walked past toward the stairs. "Follow me and I'll show you the studio."

They ascended the stairs, Luke's gaze focused on Kyra's backside even though he wasn't trying to check her out. *Damn.* Kyra still knew how to wear a pair of jeans better than any woman he'd ever met before. Even though he shouldn't have been checking for her back then, he knew from years of watching her when he thought no one was looking that she was one of those women who was just born with an extra switch in her hips and curve to her thighs.

"You better not be checking out my ass, O'Connor," Kyra said, glancing over her shoulder.

"Uh, I was just watching your feet to make sure you don't trip."

She rolled her eyes. "I'm sure you were." When they reached the top, once again Luke was caught off guard by how similar it looked to the Chicago location with regard to the decor. However, the vibe in this studio was different than any he'd felt before.

"It feels good up here," he said, walking past the grand bed in the corner covered in a plush white comforter and large beige pillows. "I'm not sure what it is that's different, but I like it."

When his eyes met Kyra's, he noted the look of surprise. "I've thought that exact same thing so many times before. Decor-wise, my sisters-in-law wanted the studio to be similar to Chicago, and although we achieved that, I remember walking into this place after the interior was finished, wondering what was different. I even told Nicole and Aaliyah, who opened this location with me, and neither one of them could put their finger on it, either."

She walked past some more furniture that Luke

assumed was staged for the next photoshoot. "Unexplained reasons like this are exactly why I like to see the current locations of businesses before finding them a new home."

"That makes you a great real-estate agent."

"Wow! Did Kyra Reed just give me a compliment?"

She smirked. "Don't let it go to your head. All I meant was that most of them wouldn't care about something as small as a feeling."

"The good ones would," he said. "Being a good real-estate agent is a lot like being a matchmaker."

"Oh, hold on," Kyra said, pulling him over to two stools. "I have to be seated to hear how you plan on justifying that a real-estate agent is anything close to a matchmaker."

"Whoa, slow down." Luke held out his arms. "I said a good real-estate agent, not all real-estate agents."

Kyra waved him off. "Some. All. You know what I meant."

He shook his head before explaining. "In real estate it's about helping a person find their next home or business. It's about showing them the different options available to them in the hopes that they will find something they love. It's about that feeling in the pit of their stomach that they get when they've found the perfect one. When they've fallen in love with the right one. Most people think being a real-estate agent is like being a salesperson, when in all honesty, it's more like being a matchmaker than anything."

Kyra observed him with an amused look on her face. "Well, well, well, O'Connor, dare I say that your words have gotten much deeper than that time you made the correlation between a garbageman and a bartender."

Luke laughed. "I was drunk when I tried to connect those two. You shouldn't hold that against me."

"Oh, I will definitely hold that against you, but seriously, I love that. The real-estate agent being the perfect matchmaker." She leaned closer to him, causing his heartbeat to quicken. "So now is the time when I ask you to use matchmaker terminology with me until you're able to find my *perfect one*."

Luke wasn't sure if it was the fact that she was leaning toward him or the way her lips curled into a mesmerizing O when she said the last word, but he wanted to kiss her. Badly. And the fact that they hadn't talked out any of their issues was only part of the reason he needed to maintain control. So it only felt fitting when he told her, "Absolutely not."

Chapter 4

"I can't believe you and Kendrick are planning another party," Kyra said to Nicole as the two of them and Aaliyah walked into Nicole and Kendrick's home. "Now you know I love me a good party, but y'all just had a ridiculously huge one a couple months ago."

The ladies had been at the shop longer than usual to finish up a boudoir photoshoot. Kyra had insisted that Nicole return home to set up for her party tonight, but she'd assured Kyra that they would arrive in plenty of time before the party. Glancing at her iPhone and noticing they had an hour before the official party kickoff, she was right.

"That party was my idea after we finished producing that romance movie in the studio. This party was Kendrick's idea because we wrapped up on that action movie he was dying to get his hands on."

Aaliyah shook her head. "Nic, you and Kendrick are the only couple I know who try to throw parties to outdo one another."

"I agree," Kyra said. "But it's so y'all."

"You're married," Aaliyah added.

"You sure are," Kyra agreed.

"So his party is your party and vice versa. It shouldn't matter which one is bigger and better."

Kyra stopped walking and turned to Aaliyah. "And that's where my agreement stops because when I get married, he better be prepared for me to outdo him in every way possible."

"That's my girl," Nicole said, slapping Kyra's hand.

Aaliyah shook her head. "Sometimes, I don't know what to do about the two of you."

Kyra and Nicole both opened their mouths to comment, but neither got a chance when Kendrick walked into the living room. "Looks like the Three Musketeers are all here."

"I hate that nickname," Kyra said, giving him a hug after Aaliyah gave hers.

"I kinda like it," Aaliyah said. "That movie was good, too."

Kendrick pointed to Aaliyah. "You see, that's why you're my favorite of Nicole's friends."

Kyra rolled her eyes, but she couldn't help but laugh at the way Aaliyah teared up at Kendrick's words. Aaliyah was already an emotional person—add pregnancy hormones to that and she was a walking cry-bomb.

"Kyra, you're just in time. I'm dying to know if anyone ever called the cops on you for people-watching?"

Kyra blinked rapidly. "Wait, what? Why would you

ask something like that? And how did you know about my people-watching?"

Her question was answered the moment Luke slid into the living room looking guilty. "My bad, Kyra. I may or may not have said something to Kendrick about it." Bryant, Aaliyah's husband, walked into the room right after, wearing an amused look on his face.

"Why didn't you tell us you knew Luke?" Bryant asked.

Kyra shook her head. "Better question. How do you know Luke?"

"When we lived in Chicago, he attended the same boys-and-girls club that we went to," Kendrick answered. "When I heard he'd moved to Cali, I knew we had to get him to a party."

Luke took a step forward and reached out his hand to Nicole. "You must be Kendrick's wife. It's very nice to meet you."

"Nice to meet you, too," Nicole said, winking at Kyra as she did so.

"And you must be Aaliyah," he said next. "Bryant has been talking about you all night."

Aaliyah's eyes widened in surprise. "How did you guess I was Aaliyah and not Nicole?"

Luke laughed and turned to Bryant. "You're right, man. She is funny."

"She is," Bryant replied, a big grin on his face. "But she's dead serious. The pregnancy has her acting a little different." As if her husband's words made it click, she glanced down at her belly and started laughing, finally understanding how Luke knew she was Bryant's wife.

"When I saw you yesterday, you didn't mention you would be here tonight," Kyra said to Luke.

"When we were together, I didn't know I was coming, either. Kendrick called me this morning."

Kyra glanced from Kendrick to Nicole. "Funny that all of a sudden, Luke was invited tonight."

"I thought the same thing," he admitted.

"Enough with the awkward introductions," Kendrick interjected. "Nicole and I still have some setting up to do before the others arrive, but why don't you all get something to eat and hang out while we finish."

"I'll help y'all," Bryant said, following Kendrick and Nicole. Aaliyah looked between Kyra and Luke before smiling and waddling out of the room behind her husband.

Great. Kyra had thought she was in for a night full of fun with her friends during which she'd be able to vent about the fact that Luke had walked back into her life. *Guess the joke is on me.* And why did he have to look so good in a pair of dark jeans and a navy polo? He was sporting that look that was a cross between bashful and sexy, his eyes darting across her face, studying her. Observing her.

"If you take a picture, it will last longer," she said with a smirk.

He smiled. "Did anyone ever tell you that your mouth may get you in trouble one day?"

"My entire life," she told him proudly. "You can give me that look all you want, but you knew I was going to call you out."

"I did," he admitted. "I guess I wanted to hear that smart mouth of yours to break the tension."

"Oh, there is a lot more where this came from."

He shook his head. "Don't I know it."

"If you know it, then I suggest you tread lightly."

Kyra glanced around the empty front room, the soft sounds of whatever holiday playlist that was coming through the Bluetooth speakers filling the silence in Nicole and Kendrick's living room.

"I love this song," Luke said as a new song started.

"Me, too. 'Santa Baby' has always been one of my favs."

"Especially Eartha Kitt's version," he added. They stood there for a few long minutes, Kyra unsure of how to fill the awkward silence.

"I'm sure you've already guessed this," she said, "but my friends wanted to give us alone time to talk. Funny thing is, I feel like this was more the guys' idea than my girls', but that doesn't make sense. Kendrick and Bryant aren't the meddling type."

"I may have had something to do with that," he admitted. "I'm not on social media much, but I remembered Kendrick and Bryant from back in the day. Also remember seeing them at a wedding I went to years ago."

"Their cousin Imani's wedding, right?" Kyra asked. "She's close with Taheim and I remember the three of you hanging out when I was little."

Luke squinted. "Sometimes your memory surprises me."

She shrugged. "My memory isn't that great." She left out the part where at one point, she thought Luke had a crush on Imani so, of course, even as a young girl, she'd paid close attention. Plus, she'd always liked Imani.

"Anyway, I reached out this morning and Kendrick hit me up, asked me what I'd been doing since I moved to LA. I mentioned you and he said you were a good friend of his and his wife and invited me to the party."

"When you mentioned me, what did you say?"

Luke's eyes widened. "Oh, you know. Just that I've known you most my life and that I'm close to your brothers. That sort of thing."

Kyra got the distinct impression that he wasn't telling her everything, but she didn't push it. "You know, we don't have to stand here and make awkward conversation. We can just join the others and help them finish setting up."

"I don't know," he said, stepping closer to her. "I kinda like making awkward conversation with you. Although if I'm being honest, it doesn't feel all that awkward. You've always been one of my favorite people to talk to."

Kyra widened her smile. "I like talking to you, too." And that meant she had a serious problem.

"So let me get this straight," Nicole said as they approached a juice bar along the beach in Santa Monica. "Your plan to deal with the feelings that you clearly still have for Luke is to drag out your attraction for as long as possible?"

Kyra nodded her head, looking from Nicole to Aaliyah. "Exactly! I can't just give in to his cuteness. I need to make him sweat a little."

"But you do expect something to happen between the two of you?" Nicole asked.

"Exactly. I see it plain as day. He's attracted to me, too."

"That doesn't sound like a good plan," Aaliyah stated. "Why would you make him sweat if you already know you like him?"

"I don't need a reason," she said as they ordered their

usual. "I just… I need to do this." There was so much that Kyra wasn't saying, but she wasn't in the mood to divulge all the details to her friends yet. Besides, she didn't expect them to understand.

"Try us," Nicole said. "We know you better than you think."

"What do you mean?"

"You just mumbled that we wouldn't understand," Aaliyah explained. "But I think we're already beginning to get it."

Crap. Luke was really messing with her state of mind if she was speaking her inside thoughts out loud. They grabbed their veggie-and-fruit juices and started walking down the path. "I won't get into all the girlie details, but I guess you can say that the crush I had on Luke growing up was the type of all-consuming crush where I didn't see anything besides him.

"Although Luke was Taheim's friend, he always took the time to ask me how I was doing or make sure I was doing my homework. It could have been my imagination, but when I turned sixteen, he started spending a little less time with me. Then at eighteen was when he really steered clear. But y'all know me. It didn't matter because I knew how I felt about him. On my twenty-first birthday, I was tired of waiting for him to notice me, so I took matters into my own hands and told him how I felt in the way I thought was best. But the night went completely wrong and ended with me in tears and him telling me all the reasons why he could never like me the way I liked him." Kyra glanced at her friends. "He made me feel like a fool. Like my feelings for him were unjustified and childish."

"Did you ever think about the alternative?" Aaliyah asked.

"What alternative?"

Aaliyah glanced at Nicole, then said, "That maybe the reason he pushed you away all those years ago was because even though you felt like your crush on him was strong, his was a lot stronger?"

"And like some men when faced with coming to terms with their feelings," Nicole continued, "when shit gets real, they run as fast as they can in the opposite direction."

"You need to figure out how you're going to deal with having Luke back in your life," Aaliyah advised.

Nicole nodded. "Because based off what we saw yesterday, he's done running. Now he's doing more of a slow jog."

Kyra sighed, wondering if they could be right. "When you two finish each other's sentences, I know I need to listen."

Aaliyah smiled. "Yep! You helped us realize how we felt about our men, so even if Luke is not the one, you owe it to yourself to figure it out."

"All he's doing is helping me find a new location for the boutique and a condo. Not exactly the type of setting for romance."

"Um, I'm sorry, but you're Kyra Reed," Nicole said. "You are never deterred from a situation. You tackle it head-on every time."

"He may not want me," Kyra said, voicing one of her fears. "He may just be trying to rebuild our friendship."

"Then rebuild with him," Aaliyah suggested. "Figure everything else out along the way. You don't always have to have the answers."

"Yes, I do," she said. "Having the answers means you're prepared. Being prepared means you won't get hurt. And if I don't get hurt, then…" Her voice trailed off, since she wasn't sure what should come after that.

"If you don't get hurt, then you aren't living," Nicole said. "And you're one of the most ambitious people I know. You always go after what you want. Don't let fear of getting your heart broken keep you rooted in place or afraid to try."

Afraid to try. Nicole's words echoed as they continued their walk. Her friends were right. There wasn't much that scared her, and if something did, she tried to face that fear as best she could.

The conversation soon changed to another topic, but Kyra's mind was still on her friends' words. She knew she didn't have to have all the answers right now, but she had some feelings she needed to sort out before she met up with Luke for more showings.

Chapter 5

Luke tried his best to conceal the smile on his face as he escorted Kyra into a space that had recently become available. "Okay, so you may not have liked the first two locations I showed you today, but I'm sure you'll love this one."

She shrugged. "We'll see. I doubt I'll find something I like for the boutique today since it's our first time looking at store locations, but I'm open to seeing everything you have on your list."

Luke smirked, thinking she was about to eat her words. "I was excited to see this space come on the market because it fits the boutique's needs if you're okay with the warehouse being in a different location."

"I love the brick exterior," she said. "But it's a little far from the area I wanted the shop to be."

"Just give it a chance. This space has been here for

decades," he said, entering a code to unlock the door. "The previous store owners decided to move locations and place this gem on the market."

The moment he opened the door, Kyra gasped. He smiled as he escorted her through the doors. "Wow," she exclaimed as they walked farther inside.

"As you can see, the main section is divided into three levels," he explained. "The second level has an open floor plan with the balcony overlooking the main floor. There are also fitting rooms on both levels."

"I love this layout," she said. "I always imagined a balcony overlooking the floor when I imagined the boutique." Kyra walked around the space, snapping pics with her iPhone. After a couple of minutes, Luke asked her to follow him.

"In addition to the rounded staircase, there's an elevator here that will take you to the third level," he said as they stepped onto the elevator. "It's divided into two parts and I think this space on the left would be perfect for the boudoir studio."

He opened the swinging doors and Kyra squealed with excitement. "This is almost better than the first two levels," she said. "And the amount of sunlight is fantastic. Our current location is great, but Aaliyah and our guest photographers are forever having to find creative ways to bring in the sunlight."

Luke smiled, loving the way Kyra walked around the empty space. His goal today had been to place a smile on her face and, luckily, he'd done just that. He gave her a few more details about the space, then told her, "And that's not it. There is one more feature to this property that I'm sure you'll love."

He nodded his head for her to follow him to the other

side of the third level. "When I saw this next section, I immediately thought about the parties you love to throw at the boutique." He motioned for her to walk in ahead of him, but instead, she just froze in the doorway and glanced around the space. Her eyes slowly took in everything.

"Luke," she huffed. "This. Is. Amazing."

"I know," he said. "Now what was that about you not expecting to fall in love with a store location today?"

She lightly hit him on the arm. "That was before you showed me a three-level space with an outdoor furnished rooftop! Are you sure you quoted me the correct price? Rooftops usually cost a fortune."

"The price is right, but I may have lied about it just coming on the market," he explained. "I know the couple selling this place and it hasn't gone on the market yet. They want to sell it by March of next year, but for now, they've just leased it out for the next three months to some art gallery who will only be in town for a short time."

Kyra walked around the deck and glanced at the bar before looking up at the lights twirled around the wooden pergola. "I could lay out in this mini courtyard all day. I wouldn't even get any work done."

Luke smiled as she fell back into a lounge chair. "Knowing you, you'd find a way to take every break up here."

"You damn right." She stood back up and walked toward Luke. "Okay, Lukey, you got me. I still want to see a few more places for the boutique that are in the area I originally wanted, but this is a real contender."

"I hate it when you call me Lukey," he said.

"Which is why I do it," she said, smirking. "So how long do I have to make a decision on this place?"

"Mr. and Mrs. Thomas aren't in the country right now, but I'd love to let them know before Christmas. Sooner would be better. I have another place to show you today, so how about we talk about it more over lunch after we visit the next location?"

Kyra laughed. "Every time we're together, you ask me to have lunch with you." She took a step toward him, but he refrained from pulling her even closer, like he wanted to do. "If I didn't know any better, I'd say you like spending time with me."

"I've always enjoyed spending time with you," he admitted. "That hasn't changed." There was so much more he wanted to say, but didn't. *In due time*, he thought. He was finally feeling like he was getting his friend back. The last thing he needed was to push her away again.

The next place Luke showed Kyra wasn't nearly as nice as the previous location. However, just like she'd asked, it was in a prime location.

"You're still thinking about the Thomas place, aren't you?" he asked as they were seated at a Thai restaurant for lunch.

"I am," she admitted, taking a sip of the water that was already at the table. "It's hard to forget a three-level place with a courtyard. I think I may call my sisters-in-law and send them the pics I took. I'm sure one of them would want to see if before we make any final decisions, but so far, that place is at the top of my list."

Luke nodded his head. "Good. Now all I need to do is help you find a condo you like just as much."

"You have your work cut out for you," she said. "I can be hard to please at times."

He smirked. "Don't I know it."

Snarky Kyra would have asked him what he meant by that comment. However, the Kyra who was now feeling slightly nervous under his gaze wouldn't dare make him explain.

"What are you doing for Thanksgiving?" he asked her after they ordered.

"Well, I thought I would be spending it with my family as usual, but my brothers and their wives are headed to France to visit Winter and Autumn's father. And my parents are on a fourteen-day cruise enjoying their retirement. So I figured I would go to Chicago and spend some time with my girl Cheyanne's family."

Luke smiled. "I remember Cheyanne. You two met in college, right?"

Kyra nodded. "Yeah, we were roommates. Been friends ever since."

"I actually ran into Cheyanne in Chicago a couple times. We also share a mutual friend."

Kyra snorted. She knew all about the mutual friend they shared and it seemed Luke had forgotten that the last time he saw her before Taheim's wedding, he'd been with that mutual friend. Instead of embarking on a topic she didn't want to discuss, she dryly said, "Nice."

For a second, she noticed the way Luke observed her and figured he noticed the change in her mood, but he must have shaken it off because he changed the topic and asked her when she was heading back home.

"I haven't decided yet, but I guess I should contact Cheyanne since Thanksgiving is next week."

Luke laughed. "Kyra Reed, never making plans too early. I guess that hasn't changed, either."

Kyra shrugged. "I make plans, I just don't believe that everything needs to be planned out. You know how we do in Chicago. There are a ton of houses I can crash at for the holiday if my nonplans fail."

"Yeah, I know. But I still couldn't do what you do. My plans have been made for months."

"What are you doing?"

"Going to St. Lucia," he said. "Did you hear that my mom moved back there?"

Kyra nodded. "Yeah, I heard that." *More like snooped on Facebook, but whatever.*

"Well, since my dad is from there, too, I wanted to take my brother, Nash, there so he could see where he's from."

"Oh, wow," she said. "That's a big deal. My brother told me you found out you had a brother not too long ago."

Luke frowned a little. "Yeah, I still haven't forgiven my dad for not telling me he had another kid out there. Nash was put into the system right after his mom gave birth to him and was adopted as a baby. He didn't even know anything about his birth parents and when he found out he was adopted a few years ago, he hired an investigator. He still doesn't know the whereabouts of his birth mother, but the investigation led him to Chicago and to me."

Kyra shook her head. "Back in the day, I remember your parents being so happy together. Never would have thought your dad had another child."

"You and me both. But my relationship with my dad has been strained for a while, so this was icing on the cake. It all took a toll on my mom. She wanted to be close to her sisters, so she moved back to her home country."

"Did you ask your dad about your brother?"

"I've been having a hard time tracking him down. I'm not even sure where he's living right now, but after talking to my mom, I figured I didn't even want his explanation. Nash and I have been getting closer and although he's nervous about going to St. Lucia, I told him my mom wants to meet him."

Kyra smiled. "Your mom always has been one of the sweetest women I've known."

"She's a godsend," Luke said with a smile. "Don't know what I'd do without that woman."

Kyra reached over the table and placed her hand over his. "I think it's awesome that you're reconnecting with your brother. Forget about your father. This is about you and Nash."

He nodded his head, placing his opposite hand over hers. "I'm trying my best to remember that." His eyes held hers, the moment making her breath catch. *This is the opposite of what you're supposed to be doing, girl!* She'd just told her friends the other day that she wanted to make him sweat a little, yet here she was, doing the opposite.

She pulled her hand away just as their food arrived. "I think you'll have a great time in St. Lucia."

"Me, too," he said, glancing at her over his fork as he took a bite. "If any of your nonplans fall through, you should think about coming with me and Nash to St. Lucia."

Kyra almost choked as she swallowed. "Uh, you can't mean that. This trip is about you and your brother getting to know each other and your mother meeting him for the first time. Pretty sure inviting your best friend's sister isn't part of that plan."

He shrugged. "I just think going to St. Lucia is better than house-hopping in Chicago. Plus, you can enjoy eighty-degree weather instead of twenty."

Oh, my God, he's serious. Kyra thought she could concoct some crazy ideas at times, but this took the cake. In fact, she could think of a couple of her friends who'd been faced with this exact decision. The men of their dreams wanted to whisk them away on a trip. In the past, she probably would've jumped at the idea, but now, she was a little baffled.

"Why are rich men always trying to fly women places in private jets and showering them with diamonds to win their hearts?"

"Private jet?" Luke blinked. "Uh, I'm not rich, but I do well for myself."

"Same difference," she said with a shrug.

He laughed. "Not really. Nash and I leave in a couple days. We'd be flying commercial, although I have first-class seats because economy seats are bad for my knees. So I'd get you one, too. And who said I'd buy you diamonds? Are you fishing for a diamond?"

Kyra's mouth dropped. "Oh, no, I mean… That's not what I meant. It came out wrong."

Luke laughed again. "For the record, I don't mind buying you jewelry if you see something you want while in St. Lucia, but let's get through our first trip together before you start getting too crazy."

Our first trip together? She wasn't sure how to handle everything he was saying, so she said the only thing she could say. "I'll think about it."

Luke nodded, pinning her with a look she couldn't

quite place. A look that seemed to hold the answers to questions she hadn't yet asked.

Despite the awkward start, the rest of lunch was enjoyable and Kyra even found herself looking forward to the possibility of vacationing with Luke, assuming she even said yes to his offer. Which she wasn't. No way.

Chapter 6

"There is no way we're letting you turn down a free trip to St. Lucia," Nicole said as she took a sip of her wine. Like most Friday nights when they were all in town, Kyra, Nicole and Aaliyah were lounging around Kyra's apartment getting caught up on missed episodes of *Grey's Anatomy*.

"Don't you think that's a bit crazy?" Kyra asked. "Who up and goes on vacation with a man when they have so much unfinished business?"

"Uh, I kinda did," Aaliyah said.

Nicole smiled. "Me, too."

"And didn't you encourage your friend Kiara to do the same when that millionaire mogul, Trey Moore, wanted to whisk her away?"

Kyra frowned. "That may have been the case with all y'all, but I fail to see the point."

"You know the point," Nicole said. "How many times do we have to tell you to quit being scared and take the opportunity to get to know the man Luke has become. Not the boy you fell for all those years ago."

Kyra sank deeper into her chair and groaned. "I swear if he wasn't still the sexiest man I'd ever seen, telling him no would be so much easier."

Aaliyah and Nicole laughed. "Said every woman who's gotten hung up on a man," Nicole said. "Sis, at least you're in good company."

"I don't want to be in good company," Kyra moaned. "I can deny it all I want, but a very large part of me wants to say yes to his offer."

"Then say yes," Aaliyah said. "Stop overanalyzing it and just say yes. It will probably be the trip of a lifetime."

"Do you think it's wrong of me to even consider it since I'll be invading on his time with his family?"

"He invited you," Aaliyah reminded her. "He wouldn't have done that if he thought you were invading his family time."

"You're right."

"Then what are you going to do?" Nicole asked.

Kyra sighed. "I'm not sure yet, but I figure I should let him know by the morning. Still more to think about."

Nicole and Aaliyah nodded and directed their attention back to *Grey's Anatomy* just as Kyra's phone rang. She glanced at the caller and told them she'd take the call in another room.

"Hey, Taheim," she said upon answering. "What's up?"

"Nothing much, sis. I told Ajay and Winter that I'd check in on you to see what plans you'd made for

Thanksgiving when a thought hit me. Why don't you come with us to France? No sense being in Chicago by yourself for the holiday."

"I already told you I'd be fine," she said. "Besides, I already tagged along with you guys on the two past trips to France. Your father-in-law is looking forward to seeing you all and his grandkids. I'll be fine."

"We just feel bad," he said. "Did you call Cheyanne to see what her family was doing?"

"Not yet. I've been distracted with work and some other stuff." Kyra cleared her throat. "I got an offer to go someplace else for Thanksgiving week, though."

"From who? Nicole and Aaliyah?"

"Not exactly." Kyra looked to the ceiling, wondering what her brother would say when she told him. "Luke invited me to St. Lucia with him."

Taheim grew quiet, then asked, "Luke invited you back to his hometown?"

"Yeah, he did."

"Are you going with him?"

"I'm not sure yet," she said. "If I say yes, would you be cool with that?"

It took a few seconds for him to respond, but Taheim finally said, "Yeah, of course, I'd be cool with it."

He didn't sound convinced, but Kyra didn't push for him to say any more. She knew her brother. Knew how he thought. He may have been clueless about her feelings toward Luke back in the day, but now he was wondering if anything was going on between them—he just wasn't outright saying it.

Truth be told, Kyra wished she had an answer to the question lingering in the air because she was clueless as well.

"Let me know what you decide," Taheim said before they ended the call.

"I'm leaning toward saying yes, but I'll text you tomorrow."

"Wow, you're really thinking about going, huh?"

Kyra took a deep breath, acknowledging for the first time that she actually was thinking about going. She hadn't said those words aloud, but by the time she hung up with her brother, she was pretty sure she was going to take up Luke on his offer to join him and Nash in St. Lucia.

"You invited her to St. Lucia with us, didn't you?" Nash asked with a smirk. Luke leaned back in his desk chair and ignored his brother as he continued to toss his mini basketball in the air.

"You can ignore me all you want, but you were the one who walked into the office this morning and said you had something important to tell me. Now all you're doing is procrastinating. I know you spent most the day with her yesterday, so you might as well just fess up."

Luke stopped tossing the ball. "Why do you think I invited her on our trip?"

"Because all you've done lately is talk about her and if I was trying to win back the heart of a beautiful woman, I'd take her on a romantic trip to the Caribbean."

"What makes you think I'm trying to win her heart?"

Nash raised an eyebrow. "Bro, I know we haven't known each other long, but we share DNA. Give me some credit, all right?"

Luke shook his head. "What was I thinking, asking her to come along? This is supposed to be a trip for you and me to get to know each other more and for me to show you St. Lucia."

"We've been catching up since we found out about each other," Nash said. "I'm looking forward to this trip, but I don't mind that you invited Kyra. Based off what you've told me, she seems cool."

"She is," he said. "She hasn't told me if she's coming or not, but I'm second-guessing why I asked her in the first place."

Nash sighed. "We've already been through this. You like her. She used to like you. Now she still holds a slight grudge that you rejected her. So you want to prove to her that you're not the same idiot you used to be."

"Something like that," Luke said with a laugh. "Are you sure you'll cool with it if she decides to come?"

"Yes, man. I'm good. I'm not some little boy wanting to spend time with his older brother when all he wants to do is lay in bed all day with his girlfriend. I'm a grown-ass man and if you want Kyra to be in your life more permanently, I want to get to know her, too."

Luke smiled. "I hope you're ready for everything St. Lucia has to offer. It's a small but mighty island. The people are great and I'm sure lots of folks want to meet you."

"I just want to learn more about my background," he said, his voice solemn. "Your dad may not have wanted to know me, but that doesn't mean I don't care to learn more about where I came from."

Luke tossed the ball to his brother and they began throwing it back and forth. "He's not the man I thought he was. Your adoptive dad is a better person than ours will ever be."

"You still haven't talked to him?"

Luke shook his head. "Nah, and I doubt I will anytime soon."

When the ball reached Nash again, he held it. "I get that, but I hope you know that if it has anything to do with me, I don't want my existence to be the reason you and your dad have a broken relationship."

"I appreciate that, bro, but it's not just you. There's other issues we have to work out."

Nash nodded. "Okay. But if you ever need to talk, just let me know."

"Thanks, man." Luke's cell phone rang, interrupting the moment. Luke answered on the fourth ring.

"Hey, Taheim, what's up, man?" At the mention of Taheim's name, Nash raised his eyebrows and walked over to Luke's desk.

"Hey, Luke, you busy?"

"Uh, not really. What's on your mind?"

Even before he asked, Luke suspected that it was about Kyra. It was confirmed when Taheim said, "Listen, man. I know I asked you to help Kyra find a condo and location for the boutique, but now she tells me that you asked her to go with you to St. Lucia?"

Nash quickly went back to his office and returned with a dry erase board. Luke mouthed, "What the hell are you doing with that?" but he had his answer when Luke wrote something down and turned the board around to show the message—*Tell him yeah and that you want to date his sister.*

Luke pushed away the board. "Yeah, I invited her to go to St. Lucia with me. You cool with that?"

"It depends," he said. "I thought you and Kyra hadn't talked in years, and now you're bringing her to your home country?"

"Well, technically, I was born here in the US."

"You know what I mean. You've never brought a woman to St. Lucia. I thought you said taking a step like that with a woman was important and you'd never do so unless you were serious about the relationship. So I'm asking you—is there more going on between you and Kyra than just friendship?"

Nash laughed and showed Luke the board again. This time it said, *Taheim is trying to figure out if you are bringing Kyra to St. Lucia to sleep with her or if you're already sleeping with her.* Then Nash erased the board and wrote another message that said, *And if you are sleeping with her, his ass will probably be on the next flight to LA.*

Luke shook his head. "We're just friends. I'm surprised you even had to ask." Nash put the board in front of Luke's face with the word *LIAR* written in all caps.

Taheim was quiet for a few seconds, then finally said, "I guess I gotta take your word for it. Something about this doesn't sit right with me."

"Man, come on. You know me. If something was going on between me and your sister, I'd tell you." Luke heard a female voice in the background, sparking another thought. "Is that Winter? Did she put you up to this?"

Taheim sighed. "She may or may not have mentioned that she suspected something was going on between y'all, so I got to thinking and figured I would call you."

Luke shook his head. *I should have known.* Taheim was great when it came to business, but when it came to treating Kyra like a woman and understanding that she wasn't a little girl anymore, he was clueless. "Listen, if anything changes in my relationship with your sister, I'll let you know out of respect." Nash shook his head and mouthed "wrong answer."

"So, Winter's not trippin'. You do think something more could happen between y'all?"

Luke pinched the bridge of his nose. "T, don't let Winter make you overthink this. I'm going to St. Lucia to introduce Nash to our family and I thought it would be nice if Kyra joined us since she mentioned not having any solid plans."

"Oh, Nash will be there, too?" Taheim asked.

"Yeah, Kyra didn't tell you?"

"Nah," he said. "She failed to mention that part."

Luke shook his head. It was just like Kyra to leave out important details. She'd rather keep folks guessing even if that meant him getting calls from Taheim about his intentions. "Well, yeah. It's a family trip that I invited her on."

"Why didn't you say that in the first place?" Taheim asked. "I mean, you my boy and all, but when it comes to relationships, you suck. The thought of you introducing my little sister to your commitment issues was messing with my head. Glad to know you were just looking out for her."

Nash shook his head and wrote *Well, damn* on the board. "He'll be looking out for her all right," he whispered.

"What was that?" Taheim asked.

"Nothing," Luke said, waving away Nash. "Nash just had a question about something. But, anyway, I got to get back to work. It seems like Kyra might be turning down my offer to vacation with us, anyway."

"Nah, man. She sounded like she was going when

I talked to her," Taheim said. "That's why I figured I should give you a call."

Luke looked to Nash, who mouthed "told you so." "Are you sure she sounded like she would be going?"

"Yeah, she definitely did. In case she forgets to text me, can you let me know if she decides to go with you? You know how she is with her secrets and shit."

"If she decides to come, I'll definitely let you know."

"Thanks, man. I knew I could count on you." They spoke for another minute before ending the call.

"Wow, I'm glad I'm not you," Nash said after they hung up. "It was hard enough watching you lie to your best friend, but listening to your voice get all high and shit was hilarious."

"Man, shut up. You were messing me up with that dry erase board."

"Bruh, that's because I was speaking the truth and you were too chicken to say what I was writing."

Luke shook his head. "All you know is what I've told you. You were just speculating."

"Whatever." Nash waved off his comment as he glanced out the window. "And you know what else I speculate?"

"I'm afraid to ask, but what?"

Nash smirked. "That you better not stumble over your words the next time you talk to Kyra like you did on the phone with her brother."

"I don't stumble," Luke said. "She's probably not going with us, so I'll do some self-reflection in St. Lucia."

Nash laughed, but just when Luke was about to ask him what was so funny, the bell at the front door chimed, indicating that someone was walking in. Just like Nash had predicted, Luke could barely form a sentence when his eyes landed on her. "Kyra. Uh, what are you doing here?"

Her long lashes batted as she looked him up and down, and as much as Luke was trying not to look at her just as hard, he couldn't help himself. She was wearing black jeans, black booties and a maroon top. Simple, yet so sexy on Kyra.

Her hair was down, flowing around her shoulders, and the colored gloss she was wearing matched her top.

"I was close by your office," she said. "So I figured I would stop by and tell you that I decided to go to St. Lucia." She glanced to Nash, then back to Luke. "If you guys will still have me."

Luke glanced to Nash, who answered, "Most definitely, we will still have you." Nash walked over to Kyra and reached out his hand. "I've heard a lot about you. I'm Luke's brother, Nash."

"Nice to meet you, Nash." Kyra looked between the two men. "Wow, I didn't think you'd look so much alike. You look just like Luke."

"Just the slightly taller, sexier version," Nash said with a wink. "And might I say that you look even more beautiful than Luke described you."

Kyra laughed. "And clearly, you're trouble. But thank you." She looked to Luke. "Is it okay with you if I still come?"

"Of course," Luke said. "I was hoping you'd come with us."

She smiled. "Great. I guess I need to pack since we leave soon."

"Yeah, I can reserve your ticket and send you over the details."

"Sounds good." She glanced down at her phone in her hand. "I should probably get back to the shop, but I appreciate you letting me tag along. I'll see you both in a couple days."

Nash didn't even wait a full minute until after she'd left before he started whistling. "Okay, bro. Now I see why you've been talking my ear off about her. You mean to tell me that she threw it at you back in the day and you threw it right back in her face? What the hell is wrong with you?"

Luke sighed. "Tell me something I don't know. That mistake has followed me around for years. I've thought about what I would do if given a second chance more times than I can count."

"Well, now is your second chance," Nash said. "She came here to talk to you in person and based off what I saw, y'all still have mad chemistry."

"You think so?" Luke asked.

"Man, get out of here with that hopeful look," Nash teased. "But, yeah, I think so. Now all you have to do is play your cards right in St. Lucia and win her over."

"I'll try," he said, finally admitting that was exactly what he wanted to do. Unfortunately, he had a feeling it was going to be easier said than done.

Chapter 7

Sitting on the plane next to Kyra had been pure torture. First, it seemed every time she adjusted herself in her seat, her hip brushed against his. Then she'd fallen asleep in her chair and conveniently rested her head on his shoulder, with her hand draped over his thigh.

If that hadn't been enough, every now and then she would softly moan in her sleep, the sound serenading Luke in a way that made it extremely difficult to rest with her so close. He'd been thanking God when they finally reached their layover, so for the second part of the flight, she was fully awake. However, that didn't stop her from brushing past him when she had to use the restroom even though he could have gotten up. He wasn't sure if she was doing any of it on purpose, but it sure as hell felt like it.

"Welcome to St. Lucia," he announced to Nash and

Kyra as he watched her get into the back of the rental car wearing her formfitting olive dress and gladiator sandals.

Nash leaned into Luke and whispered, "Bro, are you talking to me or Kyra's ass?"

Luke choked on air. "I was talking to both of you."

Nash tilted his head to the side and glanced into the car. "I don't blame you if you were talking to the booty because cutie has a nice, round one. I can see why you can't stop talking about her."

Luke shoved Nash. "Man, quiet down before she hears the crap you're talking."

"I already heard y'all," she yelled from the car. She leaned her head out the open door. "Now if both of you are done admiring my ass—which I work very hard on in the gym, mind you—can we get it moving? I'm dying to see more of St. Lucia than the airport."

Luke's mouth dropped, but Nash closed it shut. "Don't drool, brotha. You'll be with her for the next five days and no one likes a slobbery man."

"Uh, we weren't… I wasn't…" Luke stammered.

"Yes, he was," Nash said. "But she's right. We gotta go." Nash packed the last suitcase into the trunk and got into the passenger seat.

Dude, what's wrong with you? Luke had always had game and could charm the panties off any lady. Clearly, he was out of practice or out of his element because so far, he wasn't showing any of that charm to Kyra.

He got into the driver's seat and began making his way toward their destination. "I have some motion-sickness medicine in case either of you need it," he said to Nash and Kyra.

"Motion sickness. Are we getting on a cruise or something?" Kyra asked.

"No, but St. Lucia is pretty mountainous, so it has many hills, and here we usually go up and down about five to six hills a day. More if you need to get to the other side of the island."

"I usually don't get sick when driving in a car, but I'll let you know if I need any," Nash said.

Kyra nodded. "Ditto what he said."

"Sounds good." Luke turned a corner and started the ascent up the first hill. "Okay, my home is in the mountains. So, before we head there, we're going to stop by and see a few folks."

Luke glanced over at Nash, whose eyes were wide. "Relax," he told Nash. "You aren't meeting my mom today. She's visiting a friend in Barbados, so she flies in tomorrow. These are just friends."

Nash exhaled. "That's good. I really want to meet her, but I—I'm not—"

"You weren't prepared to see her right when you got off the plane," Luke said, finishing his brother's sentence. "I get it. That's why I figured I'd introduce you to a few locals first."

After twenty more minutes, they arrived at their first stop. "We're here," Luke announced.

"Ralph's Wharf," Kyra said, reading the name. "Are we eating here?"

"Not exactly," Luke explained, getting out the car. Nash and Kyra followed him to the entrance just as the door opened and a large, burly man walked out.

"Well, I'll be a monkey's uncle. If it isn't my nephew looking like he hasn't seen the sun in days."

Luke laughed. "Uncle Ralph, still cracking jokes, I see. For the record, I'm out in the sun every day."

"I doubt it, boy. Your skin too light. You need more vitamin D or a day out on my fishing boat to darken you up."

Luke heard Kyra and Nash laugh behind him. He'd really missed his uncle's island accent and the way he was always ragging on him. "Well, when you're done teasing me, I want to introduce you to my friend Kyra and my brother, Nash."

"Nice to meet you, beautiful," Ralph said, pulling Kyra in for a hug.

She smiled. "Nice to meet you, too."

"And you," Ralph said. "You look just like my nephew. I thought Luke said you grew up in California, boy. Thought you'd be darker."

Nash looked from Ralph to Luke. "Is he my uncle, too?"

Luke shook his head. "He's my mother's younger brother."

"But you're my nephew, too," Ralph said, pulling Nash in for a hug. "Here on the island, we don't do all that division crap. Family is family, so you call me Uncle Ralph."

Nash smiled. "Sounds good, Uncle Ralph."

Luke glanced at Kyra, who was watching the exchange as closely as he was.

"Well, come on inside," Ralph said. "I just got a batch of fresh fish and seafood. Y'all must be hungry after traveling."

When they stepped into the place, Luke breathed in the familiar scent. Yeah, the fishy smell may bother most, but Luke didn't mind. To him, it smelled like home.

* * *

Kyra couldn't remember the last time she'd eaten so much food. Ralph was an amazing cook and, aside from the accent, so much of him reminded her of Luke.

"This was so good, Uncle Ralph," she announced. "I wanted to eat that last crab leg, but I don't have anywhere to put it." Normally, she wasn't even a fan of seafood, but there was something about the way Ralph made it that left her craving more.

"I agree," Nash said. "I haven't eaten this good in years."

"We could tell," Kyra said.

Nash frowned. "What's that supposed to mean?"

"It means, you were smacking the entire time you ate like you hadn't had a decent meal in a while."

"Huh?"

"It's not you, Nash," Luke said. "Kyra has an issue with hearing people chew. She'll get over it."

"I don't have an issue with people chewing," she defended. "I just think that you should eat with your mouth closed. People who chew loudly are annoying because it's unnecessary. I swear, they'd enjoy their food more if they chewed properly. And don't even get me started on those who talk, then smack on food, then talk, then smack again. I could go on and on about this."

Nash blinked. "I can see that. Remind me to eat even louder next time."

Kyra threw a straw at him as all three men laughed at her expense.

Ralph smiled. "Anytime any of you want to eat well while you're here, just drop by."

"Will do," Kyra said while Nash expressed the same

sentiment. She barely knew Nash, but so far, she really enjoyed his company. He kept her laughing and, just like Uncle Ralph, parts of him reminded her of Luke. They looked so much alike.

When she'd dropped by their office a few days ago, Kyra had been taken off guard by how much the two brothers looked alike. Like replicas of each other in a way that could even pass for twins.

"What are your plans for the rest of the day?" Ralph asked.

"Since Mom gets in tomorrow, I was thinking of relaxing at the house for a bit. I had it cleaned and the fridge stocked for our arrival."

"Trista is having a party tonight at Lou's Reggae Lounge in town, so you may want to check it out."

"That sounds fun," Luke said. He turned to Kyra and Nash. "Trista is my cousin and Uncle Ralph's daughter. I guess you can call her the official island party planner."

"She's the head of St. Lucia tourism and other islands are taking notice," Ralph explained. "At a young age, my wife and I tried to control Trista, but it was no use. Better to embrace it than change her. And we were tired of cutting down bamboo trees outside her window just so she wouldn't climb out."

Kyra laughed. "Sounds like my kind of girl. My parents used to say I was the reason for all their gray hairs."

"I'm pretty sure they still say that," Luke said, smirking.

"I'm a lot better," she defended. "I tell them more information now than I ever did before."

Luke raised an eyebrow. "Not according to Taheim. Just the other day, you left out important details about this trip when you talked to him."

"Details like what?" she asked.

"Details like I was bringing Nash to St. Lucia to meet the family."

Kyra crossed one leg over the other and adjusted herself in her chair, knowing that Luke was following her every move. "I told Taheim you'd invited me to St. Lucia for the holiday. Why was it important to tell him about Nash, too?"

Luke pinned her with a look. "You know why."

"Clearly I don't," she said with amusement. "Why don't you enlighten me?"

"Kyra," he said sternly.

"Luke," she said with a smirk. "You only look at me like a sister, right? So telling him Nash would be here wasn't important, correct?"

"I'm not doing this with you," he said. "Taheim called me and didn't seem too happy that I'd asked you to come here with me."

"Taheim should have gotten a clue years ago," she said. "If he had, he never would have asked you to be my Realtor."

Luke sighed. "Just forget I said anything."

Kyra wiped her hands clean. "Already forgotten." She took a sip of her water, holding Luke's gaze. If he thought for a second she would own up to anything when he wouldn't do the same, he needed to think again.

"Oh, this trip is gonna be fun," Nash said, sharing a knowing look with Uncle Ralph. "In case you haven't guessed it, these two have some unfinished business."

"I knew they did the moment he introduced her," Uncle Ralph said to Nash. "He's been whining about this one for years."

Kyra broke Luke's gaze and looked to Uncle Ralph.

"What do you mean? Luke told you about me? What did he say?"

Uncle Ralph held up his hands. "It's not my business to repeat. But, yes, girl, I've known about you for a long time."

Kyra looked back to Luke, who had the nerve to sit there without an expression on his face. *Enough of this.* "As amusing as this conversation is, I really need to take a nap or something. Do we have many more stops or can I take a taxi to your place?"

Uncle Ralph laughed. "A feisty one you got here, nephew. You'll have your hands tied this week."

"Don't I know it," Luke said. "No need to take a taxi. We're headed to my place now." Luke looked to Nash. "Ready to hit it?"

"Yeah, let's go." As they were walking out of the restaurant after saying their goodbyes to Uncle Ralph, Nash leaned to Kyra and whispered, "Luke is always so calm, yet you rattle him unlike I've seen before. You pulling his leg or making him sweat for what he did back in the day?"

"He told you about that?" she asked in surprise.

"Not the whole story, but enough."

Kyra rolled her eyes. "Not that it's any of your business, but I'm not that petty." *Ha! Tell that lie again, sis.* She was about to repeat herself when she noticed that Nash had stopped walking beside her.

"What?" she asked. "I'm not."

"You know that saying, 'game recognizes game'?"

She shrugged. "Yeah."

"Well, I see what you're doing," Nash said. "And, yeah, you're entitled to make him sweat, but just know that

Luke isn't that great at hiding his feelings. I want to see y'all work it out. Just don't make him pay all vacation."

Kyra's face grew serious. "Although I may not care for what you're saying, I love that you care so much."

Nash smiled and glanced at Luke, who was leaning on the car looking out into the water. "We haven't been brothers long, but he's my guy."

"You've always been brothers," she said. "Just because you didn't know the other existed, doesn't make that any different."

"I guess you're right." He turned back to face Kyra. "While I have you alone, there's just one more thing I need you to keep in mind while you're here."

Of course there's more. "And what might that be?"

"If you decide to make Luke do anything stupid on this petty quest of yours, make sure I'm around to capture it on camera."

Kyra laughed so hard, she almost doubled over. "I was not expecting that," she said in between laughs.

"I wouldn't be a younger brother if I didn't capture the embarrassing stuff," he said. "Do we have a deal?"

Kyra glanced down at his outstretched hand, still laughing, and accepted his request. "Deal."

"I already don't like whatever y'all are agreeing to," Luke yelled from the car. "Now can we get out of here, or do the two of you have to conspire some more?"

"We're good," Nash announced as they reached the car. "Kyra, I want to lay down until we get there. Can you ride shotgun?"

She glanced from Nash to Luke. "Uh…"

"Great." Nash was in the backseat so fast, she didn't have a chance to really answer. Reluctantly, Kyra got in the passenger seat of the rental and they headed off.

"How far is your home?"

"Only an hour," Luke said.

"An hour? You say that like it's nothing."

Luke laughed. "On the island, it really isn't long. I live in the mountains, and with us having a huge rainforest and overall hilly terrain, an hour is typical."

Kyra sank deeper into her seat. "Would you kill me if I took a nap until we got there? The motion is getting to me a little."

"Do you want to take something?" he asked.

"No, I think I'll be good if I just rest a little."

"Okay, I'll wake you and Nash when we get there." He glanced her way before looking back to the road. "If you change your mind, let me know so I can give you something."

Kyra nodded. "Thanks, Luke. I will." The last thing she remembered seeing before she closed her eyes was Luke's smiling face.

"We're here." Kyra heard Luke's words and she gently nudged awake. She slowly opened her eyes to a beautiful glass-and-white-concrete villa surrounded by lush trees and greenery.

"Damn, bro," Nash said from the backseat. "I knew you said you had a home in the mountains, but this place is huge."

"Not huge. Just five bedrooms, four bathrooms and a pool."

Kyra glanced back at Nash, then both of them repeated Luke's words in a mocking voice.

"Stop it," Luke said with a laugh. "That came out wrong. I just meant there are much bigger mountain villas in St. Lucia than mine, but I fell in love with the place the first time I saw it."

"I can see why," Kyra said, stepping out of the car. "We haven't even walked inside and I can already tell it's going to be hard to leave."

"Then how about I give you both the tour and then we can get the luggage."

Nash nodded. "Sounds good to me."

"You've got to be kidding me," Kyra said as they followed Luke to his home. "You have a bridge over a small pool that leads to your front door?"

"That was the designer's idea," Luke admitted. "The water is only a foot deep, but she felt like the bridge would be a nice way to greet visitors."

"I fully support this designer already," Kyra said as Luke opened the front door and she stepped inside. "Although seeing this foyer and grand staircase might give the bridge a run for its money." Kyra didn't think she was impressed by many homes since she knew a lot of people with grand estates. Hell, she'd even been raised in one. However, there was something about Luke's villa that was giving her a very lush and lavish vibe that she wasn't quite sure she'd experienced before.

As Luke took them through each bedroom in his villa, her mouth dropped even more at the beauty. Nash was on such a high searching through every room, Kyra wasn't even sure when they'd lost him.

"Everything is so crisp," she said. "Was it your idea to have this white, heather gray and light blue color scheme or was that the designer?"

"The color choice was all me," Luke said with pride. "I wanted it to have that warm Caribbean vibe and

I've never been one for bold colors. This palette works for me."

"It suits you." She stepped deeper into the last bedroom and second master of the villa, her steps faltering when she noticed that the balcony doors opened into a private plunge pool separate from the main pool. "This has to be where you sleep."

Luke laughed. "Did the plunge pool give it away?"

"Heck yeah! All the bedrooms are beautiful, but who would pick any of the other rooms when they could have their own private pool."

"True," he said, stepping out onto the balcony. "That's why I want you to stay in this room while you're here."

Kyra shook her head. "Oh, no, I couldn't put you out like that. This is your home, so I'll just take one of the other beautiful bedrooms."

"I insist," he said.

Kyra shrugged. "Well, pull my arm, why don't you? I'll stay here if you insist."

He laughed. "That's the Kyra I know."

"The one and only," she said with a twirl. "But seriously, thank you for being so gracious."

"You're welcome." His eyes studied hers and she wished like hell she knew what he was searching for. "I'm just glad you were able to join us on this trip."

Kyra cleared her throat. "Me, too. So far, this definitely beats house hopping in Chicago in the cold."

"St. Lucia suits you," he said, his voice getting deeper.

Kyra's heartbeat quickened. "You can't possibly know that. We haven't even been here for a day yet."

"I know," he said with conviction. "And in case I forgot to tell you, you look beautiful today."

Kyra glanced down at her dress. "Thank you. At first, I thought it was too much for the plane, but I'm glad I wore it."

Luke looked her up and down, his eyes lingering on her legs. "I'm glad you wore it, too." At his words, Kyra's breath caught. *Okay, who are you and what have you done with the real Luke O'Connor?* The old Luke would never openly flirt with her like that, let alone check her out. If she didn't know any better, she'd say this St. Lucia heat was getting to him.

Breaking the tension, she walked away from him and past the pool so she could look out into the greenery. "At first, I couldn't even imagine living in the mountains. But now, I see what all the fuss is about."

Luke approached and leaned over the railing next to her. "Since I grew up in the States, it was an adjustment when I purchased this home. I didn't plan on getting a house that was so off-the-grid, but that's exactly what happened when I found this gem. It needed some love and care, but after the renovations, it became my dream home."

He was so close, his masculine cologne teased her nostrils. "In case you can't tell, I'm already in love with this place."

"I can tell," he said with a smile. "And if you like all this, wait 'til you see the rooftop."

"Please tell me you do not have a rooftop deck."

Luke extended his hand. "Then how about I show you rather than tell you."

Kyra glanced down at his hand, noting that she'd had more physical contact with him in the past week than she had the entire time she'd known him in her past. "Lead the way, maestro."

As she followed him through the bedroom and up a spiral staircase in the back of the home, she tried to remind herself that she wasn't the type of woman who liked to hold hands. Yet somehow, she didn't want to let go of Luke's hand.

Chapter 8

"Kyra, I swear you'll like it," Luke said, gently pulling Kyra toward a makeshift booth on the beach.

"No, I won't," she said. "I hate the water. There's nothing about it that I like. Plus, I really don't want to get my hair wet."

Nash laughed. "Said every black woman that I've ever dated."

"Shut up," she said, flicking him off. "As I recall, you didn't want to go zip-lining earlier today and Luke didn't push you on that."

"That was different," Nash said. "I'm two hundred and fifty pounds of solid muscle. Those little-ass ropes couldn't hold my weight."

"You are not two hundred and fifty pounds," Luke said with a laugh. "Since that was the weight limit, you lied to the guy so that you wouldn't have to go."

"So," Nash retorted. "Did you see the way that man looked when I told him? He knew I'd dodged a bullet. Zip-lining from tree to tree is not the black man's way."

Kyra laughed. "Oh, my God, you did not just make this a black thing."

"More of a man thing," Luke said.

Kyra rolled her eyes. "Just admit that you hate heights."

"For what," Nash said. "This is about you now. I thought you said you've ridden a Jet Ski before."

"I have," she said. "A couple times."

"So what's different between then and now?" Nash asked. "Unless you're lying."

"Lying?" Kyra exclaimed. "Dude, come on."

Luke shook his head as he listened to Kyra and Nash go back and forth as they had since they'd arrived in St. Lucia. "Y'all argue like brother and sister."

"If you weren't tryin' to get her in your bed, you'd probably be arguing with her like this, too," Nash said. "She's annoying sometimes."

"Do you think about the crap you say before you say it?" Luke asked.

Nash stuck out his arms in defense. "What? I thought that was common knowledge."

"You're an idiot," Kyra said. "And for the record, I've Jet-Skied on lakes before in a situation where I knew I wouldn't fall off."

"How could you know that?" Nash asked. "You just got lucky and didn't fall off. But I'm sure you got your hair wet."

"Why am I even arguing with you about this?" she huffed. "I'm not doing it."

"Would you do it if you were on the back of the Jet Ski with me?" Luke asked.

She frowned. "Uh, no. I don't trust either of you to not flip us over."

"I didn't volunteer," Nash said. "But if you get on with me, I'll definitely be flipping your ass off it."

Kyra whacked his arm. "Remind me to never vacation with you again."

Nash laughed. "You know you're enjoying my company."

"Nope. Negative."

Luke shook his head as they went at it again. When his mom, Athena, had called this morning and said that she wouldn't be arriving until tomorrow instead, Luke had thought he'd treat Nash and Kyra to some fun island activities. But had he known they'd be so difficult, he would have let them spend the day lounging around his place instead.

"Okay," Kyra said, interrupting his thoughts. "I'll go on the Jet Ski with you." She walked closer to Luke and poked him in the chest. "But you better not flip us over, or else I will make the rest of this trip hell for you."

Nash snorted and mumbled something under his breath. He couldn't make out his words, but he was pretty sure he shared the same sentiment.

"You've already been acting like a princess, so I'll take my chances." He led them to a guy at the booth on the beach who set them up with Jet Skis. Luke had Jet-Skied more times than he could count at a bunch of different places. However, nothing could compare to the beaches of St. Lucia.

While Nash didn't waste any time hightailing it out

into the ocean, Luke started off slow, making sure Kyra held him tight as she got used to the waves.

"I can't believe I'm doing this," she yelled as they picked up speed.

"Believe it, baby," he said with a laugh as he kicked it up a notch so he could catch up with Nash.

"Are you gonna slow down?" she yelled when he reached the speed he normally rode at.

Luke smiled slyly even though she couldn't see him. "Not a chance."

Nash was just as good on the Jet Ski as Luke was and, eventually, he heard Kyra comment on how beautiful the small islands were that they passed by. "It's really pretty," she yelled.

"I agree," Luke yelled back. "There's nothing like it." He slowed down so that she could admire one of his favorite small islands. "I took a small boat over to that island over there with my uncle a couple times when I was a teenager to do some exploring."

"You and Uncle Ralph are really close, huh?"

Luke nodded. "Yeah, he and my dad never got along, but we've always had a close relationship. Most of St. Lucia knows Uncle Ralph and whenever I visit here, he always made me feel like a son. I learned more about this island from him than my own father, who was also born here."

"You're lucky to have each other," she said. "I definitely want to get another meal or two from him before we leave."

"Oh, you'll get plenty." Luke looked to his left when he saw Nash speed past them yelling about Luke being a slow rider. "But for now, I have to show my little brother up."

"Just be careful," Kyra yelled as Luke took off. But it was no use. He was already speeding fast, passing Nash. A minute later, Nash passed him again, standing as he tackled the incoming waves. Although Luke had to remain seated because Kyra was gripping his life jacket for dear life, he managed to ride Nash's tail, almost passing him. Then without warning, his brother slowed down and began to turn, pointing ahead.

"Crap," Luke mumbled as he saw a huge incoming wave heading their way. Nash managed to turn easily, avoiding the wave, but Luke wasn't so lucky and they flipped over, both going under.

When they rose to the surface, Luke quickly flipped over the Jet Ski, but Kyra was already freaking out.

"Oh, my God, I can't believe you flipped us." She flailed her arms, glancing around the open water. "Why is the water so dark blue here? Are there big fish out here?" Her eyes widened. "Or sharks? Oh, crap, it's an ocean so there's definitely sharks, right?" In a panic, Kyra gripped the side of the Jet Ski.

"Don't do that," Luke yelled. "It will flip it back over." Unfortunately, she wasn't listening and managed to flip over again and go under. Since Luke was so close, he helped her rise back to the surface.

"Are you okay?" he asked after she stopped coughing.

"No, I'm not okay," she yelled. "We flipped over. In the ocean. Which is exactly what I was afraid of. You promised we wouldn't flip over." Kyra was talking a mile a minute, which wasn't normal for her. Luke knew she was still freaking out, but no matter what he said to try and calm her down, it wasn't working.

He wished she didn't look so sexy all heated and wet,

but she did. She always did. If asked, he'd never admit it, but he'd done his fair share of social-media stalking. He'd convinced himself he was just checking on her to make sure she was okay, and strategically hounded Taheim for details of her exes when he saw a new guy pop up on her pages. Luke always thought through his actions, but ever since he'd moved to LA, he'd done less thinking with his mind and more thinking with his heart.

"Are you going to help me back on this thing?" she asked, still in a panic. He wanted to help her. He really did. However, thanks to this whole thinking-with-his-heart thing, he couldn't help her the way she needed, but rather, in the way he'd been thinking about ever since the moment they'd shared in her bedroom back in college.

Not giving it any more thought, he gently pulled her face to his, grateful that he didn't have to tread water much thanks to the life jackets. To his surprise, Kyra melted into his kiss instantly, her hands snaking around his neck, causing him to moan as she allowed him to deepen the kiss.

There were so many times when he thought about what it would be like to kiss her again, but never had he considered it would happen in St. Lucia, floating in the Atlantic Ocean. Had the waves not continued to crash into them and the Jet Ski, he would have kept on kissing her.

Reluctantly, Luke pulled away, then gently rubbed his thumb against her wet cheek as she looked at him in surprise and arousal. *Join the club*, he thought because she'd been arousing him all freaking month. When he heard someone clear their throat, Luke finally glanced away, his eyes landing on a very amused Nash.

"Don't mind me," Nash said, leaning over the handles of his Jet Ski. "I just wanted to make sure that the dolphins didn't frighten y'all since the three of us are enjoying the show."

"What dolphins?" Kyra asked, her voice breathless from the kiss. Nash nodded to his right at two eight-foot-long mammals that Luke could barely see because they were dipping in and out of the ocean. "Oh, my God," she screamed as one of them dipped their head above the water. And just like that, Kyra flipped over the Jet Ski. Again.

"Damn, Unc wasn't kidding," Nash said. "Trista knows how to throw a party."

"She does," Luke said with a smile as they walked to the VIP section of Lou's Reggae Lounge. To be honest, he wasn't smiling because his cousin was great at planning a party. He was smiling because they'd just arrived in St. Lucia yesterday and already, Nash was calling Uncle Ralph *Unc*.

That, and the fact that he was still on cloud nine after that kiss with Kyra. A kiss he'd hadn't stopped thinking about since it happened.

"I'm surprised Kyra chose to miss out," Luke said. "She usually loves parties."

"You're joking, right?" Nash asked. "I'll admit, she was just as into that kiss as you were, but she freaked out on you after. You really need to question why she didn't come out with us?"

Luke frowned as he thought about how she'd gone from yelling at him for kissing her to being quiet during the rest of the drive home. "Yeah, I guess you're right. I didn't mean to kiss her right then. It just happened."

Nash sat down in the one of the VIP booths while

Luke took a seat beside him. "Bro, don't think about it too much. It was bound to happen sometime. You and Kyra have so much sexual chemistry, I almost thought about asking Uncle Ralph if I could crash with him so y'all could have the house to yourselves."

Luke laughed. "I think you're getting ahead of yourself, little brother."

"Yeah, okay," Nash said, raising an eyebrow.

"Oh, snap, Luke is in the building," a voice said from beside them. Luke turned and spotted his cousin Trista.

"Trista, what's good?" he asked, standing to hug her.

"Not much," she replied, giving him a hug. "Dad told me you were coming into town since it's Thanksgiving in America." She glanced over Luke's shoulder. "Then he told me you were bringing your newfound brother along with you, but I think I heard my dad wrong because he looks more like your twin."

Luke laughed. "Trista, this is Nash. Nash, Uncle Ralph's daughter, Trista."

"Hey, cousin, it's nice to meet you." Trista gave Nash a hug. "Glad you made it to St. Lucia. My dad already told me that you may look like Luke, but that y'all are opposites, which makes me glad because as much as I love my cousin, he tends to think I'm reckless."

Nash laughed. "Great to meet you, too. And, yeah, I think it's safe to say that no one is quite like Luke here."

"Agreed," someone said, clapping him on the shoulder. "Luke, my man, what is up!"

Luke turned around. "Maceo, what's up, man? Last I heard, you were married and living in Barbados."

Maceo sighed. "Yeah, I was. But that didn't work out."

"Sorry to hear that, man."

Maceo shrugged. "It was for the best. We weren't right for each other from the beginning. I think we both knew it, but we stayed together for our kid."

Luke nodded. "Trying to do the right thing. I get it." Luke waved over Nash. "This my brother, Nash. Nash, this is one of my good friends, Maceo."

"Nice to meet you, man," Nash said, dabbing his fist.

"You, too." Maceo looked from Luke to Nash. "Yo, you look just like each other."

Luke laughed. "Yeah, we've been getting that a lot."

Maceo nodded and glanced over Luke's shoulder at Trista. "Long time no see, Trista."

"Only because you stay busy," she said with a smile. "What gives? Too good for my parties?"

"Nah, just trying to get a handle on this single-dad life."

"I'm just teasing," she said. "But glad you could make it." She glanced to all three men. "In fact, I'm glad all of you could make it. But, Luke, where's this woman my dad was telling me about? Said she has your nose wide open."

Nash laughed, but Luke didn't find anything funny. "Man, Uncle Ralph needs to stop telling stories."

"It ain't a lie, bro," Nash said. "You been feelin' Kyra since you were young. It's obvious as hell."

"Bruh, why don't you share that info with a few other people in the lounge. I'm not sure they understood who you were talking about."

Nash shrugged. "Why not?" He stood on the VIP couch and yelled over the music that Luke had a crush on a girl named Kyra. A few folks standing nearby asked who Kyra was, while a few others yelled for him to get down.

"Are you happy with yourself?" Luke asked, ignoring the way Trista and Maceo were laughing.

Nash gave him a Chuck E. Cheese smile. "Very."

"Good, because you're taking a taxi home."

"Fine with me," Nash said, glancing at the front door. "I'll just take a ride back with Kyra."

"She's not here," Luke said. Instead of answering him, Nash nodded his head toward the door. Luke knew she was there before he even turned fully around, and when he did, the sexy black dress she was wearing almost made him stumble. *Damn.* True to Kyra's personality, she'd already washed and straightened her hair, but that wasn't what had Luke speechless.

Her eyes landed on them and the way her hips were swaying in that dress even under the dim lighting had him wishing they were anywhere else but in the lounge.

"Hey, guys," she said as she joined the group. "I remembered the name of the lounge and figured I'd take a taxi here. Glad I made it."

"You should have called me," Luke said. "I would have come and got you."

"I called Uncle Ralph and he called a friend to get me."

"That's my dad," Trista said with a smile. "Hey, Kyra, I'm Ralph's daughter, Trista. I've heard a lot about you. Glad to finally put a face to the name."

"Nice to meet you," Kyra said, giving her a quick hug. "I met your dad yesterday and he's already one of my favorite people."

"He has that effect on people," Trista said proudly. "And this here is Maceo, a friend of mine and Luke's."

"Nice to meet you," Maceo said, shaking her hand. "Welcome to the island."

"Glad to be here." Kyra glanced back at Luke. "Hope you didn't have too much fun without me."

"He hasn't," Nash said for him. "He talked about you the entire ride here." Luke elbowed Nash in the ribs, causing him to let out a groan. "Be a lover, Luke. Not a fighter."

"Shut up, Nash." Luke took another head-to-toe glance at Kyra. "You look beautiful."

"Thanks," she said. "You don't look too bad yourself."

"Oh, yeah," Maceo said to Trista. "Luke's in trouble with this one."

Unable to help himself, Luke asked Kyra if he could chat with her for a minute.

"Sure," she said with a nod. There weren't too many private places for them to go, so Luke pulled her deeper into the VIP area.

"Are we okay?" he asked, leaning down to whisper.

"You mean because you kissed me or the fact that we almost got attacked by dolphins?"

He laughed. "Those dolphins weren't going to attack us."

She huffed. "Yeah, okay."

"Seriously, though, are we good?"

She looked to him, studying his eyes in a way that made him feel like she was undressing him in her mind. "We're good. I know you kissed me on an impulse and didn't really mean it. Everything's cool."

"Nah, I meant that shit," Luke said. "It was impulsive, but I don't regret anything."

She smiled. "Me, neither." At her admission, his eyes dropped to her lips, eager to taste her again, but not wanting to lay it on too strong. Especially in front of a bunch of people.

"Y'all should join us tomorrow," Trista suggested, calling over to them. "Maceo and I, along with a couple other locals, are thinking about going on a hike in the rainforest."

"That sounds like fun," Kyra said, walking back over to the group. Luke followed.

"Seriously?" Nash exclaimed. "You're afraid of water, but you're down to hike?"

Kyra rolled her eyes. "How are the two of you even remotely related?"

Nash shrugged. "I just thought you were one of those women who didn't like to do anything outside. More of an air-conditioned kind of girl."

Kyra looked to Luke and pursed her lips together. "You may be down one brother after this trip."

"That's if I don't get to him first," Luke said, shaking his head as the two got into another argument. Luckily, this time, Trista and Maceo were there to run interference.

Chapter 9

"Tell me again why I agreed to go on this long-ass hike in this scorching heat," Nash yelled as they made their way up a deep incline.

"Aww, is Ashy Nashy tired when we're only twenty minutes into the hike?" Kyra teased.

"The baby talk is one thing," he said. "But you ain't gotta call me 'Ashy.' I made sure I lotioned, put on sunblock and bug spray. Ya boy is moisturized up here in these trees."

The group all laughed and Kyra took the moment to pull out her GoPro and capture a few photos and a video of Nash taking a break to fan himself with a towel. Even though she'd just met Trista and Maceo, she felt like she'd known them forever. She liked their vibe. And, yeah, Nash may annoy her, but she'd felt like she'd known him for years, too. He was like that annoying best guy friend she always wanted but never had.

"We're almost there," Trista said after another twenty minutes.

"We're almost where?" Nash asked, panting from the heat. "Luke and Kyra had agreed to go on this hike before they told me all the details."

"We're almost to Wishing Waterfall," Maceo explained. "It's a place only St. Lucians know about."

"Sounds like my kind of place," Kyra said. "I love spots that aren't overrun with tourists."

"Me, too," Luke said. "The first time Trista took me to this waterfall, I told her I didn't want to leave and could live in the trees in this rainforest."

"He really did," Trista said with a laugh. "He was only twelve then, so I believed him."

"I'd never live in the rainforest," Nash said, now using the towel to wipe the sweat off his face. "It's too damn hot. I thought it was supposed to rain a lot."

"Most of the time, it does," Maceo confirmed. "We're just lucky today, I guess."

Nash mumbled something under his breath that Kyra couldn't make out, but she was sure he was still complaining. They walked for another ten minutes until Trista announced that they'd finally made it.

"The waterfall is right over this hill," she said. "Nash, this is your chance to cool off because we're getting in."

Kyra cringed. "More water? Did Luke tell y'all that he flipped me over in the Jet Ski and we were almost attacked by dolphins?"

Maceo and Trista froze. "Dolphins bothered you?" Maceo asked. "Our dolphins are usually friendly."

Luke laughed. "They didn't attack us, but Kyra was flapping around in the ocean trying to get back on the

Jet Ski and they thought she was playing, so they were following her around."

Everyone laughed. "Okay, so maybe they didn't attack me, but those things were huge! I'm not a water person, so yesterday was a bit much." Although, had she not been locking lips with Luke, she wouldn't have been in the water at all.

She hated to admit it, but yesterday had been a great experience. However, she'd be lying to herself if she didn't acknowledge that their kiss had confused the hell out of her. Kissing Luke was everything, and even though her body was craving for more, her mind was warning her to tread lightly.

His lips had been so soft and just like the first time they'd kissed all those years ago, he'd applied the perfect amount of pressure with enough tongue to drive her insane with need, emphasis on the *insane* part. She'd put her heart out there again and kissing Luke yesterday had reminded her that if she wasn't careful, there was a possibility it would get broken again.

"You don't have to get in if you don't want to," Trista said, "but at least check it out before deciding." Kyra nodded her head and followed Trista—who was ahead of the pack—up the hill.

When they reached the top, Trista stretched out her arm. "Welcome to Wishing Waterfall, St Lucia's very own fairy godmother."

Kyra's eyes widened at the beautiful sight before her. "Wow, I'm not sure what I expected, but this is beautiful." There were only a few other people in the waterfall and when they noticed them and the others on the top of the hill, they waved.

"Do you know them?" Kyra asked.

"Yes, they are the friends that Maceo and I were meeting. If you come in, I'll introduce you."

Kyra studied the decently sized body of water. "How deep is it?"

"Hmm, no more than twenty feet in the deepest part. Only about three feet at the base."

Kyra swallowed. "Twenty feet! That's it, huh?"

Trista laughed as they made their way down the hill. "It will be fine, trust me. We brought a couple life jackets with us, so you can have one. And we have some tubes that us island folks keep stashed in an empty shed. They should already be pumped with air, so we can tie together."

Kyra watched Luke, Maceo and Nash begin removing their clothes so that they could get into the water. *Hmm...nice.* Despite her best efforts, she couldn't take her eyes off of Luke's six-pack. She'd seen it yesterday, but goodness, the man still had it.

"You guessed why we call it Wishing Waterfall, right?"

Kyra tore her eyes away from Luke and glanced at Trista. "Because you can make wishes at it?"

"Yes, that's true, but not just any wishes. There's a story St. Lucians are told in school." Trista pointed her finger to the top of the waterfall. "It's said that many years ago, right up there, there was a young woman who'd lost her fiancé at sea due to a storm that killed everyone on the fishing boat. To escape the heartache of having to face everyone in town, she had her father build her a small cabin right above the waterfall for her to live at. Every day at sunset, she'd come out of her cabin and cry up to the night sky for the love she'd lost to find his way back home her. But he never came. She waited at the top of that hill for years, crying every day for his return."

"Did he ever return?" Kyra asked.

Trista shook her head. "No, he didn't."

"What happened to her?"

"No one knows for sure," Trista said. "Yet, the way the story goes, she cried so much that, eventually, her tears turned into a stream. That stream turned into a river. And that river turned into a waterfall. When the girl's father came to the cottage to find her, he noticed this waterfall, although it wasn't originally there when he'd first built her home. He also found a note his daughter left saying that she hoped the people of St. Lucia would visit this waterfall and remember how special love can be. She hoped that their hearts would always return to their true loves because she didn't want any visitor to ever feel alone. She wanted us to be encouraged and make wishes knowing that there was someone in the world who was listening, hoping that all our dreams come true."

Kyra glanced at the waterfall. "Have love wishes ever come true as a result?"

Trista smiled. "More than I can count. Personally, I know over thirty people who have found the heart of the one they love after visiting this waterfall."

"So in a way, she scarified herself for the happiness of others," Kyra said. "That's a beautiful story."

"That's a messed-up story," Nash said, sneaking up behind them and interrupting the moment.

Kyra hit Nash on his shoulder. "Dude, I was really listening to that."

"I could tell," he said. "But why tell kids that story in school? I mean, the woman basically dies of a broken heart and we're supposed to swim in her tears and be okay with that? Nah, bruh. As a kid, that story would have done just the opposite and scared me away from a relationship." Nash looked to the whole group. "Tell you what. When I dive in, I'll make a wish, but my wish will be for all the kids who may have been deterred from love after hearing that story. May they still find their way to that one special someone."

Maceo laughed. "In a twisted way, that makes sense."

"Don't encourage him," Luke said. "Nash, you have to respect the story. It's older than you by decades."

Nash walked over to the water and waded right in. "I respect the story, bro. I'm just being realistic. I mean, was anyone concerned that this woman went missing? What father do you know that will accept a letter assumingly written by his daughter as a sign that she's okay? Especially when she's up in these hills all by herself."

Luke and Maceo went in after him. "You have a point," Maceo said. "I never thought of it that way." While the men debated the story a little more and made their way to the other people in the water, Kyra and Trista removed their clothes and began wading in slowly.

"Thank you for sharing that story," Kyra said to Trista once they'd both gotten into their tubes.

"You're welcome," she said. "I hope it helps you find the answers you're searching for. Or should I say, I hope your wish for love comes true."

"I may not make a wish."

Trista rolled her eyes. "Oh, honey, please. I see the way you look at my cousin. And I see the way he watches you. You'll make a wish before we leave today and I'd bet money that he's doing the same thing."

Kyra thought about denying it, but it was no use. She had a good poker face at times, but being in St. Lucia was making her soft. She could blame it on the heat, but there was no point doing that, either.

Maceo grabbed the rope that was keeping her tube linked to Trista's and pulled them together with the others. When Kyra's tube waded right next to Luke, she smiled, loving the smile he was giving her in return. Since they'd been with the others, they'd barely spoken to each other today, but somehow, she felt like they'd still been communicating. Whether it was the looks he was shooting her way or the private smiles he gave her when the others were occupied, their body language had been having major conversations.

When she heard Nash mention Christmas and ask the St. Lucians how their Christmas differed from the States, a thought crossed Kyra's mind. She'd been honest when she told Trista she wasn't sure if she'd be making any wishes, but now—being here with Luke—she could think of at least one wish that she wanted to make for the holiday. So without hesitation, she slowly closed her eyes and inwardly made her Christmas wish, her hands wafting over the water when she did so.

She opened her eyes, glad that the group was still engrossed in a conversation about Christmas. Only when she couldn't shake the feeling that someone was watching her did she look Luke's way and spot him—his eyes were fastened on hers.

Kyra swallowed the lump in her throat as she observed him more closely. *Crap.* She hoped he hadn't known she'd made a wish, because if he did, she didn't need him suspecting that the wish had anything to do with him. Yet, judging by the smirk on his face, he already knew it did.

Chapter 10

Luke could tell that Nash was nervous to meet his mother, but Luke wouldn't dare tell him that he was just as nervous.

"Are you okay?" Kyra asked from the passenger seat of the rental. Before Luke answered, he glanced back at Nash to make sure he still had his headphones in.

"I'm a little nervous," he admitted. "My mom is amazing, but I know this will be a lot for her. For them both."

Kyra covered Luke's hand, which was resting on his thigh, with her own. "Nash and your mom both need this and while it may be hard, you having Nash come to St. Lucia to meet her was the right thing to do."

Luke nodded. "I know you're right. For my mom, I hope this doesn't dig up memories of my father's infidelity. And for Nash, he still doesn't know his birth mother, so I hope it doesn't trigger his feelings about that, either."

"There's a good chance this will trigger emotions for both of them," Kyra said. "But that's natural given the circumstances. Until we get to your mom's house, try to think about the positive side. This trip needed to happen, and so far, it's gone well."

For the rest of the drive to his mom's house, Luke took Kyra's advice and tried not to think about everything that could go wrong with this visit, but rather, everything that could go right.

When they arrived at his mom's place, as expected, she was sitting on the porch, ready to greet them. Luke looked back to Nash as he removed his headphones.

"Is that her?" he asked. Luke nodded and all three of them exited the car. Luke was still trying to figure out if he should hug his mom first and then introduce Nash or the other way around, when Kyra made her way past both of them.

"Ms. O'Connor, it's so great to see you," Kyra said, pulling her in for a hug. "Should I still call you Ms. O'Connor?"

Athena laughed. "Yes, child, I kept my married name." Athena sat back. "Ooh, would you look at you. If you aren't just as beautiful as the day I met you."

"Thank you," Kyra said with a smile. "I've missed you."

Athena clasped a hand over hers. "I've missed you, too, sweetie."

Luke went to his mom next, hugging her tightly since he hadn't seen her in a few months. "I've missed you, Mom," he said. "But I'm glad St. Lucia is treating you well."

She leaned up and hugged him back ever so tight. "I needed this, baby. I needed my people."

Luke nodded, knowing exactly what she meant. The divorce had taken a bigger toll on her than Luke had been prepared for. "I want you to meet someone." Luke waved over Nash, who was still standing at the bottom of the stairs. "Mom, this is my brother, Nash. Nash, this is my mom, Athena."

After coming up the steps, Nash looked uneasy, like he wasn't sure what to do. Extending his hand, he told her, "Nice to meet you, Ms. O'Connor."

Instead of accepting his handshake, Athena stood from her porch chair and lightly touched his cheek. "Nash, it's very nice to meet you, too. You look so much like my boy." Athena opened the screen door. "Come. Let's go inside."

Nash smiled as he stepped into the home. "We've been getting that a lot. Guess our dad has strong genes."

Athena nodded, her eyes full of emotion. "You do look like Nick," she said. "Maybe even a little more than Luke does."

Luke took a seat next to Kyra on the couch. He wasn't sure if he should leave the room so they could get to know each other without him there, or if they should stay. When Kyra took his hand in hers, he figured that was her way of saying they should stay.

"Thank you for wanting to meet me," Nash told Athena.

"Honey, I wanted to meet you the moment Luke called and told me about you."

"So you didn't know I existed?"

Athena shook her head. "My ex-husband is a lot of things, but honest isn't one of them. Had I known you existed, I would have made Nick do right by you."

Nash visibly swallowed. "I appreciate that. I was

adopted when I was a baby and my parents are great. But I always felt a little off in my family and then they told me I was adopted."

"And you found my Luke," Athena added. "I remember how scared and excited he was to get to know you."

Nash laughed. "I was probably even worse than Luke." His face grew serious. "The investigator I hired didn't find much on my father."

Athena shook her head. "Nick has always had a wandering spirit and I didn't know until Luke was in high school just how wandering that meant. If Nick doesn't want to be found, he won't be found. That doesn't mean you should stop trying. It only means that you may not like what you find when you track him down. Luke can probably help you. Nick tends to reach out to him from time to time."

Nash frowned. "After talking it over with Luke, I'm not sure I even want to find him." Nash glanced at Luke before returning his gaze to Athena. "Do you know anything about my birth mother? Or have an idea as to who she might be?"

"I've thought about those early years with Nick many times upon finding out that you existed, but I can't recall Nick even being friends with another woman back then. I wish I knew more, but I was kept in the dark about a lot of things."

"So there was never a clue that he had another son out there?"

Athena shook her head. "Nick and I had some dark times, so I may not remember every fight we had that made him walk out, or every guy trip he went on that could have been covering for something else, but sometimes, our subconscious chooses not to see things to try and save us from the heartbreak of our situation."

Nash nodded. "I understand. Figured I had to ask."

Athena placed her hand over Nash's. "I know you already have a family, but Luke's family is your family, too. We don't do all that half this and half that around here. You are family, Nash, and when you're ready to learn more about your past, tell my Luke and he'll get you in contact with Nick. Unfortunately, he may have the answers you're looking for. But I must warn you, the years have not been kind to him. You may not like what he has to say."

"I've been preparing myself for the unexpected ever since I learned I was adopted," Nash said. "If I decide to learn more, I'll try to handle it best I can."

Athena smiled. "That's all any of us can do, Nash. And now that we've met, I hope you know that you can always come to me when you need someone in your corner."

Nash glanced over at Luke, who couldn't really read the expression on his brother's face.

"I really appreciate that," Nash told Athena.

"Good." She lightly touched his cheek once more before announcing that dinner was waiting on them all in the kitchen. "Should we eat?"

"Oh, man," Kyra said. "I'm probably going to gain ten pounds from all this good food, but I'm down to eat more." They followed Athena into the kitchen and sat around the table. It had been a while since Luke had tasted his mom's cooking, but she definitely didn't disappoint.

Conversation flowed easily as he and Kyra caught up with his mom and Nash learned about some of the antics Luke and his friends used to pull back in the day. At first, it seemed like Nash was enjoying all the stories, but as dessert neared, Luke noticed Nash seemed to be a little distant.

"Are you good?" Luke asked after dessert.

"I think so," Nash said. "But I'm overwhelmed."

"Anyone in your situation would be that way," Luke said.

"But it's not just that. It's hard, hearing stories of a life that feels like I should have been a part of, but wasn't. I mean, it's as if we've been brothers our entire lives, but we haven't."

"We'll get there," Luke said. "We can't replace the years we lost, but we can make new memories."

"I know we can and I may sound like a jealous little brother, but sometimes, it feels as if Nick already had you, so you were the son he decided to keep and I was the one he decided to throw away. And Athena can't remember some of the dark times in their relationship, but she can remember every moment of your childhood. Even the good memories with your dad."

"That's not fair," Luke said. "My mom hasn't had an easy life, either. She's still coming to grips with how her relationship with our dad went."

"Your dad," Nash said. "Not mine. I don't even know the man."

Luke nodded. "Fine. My dad." Given how quiet it was in the kitchen, Luke assumed Kyra and his mom were now listening to the conversation.

Nash pinched the bridge of his nose. "Listen, I loved meeting your mom and I thank you for bringing me to St. Lucia, but I think I need to head out." Instead of waiting to get a response from Luke, Nash said goodbye to Athena, hugged her tightly and walked out the front door.

"We can head back," Luke said, following him out the house.

Nash sighed. "I just need a minute. Some space to think. Maybe I'll get a hotel room tonight if you're cool with that."

"I don't want that, but I understand that this is hard for you," Luke said. "It's difficult getting taxis this time of night, so I'll give you a ride."

"No need," Nash said. "I texted Maceo during dessert and he'll give me a ride. He should be here any minute." Nash walked over to Luke and clasped his shoulder. "Bro, I appreciate everything you've done since we met and I love you for it. I just need some time. Seeing you and your mom… Knowing that you were able to at least grow up with Nick and get to know him… It's all harder than I thought it would be. Athena is a sweetheart just like I imagined she would be. But I need some time by myself to think about everything that's happened."

Luke clasped the back of Nash's head and brought their foreheads together as Maceo arrived. Luke was staring at the street long after they left, until he felt someone loop an arm around his. He glanced down to see Kyra, her eyes warm and comforting.

"He just needs time, son," Athena said, stepping out onto the porch. "He's a good man and his parents raised him right. But this is a lot for anyone to handle."

"I know," Luke said with a nod. "I guess I just hate feeling like I'm the reason he's overwhelmed right now. It was my idea to bring him to St. Lucia. Dad doesn't even have family here anymore, so I'm not sure why we even came."

"Because even though your dad isn't handling this situation right, you still wanted your brother to see where he came from," Kyra said. "It was the right thing to do, even if Nash is having a hard time handling it right now. He'll appreciate you later."

"How could he do this?" Luke asked, looking to Athena. "How could Dad father a son and not tell us anything about it? Even if Nash's birth mother wanted to give him up for adoption, how could he turn his back on his own flesh and blood?"

Athena walked down the stairs and met them in the street. "Who knows why your father made any of the decisions that he has. We can't spend all our time trying to figure out why he did this or that. We just have to learn to heal and accept that Nick has made mistakes that cannot be undone."

"I wish Nash could realize that," Luke muttered.

Athena glanced at her son. "Nash is a lot like you, you know."

"How so?"

"You've always needed to take a moment to process things. You've been like that since you were a boy. There are some people in this would who would have found out they had a sibling and wouldn't be doing everything in their power to incorporate them into their life. You're one of the good seeds, Luke."

Luke hugged his mom. "Thanks, Mama. Don't know what I'd do without you."

Luke glanced to Kyra. "Ready to head out?"

"Yeah, let's go home."

Luke smiled, touched that she said "home" so easily.

"Take care of him," Athena said, giving Kyra a hug. She whispered something in her ear that Luke couldn't hear, but Kyra was smiling when they broke their embrace.

The night had been more mentally exhausting than Luke would have liked, but the forty-minute drive from his mom's place with the windows rolled down and Kyra sitting beside him wasn't half-bad.

"Having you there tonight made all the difference," he told her.

"Duh," she said. "I'm kinda awesome. Shocked you never realized it before."

"Oh, I realized it," he admitted. "I've always known how great you are." He briefly glanced over at her. "Always felt how much I need you in my life."

Since he had to look back to the road, he didn't have time to see her expression, but he figured the hand that was resting on his thigh was a good sign. *I'll take it.*

Chapter 11

Kyra's heart was beating out of her chest as they walked into Luke's home after leaving his mom's place. She knew the night hadn't gone how he'd planned, but she was glad Luke had introduced Nash to his mom.

"I don't know about you," she said, walking over to his bar, "but I could use a drink or a shot."

Luke laughed, following her. "I think I need a shot. What are you in the mood for?"

Kyra scanned the liquor bottles. "Ooo, Jameson. Definitely a whiskey kinda night."

"How could I forget," Luke said, getting out two shot glasses. "You've been a whiskey girl since you were old enough to drink."

"Nope," she said with a smile. "Way before that. I was a whiskey girl since I snuck my first bottle out of my parents' liquor cabinet."

"I think I remember you getting in trouble for that," Luke said, pouring the whiskey. "Your parents found you and your friends drunk in the backyard. You were like sixteen, right?"

"I was," she said with a laugh. "Can't believe you remember that. Taheim and Ajay were pretty pissed, too. But I remember you telling me that although it seemed like the end of the world to have my entire family upset at me, it was a teenager's rite of passage to misbehave."

He nodded his head. "I did say that, but I have to admit, you scared the hell out of me, too. I'd never known someone who had to get their stomach pumped from too much alcohol."

"I didn't drink until I turned twenty after that incident," she explained. "It was really my first time having liquor, so I didn't know how my body would take to it. You would think I'd hate whiskey after that, but I like to forget that I ever had to go to the hospital."

"I could never forget," Luke said, clinking his glass to Kyra's before they both took the shot. "You looked so helpless in the hospital and your parents had told me you were asleep. I wasn't expecting that you'd wake up when I came in the room."

"I felt you there," she admitted. "I'd been out of it most the night, but something pulled my eyes open. I'd wanted it to be you and, surprisingly, it was."

"Really?" he asked, his eyes studying hers. "Pretty sure I thought you wanted it to be someone from your family instead of me."

Kyra rolled her eyes. "Luke, I had the biggest crush on you and that was the year that I finally noticed a hint of flirtation in your eyes that made me think that maybe you didn't see me as a little sister anymore."

"That hint of flirtation you saw scared the crap out of me. I'm not gonna lie—I still looked at you like a little sister back then. But it was in a rare moment when we were hanging out at one of your family's parties and I actually forgot that I shouldn't be noticing certain things about you, like how your hair fell over your shoulders or the way your eyes twinkled when you laughed." Luke poured himself another shot. "Jaleen noticed it at that same party and you called me out. Warning me that if Taheim and Ajay picked up on it, they'd kill me. Plus, I was in college and you were in high school. It just felt wrong."

Kyra played with the rim of her shot glass, nervous to ask a question she'd had for years. "I understand why you felt the way you did back then. But by my twenty-first birthday, we were both adults and our five-year age difference didn't seem that strange to me."

"It wasn't about the age thing at that point," he said, holding her gaze. "Do you remember Jessica? My ex?"

"The one you were engaged to?" Kyra asked. "Things ended right before my birthday party. I thought that may have had something to do with it, but you'd seemed fine."

"I thought I was fine, too," he agreed. "Jessica was never good for me and deep down, I knew that. She only cared about herself and what I could do for her. If it didn't revolve around making money or high social standing, she didn't want to be concerned about it. She got her hooks in me in college because she knew even before I did that I would make something of myself. I was the one who broke off the engagement after overhearing her saying to the partners at her law firm that she was only with me because it looked good and that she'd already landed more clients because they liked the person I was."

"That's messed up," Kyra said. "And you projected those feelings on me?"

"I did. And I'm so sorry because that was wrong of me. But I was in a bad place and didn't know how to get out of it. I didn't mean anything I said about you, but I knew the words would hurt and as much as I hate to admit it, I needed someone to hurt more than I was. It was an asshole move and I vowed to never make anyone feel less than after that situation. The guys had invited me down for your birthday because they knew I needed a change. Plus, I'd found out some news about my dad that had really messed up my head."

"What was it?" she asked.

Luke sighed. "Back then, I knew damn well my dad was cheating on my mom. The first time I noticed something was going on was back when I was in like the third or fourth grade. Even then, I knew Dad shouldn't have women in the house when my mom was at work. But he was my world when I was younger. I wanted to be just like my father."

"He's always been charismatic," Kyra added. "Most young boys look up to their fathers, so it's natural for you to only want to see the good."

"That may be the case, but I was an idiot. When I finally decided to take a stand against my dad, we got into a huge altercation. Punches were thrown. Words were said. Revelations surfaced. And my only regret is that it took me so long to call my father out. I didn't know Nash existed, but I shouldn't have been surprised when he found me."

"I'm so sorry, Luke," Kyra said. "I had no idea that was going on between you and your dad. But you do know that it's not your fault that Nash didn't know your father growing up, right?"

Luke shrugged. "Yeah, I know. But I still feel guilty. Every time he brings up his birth mother, I can't but wonder if she was one of those women I caught my dad with."

"You may never know, and you'll drive yourself crazy thinking about it."

"I told Jessica some of it," he said. "That mess with my dad went on for years and I confided in her only for her to tell me that I needed to get over my family issues and suck it up."

"Like you said before, Jessica wasn't good for you," Kyra said. "She didn't have a bone of empathy in her body. Besides, she never liked me, anyway."

"Most of my exes didn't like you," Luke stated. "Clearly, despite my best efforts, they saw what I'd failed to acknowledge."

Kyra swallowed. "What might that be?"

Luke held her eyes for a while, then he walked around the bar and placed his arms on either side of Kyra, pinning her still. "That I was crazy about you even when I tried convincing myself that I wasn't."

Kyra closed her eyes. "Or maybe you just think that you were because all of these stories about the past are making you nostalgic."

Luke shook his head. "Nah, I know damn well what I'm feeling. What I've always felt. I may have tried to ignore it when I didn't want to jeopardize my relationship with your brothers, but we're adults and, quite frankly, I'm tired of fighting my feelings."

Kyra opened her eyes, locking them with his. *He's dead serious.* She could tell by the way he was staring at her, observing her, waiting for her to comment on what he'd said. Usually, she could find the words, but it was hard to say something during a moment she'd waited so long for. A moment she'd craved and dreamed about in every fantasy she'd ever had.

She liked to think she was a strong woman who could make the man of her dreams sweat a little before he won her over, but sitting on that bar stool, pinned between Luke and the counter, she couldn't think of one good reason why she shouldn't be taking full advantage of this opportunity to finally get with Luke.

Pulling his head down to hers, Kyra placed her lips on his, the taste of whiskey on each of their tongues increasing her awareness of the situation. As with the kisses they'd shared before, it was as if their mouths knew what their minds were still trying to figure out.

Luke clasped her around the waist and lifted her so that she was on the counter, the move catching her off guard. She felt like she was starring in her own romantic film, but the problem was, cheesy romance movies were so not Kyra. She didn't do the pick-me-up-and-kiss-me-senseless thing. Up until college, she'd been a hard-core tomboy for goodness' sake, thanks to her brothers. Yet sitting on this counter, her long skirt pushed up as Luke's hands roamed her thighs, she couldn't even handle how hot the moment was.

"Kyra," Luke breathed between kisses. She wanted to answer him back. Had planned to say his name, too. Yet she was feeling too many emotions all at once to do anything other than soak in the moment with him.

Luke broke the kiss first and rested his forehead against hers. "Do you want this to go any further?"

She nodded. "Yes. Hell yeah."

"Then we have to go to the bedroom," he said with a laugh. "I don't have a condom down here."

"I can't wait that long." Kyra looked around the bar for her purse and spotted it. She pulled out a condom and tossed it to him. "We're good."

He looked from the condom to her. "Did you expect this would happen tonight?"

She shook her head. "No, but I figured it would happen sometime on this trip, so I wanted to be prepared. Now are you gonna keep talking or are you gonna help me off this counter and onto that soft-looking rug down there."

Luke smiled before kissing her again, his lips not leaving hers as he lifted her off the counter and gently placed her on the rug in his living room. Kyra felt like she could feel him on every part of her body as they were lying there, kissing and touching in a way they never had before.

When Luke leaned up to remove his shirt, Kyra's hands went to his pants. She unbuckled his jeans and helped him slide them down his hips, leaving him in only his boxers. She took a moment to admire his delicious-looking stomach, strong thighs and overall manly physique.

"You've always looked good," she said. "But this…" She motioned up and down. "This body is on another level."

"Thank you," he said with a laugh. "I've been working on it."

"It shows," she replied, removing her shirt without warning. Luke's eyes widened as she stood to unzip her skirt and slid it down her hips, leaving her in only her black lingerie set.

"Damn," he said, kneeling to place soft kisses on her stomach and thighs. "You look amazing." Instead of responding, she unhooked her bra and tossed it to the side with the rest of her clothes.

Luke visibly swallowed. "Was not expecting that." She slid off her panties next. "Was expecting that a little more after the bra," he said, causing her to laugh. The laugh didn't last long because Luke was pulling her down to the couch instead of the floor and widening her legs.

"What are you doing?" she asked, the question dying on her lips the moment she felt his tongue teasing her nub. She expected him to take it slow because this was their first intimate moment together, but Luke clearly hadn't gotten that memo because he was swirling his tongue and causing her to buck off the couch, showing no remorse for the way she was panting over how good it felt.

"Luke," she whispered, trying to push his head away and pull it closer all at the same time. He hadn't even been pleasing her long, and already she felt like she would burst if she didn't have an orgasm soon. "I can't take it."

"You can," he said, dipping his tongue even farther. The strokes of his tongue increased and sent her overboard as her orgasm erupted faster than she'd been prepared for. When she finally came down from the pleasure, Luke finally stood, a cocky look on his face.

"I'll never forget your orgasm face," he said.

"Ugh, please do. I'm sure it was horrible."

"It was beautiful," he said, helping her to the floor and putting on the condom. He planted her with a serious look.

"What's wrong?"

"Are you still a virgin?"

She laughed. "Hell no. I got tired of waiting for a man who was convinced we shouldn't be together, so I gave it up to the next sucka."

Luke frowned. "That was a low blow."

"And the truth," she muttered, placing a soft kiss on his neck. "Now we can reminisce more about all the ways you passed up on the best woman you've ever known, or we can participate in an activity that allows us to get naked and behave like savages. Personally, I think we've talked enough for one night."

"I've always preferred sweatier activities," he said.

She smirked. "Good choice." And just like that, he thrust inside her, causing her words to get caught in her throat. Inch by inch, he branded her, marking territory that as far as she was concerned was already his years ago. She'd compared every man she'd dated to Luke. None of her exes had measured up to the man she'd never been with, but always imagined she would.

Luke had no idea the way he'd impacted her life, but now wasn't the time for her to dwell on that. Now it was time for her to focus only on the pleasure he was bringing her way. When he was fully inside her, he stilled. Both of them breathing a sigh of relief that they were finally both in the right place at the right time of their lives.

"This means everything," Luke whispered. "Thank you."

She closed her eyes at his words. "You're welcome," she finally said as she began to move her hips. For a second, she thought Luke wasn't going to join in, preferring to stay still a bit longer. Thankfully, he put her out of her misery and began meeting her movements. Soon he was running the show and all Kyra could do was soak in every moment of it.

She wasn't sure how long she lasted, but her next orgasm snuck up on her quick and fast, her warning for Luke to get his first falling on deaf ears. She convulsed as her orgasm shook her to her core, causing her to cry out his name. She was thankful that Nash wasn't in the house to hear how unusually loud she was being. As the tremors subsided, she wasn't sure she could even take much more because every single nerve in her body felt alive. So she was thankful when Luke grunted and pulled her even closer as he welcomed his own release, the moment being much more erotic than any Kyra had ever had in her life.

Using his upper-body strength, he stayed positioned above her, careful not to crush her. "Are you okay?" he asked.

"Perfect," she replied, the sincerity in his eyes touching her heart. She pulled his head back down to hers and kissed him passionately, hoping that he understood how much this moment meant to her without her having to say the words. Judging by the way he kissed her back, he knew.

"Round two?" she asked, surprising herself. She wasn't the only one surprised as Luke looked at her, his eyes wide.

"Are you sure you don't need a break?"

She shook her head. "Nope." This time, when she kissed him, he was smiling and shaking his head at the same time.

Chapter 12

Kyra would have paid good money to see city-boy Luke out on the water fishing with Uncle Ralph, but she'd passed on the opportunity. As amazing as last night was and as much as she wanted to spend it in bed all day with Luke, she knew he needed some quality time with his uncle.

So instead, she'd decided on another mission. One that she hoped would help her traveling companions.

"What are you doing here?" Nash asked.

"I asked Maceo to give me a ride to the same hotel he'd dropped you off."

Nash stood aside and motioned for her to come inside. "How did you find my room number?"

Kyra shrugged. "A little flirting, a little French and voilà."

Nash raised an eyebrow. "Since when do you know French?"

"Since I picked up some words to help me communicate with those who may not speak English. Now are we gonna debate all day or are you going to let me be a friend and help you."

Nash took a seat on the edge of the bed while Kyra took a seat at the only chair in the room. "Help me with what?"

"Help you not spend the rest of the vacation sulking in your feelings."

"I'm entitled to some time to think," he said.

"I get that. I just want to make sure that you also realize this is the best time for you to get some of those answers you need. Ms. O'Connor may not be able to tell you exactly what you want to know, but she's a sweetheart and if you want to know more about your background, she'll be able to tell you the St. Lucian ways. Plus, this is still the country where your birth father was born and raised, meaning it's in your blood. Get to know your people."

Nash was silent for a few minutes until he finally said, "You're right. I should make the most of being here. It's just, sometimes I get frustrated when I think about how different my life could have been if I'd grown up with Luke. If his dad would have chosen to be in my life. If my birth mother would have chosen to keep me. It almost seems wrong to have had a good life but still wonder 'what if?'"

"I think that's a natural reaction," Kyra said. "We live in a society where we're always thinking about what could have happened or should have happened. When, honestly, we should be paying attention to what is, not missing moments that may otherwise seem unimportant."

Nash nodded his head. "You know, that sounds like something Luke would say."

Kyra laughed. "Yeah, well, he's a lot like my brother Taheim in that way. The two of them together probably rubbed off on me."

"Probably," he said, eyeing her with a curious look on his face.

"What?" she asked.

"Not sure," he replied. "Something seems different about you." He looked her up and down again. "I know what it is." Subconsciously, Kyra ran her fingers through her hair, thinking there was no way he would guess. "You and Luke finally had sex, didn't you?"

"What?" she gasped. "Why would you say that? And what do you mean 'finally'? I think you've been in this hotel room too long already."

Nash lifted an eyebrow. "Damn, Luke didn't waste any time putting on the charm. And when I say 'finally,' I mean the two of you are good together and I know you both have feelings for each other, so it's nice to know y'all had a good night."

Kyra shrugged. "What if the night wasn't all that great?"

"Uh, was it not great? Because I don't mind kicking my brother's ass if he did something stupid."

She smiled. "I appreciate that, but there's no point in lying. So yeah, we finally had sex and it was pretty damn amazing."

"It always is when feelings are involved," he said. "Or so I've heard."

Kyra dropped her head into her hands. "We haven't really talked about things, so I have no idea where we stand. But today isn't about me, it's about you."

"Nah, this is more interesting," he said. "I know I warned you not to hurt him, but I don't want you getting hurt, either. This is probably breaking bro-code, but he talks about you a lot and if he finally made a move, it wasn't a temporary thing. When Luke commits to something, he does so fully. When the time is right, y'all will talk it out."

Kyra lifted her head. "Thanks, Nash. I'm sure whatever it will be, it will be. In the meantime, I'm trying not to make a big deal about it."

"But it is a big deal," he said. "Luke knows that, too. I didn't know y'all back then, but something tells me that you two were going to end up together in some way eventually. If it's happening now, it's happening at the time it should."

"Wow, look at you," she teased. "Being all prophet like and whatnot."

He popped his collar. "You know me. I try my best."

"Okay, Nash, I see you."

They started talking about random topics, Kyra hopeful that the light conversation eased Nash's mind after all the deep thinking he'd been doing. She was glad when he walked her to the door and finally told her, "Thanks for this. I really needed it. And you're right, I'll call Luke later and take advantage of this chance to get to know more about our family and St. Lucia."

Kyra gave him a quick hug goodbye. "I think that's a great idea. And if at any time, you need to talk to someone who's not related or semirelated to you, just let me know."

Nash laughed. "Are you, though? Not related. Because I gotta admit, it kinda feels like you're my brother's wife giving me advice right now. I'm getting mad sister-in-law vibes."

"Wife? Ha!" *Oh, how many times I've dreamed about being that man's wife.* It was sad when she thought about it. Completely unhealthy. Out of nervousness, she started to awkwardly laugh. "Boy, please. How about you just admit that our friendship is blossoming and leave it at that."

"Deal," he said with a smirk. "But when y'all do end up together, remember this conversation because I plan to tell you I told you so."

Kyra shook her head. "I can't wait to meet someone you like so I can tease you."

"Hate to burst your bubble, but I've never been a one-woman kind of guy and I accepted that years ago."

"That doesn't mean there isn't a woman out there crushing on you," she explained.

"Nah," he said. "I'm clear up front with any woman I'm feeling, so they know the deal."

"Do you hear yourself?" she asked. "Men are so dense sometimes."

Nash stuck out his arms. "I'm just spitting facts. I even brought two girls to prom and they were cool with it."

Kyra shook her head. "And just when I thought we were getting somewhere in this friendship, you do something to remind me that you're an idiot. I'm not knocking the game because I've been known to be a bit of a playa in my day, but Nash, just because you think you're laying out the rules doesn't mean they're being followed."

Kyra spent the next hour debating with Nash the pros and cons of playing the field. And just like most topics they discussed, they couldn't agree on much. Kyra left the hotel thinking that Nash had nailed one point right on the head… This thing—whatever it was—between her and Luke had been a long time coming, and for the first time in years, everything felt perfect.

Luke glanced at his phone for the tenth time in the past hour, wondering when Kyra was going to get home. He was on one of his favorite places in his home—his rooftop. But his mind couldn't settle until he saw Kyra after the night they'd had.

He'd had a great day with his uncle and his mom and she'd picked up on his attraction to Kyra right away. In fact, she told him he'd always known, which didn't surprise him. A part of him thought a person would have had to have been blind not to catch the way he started looking at Kyra the older they got.

Except Taheim. He wasn't sure if his best friend just chose to ignore it, knowing Luke would never cross that line, or if he'd been oblivious. When they'd had the conversation about him never messing with his sister, they'd also been talking to their friend Jaleen and others. Taheim had seemed to be talking like any big brother would, but looking back, Luke wasn't sure if he'd actually had a clue. Even Kyra's brother Ajay had picked up on it once and called him out a few years back at Taheim's wedding, but Luke had denied it. Mainly because he'd been in a serious relationship at the time and thinking about Kyra would have been heading down a bad path.

He glanced at the time again, thinking she should have been home by now. Unable to help himself, he called Maceo again.

"Yes, Luke," he said dryly.

"Did you pick up Kyra yet?"

"This is crazy, you know," Maceo said. "You've been calling me most the day. The only reason I told you that I dropped her off at Nash's hotel was so that you wouldn't worry. Not so you could blow up my phone."

"Sorry, man. Just wondering where she's at."

Maceo sighed. "You know, after this trip—better yet, *on* this trip—you better tell Kyra how you feel because holding in your feelings for this long ain't healthy."

"It hasn't been that long," Luke lied.

Maceo snorted. "Brotha, who are you kidding? You think I don't remember you coming to St. Lucia and going on and on about this woman you'd known since you were younger who you compared every woman you've ever dated to? You've been in some pretty serious relationships and you've never brought any of them to St. Lucia. Yet you brought Kyra."

Luke grew quiet, then said, "I see your point. I'll talk to her before we head home."

"Thank God," he mumbled. "And by the way, I dropped her off there about twenty minutes ago."

"She's here?" Luke asked, getting up from his chair.

"Yeah, she's there. Seemed just as anxious to see you, too, if it helps."

Luke got off the roof and went into his house, finally spotting Kyra outside by the pool, sitting in one of the lounge chairs. "Found her. Thanks, man."

Maceo laughed. "Anytime, man."

Luke hung up and walked outside, noting that she seemed to be watching the sunset.

"It's beautiful, isn't it?" he asked.

She grabbed her chest. "Jesus, you scared me! I saw

the car, but couldn't find you, so I thought you went on a walk or something."

"I was on the roof," he explained. "Thinking about you and wondering when you'd get here."

She smiled. "I've been thinking about you, too. Nash says hi by the way and that he'll be here tomorrow."

Luke nodded. "I'm glad you went to talk to him. I think he needed a friend."

"He did," she said. "And he's fine. Just needed a moment to reboot."

Luke sat down on the lounger beside hers. "My mom told me to tell you hi as well and that she's glad we finally stopped ignoring our feelings toward one another."

Kyra's eyes widened. "You told your mom about last night?"

"Hell nah, but she said she could tell something was up between us when we were at her place."

"But we hadn't even had sex yet when we were over there."

"Our relationship started changing way before that," he told her, lightly running a finger up and down her arm.

She glanced down at his hand. "Yeah, that's true. But it's still crazy to me to think that last night happened after all this time. A few years ago, I'd finally accepted the fact that you and I would never be together."

"I thought you'd come to that conclusion after the night of your twenty-first birthday."

"Nope," she said. "I was hurt as hell, but I didn't finally drop it completely until Taheim and Winter's wedding."

Luke thought back to their wedding and couldn't

think of anything that happened. "Why was that the turning point?"

Kyra sighed. "Right before their wedding, I'd been hanging out with my girl Cheyanne and she'd told me that there was a friend of hers that she wanted me to meet. She'd barely had time to warn me who I was meeting before your ex-girlfriend popped up. Apparently, Cheyanne had just found out that her coworker was dating you."

"Crap," Luke said. "You must mean Meeka, right? We'd just started dating. I think we were only like a month in. I almost didn't even bring her to the wedding, but she'd been going through a lot and needed a break, so I took her as my plus-one."

"I know," Kyra said. "She told me all about you when we met and even though I admitted that I knew you through my brothers, I refrained from acting like I'd always looked to you like a friend, too."

"Cheyanne knew how you felt about me?" he asked.

Kyra nodded. "Yeah, she did. But just like any friend would, she was pissed that I still seemed hung up on you despite how you'd treated me years prior. She said she'd been talking to Meeka at work and found out she'd be at the wedding. She didn't want me to be blindsided. Plus, she didn't want me to hold out hope for a relationship that may never happen."

"I get that," he said. "But Meeka and I weren't that serious back then."

"It didn't matter," Kyra said. "Meeka was a little on the crazy side, but in a good way. She was my kinda girl and we all had fun that night. Eventually, I asked her how old she was and when I realized she wasn't that much older than me, I suddenly got very annoyed.

I mean, here I was hanging out with a pretty great woman, who even a month into her relationship seemed crazy about the same man I'd had a crush on growing up. I don't know what came over me, but at the end of the night, I told Cheyanne that I was done chasing after a dream relationship that would never happen. I needed to move on and, unfortunately, that meant letting any ideas I had about me and you die."

"That's why you were acting so nonchalant at the wedding, right?" Luke asked. "I hadn't seen you in so long and I'd been excited to finally catch up and apologize in person, but you were chumming it up with Meeka and Cheyanne most the day and it felt strange trying to steal your attention away given the circumstances and the fact that you were connecting with my current girlfriend. She was the only one you never disliked."

"She wasn't the type to get threatened," Kyra said. "Her and I clicked instantly, so, yeah, I didn't dislike her and she didn't dislike me."

Luke smiled. "Even though it was nice to see y'all getting along, I was glad when we finally did get a few minutes alone."

"When we almost kissed," Kyra stated. "I'm glad we didn't."

"Me, too," he said. "Even so, I'd wanted to. Badly."

"But you've never been that guy," she said. "You're loyal. Faithful. As much as I hate to admit this, I wasn't the one who stopped that kiss, but I was the one who started it. Yet before I even got close, you stopped me. In my mind, it was going to be a goodbye kiss, but it would have been messed up on so many levels."

"I was there, too," he said. "It took two to almost kiss."

Kyra shook her head. "Sort of. It was mainly on me. Which is why I decided to own up to my feelings, and before you left the wedding, I pulled Meeka aside and confessed to my crush on you, but told her that I wanted what was best for you and that what was best at the time was you being with her."

Luke's eyes widened. "I had no idea you told her that. She never said anything to me about that conversation."

"That's because she's cool as hell," Kyra said. "She hugged me after and said under different circumstances, she could see us being friends. She didn't give me a look of pity like I was prepared for and I respected her for that. Instead, she promised that for however long your relationship lasted, she would do what she could to make you happy, which made me happy."

Wow, I had no idea. "That explains a lot," Luke said. "Back when we were together, I was ready to propose to Meeka. She checked off every box I had. She was funny, outgoing, always the life of the party. Knew how to make me smile when I was having a bad day. Pushed my buttons in ways I desperately needed. We were complete opposites, but it just worked. The only thing that didn't work was the fact that she and I weren't meant to be each other's forever."

Kyra squinted. "What do you mean? Sounds like a match made in heaven to me."

Luke thought back to the time he was with Meeka. "I told her that I'd always imagined marrying a woman just like her and she felt what I felt. She knew I was going to propose, and in true Meeka form, she stopped it before it happened."

"Wow," Kyra said. "I didn't know that."

"Many don't," he stated. "Not even Taheim. Wasn't something I wanted to explain to folks, especially since our breakup was one of the best things that could have happened to both of us."

"How so?" she asked.

"Easy. We would have been together out of convenience and comfort, not passion and excitement. Meeka told me that the reason she checked off all the boxes on my list was because I'd grown up with a girl in my life with those same qualities. She actually brought you up and said that even though her and I shared an amazing friendship, I'd never love her as much as I'd love..." His voice trailed off as he realized what he almost said next. "Anyway, by then, you'd already moved to LA, so I told myself I had to be okay with how things were."

"I left for LA because being in Chicago was too hard," she admitted. "Cheyanne was great about not having me go out with Meeka too much because it was too weird, but suddenly, Chicago felt too small given how I felt. When Winter and Autumn told me that their sister, Summer, had two of her employees opening the office in LA, I knew it was the change I needed."

"I always wondered if I was part of the reason you left," he said.

"It wasn't just you," she confessed. "I also needed to live on my own without my parents and brothers there to help me whenever I needed it. I needed to grow up and moving to LA helped me do that."

"I'm proud of you," he told her. "You've never needed your parents and brothers to thrive, but it's amazing watching you succeed in LA without any of them there to guide you."

Kyra smiled. "Thank you. It means a lot to hear you say that." She stood from her lounge chair and straddled Luke. "What does this mean for us now?"

He placed his hands around her waist. "I know we still have more to work through, but I was hoping you'd be my girlfriend."

"Uh, aren't we skipping a few steps since we haven't even gone on a date yet?" she asked with a laugh.

"I promise to date you the way a man should, but I'm also done with us ignoring this, so I just want to put it out there that I want to date you and only you. You're too important to me for us to just casually date."

She smiled. "Okay then. In that case, I'll be your girlfriend. You just have to get both my brothers' blessing first."

Luke raised an eyebrow. "You're kidding, right? I mean, yeah, I gotta talk to Taheim and Ajay because that's what a man would do, but you want me to get their permission to date you?"

"Yes," she said. "I want you to call them right now and ask. Otherwise, this can't continue."

Luke studied her for a moment, then said, "Okay, let's get this over with." He took out his phone and went to his speed dial.

"Oh, my God, stop," she said with a laugh. "I was just kidding. Didn't think you'd really call them right now."

"I told you I'm serious about this."

"Well, serious or not, I was playing." Kyra took his phone and placed it on a table nearby. "Tell you what, my parents' anniversary party in Chicago is in two weeks. Did you plan to go?"

He nodded his head. "Of course."

"Good. Then how about we take this time to figure out how this will play out and if we see it getting more serious, we'll talk to my brothers then. Deal?"

He studied her eyes, wondering if she really thought there was any way things wouldn't get serious between them. They'd waited too long. Dated too many of the wrong people. Even with the words left unspoken, it was clear to Luke that things were already pretty serious, but he'd been the one to mess it up all those years ago, so now, he'd do things Kyra's way.

"Okay," he finally said. "It's a deal."

"Good." Her hands slipped into his basketball shorts, cupping him in a way that made him harder by the second. "Now are we done talking or is there more that you want to discuss right now?"

Luke may do some stupid stuff at times, but he wasn't a fool. So he kissed his woman the way he'd wanted to kiss her all day, and for the first time, he made love on his balcony to the woman he'd had in mind when he'd told the designer to make sure it was as private as possible.

Chapter 13

"You know, when you mentioned that we'd be having our first date right now, I didn't think it would involve you making me get in the water for the third time on this trip," Kyra said, pouting as they walked on the beach. "Did you forget what I said about not liking water?"

Luke laughed. "I didn't forget, but you came to an island. Didn't you think it would involve a lot of water?"

She shook her head. "No, because I've gone to islands before and they typically include a lot of being on land, too."

"Trust me, this is not what you think it is. I just wanted to walk to get there."

She groaned. "I know your mom is spending the day with Nash, but maybe I should have joined them because I could have sworn your mom mentioned a car—meaning, they are driving to wherever they're going."

"Be patient," he said with a laugh. "You'll like it." Twenty minutes later, they'd arrived at their destination.

"A boat?" she asked as they approached a small yacht that was sitting on a small dock.

"Yes, I'll be taking you on a cruise around the island to show you some of the best places you can only see by boat."

"Well, why didn't you say so?" she said. "I love cruising on the water. It's getting in the water that I have an issue with."

They got on the boat and Luke showed her around the vessel. "I love it," she said. "Who's driving us?"

"I am," he stated. "I've been operating boats for longer than I've been driving."

"Wow, I had no idea."

"Not surprising," he said. "I've never driven a boat back in Chicago. Most of my experience is on the open waters in St. Lucia. Are you nervous?"

She smiled. "Not at all. I'm actually more excited for it now. Feels like our first real date."

"It is our first real date, but if at any time you feel uncomfortable out on the water, let me know and we can do something else on land."

"I think I'll be okay?" She glanced to the side of the boat. "Can you take a picture of me before we take off?"

"Sure." He took out his phone and swiped to the camera. "Step a little to the right so I can get the mountains in the background."

She did as she was told. "Make sure you get that side profile of my small waistline. I'm in a competition with a few friends."

"Uh, do I even want to know?"

"Nothing serious," she said, waving off his comment.

"Cheyanne and a couple other single friends are trying to see who can keep their waistline close to what it was when we were in our late teens and early twenties. We started it when we turned thirty."

"Women," he said, shaking his head, snapping the first shot.

Kyra rolled her eyes. "Oh, no, don't do that. Taheim told me all about that mess y'all do with seeing who can have the most toned body and abs."

Luke shrugged. "Nothing wrong with staying fit."

"Or making a competition out of it," she added.

"Okay, I see your point." After Luke was done with Kyra's mini photoshoot, he snapped a few selfies of the two of them before starting the engine. Kyra wasn't new to dating, so she'd been on some pretty great dates; however, sightseeing St. Lucia by cruising around the island definitely took the cake.

"You can't really see it, but just over those mountains is Sulphur Springs, the Caribbean's only drive-in volcano."

"That sounds cool."

"It is," he said. "Maybe before we go I could take you and Nash there." Luke continued describing more of the island. Kyra couldn't remember the last time she was so engrossed with sightseeing. St. Lucia was a beautiful place, but she knew her enjoyment had less to do with the island and more to do with the man showing her around.

"I packed lunch for us," Luke told her. "I figured we could stop by one of the smaller beaches for a little more privacy and eat there. Are you down for that?"

"I'm down for anything," she said, wiggling her eyebrows.

Luke laughed. "You always were trouble." Five minutes later, he announced they were almost at the beach. "This is one of my favorite beaches, so we'll eat here."

Kyra nodded, noise from the beach catching her attention. "Uh, are you seeing what I'm seeing?" she asked.

Luke squinted. "If what you see are several men drinking beer on the beach while wearing Santa trunks and hats, then, yeah, I see it, too." As if they knew they'd been spotted, they started yelling for Luke and Kyra to come join them in a drunken slur.

"Nah, we're good," Luke said. "Enjoy yourselves."

"Maybe we head to that other small island instead," she suggested.

"Yep." They made it to the other island fairly quickly, and like they'd hoped, it was almost deserted. "That's much better," he said, dropping the anchor.

"How are we getting to the island?" she asked.

"With the Jet Ski I have on board," he said. "I just have to lower it into the water."

"Great, another Jet Ski," she said sarcastically. "You see, this is the whole getting-into-water part that I was afraid of."

Luke laughed. "You'll be fine. I'll station it and all you'll have to do is sit on it after I get on."

"Okay," she said hesitantly. "Are you sure it's safe to leave the boat in the middle of the water?"

"We're not that far from shore. Nothing will happen to it."

Kyra nodded and followed Luke to the back of the boat while he lowered the Jet Ski into the water and got on before she did. "Can you put that backpack on?" he asked. "Everything we need is in that bag."

She nodded and put on the backpack before accepting Luke's extended hand to help her get on the Jet Ski. "We made it," she said as they neared the beach. "We didn't fall into the ocean like last time."

Luke laughed. "I was going about ten miles per hour, but I guess you're right. Glad we made it." After they got off, he pulled the Jet Ski onto the beach and walked them over to a section with palm trees that provided good shade. Then he opened the bag, pulled out a large blanket and spread it out for both of them to sit on.

"Is there food in there, too?" she asked.

"Of course." He removed two sandwiches, chips, two bottles of water and two thermoses.

"Are these Uncle Ralph's famous sandwiches?"

"Sure are. I picked them up early this morning. And I also got some of Trista's bomb rum punch since I don't remember you trying it at the lounge the other night."

"Nice! She told me about it, but no, I didn't get to try it." She glanced around the beach at a family that was on the opposite end and the greenery behind them before digging her feet into the white sand. "It's beautiful here. You can tell this beach isn't used too much."

"St. Lucia has so many beaches to choose from, but, yes, this one is secluded and just as nice as the others. Back when I was in my early twenties, Trista and Maceo told me this beach was where most of them used to run off to and have sex. You can get here by car and it's a pretty far drive from where they grew up, but I imagine having sex here would be pretty memorable."

Kyra placed her hand over her chest. "Why, Lukey, did you just suggest sex on the first date? What kind of woman do you think I am?"

His eyes widened. "No, that's not what I meant. It's

just being here with you made me realize that I've never had sex on the beach. But it wasn't to imply anything."

She laughed. "I'm just messing with you. Did you forget that we've already had sex twice before our first date?"

"I know, but I still wasn't trying to make you uncomfortable. I want this date to go perfect."

She couldn't help the smile that crossed her lips at his words. He was nervous and it was so adorable. Didn't he know that she enjoyed anything they did together? Even the activities that she'd previously never enjoyed?

What part of "I've long had a huge crush on you" didn't he understand? In some ways, she felt like she'd waited most her life for the chance to have these moments with him, and now that they were happening, she was determined to make the most of them.

Her only hesitation so far had been yesterday, when she'd found out why Luke and Meeka had broken things off. She'd had no idea she played a part and it seemed as if Luke was close to saying some words he wouldn't have been able to take back once they were out there in the universe, but he'd caught himself and she was glad for that.

If they fell in love—and not the kind of "I got love for you" that they'd always had—she didn't want to second-guess anything. She didn't want to wonder if he meant it or if it would change next week. They'd had some pretty eye-opening conversations since arriving in St. Lucia, but Kyra was curious to know how dating Luke would be in LA without the beauty of St. Lucia serving as a backdrop to the time they spent together.

And don't forget to protect your heart. It might sound crazy considering it was just their first date, but in a way, she felt like she was moving too fast. Ten years seemed like a good amount of time to get her heart back intact, but deep down, she was nervous about the possibility of being rejected by Luke again. Still, she didn't want to ruin their date by letting her insecurities about Luke steal the show.

Luke brushed some sand off his calves and shot her a sexy smile, so, of course, the only thing she wanted to do to him was precisely what he'd accidentally suggested. Kyra glanced down at where the family was, grateful to see they were gone, leaving only her and Luke on the beach under the palm trees.

She lifted herself from the towel and straddled him, loving how his hands automatically wrapped around her waist. "What are you doing?" he asked.

"Isn't it obvious?" She placed a soft kiss on the side of his neck and tugged at his red swim trucks. "Did you bring a condom?"

He nodded and unzipped the front pocket of the bag to pull out a condom. She slightly lifted her hips so that he could slip it on, and while he did so, she untied the sides of her olive-colored swimsuit.

Luke opened his mouth to say something, but she didn't give him time as she buried him deep inside her, the sensational feeling causing both of them to moan into the sky.

"I didn't expect for this to happen," he mumbled, his eyes following her every move as Kyra slowly began to rotate her hips.

She smirked. "I did."

"You shouldn't be so sexy," he said in between the kisses he was placing down her collarbone.

"We're allowed to be freaks right now," she said breathlessly. "We've waited too long to get to where we are. So, my suggestion? We make up for lost time."

Luke laughed. "I like the way you think." A few seconds later, his laughing was cut short as she adjusted her hips and began to ride him in a way that had him gripping her just so he could hold on.

Being with Kyra was everything he ever imagined it would be. She consumed his thoughts so it made perfect sense that she'd consume his body as well. Originally, Luke had thought that they'd be taking their relationship slower, but he'd underestimated the neediness they would both feel upon waiting so long to be together.

In past relationships, his exes had accused him of never fully sharing himself with them. He was a nice guy. One of the good ones, they'd say. However, there was an emotional wall Luke had built up around his heart, and although he knew his father had a lot to do with that, so did Kyra.

She'd always been the precious fruit he shouldn't have, but craved like nobody's business. A rare rose among the thorns and even though a five-year age difference didn't seem like a lot now, back then, it hadn't always felt right to have a crush on his best friend's little sister. Especially when said little sister was probably one of the hardest people in the world to ignore.

Kyra demanded attention whenever she walked into a room and since he was constantly at the Reed house, she walked in and out of plenty of rooms while he was there. He didn't think he could ever forgive himself for making her feel like she was anything less than special to him back then; however, it was true what they said. Men took longer to mature than women.

"I'm close," she whispered, tossing her head back, her moans teasing his ears.

"Me, too." He gripped her hips even tighter and angled his so that he could sink deeper into her wetness. The move must have been just what they both needed because she cried out at the same time that he groaned.

Kyra's orgasm hit her first, her convulsions bringing him even closer to the edge. Using all the strength that he had, he reached between them and found her nub, teasing her in a way that he hoped would make her come again despite the fact that she'd just had a release.

A few minutes later, Kyra was bucking in his lap, her moans turning into screams of passion as she rode out another pleasurable wave, this one bigger than the last. Luke couldn't hold on after that and he soon followed her, releasing his own pleasure, his grunts loud and foreign to his ears.

"I think we're getting the hang of this," she said breathlessly after they both began to come down from the climax.

Luke laughed. "Pretty sure no one does it better."

She smiled, gently nudging her head underneath his neck. "Pretty sure you're right."

There was so much more that Luke wanted to say. Like the fact that the reason it felt so freaking good was because when it was right, it was right. Kyra was the woman he was always meant to be with—it just took him a while to get on board. Now all he had to do was convince her it wasn't too late for them, but rather, they were right on time.

Chapter 14

"I don't like it," Kyra said for the third time that day.

Luke rubbed his forehead. "I'm starting to think there isn't anything you will like." It was the third condo he'd shown Kyra that morning and just like the others he'd shown her earlier, and the day before, she didn't care for it.

They'd gotten back from St. Lucia four days ago and even though their dating life had been great so far, their Realtor-and-client life was anything but.

"What's wrong with this place?" he asked.

Kyra glanced to the ceiling. "Do you hear that noise?"

"What noise?"

"Those heavy-footed neighbors."

Luke stopped talking and listened, barely hearing a footstep. "They aren't that loud."

"To me they are," she said. "Nope, this won't do. What's next?"

Luke glanced at the time. "Kendrick mentioned watching tonight's football game at his place. Not sure what the women are doing, but I'm bringing Nash so he can meet them. Did Nicole mention anything to you?"

Kyra nodded. "Yeah, we're supposed to hang out at her place, too, but while y'all are in the basement, we'll be catching up on *Grey's Anatomy*. It's kinda our thing."

Luke laughed, pulling her toward him. "I'm glad we'll be in the same vicinity tonight. Is it cool if I stay at your place again tonight, or do you want some time to yourself?"

She looped her arms over his shoulders, her lips close to his. "I'm not tired of you yet, Mr. O'Connor, so you should plan on spending tonight and tomorrow morning in bed with me."

There was a smile on his lips as he kissed her the way he'd been doing since they finally started dating. And as much as he hated to admit it, she was right about the condo. Luke would never let anyone interrupt him kissing his girl, but even consumed in Kyra's bliss, he could hear the neighbors upstairs walking around.

When it got even louder, he broke the kiss. "What the hell are they doing? Jumping around?"

"I told you," she said. "It sounds like a stampede up there."

"Let's get out of here," he suggested. "I have a feeling the fellas want to ask me about you and I'm sure Nicole and Aaliyah want to do the same."

"You really think Kendrick and Bryant are going to ask if we're together?"

"Yeah, because Kendrick was already asking me a million questions when he called about the game."

"Do you think they'd tell my brothers?" she asked warily.

"I doubt it since they don't talk that much, but I'll mention it just in case."

She nodded her head. "Thank you." She placed another kiss on his lips, but it was cut short when they heard the footsteps start back again. Kyra rolled her eyes. "You're right, let's go."

"I knew St. Lucia was going to be amazing," Nicole said. "And your first date on the beach sounds really romantic."

"You can tell he's so into you," Aaliyah added. "His face was glowing when the two of you walked in."

She'd only been at Nicole's place for the past half hour, but it seemed *Grey's Anatomy* was the last thing on their minds. They'd begun questioning her and Luke the moment they walked into the house.

Nash hadn't helped them out at all and had even decided to introduce himself to the group so that they wouldn't have to divert their attention away from grilling her and Luke. It had worked for a couple of minutes, but then, the group became engrossed with getting to know Nash and, not surprisingly, he fit in perfectly.

"I can also tell how close you and Nash are," Nicole said. "I know you just met, but I would have believed you if you'd told me y'all had been friends for years."

Aaliyah nodded. "I agree. He treats you like a sister already."

"He's a pain in my side," Kyra corrected. "Like the

brother I never wanted because I already have two of those."

Nicole adjusted herself in her chair. "Speaking of brothers, when do you plan on telling yours that you're dating one of their friends?"

Kyra sighed. "Honestly, I doubt Ajay will care. Sometimes he treats me more like an adult than Taheim does. However, I'm dreading Taheim finding out. I haven't told Luke this because I don't want him to freak out any more than he already is, but I'm really nervous about this coming between them. Taheim was clueless about my feelings for Luke growing up and he treats me like a little girl sometimes."

"Luke doesn't seem like he's freaking out to me," Aaliyah said.

"He doesn't, but I know him. Taheim is his best friend. And the last thing he'd want to tell his best friend is that he's sleeping with his sister."

"Well, yeah, if Luke says it like that, it won't be good," Nicole stated. "But anyone around the two of you can tell it's more than that, so if he handles it the correct way, Taheim will understand."

Kyra sighed. "He has to understand because it has taken me way too long to get to this point with Luke for Taheim to mess it all up."

"I'm loving this new you," Aaliyah said, waving her hand up and down at Kyra. "Before you left for St. Lucia, you were so confused about you and Luke. And now you're ready to defend your relationship with your mind to anyone who comes between the two of you, whether it's your family or not. It's so Romeo and Juliet."

Kyra leaned to Nicole and whispered, "Uh, has she been watching more classic romance movies lately?"

"It's the worst," Nicole confirmed. "She was bad enough before she was pregnant, but Bryant said all she wants to do is watch sappy films and cry about you. And we both know Bryant is not the type to watch that cheesy mess."

Aaliyah waved a hand. "Hey, I'm right here. I can hear you both, you know."

"We know," Nicole replied, deadpan.

"For the record, Bryant can be a sap sometimes, too, so he happily watches those movies with me."

"No, he doesn't," Kyra said with a laugh. "But he loves you and your sappy romantic pregnant self, so your husband is willing to do whatever he can to make you happy."

"And I make him happy in other ways, too." She grinned and shook her feet like a little kid. "You know, pregnant sex is the best sex."

Nicole shook her head. "Kendrick and I tried that and it didn't go too well once I got to be six months pregnant."

Aaliyah perched up in her chair. "There's a trick to it that helps him get deep without your stomach being in the way. As soon as Bryant and I figured it out, we've been making love that way ever since."

As Aaliyah and Nicole dived into a conversation about pregnant sex and post-baby sex, Kyra took the time to let her thoughts breathe for a moment. She hadn't had a chance to really think about everything that transpired in St. Lucia since they'd returned, but her gut was telling her she needed to have a plan of action for when she and Luke went to Chicago next week.

Their relationship was really beginning to take shape and, yeah, she wanted to act like a big girl in front of her friends, but deep down, she was also coming to terms with the fact that she'd been running from serious relationships since Luke's rejection.

Now that he was texting throughout the day and randomly dropping off lunch to the shop, or letting her talk to his mom via FaceTime when she called and they were together, everything was beginning to feel *very* real.

Tread carefully, girl. She'd spent years giving her friends advice and convincing them to follow their hearts, so it was time for her to do the same. If only she could stop her inner thoughts from creeping in just when things were starting to get good.

"Yeah!" the men yelled when the team they were rooting for made a touchdown. Since he'd arrived, they'd been engrossed in the game, which Luke appreciated since he hadn't expected to walk right through the door and be questioned about his relationship with Kyra.

However, now that it was halftime, he noticed Kendrick and Bryant exchanging looks and Nash smirking like he knew what was coming.

"I'm guessing St. Lucia was really good for you and Kyra," Kendrick said.

Luke nodded. "Yes, it was pretty good. No complaints."

"So y'all are together, right?" Bryant asked. "Dating and all?"

Luke laughed. "Yeah, man, we're together. It's been a long time coming if you ask me."

"He's downplaying it," Nash said. "At first, this dude was stumbling over his words when we picked up Kyra for the airport and the awkwardness continued until the two of them finally acknowledged that what they had was more than friendship. I'm telling you, fellas, I felt like cupid out there."

"Bro, you didn't do anything," Luke said. "Except annoy Kyra."

Nash shook his head. "Not true. I gave her some good advice on this trip. I was something like a counselor." Kendrick and Bryant laughed.

"We should have left you back in St. Lucia."

"You already know I loved it there, so that would have been fine."

Luke smiled at Nash's statement since he had wanted so badly for his brother to enjoy St. Lucia and, luckily, everything had worked out. His mom had even told Nash that he felt like a son to her since the two of them bonded after spending the day together. Uncle Ralph and Trista had expressed the same sentiments. St. Lucians had welcomed Nash with open arms and even though he didn't get some of the answers he'd wanted, Luke saw a sense of acceptance and appreciation from Nash that he hadn't seen before. *Which is why you need to be honest about everything.* Luke knew he needed to circle back to Nash about their father, but things had been going so good, he'd been putting it off. But seeing Nash fit in so well with everything in his life, Luke knew the longer he waited, the harder it would be to talk to Nash.

"Have you told her brothers yet?" Kendrick asked.

"Nah, I haven't. Kyra and I are going to tell them next weekend after her parents' anniversary party."

"I heard about that," Bryant said. "My dad and Aaliyah's aunt are going."

"I'm not surprised," Luke said. "Folks tend to move out of Chicago, but y'all know how it is. We tend to stick together regardless." Luke cleared his throat. "Which brings up the fact that I hope you fellas can keep my relationship with Kyra under wraps until we can tell her family?"

"Say no more," Bryant said. "We've all been there. That's your business to tell, not ours." Kendrick agreed and Luke thanked them both.

"Seriously, though, I'm proud of you for making things right between you and Kyra," Nash said. "I may tease you both, but it's nice to see you together. Don't worry about what her family will say because anyone can tell you two are good together."

Luke smiled. "Thanks, man. I'm still surprised we're together after all this time. This feels differently than my other relationships. It feels like I'm finally with the woman I'm supposed to be with."

"I know the feeling," Kendrick said. "It was like that with me and Nicole, too. I fought my feelings for her for a while, but when I finally accepted them, there was no turning back."

"Aaliyah and I were a little different," Bryant stated. "I knew she was it for me a while before she even decided if she liked my ass or not. I still fought it when my feelings slapped me in the face, but I'm so glad she's mine."

The room got quiet, each man thinking about the woman who'd stolen their heart, until Nash broke the moment when he said, "Damn, y'all could be the poster men for dudes like me who don't want to settle down for fear of becoming soft. These women have y'all in here talking about feelings and emotions during halftime instead of drinking beer and catching up on sports news."

Kendrick looked to Bryant, who shrugged. "You're right, man," Bryant said, taking a swig of his forgotten beer. "Aaliyah is hormonal right now and I swear,

I found myself changing as a result of all the things she's been experiencing. I even caught her crying in the bathroom the other day because she had to kill an ant, and after she gave a moving speech about why the ant should have lived, I found myself damn near in tears." All the men laughed.

"Nicole was like that when she was pregnant, too," Kendrick said.

"Where is your daughter, anyway?" Luke asked.

"My mom took her to Europe for some work she's doing," Kendrick said.

"I swear, that little girl travels more than I ever did," Bryant added.

All the men nodded their heads in agreement as Kendrick explained, "Nicole has been giving me the hint that she's ready for more kids. She's also been making me take all these love-language quizzes," Kendrick admitted. "She said it will make us feel more connected to one another. I knew it was bad when I almost texted you guys to ask you what your love language was."

Luke laughed. "Kyra and I are just starting out, so I haven't been faced with any of that stuff yet."

"Beware, my brother," Kendrick said. "It's coming."

The game continued and Luke appreciated having men he could talk to about Kyra, considering he couldn't talk to some of the other men in his life. Soon, the doorbell rang and Kendrick stood to get it, but he stopped when he reached the stairs.

"I got it," Kyra yelled down to the basement. A couple of minutes later, she came downstairs with a carton of drinks in tow.

"Who was at the door?" Kendrick asked.

"I had some veggie juices delivered for the ladies.

We love this stuff and can't watch *Grey's Anatomy* without it." She took a sip of her drink and walked over to Luke. "Here, try some."

Luke eyed the green concoction and shook his head. "No thanks. I think I'm good with beer."

"I get it," she said. "I used to hate it at first, but it's good for you. Much more nutritious than beer." She leaned down to whisper in his ear so that the others wouldn't hear. "And word has it, this juice increases your stamina in the bedroom."

Luke lifted an eyebrow and took the cup, taking a large sip. "Hmm, that's actually better than I thought it would be."

"Good," she said with a smirk. "Because I brought four. That one is for you." She took another cup out of the carton and took a sip as she winked at him and went back up the stairs.

"This really is good," he said to himself. He turned his head back to the game and sipped the juice. When he noticed the room was rather quiet, he turned to see three sets of eyes staring at him curiously.

"Told you it would happen sooner than you think," Kendrick said.

"And Kyra can't whisper at all," Nash added.

"Is it really good?" Bryant asked. "Aaliyah has been trying to get me to try that for months."

"You should try it," Luke said. "It takes a couple sips to get used to it." The conversation once again turned to a topic that made Nash groan in frustration.

Chapter 15

"How in the world is it time for Chicago already," Kyra said as they made their way to the restaurant her parents owned where they were meeting the family for the anniversary dinner. They'd closed the entire place for the occasion and although, normally, Kyra would have come into town early to hang out with her family, she hadn't been ready for all the questions she was sure she'd get about Luke.

The past few weeks with him had meant more than she'd ever imagined, and now they were in the city they both grew up in and all Kyra could think about was trying to keep her distance from Luke so that her family wouldn't pick up on anything.

"It will be fine," Luke said, placing a soft kiss on her lips. "It's your parents' fortieth anniversary. Everyone in attendance will be busy congratulating them and celebrating. They won't have time to think about us."

"I hope you're right," she muttered as they arrived at the restaurant and parked. Walking around the corner, Luke continued to say encouraging words, but it wasn't working. She'd feel better once they got through the dinner and told her close family that they were dating.

They opened the door to the restaurant and were welcomed by her parents and some family friends, who were all eating, drinking and celebrating.

"Sweetie, you made it," her mom said, pulling her in for a hug.

"Hey, Mom. Happy anniversary!"

"Is that my sweet pea?" her dad asked, pulling her toward him. "I've missed seeing you around here. Are you sure you aren't ready to move back home?"

"Not yet, Dad," she said with a laugh. "But I'm sure you already knew that."

He shrugged. "It was worth a try."

"Your brothers are on the second level," her mom said, looking from her to Luke. "Luke, honey. Glad you could make it."

Luke leaned down to hug Mrs. Reed. "I'm happy to be here. You know, you and Mr. Reed have always been like second parents to me."

"And you're like a son to us," she said, beaming just as Kyra's dad pulled Luke into a conversation about real estate.

"So you and Luke, huh?" her mom asked once her dad was distracted.

"We traveled here together if that's what you mean."

"That's not what I meant and you know it." Mrs. Reed leaned closer to Kyra. "You both seem happier than I've ever seen you. Took him long enough to notice how special my baby girl is."

Kyra's eyes widened. "You mean, you suspected something was going on in LA?"

"Child, please. I'm your mother. You've had a crush on that boy since you were a little girl and I suspected the reason you stopped coming around whenever you heard he was at the house visiting was because he didn't know how to accept his feelings."

"I guess it was something like that," she said. "I don't think he liked me like that back then, though. His feelings seem more recent."

"Sweetie, please tell me you're not that blind. That man has liked you for far too long and dated many women who weren't right for him to try and fill the void of the one who was. And I wasn't the only one who noticed. Your dad and Ajay brought it up to me years ago, especially after Taheim's wedding, when things seemed awkward between you. We could all tell how you two felt about each other, but it wasn't our place. Y'all had to get there on your own and judging by the way he keeps smiling over here at you while he talks to your father proves that you both have come a long way."

Kyra smiled. "Yeah, things have been pretty great in LA. We're officially boyfriend and girlfriend now."

"Aww, thanks for telling me that, baby," her mom said, giving her a hug. "Athena called me while you were in St. Lucia and gave me an update, but I told her I'd hoped you would tell me yourself when you're ready."

Kyra rolled her eyes. "I should have known you and Mrs. O'Connor were talking about us. She kept giving me this look while I was there and it made me feel like I was missing something."

"You're our kids. Of course we were talking about you. We knew the two of you would end up together eventually, we just didn't know it would take so long. Athena is ready for some grandbabies and I'm ready to see my daughter become a mom."

Kyra blinked. "Uh, moving a little fast, don't you think?"

"Absolutely not. You've known each other most your lives. In some situations, I agree, a couple should date first for a good amount of time before moving to the next step. However, in this case, sweetie, you both aren't getting any younger. You've never felt about any man the way you seem to feel about Luke."

Kyra sighed. "Yeah, you're right. He's always had my heart."

"And you've always had his. I liked that loud-talking girl he dated—um, what was her name?"

"Meeka," Kyra informed her.

"Right, Meeka. They were good together, but not the way you and Luke are together. I always thought that if they'd ended up together, he always would have wondered 'what if?'"

"He said something similar," Kyra confessed. "Do you think Taheim ever picked up on our feelings for one another?"

Mrs. Reed waved off her question. "That son of mine was too busy chasing around anything in a skirt to notice that his best friend had feelings for his sister. But now, I think he may suspect something thanks to Winter planting the seed."

"Guess that means we should talk to him."

"You should," Mrs. Reed said. "The others are waiting upstairs for the conversation."

"Dang," Kyra gasped. "They couldn't even wait until after your party."

"No, they couldn't. You know your brothers. Besides, your father and I are ready for you to talk to them so that the party can continue without any awkwardness. Your brothers are reasonable. Just talk to them."

"Okay," she said with a sigh. "I'll tell Luke we have to talk to them now."

"Good. And word of advice, please let Luke do most of the talking. Your brothers will want to hear from you, too, but they need to hear from Luke more than they need to hear from you."

Kyra nodded. "Understandable. I will."

"Is it just me or does it feel like we're walking before a jury ready to defend our relationship?" Luke asked.

"It does," Kyra said with a laugh. "But we have to get this over with and my mom told me now was the time."

Luke nodded. "I still can't believe my mom told your mom before we got a chance to."

"I'm relieved," she said. "Your mom told my mom and my mom told my dad, so they were already used to the idea before we got here.

"Is Nash going to make it to the party?"

"Not sure," Luke said. "The plan was for him to come, but we had a big corporate office stop by looking for a property ASAP. So we have a lot of work ahead of us and Nash is leading that charge. He said if he can get away, he may stop by tomorrow for the brunch."

Kyra nodded. "Sounds good. I just thought he'd make a good buffer."

Luke stopped once they were around the corner from where her brothers were at and pulled her to him. "Maybe this will help ease your tension." He dropped his lips down to hers, kissing her in a way that he hoped would distract her. He knew she'd rather be doing anything other than talking to her brothers right now, but Luke hoped she knew he would be by her side every step of the way.

Once he felt some of the tension leave her shoulders, they both took a deep breath and rounded the corner. Luke had figured that his friends would be engrossed in conversation or something, but to his surprise, when he and Kyra walked in on them, everyone glanced at them as if the topic of the hour had finally arrived.

Luke had expected Taheim, Winter, Ajay and Autumn to be there, but he hadn't expected to see his other best friend, Jaleen, his wife, Danni, and Winter and Autumn's sister, Summer, along with her husband, Aiden.

"Uh, hey, everyone," Kyra said, seemingly as surprised as Luke was.

"Hey, sis," Taheim said, standing from his seat. "Hey, Luke."

"Hey, man," Luke said, prepared for what would come next, but dreading it nonetheless.

"Care to tell me why you waited so long to tell me you were sleeping with my sister?"

Winter hit Taheim on the arm. "I told you to ask him if they were dating, not imply they're sleeping together."

Taheim shrugged. "Figured I would skip the obvious since we already know they are dating."

"How would you know that?" Kyra asked.

"Mrs. O'Connor posted a picture of y'all on her Facebook page. Anyone with a set of eyes could tell."

Luke shook his head. *Note to self: tell my mom she doesn't need to post everything on Facebook.* "I think that's a private question, but we've been officially dating for a couple weeks now. Had I not had my head up my ass, we would have started dating years ago."

"Way to tell him, Luke," Jaleen said with a laugh. In turn, Danni hit his arm as well. "What did I say?"

"Let them talk this out," Danni said. "They don't need any feedback from the peanut gallery."

"Then why are we all in this small-ass room looking like this is a scene from *The Godfather*?" Jaleen said. "Besides, Luke has had a crush on Kyra for years. I'm shocked he waited this long to get her in his bed." Danni slapped his arm again and Taheim pinned him with a hard stare.

"You're not helping, Jay," Luke said.

He shrugged. "My bad, dog. I'll take my wife's advice and shut up."

"Good idea," Ajay said, standing from his chair and walking over to them. "Unlike Taheim, I've always known how you guys felt about each other, but I think we should talk about this more privately." Ajay glanced to the group. "Do you all mind if Taheim and I talk to Luke?"

"Can I stay?" Kyra asked.

Ajay shook his head. "Nah, sis. We need to talk without. But give us ten minutes and everyone can come back in so we can enjoy the rest of the night."

Everyone began filing out of the room. "You got us kicked out," Aiden whispered to Jaleen on the way out. "This was the most entertainment I've had in months."

Once the room emptied, Luke remained standing and faced Taheim and Ajay. "It was never my intention to keep you both in the dark for long," he said. "Kyra and I just needed to do this without the input of the people who mean the most to us."

Ajay nodded. "You and I have had this conversation before. I've always known how you felt about her, so I get it."

Taheim looked to Ajay. "I didn't have a clue. Why didn't you tell me?"

"Because you still look at Kyra like she's a little girl instead of a thirty-one-year-old woman," Ajay answered. "When I talked to Luke, he was still in denial about how he really felt, so I didn't think I needed to tell you anything."

"I was in denial for years," Luke said. "At first, I blamed it on my relationship with the both of you. Then I convinced myself our age difference had more to do with it. But to be honest, I never thought I was good enough for Kyra. Not after I found out how much my dad was cheating on my mom and how much his dad had cheated on my grandmother. He said it was in our blood to suck at marriage and somewhere along the line, I started believing him."

"You were always a better man than your father was," Taheim said. "And any man who will walk out of his son's life after breaking apart his family isn't a man at all. I agree, you're not good enough for Kyra, but that's only because I feel like no man is good enough for my sister."

Luke nodded. "Fair enough. I'd be the same way if I had a sister."

"You're a good guy," Ajay added. "But I'm sure you already know how much Kyra means to us. We'd kill for her and hurt anyone who would dare hurt her. You may be fam by choice, but we wouldn't hesitate to put you in your place if you ever did anything to hurt her."

"I understand," Luke said. "I wouldn't expect anything less and I'd never do anything to purposely hurt her."

"So it is serious then?" Taheim asked. "You aren't just dating her just because?"

"It's very serious," Luke exclaimed. "She's it for me, fellas. I know it's too soon to start talking to her about marriage, but I'm dating her now with the goal of marriage in mind. I think it's never worked out with those other women because I was always meant to be with Kyra. She makes me want to be a better man and my only regret is that it took me so long to get to where I'm at with her today."

Taheim looked at Ajay, the two of them sharing a smile. "In that case, we give you our blessing to date our sister."

Luke nodded his head. "I appreciate it, man, and I'm sure Kyra will, too."

"She never needed our blessing, but we figured you would want it," Ajay said. "Kyra's gonna do what Kyra's gonna do despite how we may feel about it."

Luke laughed, his heart full now that he'd spoken with his friends. "Ain't that the truth." The three of them caught up some more before the others began coming back into the room. Luke was glad the conversation had taken place when they arrived because now he could focus on having fun and enjoying himself. However, while he enjoyed catching up on everyone's lives, he was even more grateful that he'd kept his downtown condo because he'd always imagined having Kyra up there with him, seeing the sunrise over the lake from his bedroom balcony. There was nothing like a St. Lucia sunrise and sunset, but he'd like to think his little Chicago haven was a close second.

Chapter 16

"Okay, sis, spill the details," Winter said, taking a sip of her mimosa. "We wanted to ask last night, but the group never parted long enough for us to get the inside scoop."

Kyra laughed as she looked at Winter, Autumn, Summer and Danni, who were all looking at her expectantly. Unfortunately, Nash hadn't been able to fly to Chicago, so Kyra and Luke still had no one they could redirect the attention to.

At the start of brunch, Kyra had assumed everyone would be talking about her parents' party last night, but instead, everyone was spread out at different tables and her sisters-in-law and friends had managed to corner her in a separate section.

"We've heard some of the story from Nicole and Aaliyah," Danni said. "They called to check on us and couldn't stop gushing about how cute you and Luke were."

"She's right," Summer confirmed. "Then we got here and realized that Winter and Autumn hadn't gotten to talk to you yet."

Kyra shook her head. It seemed even if she and Luke had thought they could still keep their relationship a secret, it wouldn't have worked. They were the talk of their group. "Well, since it seems to be common knowledge, I've had a crush on Luke for years. But on my twenty-first birthday, when I'd finally gotten enough courage to tell him how I feel, he rejected me in the worst way he could have." She shivered even still thinking about it.

"Men are dense sometimes," Winter said. "It's obvious that he felt the same way and couldn't handle it."

"It's obvious now," Kyra stated. "Back then, it really wasn't."

"He's clearly trying to make up for lost time," Autumn said. "He hasn't stopped looking this way since we all sat down."

Kyra glanced toward Luke, who smiled back at her. Not that she could have stopped it, but her heartbeat quickened at the sight of him.

"Y'all are too cute," Summer said. "I understand what it's like to have feelings for someone and it feel like it takes you forever to get to where you are today. It was like that with me and Aiden, too. My advice is to make the most of it now. Don't focus on the time lost, but rather, the time you have now. Together."

Kyra swallowed back some emotion. "I've been telling myself that every day, but it helps to hear a reminder. I guess a part of me is also nervous because the man I'm started to get real feelings for is the same man who broke my heart all those years ago." Kyra looked back to the women. "I won't drag out the details, but he said words to me that night that I have never forgotten. In a way, those words molded how I handled the men that came after him."

"That's a tough pill to swallow," Winter said. "Have you told Luke how much he hurt you?"

"Sort of, but I'm not sure. I wanted to spend time making him pay for what he did while he helped me find a condo and a space for the new shop. I wanted him to feel that pain I'd felt back then."

"Guess that didn't work out," Autumn said. "Or did it?"

Kyra shook her head. "I failed miserably because instead of spending time with him to make him sweat it out, it just reminded me of all the reasons I fell for him in the first place."

"Ain't that how it always goes," Danni said with a sigh. "Men walk out of our lives, drive us crazy in the process, then walk back in and all you're thinking about is how much you will make him pay, but instead, you end up falling further in love."

"Cupid is cruel," Summer added. "But now is the time for you and Luke to work through all those feelings you have. Men think that they can just proclaim their love while all we're doing is waiting for them to do so when that's not the case at all. Just like he needed time to figure out how he felt about you, you should be given that same courtesy to work through your feelings about him now."

"We all know Luke's a good man," Winter said. "But, sis, he's talking to the guys about spending forever with you. To him, he's acknowledged how he feels and he's ready to go out and buy a ring. And as sweet as that is that he finally caught a clue, you have to be okay with knowing that you are allowed to take the time you need to figure things out."

"You don't work on his time schedule," Autumn stated. "You work on yours and you don't want to go into a marriage with resentment for things that happened a decade ago, when maybe all it takes is a conversation to work it out."

"But what if he thinks we've already worked through it?" Kyra asked. "In St. Lucia, we had a conversation about that and he apologized. Honestly, ladies, he's apologized for it so many times throughout the years, that I'm starting to wonder if something is wrong with me because I can't seem to shake how I feel. I accept his apology, but a part of me is still upset for what he did and I know it makes me so spoiled for saying that."

"It doesn't make you spoiled," Summer said. "You are allowed to still be upset over something that changed who you are as a person. You don't have to apologize for needing time to figure *you* out. Too many times, women apologize for having too many emotions about a situation when we are rightfully allowed to feel whatever we want, whenever we want."

"What if what I need is to take a step back from dating?" she said, her voice cracking. "Am I completely insane for finally getting the man I've always wanted, but taking time to process everything that has happened?"

"You're not insane," Danni said. "And if Luke truly loves you, he'll understand that you need time."

Autumn placed a hand over Kyra's. "It's understandable that you need to process the fact that you and Luke have finally gotten together because you've spent the better part of your life thinking it would never happen."

Kyra took a sip of her mimosa. "We haven't said 'I love you' yet."

"That man loves you," Winter said. "And you love him. We all see it whether you've said the words or not."

"I stopped believing in fairy tales the day he rejected me," Kyra confessed. "And then up he pops into LA, making me remember all the reasons why I feel for him in the first place."

"Ugh, men," Danni said. "With their goofy grins and sexy smiles and masculine swag. I swear, if I didn't love Jaleen, I'd be ready to kill him with the mess he's always putting me through."

Autumn sighed. "Then, when life knocks you down and reminds you that you don't have everything under control, there they go, saving the day by helping you remember that you are a strong black female and were made to overcome obstacles and rise above all adversity."

"Amen," Winter said, nodding her head.

"Ditto," Summer said. "Then they make sweet love to you, making you feel more beautiful than you ever have in your life, and next thing you know, you're pregnant and pushing a small human out of your tiny hole."

Kyra was glad she'd finished her drink because she would have spit it across the table. "Uh, not there yet, guys, and based off how you described that, I think I'm good for now."

"We always think we're good," Autumn stated. "Until that test shows up positive. I love our kids, but my hips haven't been the same since I pushed those rascals out."

"But the sex is worth it, though," Winter said, a dreamy look on her face.

"Ugh, I'm trying to forget that two of you are married to my brothers."

Winter's eyes widened. "Oh, right. Glad you reminded me before I started describing what Taheim did to me last night."

"Oh, my God, I can't with you," Kyra said with a laugh. She'd been trying to get Winter to filter her sexcapade conversations since she started dating her brother.

"I can share instead," Summer offered. "Since no one is related to my husband."

Kyra nodded. "Please do!"

"Then Kyra can tell us how good Luke is in the bedroom," Winter suggested, wagging her eyebrows.

"Now that, I can talk about," she said with a smile. "Let me just say, it was well worth the wait to finally get to sample some of Luke O'Connor."

"I knew it," Autumn said with a smirk. "I bet y'all had sex first, talked after, right? Too much sexual tension to hold off on that convo."

"Wait, don't answer that," Danni said. "This calls for more drinking. Where is the waiter?" Danni glanced around. When she finally spotted him, she lifted her empty glass in the air. "Buddy, we need another round of mimosas." Kyra wasn't sure if it was because the waiter could tell that Danni meant business or if he was just a fast server, but three minutes later, they had a fresh round of mimosas and the stories started flowing.

Kyra had really needed to talk to her girls, but now that she'd gotten advice and decided to be honest, she didn't know how to act toward Luke. A part of her wanted to save the conversation for when they got back to LA tomorrow, but he'd been sweet all day, placing soft kisses on her cheek even when her family was around. And he'd made sure she'd stayed hydrated despite the fact that she'd only been drinking mimosas.

He'd even been fielding questions from her relatives all day, playing the role of perfect boyfriend, and it seemed everyone in her family had agreed. They were great together. And her sisters-in-law and friends were Team Luke, even though they also encouraged her to be honest with him about what she was feeling.

"Is everything okay?" he asked, after he'd given her a tour of his condo.

"Everything is fine," she said, taking a seat beside him on the couch. He looked like he didn't quite believe her, but he didn't push her.

"Do you want to watch a movie? I think one of the *Avengers* movies is on HBO right now."

"That would be great," she said while he flipped to the channel. They'd watched movies together while they were in LA, so she curled up into his side just like she did when they were back home. The only problem was she still couldn't ignore what was going on in her mind.

"Actually, I lied before," she said, sitting upright. "Everything isn't fine."

Luke muted the television. "What's wrong?"

Kyra sighed, trying to find her words. "How do you feel about me?" she asked.

He smiled. "I care about you more than I've ever cared about anyone in my life. Even more than that, but I'm not sure you're ready to hear the words."

"I'm not," she said. "Because my gut is telling me

that you're in love with me and the problem is, I'm in love with you, too."

"How is that a problem?" he asked hopefully. "We haven't said the words, but we know we're in love with each other. Have been for years."

"That's just it," she said. "I haven't known you felt that way for years. You only just told me how you felt about me recently. I've spent so much time convincing myself that my feelings for you were only one-sided and now, you come back into my life telling me that was never the case."

"It wasn't," he stated, taking her hands in his. "I just wasn't ready to accept my feelings."

She nodded. "I understand, but regardless, our past changed me in a lot of ways. And now that we are together, I'm just so unsure about things."

"Unsure in what way?" he asked.

She closed her eyes, then opened them to find a pair of sympathetic ones staring back at her. "This is so hard for me," she said, her voice slightly breaking. "To finally be with the man who broke my heart and changed the way I viewed every relationship after that moment is more difficult than I ever imagined it would be. How do you put your feelings aside after all this time?" she asked.

Luke studied her eyes. "I don't know. I knew I'd hurt you that night, but I guess I never knew I'd caused you so much pain."

"You did," she said, unshed tears drifting to her eyelids. But she refused to cry. She'd never been a crier and she wasn't going to start now. "You've finally realized that I'm the woman you've always been meant to be with and as much as I've waited most my life to hear that, a part of me still sees you as the man who walked out on me after I bared my soul. The man who rejected my love in a way that hit me harder than I ever could have imagined."

Luke leaned back on the couch, surprise evident in his features. "I am so sorry that I put you through that, Kyra. If I could take it back, I would."

"I know. But you can't, and honestly, I'm not sure I would even want you to. I became a woman that night. Up until then, my life had been going how I'd expected with not many twists and turns, yet you came and turned my world upside down whether you meant to or not. It's not fair of me to still be harboring these feelings toward you when you've apologized to me time and time again. But they are there, lingering beneath the surface, and I'm worried that if I don't address them, this won't go any further."

"What are you saying?" he asked, looking defeated.

"I'm saying that I need time to think," she said. "I'm not saying we have to break up, but I do need a break to figure out how to get over this."

"That's the same as breaking up," he said. "Can't we work through it together?"

She shook her head. "I need to work through this on my own. But I don't expect you to wait around for me. So date, go out, do whatever you want to do."

Luke frowned. "I don't want anyone but you, so I'll wait for you. Take all the time you need."

Kyra released Luke's hand and stood. "I'll stay at Autumn and Ajay's tonight, but I'll see you at the airport in the morning."

"So you're really leaving right now?" Luke said. "You can't just stay here tonight?"

She shook her head. "I could, but I don't think that would be good for either one of us. Just like I need time to process things, you do, too. Having me here would just be a distraction."

"It wouldn't be," he said, shaking his head. "We've spent every night sleeping beside each other since we started dating. I don't think I'll be able to sleep well ever again if you leave."

"You'll be fine," she said as she grabbed her purse and walked over to her traveling duffel, which was still by the front door. "This is hard for me, too, Luke, but I hope you'll respect my wishes. I'll text you when I get to Autumn's."

Without giving it another thought, she shut the door and began walking toward the elevator. Halfway there, she almost thought about turning back, but she reminded herself that she needed this. She owed it to herself to figure out why, after finally landing the man she'd always wanted, she was feeling a little overwhelmed by everything.

Chapter 17

"Enough of this," Nash said, cutting off the television.

"I was watching that," Luke said, reaching for the remote.

"Not anymore. You've spent the week going to work, then the gym, then sitting here watching all these horror movies every day."

"That's because horror movies have little romance," Luke said. "And when they do, one of them usually dies."

Nash shook his head. "How many times do I have to tell you that Kyra telling you she has to do some thinking is temporary. Anyone who knows the two of you knows that you will be back together in no time. You know what's not fair? Subjecting me to having to watch you pout every day."

"I don't pout," he said. "Men don't pout."

"Oh, but you do, brother, and trust me, it ain't cute."

"You don't know for sure that we'll get back together. She could decide she's done for good."

"Luke, she was hurt for years over how you rejected her, so do you both a favor and let her take all the time she needs. She's allowed to, bruh."

"I know and I told her I was cool with it, but I'm not," he said. "I don't want to get her only to lose her again. It took us too long to get to this point. And I refuse to let that man be right."

"What man?" Nash asked. "Kyra is dating someone else?"

"What? No, she isn't." Luke grew quiet, choosing his next words carefully. "Back in the day, my dad— our dad—was the first one to pick up on my feelings for Kyra. Said he noticed how I was always watching her, enjoying her company. I told him that we were just friends, which back then, we were. I mean, I was young and at one point in time, I really tried to treat Kyra as if she were a sister. Hell, for many years, she *was* like a sister to me." Luke sighed. He needed to own up to some stuff because how he treated Kyra on her twenty-first birthday wasn't the only thing weighing heavy on his heart. "I guess now is a good time to tell you that I lied before when you asked me if I'd ever suspected that he was cheating on my mom, because the truth is, I did suspect it. I even caught him a few times."

For a split second, Nash looked surprised. Then, he shrugged and said, "I figured. Had this gut feeling."

"You did?"

"Yeah, I can tell when you're lying. I figured you had your reasons for not telling me."

Luke frowned. "When your investigator found me, I was mad at myself for not questioning my dad more.

For not telling my mom what he was up to earlier. For not being the type of brother you needed me to be."

"Luke, I don't blame you for that man disowning me," Nash said. "You were a kid. He was an adult. I asked you if you suspected he'd stepped out on Athena, but I feel like I knew the answer before I even asked."

"I shouldn't have lied about it," Luke admitted.

"Nah, you shouldn't have. But we still have a lot to work on to build that trust with each other. I mean, I trust you, but I know you have your secrets just like I have mine."

"You're right," Luke said. "And I know you always say you wish you knew him, but be glad you don't. He wasn't a good man. He pretended to be and I let my friends think he was, but he wasn't."

"When I spent the day with your mom, she pretty much said the same thing."

"It's the truth," Luke continued. "He was the type of man who made you believe that if he wasn't worth anything, then you wouldn't be worth anything, either. He cheated on my mom, said my grandfather cheated on my grandmother. He made certain things seem like they were just the way of life and I knew better, but he was my dad and I wanted to keep my relationship with him intact."

"I'd probably felt the same way," Nash admitted. "Even knowing the type of man he is, I still want to meet him even though I try to convince myself I don't have to."

Luke nodded his head. "That's understandable. And even though I've mentioned it before, if you really want to track him down, I think I can. There's a few States he seems to frequent, depending on the time of year."

"I appreciate it," Nash said. "And when I'm ready, I'll let you know. In the meantime, you got to figure out a way to not let him take more from you."

Luke squinted. "What do you mean?"

"Well, you waited a while before you told your mom that your dad was cheating on her. You waited over a year to tell me that you knew our father had been cheating. You waited over a decade before you admitted to yourself and Kyra how you feel about her. Bruh, you pull the trigger fast when it comes to other aspects in your life, but the more serious the issue, the more you hold back information."

Luke sunk deeper into the couch—Nash's words were really getting to him. "You're right," he admitted. "I guess in a way, I've never wanted to see someone hurt or, better yet, I didn't want to be the bearer of bad news."

"That's not healthy, man," Nash said. "You can't go through life keeping so many secrets and carrying around so much baggage. Especially when that baggage isn't only yours to carry."

Call it brother's intuition, but as Luke looked to Nash, it was almost as if he could tell Nash knew what Luke needed to say. Like he had a feeling that the last secret Luke was keeping was important.

"I promise you, I did not think about this until a couple days ago," Luke said honestly. "But I know— I may know—" *Crap.* He couldn't even get the words out.

"You think you know who my birth mother is, don't you?" Nash asked.

Luke sighed, partially in relief and partially in guilt for not realizing it sooner. "Yeah, I think I do. That day our father had the conversation with me about Kyra, he mentioned something about wishing she was at least eighteen. It had thrown me off, but I knew what he was fishing at. She was, like, thirteen at the time, and like I said before, I really did look at her like a sister at one point. But the anger I felt when her and Taheim stopped by the house one day and I caught our father looking at her in a way he shouldn't have, it disgusted me. I never invited them over again after that."

"Understandable," Nash said, clenching his jaw. "And I feel like I'm really not prepared for what you're gonna say next."

"Want to shelve the conversation for another time?"

Nash shook his head. "Nah, keep going. I can handle it."

Luke took a deep breath. "Not only was that the day he stopped being my father, but something in me snapped. I was graduating soon, anyway, and I remember distancing myself from Taheim and Jaleen because I couldn't cope with anything." Luke cleared his throat. "When I was visiting home that summer after college, there was a woman waiting outside the house when I got there. Right away, I noticed that she was that same young woman I'd caught in the house. She seemed out of it and I didn't know if it was drugs or what, but she was rattling on about our father making her life a living hell and that she gave away the most important thing in her life because of him.

"When I asked her to explain, her eyes widened and she recognized who I was, too. Even though I wasn't trying to run her off since all I wanted was answers to my questions, she made up some lie about being a Jehovah's Witness and left. I never saw her again and I put the entire incident behind me. I truthfully have not thought about that in a while."

For a few minutes, neither brother said anything and Luke wondered if he'd laid too much on Nash too soon. However, he was grateful when Nash said, "It's because of Kyra. That's why you didn't remember."

"Huh?" Luke asked.

"Since you're five years older than Kyra, I assume growing up, liking her felt wrong, correct?"

Luke nodded. "It did."

"And knowing you, you didn't want any sign of thinking you were like our father, so you pushed that shit far from your mind."

Luke swallowed, unsure of how he should feel since he'd never heard anyone voice his biggest fear out loud before. "Yes, that's right."

Nash shook his head. "Luke, from what I've heard, you sound nothing like our father and all that asshole did was put you in a position to have to lie to those close to you. I appreciate you telling me about that woman you caught outside your house and, yeah, she could be my mother. But while I was listening to you, all I was thinking about was how unimportant both of my birth parents are right now."

Luke's eyes widened, as he was surprised by Nash's admission. "You're not upset with me for not remembering?"

Nash shook his head. "Nah, bro. I'm tired of getting upset with the wrong people. My parents are amazing and I've had a good life. The best thing to come out of learning I was adopted was meeting you and Athena. I'm not saying I'll never want to meet our father or find my birth mother, but I'm good right now with the blessings I've been given."

Nash leaned to hug Luke and he accepted the hug.

He was surprised by how mature Nash was handling everything and made a mental note to take some cues from his brother...even though he'd never tell him that.

"We can talk more about all this deep shit later, but now, you need to come up with a plan of action for how you're going to get Kyra back," Nash announced.

Luke laughed. "I thought you told me to give her the space she needs?"

"I did. But if she decides to drag this out too long, you have to win back the woman you love and convince her that you're not the same man you were years ago. Let her know that her heart is safe when it's in your hands."

Luke nodded. "Thanks, bro. I needed that wake-up call and to get that stuff off my chest."

"You're welcome. Just remember to name your first son after me. Nash is a pretty dope name."

"What if Kyra and I have a girl?" Luke asked, entertaining his brother's idea.

"Nashena after me and your mom."

Luke frowned. "Ugh, that's a horrible name for a girl. Kyra would never go for it."

"I happen to think it's a great name for a female."

Luke shook his head. "Nah, that was pretty bad."

"Okay, name her Nashay then. Or Nashika."

"Do you ever want her to get a job?"

"Low blow, bro," Nash said. "I happen to think those names are pretty damn good."

"Tell you what," Luke said. "How about I thank you by making you my best man instead because Kyra may need some convincing, but I plan on marrying that woman."

"Best man," Nash said in surprise. "But what about your friends, like Taheim?"

"Taheim is my best friend, but you're my blood. My brother. The only I got."

Nash smiled. "Thanks, man, I'd be honored." They hugged it out until Nash got a thought. "You don't think we have any more siblings running around, do you?"

Luke's eyes widened. "Damn, you never know. We could."

"Hmm. Maybe I'll get my private investigator on it when we're ready to tackle that."

Luke nodded. "Sounds like a plan."

"We close in ten minutes," Kyra yelled when she heard the front door of the boutique open.

"Kyra, is that any way to greet your mother?"

Kyra looked up from the register. "Mom, what are you doing here?" She walk-ran to the front door and gave her a hug.

"I know I just saw my baby girl, but when Winter and Autumn got back to Chicago and told me that you and Luke were taking a break, I knew I had to come out here and talk to you."

Kyra frowned. Her sisters-in-law had only been in LA for a few hours to view the new location, and not surprisingly, they loved it just as much as Kyra did.

"I know you're probably disappointed in me because we were finally together and I went ahead and ruined it."

"Sweetie, you have it all wrong. I'm not disappointed in you. I'm proud of you for realizing that you needed some time to figure out what it is that you want. If Luke isn't it, then you owe it to yourself and him to put that information out there."

"That's the problem," Kyra exclaimed. "Luke is everything I want and more, yet for some reason, I can't shake this feeling I have in the pit of my stomach, replaying how he rejected me back when I was in college."

"I think I know why," her mom said, motioning for Kyra to join her on the bench by the fitting room. "Kyra, you've always gone after what you wanted no matter whether it be in school, or sports, or your career. Your father and I have always admired your tenacity to take life by the horns and make the most of your opportunities. When it came to Luke, you didn't tackle your feelings for him any differently than you have everything else in your life.

"You knew you wanted him as soon as you hit adolescence. Maybe even before then. Your father and I began to notice little things, like the way you'd ask him to help you with your homework. Or the way you would play in the yard with your brothers all night when Luke was with them rather than going to bed, something you never did when Luke wasn't around. And you know what else your father and I noticed?"

"What?" she asked.

"We noticed how much Luke cared for you right back. We noticed that even if he wasn't good at a subject, he would study up on it just to help you out. We noticed that when you all played in the backyard and you got so tired that you'd fall asleep in the grass, he was picking you up and bringing you inside. From what we saw, Luke never looked at you inappropriately when you were growing up, but it became harder and harder for him to ignore as you got older. By your eighteenth birthday, the boy was doing everything he could to ignore your flirting. By nineteen, he was downright rushing out the room when you were visiting from college and he was in town from grad school. At twenty, there was one time we couldn't even get him to come by the house at all. And at twenty-one, I wasn't sure what happened around that time, but I could tell something shifted between you two because that's when you started avoiding him at all costs."

"Why didn't you ever say anything?" Kyra asked.

"I figured you would talk to me if you needed to. Besides, I wanted you to distance yourself from Luke because you needed to grow on your own without chasing after that boy."

Kyra frowned. "Maybe I should have run a little faster when he popped up in LA."

"It wouldn't have worked," her mother said. "Once Luke decided to chase after you this time, you didn't stand a chance. No woman does when it comes to loving the right man."

"You think he's right for me?" she asked.

"Of course I do. You've always been right for one another. You were just in different places in your life. But now, you're at the right place at the right time."

Kyra sighed. "I thought so, too, but I can't seem to shake this eerie feeling."

"You're worried the other shoe will drop," her mom explained. "You're worried that now that you finally have him, something will happen and you'll lose him again. It's a natural reaction, but based off what I saw, you don't have to worry about that with Luke."

"How can you be so sure?" Kyra asked. "How can I know if I won't get my heart broken again?"

Her mother gently cupped her cheek. "No one can know that for sure, baby girl. Love is all about taking risks and hoping that it works out for the best. What I do know is that Luke didn't just up and decide he loves you. That boy has loved you since the day he met you. And at Taheim and Winter's wedding, even though he was dating someone, he only had eyes for you. He couldn't help it. He's always watched you. Observed you. Checked to see if you were okay. Randomly asked me and your dad how you were doing when he didn't want to ask your brothers. I'm not saying you shouldn't take the time you need to work through your feelings, but you shouldn't pass up on a great love because you're scared to put yourself out there again."

Kyra took a deep breath, letting her mom's words soak in. "I hear you, Mom. I'll definitely keep all of that in mind."

She smiled. "Good. Now that that's settled," her mother said, clapping her hands, "it's time for you to put me to work. Winter mentioned that you may be placing an offer on a new boutique soon, which means, you need help packing."

Kyra reached over and pulled her mom in for a hug. "I love you, Mom. More than anything."

Her mom patted her and ran her fingers through her hair, just as she'd done since Kyra was little. "I love you, sweetie."

Chapter 18

Luke was a nervous wreck as he waited near Santa Monica Pier for Kyra to show up. When she'd called and asked him to meet her there, he'd said yes almost immediately. Back in Chicago, he'd had no idea that taking time to think meant he wouldn't be communicating with Kyra for two weeks. Two excruciating long weeks in which he drove Nash crazy.

His phone rang, interrupting his thoughts. He'd hoped it was Kyra, but was disappointed to see it was Taheim. "Hey, T, what's good?"

"Hey, Luke, at least you sound better than you did a few days ago."

"Your sister asked to talk today, so I'm hoping it's good news."

"I think it will be," he said. "But that's actually not what I called for. Winter is pregnant again and though it's too early to tell if it's a girl or a boy, I was hoping you could be my child's godfather."

Luke stopped pacing. "Me? Are you sure?"

"Of course I'm sure. You're one of my best friends and my child would be lucky to have you as a godfather. And I guess I should let you know that we plan on asking Kyra to be the godmother."

Luke smiled. "This truly means a lot to me, man. Yes, I will be your child's godfather and I promise to take the responsibility seriously." Luke knew how careful Taheim and Winter had been in choosing godparents for their other two kids, so he could only imagine that they had chosen him and Kyra just as carefully.

"I needed this news," Luke said. "You called at the right time."

"I had a feeling," Taheim stated. "Just remember, Kyra loves you. Before you ask, no, she hasn't told me anything, but I know my sister. You two are going to end up together. Just keep your head up."

"I will, man," Luke said. "I just miss her so much. As soon as I see her, I'll feel better."

Taheim laughed. "Man, it's still hard hearing you talk about her like this. I made myself sick the other day thinking about everything I know you've done with other women, realizing that now, that woman is my sister."

"What do you want to know?" Luke teased.

"Not a damn thing," Taheim said, practically yelling into the phone. "In fact, I'm mad I even started the conversation down this road. How about you just give me a call later after you see Kyra."

"Okay," Luke said with a laugh. "Thanks again for this great honor."

"You're welcome, Luke. Thank you for accepting the responsibility." Luke said his goodbye and hung up the phone, then resumed his pacing. Five minutes later, he was still too anxious to stand still.

"I can't wait much longer," he said to himself as he glanced at his phone.

"You got here too early," a voice said from behind him. He turned to find Kyra wearing a white crop top and long black maxi skirt. She was looking so delicious, he wished they could skip the talking part and go straight to the kissing part. "Do you want to take a walk?" she asked.

He nodded. "Sure." Luke felt nervous, as if he wasn't meeting with someone he'd known most of his life. Awkward or not, he was happy to see her. "I've really missed you," he confessed.

She smiled. "I've missed you, too."

Okay, that's a good sign. Luke felt himself stand a little taller with her admission. They walked in comfortable silence for a few minutes before Kyra broke it.

"Do you remember about a year before Taheim met Winter, it was around Christmastime and you stopped by my parents' house to drop off a bottle of rum?"

Luke thought back to that day. "I remember. I'd gone to Puerto Rico for business and brought back a really nice bottle of rum for your parents that I got from the Bacardi factory."

"They were excited to see you since it had been almost a year since you'd dropped by," she said. "I remember the surprised looks on their faces when you called."

"You were there?" he asked in surprise. "I don't remember you being home when I was there."

"I'd been visiting that day, too, but I told them I was

leaving before you got there. I was still really hurt back then and it was pretty raw. I didn't think I could face you without getting pissed off all over again, so I dipped off. Or at least tried to."

"You stayed?" he asked.

"More like watched you from the backyard window," Kyra said with a laugh. "Looking back, it seemed pretty creepy to watch you from afar, but I'd missed you and needed to see you even if you didn't see me."

Luke nodded. "I know the feeling. I hate to say it, but I'd only visited your parents because I'd missed you and you still weren't talking to me."

"Really?" she asked. "You'd missed me?"

Luke sighed. "Kyra, when I'm not with you, I always miss you. That's never changed no matter what state we live in. I love your parents, but I was missing you like crazy and I didn't want to keep asking your brothers about you because I figured they would catch on to how I felt. So I'd ask your parents and they were so proud, they always kept me updated. For a while, I wondered if they'd picked up on anything, but I'd stopped myself from asking."

"They did," she said. "They picked up on our attraction, but my parents weren't the type to make things awkward so they left it alone."

"I was really glad when we ran into each other downtown," he said. "It felt like fate had been on my side."

"I'd felt the same way," she admitted. "I remember stumbling over my words because I didn't know what to say to you. I'd heard that you and your dad had grown distant, so it seemed like a safe topic to bring up, but I regretted it the minute I said anything."

"You shouldn't," he told her. "That day, I'd needed to

vent about him. To say how I really felt without having to explain too much. When you hugged me that day, I couldn't remember ever needing a hug that badly before. I knew you were still upset at me, but you put your feelings aside to offer me comfort."

"I did, but I was thinking back to that moment earlier today and I realized that there were so many moments in our lives where we were there for each other in ways we never really paid attention to." She cleared her throat. "Luke, I said I needed some time to think and to gather my thoughts and I appreciate you for giving me the space to do so."

Oh, no, he thought. *This is it. She's either willing to make it work, or she wants to end it for good.* Luke couldn't imagine it being the latter. He felt like they were just getting started. There was so much more life to live together and he'd never forgive himself if he didn't tell her that.

"I love you," he blurted out. "And not just in the we've-known-each-other-most-our-lives kind of way, but I'm in love with you and I have been for longer than I can remember." He stopped walking and stood in front of her. "Kyra, these past couple weeks have been some of the toughest weeks I've ever had because all I wanted to do was spend that time with you. There aren't enough apologies in the world for letting you chase me for all those years without me chasing you back because, baby, I wanted to chase you more than you realize. You deserve to be chased every damn day because you're special and loved. More important to me than anyone in my life."

Her eyes watered, which Luke hoped was still a good

sign. "That was beautiful," she said breathlessly. "And much better than the speech I was going to give."

He studied her eyes. "Give it, anyway."

"Okay," she said. "Luke O'Connor, I want to thank you for being patient with me, but I don't need any more time apart because all I've learned in these past couple weeks is how much I love you and want to spend as much time with you as I possibly can."

He grinned, finally feeling the tension leave his shoulders. "Why didn't you start with the I-love-you part?"

She shrugged. "I don't know. It just came out that way. Do you want me to take it back? Because I can arrange that, too."

Luke laughed. "There's my sarcastic girl. I almost had you in tears. Wasn't sure who I was dealing with for a minute."

She punched him in the shoulder. "Keep teasing me and I won't give you the surprise I had for you today."

He raised an eyebrow. "Is this a surprise I can watch? A surprise I can eat? Or a surprise I can touch?"

"All three depending on how you look at it," she replied, waggling her eyebrows.

"Damn, what are we still doing walking around this pier then?"

She laughed. "Actually, I really wanted to ride the Ferris wheel. Don't ask me why, but I was thinking about how this conversation would go and thought ending it on the Ferris wheel would be nice. Especially since the entire thing is decorated in Christmas lights! I mean, who gets to ride a Ferris wheel decorated in holiday lights?"

"Random, but I'm down for it," he said, pulling her to him. "As long as I get to spend the rest of the night kissing you senseless to make up for all the time we missed."

"How many kisses would you say we missed in a day?"

"Um, at least one hundred a day," he said.

"Guess that's a whole lot of making up," she stated. "Tell me, do these kisses all have to be on my face? Or are there some other places you can kiss to make up for lost time?"

"Oh, there are definitely some other places in need of my intimate attention." His eyes dropped down to her lips. "But for now, I'm going to kiss the pair I've been looking at since you got here." With that, he dipped his mouth to hers, capturing her lips in a hungry kiss that had him groaning aloud.

He heard a few people clap and a few others tell them to get a room, but Luke didn't pay them any mind. He was too busy kissing the woman who owned his heart. The woman who'd helped him realize what it meant to not just have love for someone, but to truly love someone.

It almost seemed like they'd had to go through every obstacle they'd faced in order to ensure that they'd end up in this exact moment at this exact time.

"Mmm, that was nice," Kyra whispered against his lips. "Maybe we should skip the Ferris wheel and head back to my apartment to pack?"

"Pack? Where are you going?" he asked.

"Did you forget my lease to my apartment was up last week? You didn't finish your job, Mr. Real Estate Matchmaker."

Luke's eyes widened. "Damn, can't believe I forgot about that."

She playfully swatted him on the shoulder. "It's about to be Christmas soon and I'm going to be homeless! The only good thing about being homeless in LA around a holiday is that hopefully, I can put one of those red tin cans right next to a tent in Hollywood and collect money. Folks are more giving at Christmas."

"You are so dramatic," Luke said with a laugh. "Why aren't you staying with Nicole or Aaliyah?"

"I didn't want to impose on them. I figured maybe I need to just do a month-to-month lease until I find the perfect place."

"You can stay with me and Nash," Luke said without giving it a second thought.

"Uh, I appreciate the offer, but you both are still bonding. I'd just be in the way."

Luke took out his phone and called Nash. He answered on the second ring. "Hey, Nash, I have a favor to ask you?"

"Hey, Luke. Need me to help you serenade Kyra or something? You can pick any song, but I draw the line at Christmas music."

Luke laughed. "Nah, bro. We're back together. No serenading needed."

"Congrats."

"Thanks," he said. "Kyra's lease is up and she's living in a hotel. Would you mind if she stayed with us until we find her a place?"

"Put me on speakerphone," Nash said. Luke eyed his phone curiously, but he did as Nash asked. "Hey, Kyra, can you hear me?"

"Hey, Nash! Yeah, I hear you."

"Okay, so now that you're both listening, yes, I'm cool if Kyra stays with us for a while," Nash said. "But did either of y'all think that the reason she never found the perfect condo is because you both were supposed to find a condo together?"

Luke raised an eyebrow. "Uh, my stay in LA was supposed to be temporary, though."

"Is that still the case now that you and Kyra are together?" Nash asked.

Luke gave a goofy smile that matched Kyra's. "Nope. I guess not."

"Exactly. I love you and everything, bro, but I need my own space. I haven't had a roommate since college. And I think it's pointless for you to look for a condo and Kyra to look for a separate condo when y'all are gonna be together all the time, anyway. Save money and save yourselves the headache of packing a bag every night."

"You know what, Nash," Luke said. "I like the way you think, brother."

"That's probably one of the best ideas you've ever had," Kyra added.

"That's what I've been saying all along," Nash said. "I'm pretty amazing. And that's why you'll name your first daughter Nashonda after me."

Kyra gasped. "Nashonda? That's a hideous name."

"It's better than some of the others he came up with," Luke said.

"I find that hard to believe," Kyra said with a laugh. That laugh died on her lips as Nash started going through his list of baby names. To Luke's surprise, the names actually got worse as time went on.

Epilogue

Kyra couldn't believe everything they'd accomplished in three months. Not only had they closed on the Thomas property, but the Bare Sophistication ladies in Chicago and Miami had also come together to make sure the LA boutique was ready for the grand reopening.

On top of that, Kyra and Luke had finally found a condo that they both could agree on, and so far, living with Luke was even better than she ever imagined it would be. They'd needed to get out of Nash's place because they were driving him crazy. They hadn't been fighting or anything, but Nash had said it was too lovey-dovey in his bachelor pad and that hanging out with Luke's friends was making him question his bachelorhood.

Luke and Nash still hadn't heard much from their father, but Kyra felt like their relationship was better without him in it. Plus, Luke's mom and Nash were also getting closer. Already, they were planning another visit and Kyra couldn't wait because as crazy as it sounded, she was missing those beautiful St. Lucia beaches.

"It's almost time," Nicole said, speaking to all the ladies who were gathered inside the boutique while their families, friends and others in the public and media waited outside the shop.

"I can't believe it," Winter said. "This may just be my favorite location out of all the boutiques."

"It's definitely my favorite," Summer said. "Danni and I are already talking about searching for a new storefront for Miami."

"I think we'll look at upgrading in Chicago, too," Autumn said. "Can't let LA get all the fun."

"I just love this sisterhood," Aaliyah said, clasping her hands together. She had given birth to a healthy baby girl two and a half months earlier, but Aaliyah was still hormonal and emotional. Kyra and Nicole had both told her it was possible she'd turned around and got pregnant again, but she refused to believe them.

"I agree," Nicole said. "I can't imagine what my life would have been like had I not joined the Bare Sophistication team."

Kyra looked to Winter, Autumn, Summer and Danni knowing that they felt the same way, especially since three of them had founded the boutique chain. "I love y'all," she said to everyone in the room.

"Can we have a *Baby-Sitters Club* moment?" Aaliyah asked.

Autumn glanced around the room. "What's that?"

"It's when we all stand in a circle and hug each other," Kyra explained. "She's been making us do this for a year now."

Summer laughed. "I'm all for hugging it out. Let's do this." All seven women hugged, each grateful in their own way for their Bare Sophistication journey. A knock on the window made them break their embrace.

"It's showtime," Kyra announced. "Ladies, you ready?" They all nodded their heads and filed out of the boutique, where they were welcomed by a huge crowd of people who were clapping and screaming for them.

"Thank you all for coming to the grand reopening of Bare Sophistication Boutique and Boudoir Studio in Hollywood," Kyra announced. "We are so appreciative of all the amazing people who have helped make the Bare Sophistication brand a success. When Winter, Autumn and Summer initially created this idea, they had no idea it would be so well received. Not only am I so proud of my sisters-in-law, but I'm equally proud of these strong black women standing beside me who have poured their blood, sweat and tears into this business." Kyra turned to the women. "Ladies, I am a better woman because of each of you." They each blew her kisses and Aaliyah, who was standing beside her, gave her a tight hug.

"To our parents, spouses and partners, we couldn't do this without you. To our friends and loyal customers, thank you for supporting the brand and help making Bare Sophistication shine." She made sure the red ribbon was in place and Nicole was nearby with the big scissors.

"And without further ado, we'd like to—"

"Hold on," a voice said, cutting her off. *Why does*

that sound like Luke? she thought. When he made his way through the crowd, she saw that it was Luke.

"Uh, baby, I'm kinda in the middle of something."

"I know," he said, taking the mic. "But considering we've had a pretty busy few months, I couldn't think of a better time to do this." He cleared his throat and everything around them quieted as Kyra realized what was going on.

"Oh, my God," she said, her hand flying to her mouth.

"Kyra Monica Reed, I am so in love with you and have been for most of my life. You amaze me in so many ways and because of you, I'm a better man. I know that I still owe you so many dates, but I honestly can't imagine going on another date with you as just boyfriend and girlfriend." Luke got down on one knee and opened a ring box that revealed a huge princess-cut diamond.

"It's beautiful," Kyra whispered.

"Not as beautiful as you," he said. "Kyra, would you do me the honor of making this official and becoming my wife?"

She nodded her head. "Absolutely!" He slipped the ring on her finger and stood to give her a kiss. Kyra could hear the crowd cheering in the background, but she couldn't bring herself to break apart from him. Grown-up Kyra was ecstatic and ready to spend the rest of her life with this man, but little-girl Kyra was running around outside in circles and screaming, "He finally did it, y'all!" She'd wished she could tell her young self that the patience paid off because she landed the man. Better yet, he landed her because she was a catch and she knew it.

The ribbon cutting went on without them, but she didn't care. In fact, she would have stood outside the shop and continued kissing Luke if she hadn't remembered something.

"What are you doing?" Luke asked when she took out her phone.

"I have to text your cousin Trista," Kyra said.

Luke raised an eyebrow. "Now? Why?"

"Because the rest of my wish came true," Kyra said, shooting a message over to Trista. "I thought that story was so fake, but the wish I made at Wishing Waterfall came true."

Luke smiled. "Did you wish for us to be together?"

"Technically, I wished for us to be together by Christmas, which we totally were," she said. "Then, I wished for us to engaged before Easter, which we are."

Luke shook his head. "Of course, you made two wishes."

"Three, actually," she said, holding up three fingers. "I may or may not have also wished for our wedding to be in Alaska."

He frowned. "You can stop texting her because that part hasn't come true yet. And by hasn't, I mean, it will never come true. I don't want to get married in Alaska."

"Baby, we gotta be different," Kyra said. "Most the folks we know have already gotten married and done so extravagantly. Do you know what that means? Means Alaska is the only thing that will top it."

"But you don't even like the cold," he said.

She rolled her eyes. "We have to work on this husband-and-wife thing before we say our vows," she said. "Basically, whatever I say goes and whatever you say, doesn't. Got it?"

He opened his mouth to argue with her, but Kyra beat him to it by shutting him up with a kiss. Granted,

Alaska may not be the best place to get married, but wherever they chose, she was fine with it. A wedding was just semantics, anyway. She was already the happiest she'd ever been having landed a great career, amazing friends, a supportive family and a life partner who did crazy romantic things like propose in front of a huge audience. He made life more interesting and, more importantly, he loved her for her.

* * * * *

HOLIDAY BABY SCANDAL

JULES BENNETT

To all the readers who've asked about Ryker...
you're welcome.

One

With one hand clutching the forgotten cuff links and one hand firmly over her still-flat stomach, Laney pulled in a deep breath and willed courage to make an appearance.

She was an O'Shea, damn it. She didn't back down in the face of fear. Fear was nothing but a lie. A bold-faced lie capable of defeating most people. Laney wasn't most people.

She'd come this far, all she had to do was knock…and make a life-changing confession to a man she'd been in love with since she was old enough to notice boys. Forget the fact he'd been ten years older. Age meant about as much to her as fear did.

Tears clogged her throat as emotions threatened to overwhelm her. Whatever his reaction, she owed him the truth. But if he rejected her, the pain would slice deep.

Laney pushed aside the hurt, the fear and the nausea, and pounded on Ryker Barrett's front door.

No turning back now.

Ryker had been part of her life since she was a child. He'd worked for her father, was best friends with her brothers. Her family had taken him in when his own had turned him away. He was mysterious, intriguing and frustrating.

And for the past five weeks he'd been pretending nothing had happened. He gave no hint that he even recalled tearing her Chanel dress from her body before holding her against her hotel room wall and bringing her every desire to life.

Nope. It was business as usual. When she'd had to feed him information via email or text for O'Shea's auctions, he'd never given any indication that their one heated night had made an impact on his life whatsoever. Was he that emotionally detached?

Well, he was about to sustain one hell of an impact. He may try to ignore her, but there was no way he could ignore the consequences of their night.

The door swung open and the entire speech she'd rehearsed all morning vanished from her mind. Ryker stood before her wearing only a pair of running shorts, a tatted chest and glorious muscle tone.

She'd never seen him this way. The man who traveled the globe in designer suits, the man who donned a leather jacket and worn jeans to blend in when necessary, had never presented himself in such a beautiful, natural manner. He should do this more often.

Casual as you please, Ryker rested a forearm on the edge of the door and quirked a brow as if she'd disturbed him. Yeah, well, he deserved to be put out. She'd been fighting her feelings for him for years.

Rage bubbled from within as she slapped his cuff links against his bare chest and pushed past him. In all the years she'd known him, Laney had never come to his house in Boston. When they met, it was always on neutral ground, usually at the O'Shea family home her brother Braden now lived in.

As infuriating as Ryker could be, Laney was the first to admit that her family would crumble without him. He may be the "enforcer," the guy who kept them protected and took the brunt of any backlash they ever faced, but he could easily cut ties and leave. This billionaire never threw his money around like most men she knew. Loyalty meant much more to Ryker than finances ever would... one of the many reasons she was drawn to him.

The door closed at her back. Laney shut her eyes and tried to forget the intensity of their complicated relationship, tried to ignore the way her body instantly responded to this man. She was here for one reason. And the fact that he worked for her family, was practically *part* of her family, wasn't making this confession any easier.

"If you're here regarding the painting in L.A. that you emailed me about last week, I've already—"

Laney whirled. "I'm not here about work."

Crossing his arms over his broad chest, Ryker widened his stance and gave a brief nod. "I can't believe it took you this long to come to me."

Laney's heart kicked up. So he knew she would bring up that night, and he'd what? Been waiting on her? Jerk. Uncaring, unfeeling, stupid, sexy jerk. Why couldn't he put a shirt on? She was trying to keep her anger going, but lust was creeping into the mix.

"You could've come to me," she threw back. "Or, I don't know, actually talked to me when we were exchanging work information."

The O'Sheas were a force all their own, known around the globe for their prestigious auction houses. Laney had ignored the whispered "mafia" or "mob" rumors her entire life. She knew full well what her family was, and she was a proud member. They remained on the right side of the law thanks to the connections her late father had made and the ones her brother Braden, who was now in charge, and her other brother Mac continued to work at.

And Ryker Barrett, other than starring in her every fantasy for years, was the family's right-hand man, security detail and any other job they needed him for. He did the dirty work and lay low, staying out of the limelight and behind the scenes.

Laney waited for him to say something, anything, but he stood there staring at her, which only made her nerves worse. How could he have so much power over her? She was an O'Shea, for crying out loud, and he was just standing there.

Standing there looking all half-naked, sexy and perfect.

Focus, Laney.

Ryker held up the cuff links. "Was this all?"

Laney narrowed her eyes. "Am I interrupting something?"

Or someone? It hadn't even occurred to her that he may be entertaining. A sick feeling in the pit of her stomach grew, and she hated the spear of jealousy that ripped through her.

"Yeah, my morning session with the punching bag." Which explained those perfectly sculpted arms, shoulders and pecs, though Laney figured he used a punching bag as a means of releasing his emotions rather than to stay in shape. Ryker was the epitome of keeping to himself and never letting anyone get too close. So what did that say about that night they shared? Clearly he'd thrown all of his rules out the window because they'd been as close as two people could get.

Nausea pushed its way to the front of the line, bypassing her worry, her fear. Laney closed her eyes, waiting to see if she needed to find the bathroom or take a seat and let the wave pass. *Please, please, just pass.* Of all times to appear vulnerable, this was not the one.

"Listen, I get you want to discuss what happened," he began, oblivious to her current state. "I take the blame. I shouldn't have followed you into your room and—"

"Ripped my clothes off?" she finished, holding a hand to her stomach and glaring across the room at him. "I'm not sorry it happened. I've been waiting on you to notice I'm not just Mac and Braden's little sister. I've fantasized about you ripping my clothes off, and I don't even mind that you ruined my favorite dress. So, I'm not sorry a bit. I'm only sorry about how you treated me after."

Other than the muscles ticking in his stubbled jaw, Ryker showed no emotion.

"This wasn't just some one-night stand," she argued.

"It was."

Okay. That hurt—the truth often did—but still. They were more, so much more, than a quick, albeit amazing, romp.

"How dare you act like I was just some random stranger?" she yelled, throwing her arms out wide. "I've known you almost my whole life. You think it's okay to have sex with me and—"

He moved in a flash, gripped her shoulders and hauled her against his bare chest. "No, I didn't think it was okay, but I couldn't stop. Damn it, Laney."

Ryker released her and took a step back, letting her go as if she'd burned him. "I couldn't stop," he whispered.

She had to get out of here. The last time they'd been alone his control had snapped, and he was barely hanging on by a thread now that she was in his living room, on his turf.

He'd purposely been avoiding her since their one-night stand, only communicating through texts for stuff related to O'Shea's. They'd been working together for the past several years. He could admit that when she came on board, his job had become so much easier. With her being able to dig deeper, to infiltrate systems he never could've…she was invaluable. Laney's computer hacking skills were eerily good. If she ever worked with the wrong crowd, she could be dangerous. Granted, some considered the O'Sheas the wrong crowd, but whatever. He couldn't do his job without her, so avoiding her altogether wasn't an option.

The torture of working so close together was worth it, though. Even the slightest communication with Laney kept him going. He shouldn't enjoy the pain of being so near, unable to fulfill his every desire, but he chalked up his masochistic tendencies to his less than stellar childhood.

When he wasn't on assignment, he typically would hide out at his home in London or take a trip to some random destination just because he could and had no ties. When he was in Boston, he was too tempted to give in to his desires for his best friends' and bosses' little sister.

When Laney started to reach for him, Ryker held up a hand. "No." If she touched him, this whole distance thing would crumble. He'd been playing with fire when he'd grabbed her a second ago...but damn if she didn't feel good against him.

This had to stop. He owed it to the family who saved him from a living hell. For years he'd ached for her, watched from afar as she grew into a breathtaking woman who managed to slip beneath his defenses. When she'd dated other men, it had nearly gutted him, but what right did he have to say anything?

She was the mafia princess, and he was the family... problem solver. He'd been involved with a lot of dark deeds before her father passed away and left the family business to Braden. Now they were all on the path to being legitimate. But legitimacy didn't change what he'd done in the past. And no matter that his bank account had more zeroes than any one person would need, that didn't change the fact he wasn't worthy of Laney. Not only was she the daughter of one of Boston's most powerful men, but she'd never made it a secret she wanted a large family, complete with babies and pets. He opted for lovers in other states and countries, to keep things physical and void of all emotions.

To put things simply, they were on opposite ends of this warped world. Since Patrick's death months ago, Braden and Mac protected her, and rightfully so, from the harsh realities their family faced each day. Actually, Laney's protection had also been part of Ryker's job.

Not that he needed the money or the job. But he owed the O'Sheas. Anything they asked for, he would provide or die trying. And it was all of that watching over Laney that had damn near done him in.

Blowing out a breath, he shook his head and faced her, but froze. Laney had stepped back and was leaning against the wall. Her closed eyes, her long, slow breaths had him narrowing the distance between them.

"Laney?" He was near enough to touch her, but kept his hands to himself. See? He could do it. He'd just be right here in case she needed something…like his hands on her.

With shaky fingers, he shoved her hair away from her face. Her lids fluttered open, but a sheen of sweat had popped up over her forehead. Was she that nervous about being here?

"I know you don't want me here, but I have to tell you something."

She pushed from the wall, swaying slightly.

Now he didn't resist contact. Ryker grabbed her around the waist and held her against him. "Are you all right?"

"Let me go."

Those vibrant green eyes came up to meet his. The punch to his gut instantly forced him back to that night, to her pinned between his body and the wall. She'd panted his name as she'd clung to his back. Never had he experienced anything so…perfect. And he didn't deserve one second of her affection. Mac and Braden would kick his ass if they knew… Well, they'd try, anyway. He could handle himself in a fight, but he deserved at least a punch to the face over the way he'd seduced Laney like she was just another woman he'd met on one of his trips. Laney was nothing like those other women, and he needed to remember that.

Ryker dropped his hands but didn't step back. He couldn't, not when she still seemed so unsteady and his body was wound so tightly. She was a drug, his drug. They were bad for each other for too many reasons, yet he wanted more.

"I'm pregnant."

Ryker stilled. Had she just…

What the hell? He hadn't heard her right. No way. When they'd been in Miami, he hadn't planned on having sex with her after the party at the new O'Shea's location, but she'd assured him she was on birth control. So, no. He hadn't heard right.

But Laney continued to stare up at him, and Ryker waited for her to say something else, anything else, because there was no way in hell…

"I'm sorry." Laney leaned her head back against the wall and shut her eyes once more. "I didn't know how else to say it. I mean, there's really no good lead-in to something like this."

Pregnant. As in, a baby. Their baby.

Ryker turned away as dread consumed him. How the hell had he allowed something like this to even be a possibility? A child was definitely not something he ever wanted in his life. No damn way would he purposely bring an innocent baby into this world. Into his darkness.

"You said you were on birth control."

He didn't mean for the words to come out as an accusation, but he was confused, damn it. And angry. Angry at himself, because had he kept that control of his in line, Laney wouldn't be dropping this bomb.

"I was." She pulled in a breath and squared her shoulders. "I had to switch the one I was on and started a new one the week before Miami. I don't know if that's why it happened. I just don't know…"

He remembered so clearly her tugging his shirt over

his head and telling him she was on birth control, that she had just had a physical and was clean. He knew full well he hadn't been with anyone for a while, and he'd never gone without protection. So in their frantic state of shedding clothes and getting to the good stuff, they'd had a two-second conversation about contraception.

So here they were. Laney was expecting his child and he was…screwed. Literally.

Bracing his hands on the antique table behind the sofa, Ryker dropped his head. He'd kept his hands, and all his other parts, to himself this whole time. Out of respect for the family who took him in and saved his life, Ryker hadn't given in to the one desire he'd had for years. Until Miami, damn it. How would he ever make things right with the O'Sheas?

Patrick had taken Ryker in at the age of twelve when Ryker had stood up for Braden and Mac on the playground, and the boys had become best friends. Ryker had instantly become like family, but he'd never thought of Laney as a sister. At the time, he'd ignored her because she was so much younger. But by the time she graduated high school, Ryker was deep in the family business, and more than aware that his dirty hands should never touch the sophisticated Laney O'Shea.

When her computer hacking skills were made apparent, Ryker knew she'd be an asset. He'd just had no idea how difficult it would be to work with her. He could afford to hire anyone to do the behind-the-screen work, but he trusted only her.

Braden and Mac were going to kill him. They would kill him and bury his body, and no one would ever know…and he deserved nothing less.

Damn it. Ryker blew out a breath. This was how he

repaid the family who trusted him, who was loyal to him when no one else cared?

"This isn't your fault."

Her soft voice washed over him, and he let out a curt laugh. "No? Am I the one who pushed his way into your room, tore that dress off and demanded you wrap your legs around me? Or was that another man?"

He threw her a glance just in time to see her flinch. Great. Now he was being an ass. All of this was on him. Laney didn't deserve his anger—she was just as innocent as the child.

His gaze dropped to her flat stomach, and fear engulfed him. Images of his biological father flooded his mind, and Ryker vowed that second to never be that man. Never would he lay a hand on his child, never would he choose the next fix over putting food on the table.

Ryker's childhood may be a sad cliché, but that was life and all too often kids were mistreated while other adults turned a blind eye to the abuse.

Ryker looked down. Random scars covered his knuckles, his forearms. His life was made up of more ugly than anything else, yet this beautiful, vibrant woman stood here giving him something so precious and all he wanted to do was...

Hell. What did he want to do? He never wanted Braden or Mac to find out about the night he'd spent with their baby sister. Not that he was afraid of them. He could handle anything thrown his way—almost anything.

They trusted Ryker to keep the family safe, to keep all threats away. Wasn't that why he'd been ordered to follow her back to her hotel that night? Because there had been a threat against her?

For years he'd kept asshats away from her. A few

months ago he'd had to use physical force and pull some major strings to get her ex out of her life. The man had made a menace of himself and had started harassing Laney. He hadn't told Laney what happened, and he never would, but he knew she wondered. Wondered if Ryker had done something sinister. And maybe that was for the best. Maybe she wouldn't get those stars in her eyes like she'd had when they were intimate in Miami.

Pushing off the table, Ryker ran a hand down his face. Stubble rustled beneath his palm, and he honestly had no idea what to do next. He'd never faced something this life-altering, this damn scary.

"I don't expect anything from you." Laney stood straight, apparently feeling better. Her coloring was back. "But I wasn't going to keep this a secret, either. I know you don't want anything to do with me—"

"Stop saying that," he growled. "You have no idea what I want."

She tipped up her head, quirked a brow, as if issuing a silent challenge. "Enlighten me."

If only things were that easy. If only their relationship was about sex and nothing else. *If only* was the story of his entire messed-up life.

"I will be here for this child," he told her, turning to face her fully. "I'll keep you protected."

"You've been looking out for me for years."

He took a step forward. "Not like this. If you think I was protective before, you haven't seen anything."

Laney rolled her eyes. "Don't do this. Don't be overbearing. If I hadn't gotten pregnant, I know you would've gone on to ignore me on a personal level. That night we spent together wasn't supposed to happen, but we were on that path for so long, it was inevitable."

He hated when she was right. Hated even more that every night since then, he'd had to replay it over and over in his mind because he would never be that close to her again. And she'd ruined him for any other woman.

"I can take care of the baby and myself just fine." She glared back. "But I don't want my brothers to know just yet. I'm not ready."

As much as he hated hiding from anything that threatened him, he was in total agreement. Braden and Mac would find out soon enough, but for now, just no. First, he and Laney had to grasp this news themselves.

Ryker took another step until the gap between them was closed. "Let's get something straight now. I will take care of you and our baby. You need anything, I'm providing it. You won't shut me out. If I have to haul you off to my home in London and watch you personally, I will."

Laney snorted. "Really? Now you choose to let me in?"

"I don't have a choice," he muttered.

And maybe he never had…not where Laney was concerned.

So how the hell did he even attempt to keep his loyalty to this family when he'd betrayed them? And how was he going to be closer to Laney than ever before and keep his hands off her?

Ryker Barrett had lived through some rough times, but he had a feeling he was entering a whole new level of hell.

Two

How cute was he, thinking he could be all protective and overbearing? Poor Ryker. He clearly forgot he was dealing with an O'Shea. She may be the baby sister, she may be the one everyone loved to keep safely tucked away behind the computer, but she knew more than they'd ever realize. She wasn't naive, and she wasn't blind.

And going to London? Not an option. She was working on something right here in Boston that was so near to her heart, she refused to walk away. Pregnant or not, she'd see this project come to fruition.

Once she'd left Ryker's house earlier, she headed home, changed her clothes and went for a run. Her doctor had informed her that keeping up with her regular exercise routine was perfectly fine. She needed to release some pent-up energy and blow off steam anyway. Perhaps she should've joined Ryker in his punching bag workout. Although she feared he'd have pissed her off and she'd have ended up socking him in the face to knock some sense into that thick head of his.

Why did she have to be attracted to such a stubborn, frustrating man? Why did she still have to feel how amazing he was weeks after their encounter? The imprint of his powerful touch would be with her forever. Laney had always wondered if the reality of being with Ryker would measure up to the fantasy...and it was better. So much better than anything she could have dreamed up.

But now that she was pregnant, she wasn't going to use the child as an excuse to get closer to him. She wasn't a pathetic, desperate woman. She may have loved Ryker for as long as she could remember, but she would never use an innocent child to get a man.

She'd worried about telling him, though. Worried because she knew enough of his childhood to figure out he probably had no dreams of becoming a father. Ryker never spoke of his birth family—his family had become the O'Sheas the instant Mac and Braden brought him home after school one day. All she knew was that his first twelve years had been hell, and nothing any child should have to go through.

Ryker may be ten years older than her, but that didn't make him out of her reach. By the time she'd been old enough to notice boys, she'd had eyes for only one man. Oh, she'd dated, but nobody had captured her attention like Ryker. And for years he'd ignored her.

Then one night, as if the dam had broken, he'd quite literally torn off her clothes. Never had Laney been so thrilled, so relieved to finally have a dream become reality. But no dream could've ever prepared her for the experience Ryker gave her.

Laney pulled her damp hair into a loose topknot. Now that she'd exercised and showered, she was ready to get some work done. Her brothers were so close to finding their family's missing heirlooms, and she so wanted to be the one to crack the mystery.

For years, decades actually, their family had been searching for nine missing scrolls. The precious documents dated back to the sixteenth century, when one of their ancestors, an Irish monk, transcribed some of William Shakespeare's work. The scrolls had been handed down from generation to generation.

But when the Great Depression robbed so many people of their normal lives, the O'Shea family lost their home and everything inside. The home actually ended up falling into the possession of Zara Perkins's family, which was how Zara and Braden met. Braden had thought that cozying up to the pretty event coordinator and getting inside her house would help in their search. Little did Braden know he'd fall in love.

The scrolls weren't found, so now the search continued. And Laney would love nothing more than to be the one to find the missing treasure. Her entire life she'd been sheltered, kept at an arm's length from the dangers of the family business. If her father and brothers hadn't needed her mad computer skills, she had no doubt they wouldn't have told her a single thing.

Well, if she found these scrolls, they'd have to acknowledge just how much she brought to the table and how she wasn't afraid to get her hands dirty. Family meant everything, and, now more than ever, she was determined to take a stronger role in the business. Proving to her brothers, to Ryker, that she could keep up with them wasn't going to be a problem. She was an

O'Shea. Determination was ingrained in every fiber of her being.

Laney pulled up her email and slid a hand over her flat stomach. This baby would be so hardheaded and strong. There was no other option, considering the genes.

Scrolling through messages, Laney tried to forget Ryker and his demanding ways. But it was those demanding ways that had rocked her entire world at a hotel in Miami.

Maybe she could distract herself with some online Christmas shopping. Maybe that would take her mind off Ryker and the fact she now carried his child. Laney couldn't help but wonder how her overbearing brothers would react to this news.

Dread filled her stomach. How would Zara take the pregnancy? She and Braden had miscarried a child several months ago. Were they trying for another one? Laney hated to pry, but she also didn't want to seem insensitive. Especially if they tried and were unsuccessful.

Oh, they'd be happy about the baby, but privately would they be hurt? Laney loved Zara like a sister and didn't want to cause her any more grief.

With Mac and Jenna planning a wedding, Laney seriously hesitated to say anything to anybody. There wouldn't be a perfect time, but at least she could wait for a better time.

Laney clicked on an email she'd been waiting on. Her offer had been accepted. Finally. She'd been wanting this news for over a week, and the timing was perfect. One more step closer to her goal of revamping an old, run-down building in Boston's south side… Ryker's old neighborhood.

She'd set these plans in motion before Miami. Over

the years, she'd heard Ryker talk about unfortunate kids, never of his own childhood, but she knew his worry stemmed from where he'd come from. So Laney wanted to help. She hated the idea of kids feeling like there was no hope, no one there who really cared about their future.

Her father had instilled in her that commitment. To help the unfortunate. When he'd taken in Ryker, he'd done so without another thought. If more people reached out like her father had, maybe this world would be a bit brighter.

She was keeping the project a secret because she wasn't in it for the praise or the recognition. And she definitely wasn't out to make the O'Shea name look better in the community, which was what many would think if they knew she was involved.

Laney starred the email and laid her phone on the desk in her office before taking a seat. It had gotten so dark since she'd finished her run. She longed for summer and sunshine, where she didn't have to worry about getting back in time before sunset. She also wondered if running alone was the smartest choice. She always had done it by herself to clear her head and think, but now that she was pregnant, she felt more vulnerable.

From the time she was little, her father had taught her to always be aware of her surroundings. But now she should take a few more precautions. Even though she lived in Boston and the streets were bustling with people, she might want to consider using her treadmill or finding a jogging partner.

A laugh escaped her as she thought of Ryker. She couldn't quite imagine the brooding man throwing on a pair of sneakers and running. No, he was more of a boxer type, a guy who lifted heavy weights, or did pull-ups with one arm. He was all strength, all power.

And the thought of all of that excellent muscle tone had Laney attempting to focus on something else. Anything.

Christmas shopping. Right. That's what she'd been planning to do. Why go to the stores and fight all the crazies when she could go braless at home and have everything delivered right to her door...wrapped even.

Online shopping was glorious.

She also had a few final touches to put on the O'Shea's holiday party they were having for the staff at Braden's house in two weeks. The annual event had grown even more since Mac had opened satellite offices in Miami and Atlanta.

Still, Laney loved working on the party and Zara was a professional coordinator, so her sister-in-law had done the majority of the work this year. Laney just needed to order the centerpieces she and Zara had agreed on.

She'd just opened a new browser to search for a dress to wear to the party when her doorbell rang. Glancing quickly at the monitors, she saw Ryker's hulking frame. He kept his head down, shoulders hunched against the brisk December air. He never came to her house...just like she had never gone to his. He'd followed her home before to make sure she was safe, but he'd never popped in of his own accord.

Who knew it would take a pregnancy to get him to come for a visit?

Pushing away from her desk, Laney headed toward the front door. Darkness had set in and snow swirled around, bright flakes catching in the streetlights.

Laney flicked the lock on her door and opened it, immediately stepping back so Ryker could come in out of the cold.

Without a word he strode inside. Those heavy black boots were quite the contrast to her bare feet with polished pink toes. And that was barely the beginning of all the ways they differed.

Laney closed out the cold and set the dead bolt. Crossing her arms over her chest, she faced the man she'd been half in love with since she was a teen.

"This is a surprise," she told him. "Did you come to talk or is something wrong?"

"I need to head out of town."

Laney nodded. His rushing out of town was nothing new. He did so many things for the family. The O'Sheas had gone global with their famous auction houses. Ryker sometimes traveled to obtain relics or random pieces for a specific auction. He'd been known to procure heirlooms that had been stolen. Some may look at him as a modern-day Robin Hood since he returned items to their right owner.

He also was known to go to his home in London for a quick escape, but he was always a text or call away. He put her family first above all else.

"I'm leaving in the morning, and I'll be gone a few days."

Laney tipped up her head. "You never tell me when you're going out of town unless you need my computer skills to pull up the blueprint of a building. If that's what you—"

"I'm not here for the blueprint."

The way those black-as-night eyes held her in place had her shivering. Why did she let him have such power over her? He had more power in one stare than most guys did in a kiss. And she'd dated some great kissers.

"Then why are you here?" She was proud of her strong tone but worried about what his answer would be.

"Are you feeling okay?" he asked, his eyes dropping to her stomach, then back up. "I didn't ask earlier. Or, hell, maybe I did. It's all still kind of a blur."

So he was here about the pregnancy. She should've known he wouldn't stay too far from her. He'd always been protective in that overbearing, bouncer kind of way.

"If you're going to hover, don't waste your time."

She didn't want to sound ungrateful, but she didn't want a babysitter. She wanted him, damn it. She wanted him to see her as a woman. As the woman he'd let down his guard with several weeks ago.

Up until then, she'd always thought he saw her as Mac and Braden's little sister. Someone he helped when necessary, but who was more family than anything.

"If I want to hover, I damn well will," he growled. "You're having my child. You're part of a very well-known family, and it's my job to protect you."

That was the crux of the entire problem. The slice to her heart shouldn't surprise her. Did she honestly think that after they'd had sex he'd come around? That when he knew about the baby he'd profess his undying love to her? No, but she'd at least hoped for him to treat her like…hell. Was it too much to ask for him to act like he cared about her as more than his friends' baby sister?

"I don't want to be your job."

Laney turned before he could see the hurt on her face. Heading back toward her office, she couldn't care less if he let himself out or if he followed. Trying to capture

Ryker's attention for so long was exhausting. She sure as hell didn't want it now due to a job or a baby. She wanted him to look at her for her. Nothing else.

Apparently that was too much to ask. With his traveling schedule, he probably did hookups and one-night stands. She'd never seen him in any type of a relationship or even heard him mention seeing someone. Laney thought she may take way too much delight in that, but whatever.

Just as she reached the threshold of her office, a hand clamped around her arm and spun her.

"Don't walk away from me."

Laney raised her brows. "You're not in charge of me, no matter what my brothers tell you to do. I can get along just fine without being coddled."

"Would you quit acting like you're so put out? Your brothers care about you and only want you safe."

Laney jerked free of his hold but kept her eyes on his. "And what about you, Ryker? Do you care about me?"

"Of course I do."

Laney swallowed. "As a brother?"

The muscles along the stubbled jaw ticked. "I'm not doing this, Laney. I'm not hashing out my feelings or letting you get inside my head."

Of course he wouldn't. Ryker would never let anyone in because he was made of steel. She'd never seen him show emotion, other than frustration and anger. But he never talked about what drove him to those feelings. The clenching of the muscles in his perfectly squared jaw indicated he was angry. Other than that, he played his cards seriously close to his chest.

"Whatever." She waved a hand in the air. "I'm feeling fine. There. Now you've checked up on me, and you can go on your way, guilt-free. This all could've been done in a text."

"Maybe," he agreed. "But if you were feeling bad you'd lie, and I wanted to see for myself."

Laney went for broke. "I think we both know between the two of us who would lie about how they feel."

When he remained still, silent, Laney was done. They were getting nowhere, and she wasn't in the mood to play games or whatever the hell else he wanted.

"I won't keep you out of the baby's life, but I don't want your attention just because I'm pregnant. I've waited for years for you to notice me. I thought Miami was something, but I was clearly mistaken, since you ignored me until you knew I was having your child."

All of that was so hard to admit, but at this point what did she have to lose? She wasn't one to hide her feelings, which only made Ryker squirm. Good. He deserved it.

The second she jerked the door open, a burst of cold air rushed in. "If you're done here…"

Laney turned and stared out at the blowing flakes. She didn't want to look at him, not when she still craved him. Putting up some type of emotional barrier was the only way she'd survive this.

Heavy boots moved across her hardwood floor. Ryker stopped right in front of her but kept his gaze out the open door. Laney stared at his black, leather-clad shoulder. The smell of his jacket, the familiar woodsy cologne and the unmistakable scent that she only associated with Ryker assaulted her senses. Why did he have to be the one to hold her emotionally captive?

"I've noticed you," he whispered as he remained rooted inches from her. "I've noticed too much for too long."

Laney's breath caught in her throat.

"But Miami won't happen again." Turning, he locked those dark eyes on her. "I'll check on you while I'm away."

And then he was gone. Shoulders hunched against the blowing snow, head down, Ryker walked off her porch and down the walk toward his car. Despite shivering, Laney waited until he was in the SUV with the engine running before she closed the door…but not before she caught him looking back at her.

Just that glance from a distance was enough to have her stomach doing flops, her heart pounding.

Ryker may be checking on her because of the baby, something she couldn't be upset about, but his telling words gave her hope. He'd noticed her. And from the way he seemed to be angry about it, he'd clearly been fighting with himself over the fact for a while now.

Laney leaned back against her door and wrapped her arms around her abdomen. She had no idea what was going to happen now that she and Ryker were on this journey, but one thing was perfectly clear. They were in this together, whether he liked it or not.

Three

"I don't like this."

Ryker's cell phone lay on the console as he watched the house across the street. With Braden on speaker, Ryker could focus on who was coming and going.

"I'm not a fan myself, but I think there's something here," Ryker replied.

This was his first interaction with Braden since Ryker discovered Laney was expecting. The guilt of his betrayal weighed heavily on his chest. The O'Sheas had been everything to him over the years, and he'd purposely kept his distance from Laney because he knew what would happen if he touched her. Just one touch, that's all it would've taken at any given time for him to snap.

But she'd mouthed off at the party and between her sass and that body-hugging dress, his self-control had finally expired.

Damn, the woman could tempt a saint…not that he

was anywhere near that holy. But he'd completely lost it in Miami. Years of pent-up frustration, the fact she'd been receiving threats and not sharing that information, and the way she'd looked in that short black dress had been the combination for his undoing.

"How long are you going to wait?" Braden's low tone cut through the memories.

Ryker rubbed the penny between his thumb and index finger, hating the way he carried the damn thing around like some good-luck charm. He was pathetic for even still having it, but the reminder of where he came from always needed to be front and center.

"I've seen a member of the DeLuca family go in, but nothing else."

The DeLuca family was known for organized crime. Thugs, actually. They didn't even compare to the O'Sheas, though Ryker thought some members of law enforcement would lump the two families in the same category...or prison cell.

"What activity has Laney uncovered?" Braden asked.

Ryker raked a hand down his face. "She's seen some email chatter with several family members discussing moving a package. When she dug a little deeper, she found they have an old trunk in the basement that contains some documents. But we have no clue what they are."

Ryker didn't know how the coveted scrolls would've ended up hours away from where they were last seen or how they were in a basement belonging to an organized crime family, but this was the strongest lead they'd had in a while. Ryker had followed every tip that had popped up. He'd been to London twice, Mexico, Paris and several US states.

When Patrick passed several months ago, he had one dying request. He wanted the scrolls found and returned to the O'Shea family. He'd tried for years to recover them but to no avail. Ryker fully intended to finish the job… it was the least he could do for the people to whom he owed his life.

"Damn, Laney is calling me," Braden stated. "Keep me posted no matter what happens or what time it is."

Laney was calling? Was she okay? Did something happen?

Every time he'd thought of her since Miami, all he could think about was the way she came apart in his arms. She'd been so responsive, so passionate. Now when he thought of her, all he could think was that she was carrying his child. His. Child.

The words didn't seem real even in his own mind. How the hell was he going to take care of a baby? What did he know? His father had only taught him how to get high, get laid and steal. The essentials of every childhood according to dear ole Dad.

Ryker kept his eyes on the house, but his mind wasn't on the job. Damn. This was why he never got involved with anyone. His loyalties were with Braden and Mac now. And by default, as their baby sister, Laney. If he was worrying about anyone, especially a woman, he wouldn't be able to concentrate on the task at hand. And the task sure as hell wasn't Laney.

She'd called Braden, not Ryker. That shouldn't bother him, but it did. There was no denying that he wanted to be the one she called on when she needed anything. But he couldn't be that deep in her life and keep his distance at the same time.

His mind went into overdrive. If something was going

on with the baby, she wouldn't have called Braden, that much Ryker was sure of.

Ryker disconnected the call. The penny was heavy in his hand. Over the years, he'd tried to tell himself that the souvenir from the best day of his life was ridiculous and childish to keep. Yet each day he left his house, he grabbed his keys and the penny and shoved them in his pocket. He couldn't seem to let go of his past.

Story of his life.

After another hour of waiting, which brought the grand total up to six, Ryker decided to call it a night. Laney would let him know if more activity came through her. She'd managed to tap into several areas: emails, private messages on social media, a cell phone.

Ryker always marveled at how crazy brilliant she was. She was seriously the brains behind the operation when it came to research and hunting down people. For years, she'd managed to find anything online, while Ryker did the grunt work. They were a team in a sense, but he never wanted to look at things that way. If he did, then he'd have to admit there was a relationship. And even when their dealings had been platonic, he couldn't analyze things too deeply when it came to Laney.

The woman could make a man forget everything else in this ugly world. She had beauty, grace and a stubborn streak he couldn't help but admire.

And now she was having his baby.

Pulling himself up straighter in his seat, Ryker brought the engine of his SUV to life. Snow covered the streets and showed no sign of stopping soon. December in New York was just as brutal and unpredictable as in Boston.

Cranking up the heat, he maneuvered through the

streets toward the hotel. Another cold hotel. He always booked a suite. Mostly because growing up he'd lived in a one-room dump of an apartment. Now that he could afford to stay anywhere or buy anything he wanted, he fully intended to take advantage.

But he'd never look at another hotel the same after Miami. Laney changed everything.

He couldn't even wrap his mind around the fact he was going to be a father. What the hell did he know? His own father had used him as a punching bag when he was awake and only half drunk. Ryker never wanted marriage, kids, the minivan experience. He was just fine with the job he had. Though Braden and Mac would never tell him this was a job, to them he was simply a brother, a best friend.

Which made this pregnancy so much harder to comprehend. He couldn't come to grips with how he should deal with it, so how the hell could he figure out how to tell them?

Laney was such an innocent. They'd worked for years to keep her safe, to keep her behind the scenes. Ryker had made enemies all over the globe. Now that Laney was pregnant, he would have to be twice as diligent about keeping those he cared about safe.

Yeah, he cared about her. Too much. Being ten years older than her, he'd not paid much attention when he first came to the O'Sheas as a teen. Then he'd been out of the house mostly doing grunt work and earning his way in the family, so he didn't have to go back to his former hellhole.

By the time he'd started coming around the house more often, Laney was a teen herself and he was a bastard for looking at her twice. If Patrick O'Shea had ever thought Ryker was eyeing his daughter, Ryker doubted he'd still be here.

But Ryker had respected the man more than anyone. Patrick had shown him what a true father figure was. Patrick had cared for his children, put them first and kept them protected at all costs. He had demanded loyalty, and there was nothing Ryker had wanted to give him more.

Which was one of the main reasons he wanted to be the one to uncover the scrolls. Patrick was gone, but Ryker still wanted to do this one final job for the only real father he'd ever known.

And all the more reason Ryker needed to keep his hands to himself where Laney was concerned. Patrick had been extremely protective and cautious when Laney wanted to date certain men. There were guys who wanted to date her simply for her last name or because they thought they could get into the family and wanted to use her as a warped version of a job interview.

Ryker had done neither of those things. He'd just gone straight to taking her against a wall and getting her pregnant like a loser.

One thing was for sure. He may not be father material, but he wasn't about to ignore his responsibilities. If he had his way, he'd whisk Laney and their baby away and tuck them safely in his home in London…or he'd buy a damn private island. Anything to keep them safe.

He had the funds, that wasn't the problem. No, the problem came in the form of a beautiful, stubborn, Irish goddess who would rather argue with him than listen to reason.

Ryker pulled into a parking spot right outside the window to his room. Always on the ground floor, always near an exit.

Fear overwhelmed him for the first time in years. Not for himself but for Laney and their unborn child.

When he got back to Boston, they were going to have to talk. He couldn't outrun her any longer. He may not want a relationship with her, or anyone else for that matter, but he'd make damn sure she was taken care of… regardless of the cost to his own heart.

Most would say he didn't have a heart. Ryker would have to agree. But Laney made him feel, and he could see the train wreck coming. Someone was going to get hurt.

When Laney had called her brother because her Christmas decorations were too heavy for her to lift, she hadn't even realized the time of night. But here he was hauling box after box into her living room.

"Why do you have so much stuff to put up for only one month?" he growled as he sat the last box beside her sofa.

"So you can enjoy it when you come to visit." Laney smiled and patted his cheek. "Just think, in about four weeks you can come back and take this all back up to my attic."

"I'll hire someone. Hell, just leave it up all year long. I won't judge."

Laney pulled the lid off one box and stared down at the contents. Christmas decorations were her crack. She loved everything about them. The lights, the glass ornaments that belonged to her mother, the garland she strung over her mantel and down her staircase. Everything was so magical, so perfect, and it made her remember how amazing her childhood had been. A house full of family and laughter, the parties they'd thrown in the O'Shea ballroom.

Tears pricked her eyes. She wanted that for her baby.

She wanted her child to know the meaning of family gatherings. There was nothing more valuable to Laney than her family. She needed them now more than ever, but she had no idea how to tell them a little O'Shea was about to join their ranks.

She wasn't afraid of how they'd react to the baby; her brothers would welcome another O'Shea. But how would they treat Ryker? He was such a staple in their family, and he was so much more to Braden and Mac than just an employee. He was…everything.

Laney sighed and blinked back tears.

"Hey, you okay?" Braden stood beside her, bending to look her in the eye. "Oh, damn. Please don't cry. I'll help take them down later, I swear."

Why was it that the strongest of men couldn't handle a little water?

"I'm fine," she assured him, waving a hand. "It's late and I'm tired. That's all."

His dark brows raised in disbelief. "And you opted to start decorating now?"

"I've got a lot on my mind." Wasn't that an understatement. "I'll work on this until I think I can fall asleep."

Crossing his arms over his chest, Braden straightened and pinned her with his eyes. "Is there a problem I need to know about?"

Laney picked up an ornament and began to peel away its bubble wrap. "Just worrying about my brothers. Nothing new."

That wasn't a total lie. She always worried about them. Their business kept them busy, traveling, sneaking around. Thankfully they had enough law enforcement in their back pocket to keep them out of the hot seat, but still. Laney always worried something would happen. There were worse fates than being arrested.

"We're all fine." Braden took the ornament from her and waited until she turned her attention toward him. "I'm asking about you. Are you still receiving threats? I'd hoped after Shane—"

"Stop worrying about me."

She didn't want to talk about her emails or Shane. Ryker had taken it upon himself to...handle the problem of Shane when he'd attempted to abduct Laney from in front of her home in Beacon Hill. Shane had been the bane of her family's existence for years, but he'd crossed the line when he'd harassed Braden's wife, Zara. When he'd tried to grab Laney, Ryker had had enough.

And Laney knew the way Ryker had managed the situation had been an issue between him and Braden. Since Braden had taken over the family business after their father passed, he'd been adamant about going legitimate, and that included how they took care of their enemies. Ryker insisted that ending their old practices so suddenly would make them look weak and invite retribution.

Laney was still unsure what happened to her ex, but she was fine about being kept in the dark regarding that.

"Why don't you get back home to your bride?" Laney suggested. "It's late. I'm just going to sit here and tear up a little over Mom's things."

Braden looked as if he wanted to say more. That intense stare could make even the most seasoned criminal break, but Laney wasn't caving. She'd grown up around strong-willed alphas her entire life. Not much fazed her.

"If you have any issues, you call me or Ryker immediately."

Laney nodded, though if she had an issue she'd deal with it herself. She wasn't a helpless female.

Once she hugged her loving, overprotective brother good-night, she reset her alarm and glanced around at the mess. The tree sat completely naked in the corner near the fireplace where she always put it. She wasn't even sure at this point if she had any working lights. She tried to buy new ones each year, but, well, this year had been a bit exceptional and her mind had been elsewhere.

Laney found the box with her garland and decided to work on the staircase. That would be simple enough and keep her mind occupied for a few minutes.

She'd barely started when her thoughts drifted to Ryker. There was always a level of fear anytime she knew he was working. But the not knowing was frustrating. She knew the lead he was working on, she'd supplied him with the intel, but she didn't like how he insisted on going out alone. He always stayed just detached enough to be in the know but keep to himself. Damn frustrating man.

Laney carefully wrapped the banister, fluffing the greenery as she went. This time next year she'd be playing Santa and buying the baby's first Christmas things— tacky bibs and ridiculous ornaments would be welcome here.

What would her world be like with a child? Laney smiled. As scared as she was to tell her brothers, as worried as she was about what this meant for her and Ryker, there was no way Laney would change one single thing about Miami. This baby would never question how much he or she was loved, and the first person to call this pregnancy a mistake would be throat punched.

The thought of Ryker holding a baby was nearly

laughable. She'd never seen his softer side, though she knew he had one. He cared for her, even if he opted to show it in Neanderthal-type ways.

Those whispered words before he left kept playing through her mind. She wished he'd stayed so they could talk, but he was prone to run rather than discuss his feelings. Well, he couldn't hide from her forever. Eventually they had to talk about the future and their baby.

Laney's cell chimed from the living room. She hurried down the stairs and carefully maneuvered the minefield of boxes. She found her phone on the coffee table next to a wreath that was in desperate need of fluffing. Because of the time of night, she figured the text would be important.

And she was right.

Ryker's name lit up her screen, and she swiped her phone to read the message.

Nothing new tonight. Anything come through on your end?

Work. It was always work with him. A sliver of disappointment speared through her as she replied.

Nothing. I'll keep you posted.

Her thumb hovered over the Send button. She wanted to make this more personal. She wanted to say…something. But Ryker was all work. What would he say if she asked personal questions or called him out on what he'd confessed to her earlier? Could he talk about his feelings when he wasn't looking her in the face? She understood that. She totally got how people were more apt to open up when they could hide behind an electronic device.

She hit Send but immediately started typing another message.

Earlier when you said you think about me, why were you angry about it?

Laney sent the message before she could change her mind. She wanted to know. She deserved to know, but the screen seemed to mock her as no reply came. She waited several minutes, but still nothing.

Fine. She wasn't going to beg. Yes, she would give anything to get inside that head of his, but she didn't want to have to beat the information out of him.

The second she laid her phone down, it chimed once again. Laney stared at the screen. She almost didn't want to read the message, but she hadn't been raised to give into any fear.

Because it isn't right.

Laney resisted the urge to roll her eyes as she contemplated her reply. There was so much to be said, it was too much to text and should be said face-to-face.

But he wasn't completely closing her out, so she went for it.

Whatever you feel can't be helped. Why fight it?

Laney jumped when her phone rang. The cell bounced from her hand and onto the sofa, hit a box and landed on the floor. She snatched it up, thankful the screen wasn't cracked, and she was a bit surprised to see Ryker's name.

"I didn't think you'd actually talk to me," she answered.

"You wouldn't leave me alone until I did."

Laney smiled. Just that gruff tone had her nerves calming. Ryker could always make her feel safe, at ease. Even though they argued and got on each other's nerves, he was her comfort zone. Banter was their normal. Normal was so vanilla. What she and Ryker had, well…that was more Rocky Road.

"Where are you now?" she asked, scooting a box over and taking a seat on her couch.

"Hotel."

"Plenty of time to talk, then."

Ryker's heavy sigh resounded through the line. "I'm not in a chatty mood."

"Have you ever been?"

"What do you think?"

Laney toed the disorderly wreath aside and propped her socked feet on the coffee table. "Maybe it's time you stop fighting whatever you're feeling and just go with it."

The laugh that escaped him was void of any humor. "Life isn't that easy."

"It's your life, isn't it? Make it that easy."

"You think I enjoy pushing my level of self-control?" he asked, his voice gravelly, as if fighting back anger. "I have a responsibility to your brothers. I have a responsibility to you." He let out a deep sigh. "To our baby."

Laney's heart clenched. Closing her eyes, she dropped her head back on the cushion and focused on not botching this. Ryker was so much more to her than she could even put into words, but he may never comprehend that.

"You have a responsibility to yourself," she said softly. "You owe my family nothing. I know you think you—"

"I owe your family everything. And I've betrayed them."

His last words came out on a strangled breath. Laney stilled. Did he honestly believe that? Was he that torn up over the baby that he truly felt he'd gone against her brothers? Why did everything have to come back to his sense of loyalty to her family? They trusted him, they knew him better than anyone else and they might be angry, but they would still love him.

Tears pricked her eyes, and she cursed her stupid pregnancy hormones. Tears had no place here. She was fighting for what she wanted, what Ryker wanted. Hell, what they deserved.

"If that's how you feel, then there's nothing I can say. If you don't want anyone to know this baby is yours, we don't have to say anything. I can just say I'm not involved with the father and not tell my brothers any name at all." Though it would kill her. Pain like nothing before speared through her at the thought of Ryker not being involved. "I can't make you want—"

"That's the whole problem," he yelled. "I want, damn it. Too much. But I'll never turn my back on you or this baby."

Laney picked at the hem of her T-shirt and swallowed a lump of remorse. "Right. Responsibilities."

"Laney—"

"It's late. I'll let you go."

She ended the call, dropping the phone into her lap as she battled back tears. Why did he have to be so noble, yet so ignorant at the same time? Why did he feel that he had to sacrifice his own happiness in order to fulfill some past debt? Ryker had more than proved himself to this family.

At least he hadn't agreed to being left out of the baby's life. That would've gutted her. But he still only saw her as a responsibility, and Laney feared she'd never be more in his life.

Four

"We need to get inside that house."

Braden nodded in agreement. "How soon can you get back? I don't want them moving that trunk."

Ryker leaned back on the leather sofa in Braden's study. He'd left New York after staying an extra day longer than planned, and had driven straight to Braden's house. He hadn't called or texted Laney after their talk on the phone. He'd revealed too much, she'd gotten too close to the raw emotions…emotions he feared he couldn't hide forever.

Damn it. He hadn't even been aware of suppressing them, so how the hell did he continue to hide them?

"I can go as soon as I get the blueprint."

Braden came to his feet. "Great. Laney is due here anytime."

The blueprint was a pathetic excuse to see her again.

He could've gotten it the other day when she offered, she could've also emailed it. But, he wanted to see her, touch her, consume her. But reality was cold and harsh. He'd had her once, and that would have to stay with him forever because he couldn't let his guard down again.

He'd not only betrayed Braden and Mac by slashing right through their trust, but he'd let Laney down, as well. He should've had more control in Miami, should've walked her to her room and kept going once he knew she was safe. How could he have let his all-consuming need for her change their entire lives?

"Ryker?"

Jerking his attention back to Braden, Ryker stood. "Lost in thought. What were you saying?"

"Laney just pulled in."

Ryker glanced to the monitors and saw Laney stepping from her car. While it had stopped snowing, the ground was blanketed in several inches. Braden's drive and walk had been cleared though.

He tried not to watch as she pulled her coat tighter around her waist or how her long, dark hair blew in the breeze. He didn't have to concentrate too hard to still feel that hair over his body. Ryker clenched his fists and ordered himself to get control before she stepped inside. This would be the first time the three of them would be together since he'd found out about the pregnancy. He couldn't give anything away. He couldn't—

On the screen, Laney slipped and went down. Ryker tore out of the study, down the hall and through the foyer. He whipped open the door, oblivious to the wind and the bitter air. Laney had a gloved hand on the bumper of her car and was pushing herself up.

"Stop." Ryker slid his arms around her waist. "Lean into me."

Laney pushed her hair away from her face and looked up at him. "I'm fine. Embarrassed, but fine."

Ryker didn't let her go as she came fully to her feet. "Is she okay?"

Ryker glanced over his shoulder to Braden who was coming toward them. "I think so."

Laney tried to push off Ryker, but winced. "Okay. Just give me a second."

His hands flattened over her stomach as his heart sank. "Laney?"

Her eyes held his. "It's my ankle. Just sore. I'm okay."

How did she know? Could she be sure the baby was okay? Ryker didn't know how hard she fell. Hell, he didn't know anything about pregnancies or babies, but seeing her go down had nearly stopped his heart.

Scooping her up in his arms, and careful to avoid random ice patches, he stalked past Braden and into the house. Zara rushed in from the kitchen, her dark hair flying around her shoulders.

"What happened? Laney?"

"I'm okay." Laney waved a hand. "Just slipped outside and my ankle is sore. Ryker is being overbearing as usual."

Considering he'd been that way with her for years, this wasn't out of the ordinary. He didn't give a damn if it was. Seeing Laney go down like that had ripped something open inside him. In the brief seconds it took him to get outside, all he could think of was their baby. How the hell was he going to handle parenting?

"I'll get some ice," Zara told them.

Ryker gently laid Laney on the chaise in the formal

living room. Her hand slid against the side of his neck as she let go. Even though she had gloves on, just that simple touch took him back to Miami when she'd—

No. That was then. A mistake. He couldn't live in the past. He'd vowed to move on and that's exactly what he had to do if he wanted to get their intimacy out of his life.

Unfortunately, Laney had imbedded herself into his soul…and he thought he'd sold that to the devil a long time ago.

But he felt her. When she looked at him, he swore he felt her. That delicate touch, the tender gaze. She was hurting now, and he needed to focus.

"I'll call our doctor," Ryker stated.

Laney immediately started to shake her head. "I just went down wrong. I'm fine. I didn't fall hard."

"Let's get your boot off and look at your ankle." Braden went to unzip her boot. "Can you move it at all?"

She wiggled her foot, and Ryker watched her face for any sign of discomfort. When her bright eyes flashed up to his, he had to tell himself not to look away. She could draw him in so easily…and she knew the power she possessed.

"It's a little swollen," Braden commented. "I'd say you're fine. Just stay off it for a while."

Laney smirked. Freakin' smirked at him like a child who'd been playing parents against each other. Ryker narrowed his eyes. "I'm calling the doctor anyway just to be safe."

Before he could slide his cell from his pocket, Laney laid a hand on his wrist. "I'm fine." Her eyes bore into his, completely serious now. "I promise. I'd know if I needed to be seen."

She didn't look away, her grip tightened. Ryker blew

out a breath he wasn't aware he'd been holding. Of course she would get a doctor here if she thought she needed one. Laney loved this baby and wouldn't make poor choices. Still, for his peace of mind, he'd feel better if she was seen.

"Relax," she whispered, her eyes darting toward her brother.

Yeah. Relax.

Ryker took a step back and glanced down at her ankle. He needed to get a grip. Being cautious and protective was one thing, but acting like a hovering boyfriend was—

Seriously? How had that word even popped into his head? He wasn't her damn boyfriend. This wasn't junior high. But she was right. If he didn't get a grip, Braden would wonder what was going on, and that wasn't a topic he wanted to dive headfirst into right now.

"Here you go." Zara came back in and placed an ice pack wrapped in a towel over Laney's ankle. "Let's put a pillow under you to keep it propped up."

Ryker stayed back as Braden and Zara got Laney situated. He wanted to scoop her up and take her back to his house where he could take care of her. He wanted her tucked away behind his state-of-the-art security system where she'd be safe at all times. But none of that was possible. She'd never be at his house on personal terms. He'd never see her in his bed.

Ryker reached into his pocket, his fingertips brushing over the penny. The reminder he wasn't cut out for family life.

"Do you feel like working?" Braden asked. "I hate to ask, but time is of the essence."

Laney shifted on the sofa. "I can work. My laptop is

out in the car, though. I was walking to the passenger side to get it when I fell."

"I'll get it."

Ryker needed more cool air. He needed to get his heart rate back to normal and to chill out. Laney had had to talk him down, and that had never happened. Damn it.

She may not want a doctor, but one thing was certain. When they left here, he'd be driving her. Whether they went to her house or his, that was her choice, but they'd be leaving together.

Laney concentrated on digging up the layout of the house Ryker needed to get into. Her ankle throbbed more than she wanted to admit, but she was absolutely certain nothing else was hurt. The baby was fine. If she even thought for a second that something could be wrong, she'd have a doctor here. But she honestly hadn't fallen that hard, just turned her ankle on the sliver of ice she hadn't seen.

Zara and Braden were in the study. Her brother had told her to yell when she found something because he was helping his wife work on finalizing the company party.

Laney's sister-in-law was a top-notch events coordinator and in high demand. The way Braden supported her business was adorable. He was proud of his wife, and their love was evident whenever they were around each other.

The miscarriage they'd suffered a few months ago had only forged their bond even deeper. But Laney still couldn't bring herself to tell them about her own condition.

"Will you stop brooding?" Laney's fingers flew over the keys, but Ryker's presence was wearing on her nerves.

"I'm waiting."

She glanced over to him and raised her brows. "You're leaning in the corner with your arms crossed, and you've been staring for twenty minutes. That's brooding. I can actually hear your frustration."

When he pushed from the wall and strode over to her, Laney realized she'd poked the bear. Fine. At least he was showing emotion.

Ryker loomed over her, hands on his narrow hips. "How much longer until you have something?"

"I'm downloading the blueprints now."

"Good. Then we're leaving."

Laney jerked back. "Excuse me?"

He leaned down, pinning her with those coal-black eyes. "You heard me. I'm driving. The destination is up to you."

O-kay. The clenched jaw and the no-nonsense tone told her he wasn't giving her an option.

"Fine. We're going to my house. I have things I need to get done."

Ryker shoved his hands in his pockets. "Not with that ankle. You're relaxing, and if I even think you're trying to put weight on it, I'll have the doctor at your house so fast you won't know what hit you."

Laney believed him. He didn't take chances with her on a good day, but add in a pregnancy and a fall, and Ryker was dead serious.

"Oh, don't worry." She offered him her sweetest smile. "I plan on letting you do all the work."

Poor guy. He had no idea he was about to be covered head to toe in glittery garland, lights and delicate glass ornaments. She'd most certainly have her phone at the ready to snap some pictures of Ryker decorating her house.

"Oh, here we go." She glanced back at her screen, surveyed the pages that had downloaded and quickly emailed them to Braden and Ryker. "All done."

Ryker stalked from the room. There was no other word to describe his movements. He was angry, most likely with himself, or maybe with her. Whatever. He was about to be doused in Christmas happiness. He wanted to order her around and demand he leave with her? Fine.

Laney hesitated for a second but quickly pulled up her emails. Nothing new on the property in Southie. She'd had some contractors survey the building so she could get some quotes. After she signed the paperwork next week, the place would officially be hers and she could get to work. She seriously wanted the place open by spring so kids could come and play when the weather got nicer.

Opening the community center in Ryker's old neighborhood was perfect. She couldn't wait to have children filling the place. Children who may not have an exemplary home life and just needed a break.

Laney wondered where Ryker would be today if someone had intervened and helped him earlier than her father had. Would he still be part of their lives? Would he still be as hard, as jaded as he was now? He'd made it a point to be her personal security detail from the time she was a teenager. Was that because no one had protected him?

Laney's heart clenched. Had his worry for her led to whatever happened to her ex?

No. She wouldn't believe that Ryker would do anything to him beyond a few harassing calls and texts. Ryker could be over the top at times when it came to people he cared about, but she truly hoped he hadn't done anything rash.

Laney swallowed as she closed her laptop. Ryker cared about her. Beyond their intense night together, he'd admitted as much…and he didn't mean the sibling type of caring, either.

Ryker may think he'd been keeping her safe, but she always had his back, too. She held the reins with the intel coming in, and she chose what to feed him and what to keep to herself.

Laney would be even more diligent now that he was going to be a father. There might be times she made sure he didn't get a case because of the danger it posed to him, and she'd deal with the backlash from her brothers. Ryker needed someone to look after him; he was long overdue for it, actually. And Laney was just the woman for the job.

Five

The second Ryker stepped into Laney's house, he froze. He'd been duped. He glanced at her, only to see a smirk on her beautiful face. Now she mocked him.

Why did he find himself so attracted to her again? Oh, yeah. She was sexy as hell, and she took charge. A perfectly lethal combination to his senses. If he were ever considering a relationship, those were the qualities he'd look for. But a relationship with Laney was not only risky, it was suicide.

"Don't even tell me I'm decorating."

Laney leaned on him because she wouldn't let him carry her, yet she was limping slightly. Stubborn woman.

"I can do it, but you'll just get all grouchy and make me sit down."

Ryker reset her alarm system, still wishing he'd ignored her request and gone to his own house. After escorting her over to her sofa with an attached chaise, he got her settled and pulled off her boots. He grabbed one of her fluffy yellow throw pillows and set it beneath her ankle.

"Still sore?" he asked, glancing down at her, trying to ignore how perfect she looked all laid out.

"It's fine."

Ryker crossed his arms over his chest and sighed. "You've said that at least five times since it happened, which means it's anything but fine."

Laney tipped her head back on the cushion, her hair falling around her shoulders. Try as he might, he couldn't help but recall how all those strands felt on his bare skin. A memory he prayed never diminished. He needed that to keep him going, especially since he'd never have her again.

"Stop hovering. My ankle is fine, the baby is fine." She laced her fingers over her abdomen. "Do you want to put the lights on the tree or would you prefer to decorate the mantel?"

Ryker narrowed his eyes. Testing his patience was a surefire way to get him to take her back to his house. Did he look like a damn interior designer?

"Maybe you didn't notice, but I don't do Christmas."

"I always buy you a gift. In fact, you're the first person I buy for."

Yeah, and he'd kept every single one of them. He always felt like a fool for not buying her something, but what would he get her? What was an appropriate gift for a woman he wanted but couldn't have? So he never did gifts…for anyone.

"You don't have to buy me gifts," he growled. He'd rather put up lights than get into this uncomfortable topic.

Laney shifted on the chaise and patted the spot beside her. "You're staring down at me like I'm a bug on your shoe. So, either sit down, get to work or leave."

Ryker loved how she always spoke her mind. Except when she kept revealing her feelings for him. Nothing good could come from her making an impossible situation even more difficult.

And if he sat next to her, he'd want to touch her. Touching would lead to what they both truly wanted, and he refused to betray this family again by giving into his selfish desires.

Ryker turned and grabbed a box. "What's in here?"

From the corner of his eye, he saw Laney's shoulders fall, her eyes close. He'd hurt her. He couldn't sit close to her. Didn't she get that? She had to understand this wasn't about them. There was so much more to it than just a man and a woman who were attracted to each other. So he'd have to keep his distance…as much as possible, no matter how much he wanted her.

"That's the ornaments," she told him. "I have a bag of lights I just purchased. It's on the steps. There's also a bag from All Seasons there, but be careful because I just bought the cutest Nutcracker there."

Fine. He'd put the damn lights on the tree. He'd decorate her house to put a smile on her face. He knew full well how much Laney loved Christmas. She used to go to her parents' house, which was now Braden and Zara's, and cook an elaborate dinner on Christmas Eve. She'd pass out gifts she'd bought and wrapped in thick, sparkly paper. Most likely she'd hand tied her own bows, too. Laney's face would light up as she sat and watched her family open their gifts. Ryker was always so mesmerized, so humbled he got to experience Christmas with them.

Damn it. They were his family. The only family he'd truly considered his own—the only one that mattered.

He'd just reached the steps and spotted the bag when Laney's soft voice stopped him.

"I know you don't want to be here."

Ryker glanced over his shoulder. Those bright green eyes locked him in place from across the room.

"I never said that."

Smiling, she said, "You didn't have to. You regret sleeping with me. Probably feel trapped because I'm pregnant. And I'm positive you think you betrayed my brothers. But please, don't patronize me or pity me. I'm fine on my own, Ryker."

When she held her ground and didn't glance away, he ignored the bag and started back toward Laney. She was a strong woman, what man wouldn't find that a complete turn on? She was everything he'd want in a woman, but she was the little sister of his employers, his best friends. She was off limits. And he'd ignored that unwritten rule.

Taking a seat on the edge of the chaise, he faced her. "I don't regret sleeping with you. I've tried, but I can't even lie to myself."

She reached out, tracing his scarred knuckles with her fingertip. "That's something, at least."

"I don't feel trapped," he went on. "I feel sorry for you, for this baby. I know nothing, Laney. The most impressionable years of my childhood were spent in hell. I couldn't begin to tell you what a baby needs. I don't even know how to help you adjust to this. I'm not made to be in a relationship or to be a parent. But that doesn't mean I'm turning my back on you guys. It just means…"

Ryker shook his head and turned away so he didn't have to look her in the eye. Apparently she was the stronger of the two. "It means you deserve better, and this is what you've got."

He barely heard her shift before her fingers threaded through his hair. "There's nobody better than you, Ryker. You're a fighter, you're noble and you're loyal. I know you'd do anything to keep me and this baby safe. What makes you think I'm so unlucky?"

Reaching up, he gripped her wrist, but didn't pull her hand away as he turned to meet her questioning gaze. "Because you deserve a man you can share your life with. You're the type who wants a family, who wants that big Christmas morning celebration with chaos and Santa stories. I can't give you that."

Laney smoothed his hair from his forehead. He should stop her. He should remove her hand, but he was such a selfish bastard. One more touch. He just needed one more and then he'd get up.

"Have I asked you for anything? You're already family. Just because we're having a baby doesn't mean you have to marry me."

Just the thought of marriage had him trembling. He traveled too much, took too many risks to bring a wife into the mix.

Laney's hand fell to her lap. "I didn't realize you were so put off by the thought of marriage. Glad I didn't propose."

She'd tried to make light of the situation, but the hurt in her tone gave her away.

"Laney—"

"So, if you want to bring me that sack of lights, I can

get them out of the boxes, and you can put them on the tree."

He stared at her another minute, to which her response was to stare right back, as if daring him to turn the topic back around. Ryker didn't necessarily want to get into a verbal sparring match with her, so he nodded and went to get the bag.

He'd thought Christmas decorating was torture, but seeing Laney hurt, knowing he'd caused her feelings to be crushed, was even worse. He was going to have to learn how to make her smile again or…what? It wasn't as if he could remove himself from her life. He worked for her family, and she was having his baby.

For once in his life, Ryker had no idea what the hell to do. He'd lived on the streets, he'd fought for his next meal and he'd taken risks that not even Mac or Braden knew about. But the shaky ground he stood on with Laney was the scariest thing he'd ever had to face.

Laney wasn't sure what was more amusing, Ryker cursing at the tangle of lights that had somehow wrapped itself around his shoulders, or Spike and Rapture continually getting into the tree and swatting at Ryker's hand.

Poor cats. They thought Ryker wanted to play each time he reached for another branch. Most of the time her cats kept to themselves, ignored her completely. But the excitement of the tree and the boxes had brought them out of hiding.

Laney realized she had completely forgotten about the pain in her ankle. The entertainment in her living room was more than enough to keep her distracted.

But part of her couldn't help but drift to the "what-if" state. The scenario right now with Ryker decorating,

Laney pregnant, resting on the chaise, the fire roaring and the cats playing, it was like a scene from a Christmas card.

Laney couldn't lie to herself. She wanted that Christmas card. She wanted to have a family like the one she'd grown up in. The O'Sheas were Irish—they knew how to do family gatherings. She had always dreamed of having her own home, having a husband and children. She'd never seen her future any differently.

Perhaps she was going about her plan in the wrong order, but she still had every hope of having children and a husband.

So, how would Ryker fit into this mix? He wasn't exactly the type of man she'd envisioned when she'd been doing her daydreaming. She'd never thought of being with a man who had scarred knuckles, tattoos, constant scruff along his jawline and an attitude that matched that of her cocky brothers.

Still, Ryker was absolutely everything that got her excited. He turned her on and made her want more—and not just physically. Ryker always made her feel safe, even if he drove her out of her mind.

Perhaps that's why she was so drawn to him. He didn't back down, he didn't care what her last name was and he matched her wits.

Laney stared across the room as Ryker reached toward the top of the tree for the last section of lights. So what if she was admiring the way his T-shirt rode up when he reached or the way his worn jeans covered his backside.

"Why are you staring?"

Laney blinked, realizing Ryker had glanced over his shoulder. Oops. Oh, well, it wouldn't be the last time she'd be caught ogling.

"I've never had a hotter decorator," she told him with a smile. "Next you can start on the ornaments."

Ryker turned. Hands propped on his hips, he shook his head. "This isn't going to work. Whatever is in your mind, get it out."

Laney shifted on the chaise to prop her elbow on the arm. Resting her chin in her hand, she raised her brows. "I don't know what you're talking about."

"The innocent act also doesn't work on me."

Laney laughed. "No? Offering to strip my clothes seemed to work."

Ryker's stony expression told her he didn't find her nearly as amusing as she found herself.

"Listen, we're going to have to learn to get along," she told him. "We can't always be griping at each other. You need to relax."

"Relax? You think I'll ever relax, especially now that you're having my child?"

Laney shrugged. "Shouldn't I be the one freaking out? I mean, I'm carrying the baby."

Ryker raked a hand over his jaw, the bristling of his stubble against his palm doing nothing to douse the desire she had for him. She recalled exactly what the coarse hair felt like on her heated skin. She'd give anything to feel it all over again.

"Are you that worried about my brothers?" she asked. "I mean, once they find out about the baby, they'll get used to the idea of us being together."

"We aren't together."

Laney met his dark gaze. "We could be."

Laying it all out there was ridiculous. Her hint was about as subtle as a two-by-four to the head, but she wanted him to see that they could at least try to be more.

"No, we can't." Glancing around the room, he located a box marked Ornaments and pulled off the lid. "You know why and I'm not going to discuss this every time we're together. I already told you I'd support you and our baby."

"I don't want your money." Laney swung her legs over the side of the chaise and pushed off, using the arm of the sofa for support. "I want you to stop dancing around this attraction. We already know we're compatible between the sheets."

"Sit down before you hurt yourself." In three strides he'd reached her and was ushering her back down. "I hope you don't care how the ornaments are put up because I've never done this before."

Laney didn't budge, but it was difficult to hold her ground when he was pushing her and she was putting her weight on one foot.

"Why are you so stubborn?" she demanded, then waited until he looked her in the eyes. "Seriously. Can't you just tell me why you won't even consider giving this a chance?"

His fingers curled around her shoulders. "Because you see something in me, in us, that isn't there."

"I see potential. I see a man who wants something and never goes after it. He's too busy working his ass off for everyone around him."

The muscles in his jaw clenched. "That's enough, Laney."

"Is it?" she threw back. "Because I don't think it's near enough. I think you need someone to tell you just what the—"

His mouth slammed onto hers. For a split second she was stunned, then she was thrilled. Finally. He was finally taking what he wanted.

Those hands moved from her shoulders at once. One went to the small of her back, pulling her closer to his body. The other crept up beneath her hair, fisting it and jerking her head just where he wanted it.

Laney held on to his biceps to steady herself. A full-on attack like this required a bit of warning. She supposed her warning had been his intense gaze, the way he stalked across the room toward her. The way he'd torn her dress weeks ago.

Ryker broke the kiss, his forehead resting against hers. "You have to stop."

Excuse me? "You kissed me."

"To shut you up," he growled. "I can't keep fighting this with you. You push and push until I snap."

"Maybe I push so you can see what it is you're missing."

Ryker pulled in a deep breath and took a step back. His arms dropped to his sides. "Believe me, I know what I'm missing."

If she'd ever met a more frustrating man, she couldn't recall. "What would you do if I quit pushing?" she countered. "Maybe one day I'll give up, move on. What would you do then?"

Six

Ryker shoved his hand in his pockets, a futile attempt at reaching for her. There was nothing he wanted more than to take her and rip those clothes off and make use of that sofa.

The penny in his pocket mocked him, reminding him of where he came from, of who he actually was. If he were a better man, a man who could offer Laney and their baby something of worth, he wouldn't think twice about taking her up on her offer.

"I won't wait on you forever," she whispered. "I feel like I've already waited most of my life. We had one night and you flipped out. And that was before you found out about the baby."

Ryker didn't know what to say. He didn't do feelings, and he sure as hell didn't discuss them. Laney was right, though. He'd flipped out after their night together.

Never in his life had he ever felt something so perfect—he didn't deserve perfect. In the midst of betraying the only family he'd ever loved, he'd found a dose of happiness he never knew he was longing for.

"I think we're done here." Laney eased herself back onto the chaise. Clearly she'd taken his silence as rejection. "I'm tired. Set the alarm on your way out."

"You think I'd leave when you're this upset?"

Laney's bright green eyes misted. "I'm not upset. I'm exhausted. I've beat my head against the proverbial wall for too long, and now I have a child who needs my attention. I have to look out for myself now, and if you can't see what we could be, then we have nothing left to discuss."

Getting shut out was not what he wanted, damn it, but he couldn't let himself in, either. There was no right answer, but there was an answer that would keep Laney and their baby safe.

"We need to tell Mac and Braden soon." Ryker ignored the pain in his chest. Pain was just a by-product of doing the right thing for those he cared about. "I'll do anything for you and our baby, Laney, but I can't be that perfect man in your life. You know why."

She kept her focus on her lap where her hands were folded. "I know you're a coward, so maybe you're not the man I want."

Her harsh words gutted him. The idea of her being with anyone else made him want to hit the faceless bastard. How could Ryker let her go so easily?

Because she was an O'Shea. Her father had taken Ryker in when he'd been on the verge of going down a path of complete destruction. Respecting Patrick, keeping his relationships with Mac and Braden, that's what

Ryker needed to do. He'd built his entire life around working for them, taking risks to keep them safe and going through hell in keeping his distance from Laney.

He'd failed. His penance would be to let her go.

"Let me at least help you to—"

"I don't need your help." Laney held up a hand, her lips thinned in anger, though her eyes still held unshed tears. "Since you won't take a chance, then I have nothing left to say to you right now. I'll let you know when my doctor's appointment is, and I'll fill you in on work. Other than that, we're done."

Swallowing, Ryker nodded. "I'm going back to New York since you got me the blueprints of the DeLuca property. I don't know when I'll be back, but shouldn't be more than a couple of days."

When she said nothing, Ryker moved around the coffee table and the storage boxes. He grabbed his coat off the hook by the front door and had just jerked the leather over his shoulders when her soft voice stopped him.

"Be careful."

With his back to her, Ryker closed his eyes.

"I may be angry with you, but I still care and I want you safe," she went on. "Your baby is counting on you to be here."

His baby. Words he never thought would come to mean so much to him.

"I can take care of myself." He opened the door and typed in the alarm code.

He thought he heard her mutter, "That's what scares me," before he closed the door, but he didn't stop to ask. The bitter cold whipped around him. Ryker pulled his jacket tighter around his shoulders and made his way off her porch and toward his SUV. Walking away from

Laney was the hardest thing he'd ever done. Before Miami, he'd always thought not knowing what being intimate with her felt like was the worst thing, but he'd been wrong. Because now he knew. Now he was fully aware of how perfect they were, how compatible they were. Now he had to live with the knowledge that he'd never have something that amazing in his life.

As Ryker slid behind the wheel of his car, he cursed himself. In the long run, this was the right answer. He'd been teetering on the wrong side of the law for so long, and he should finally feel good about a decision he was making.

So why did he feel like hell?

"It's a trap." Laney gripped her phone and tried not to panic as she left Ryker a voicemail. The third in as many hours. "Don't go inside. It's all been a setup."

She stood in Braden's office, staring out the massive wall of windows that overlooked a snow-blanketed backyard. She'd come here after her first call and several texts had gone unanswered. It was late, too late to be worrying about Ryker and this damn job. She should be at home asleep. Ryker should be safe in his hotel room. But she'd been given intel that the DeLuca home was going to be empty around eight in the evening, and Ryker had been given the green light to go in, check the trunk in the basement and get out before they arrived back sometime around midnight.

It was now one in the morning, and nobody had heard a word.

"Find out something, damn it." Braden's frustration level was just as high as hers as he shouted into his cell. "Call me back."

Laney turned to face her brother. "Anything?"

"I called one of our FBI guys in that area, and he's looking into where Ryker is."

Which meant they still knew nothing. Laney tamped down her fear because Ryker had been in sticky situations before. For years she worried each time he went out, but he'd always come back. On occasion he'd dodge the topic of why he had new scrapes or bruises, or a run-in with the law, but he always returned.

All Laney could think of was how they'd left things last night. Why had she told him that she was done? If he came back right now and told her he wanted to give things a shot, she'd be right there with him. He was it for her.

Laney smoothed her hand down the front of her tunic and over her flat stomach. She needed to remain calm for the baby. Ryker was okay…he had to be.

"He'll be fine," Braden assured her. "It's Ryker. You know he's probably somewhere laying low. Most likely he's hiding in that house with his phone on silent and dodging the DeLucas. You know he loves a challenge."

Laney jerked the leather chair from behind the desk and sank into it. "You're not helping. It's all my fault for giving him that information."

"Laney, you were going on a lead. That's all."

Exhaustion had long since set in. She hadn't slept well after Ryker had left last night. Then today she'd been searching for the root of her troublesome emails that had been sent a couple months ago when she'd gotten another bit of information on the DeLuca property. She'd instantly noticed something was wrong when the chatter turned to humorous banter about a setup. She'd almost gotten sick. After her texts to Ryker went unanswered, she called. And called.

She hadn't suffered much morning sickness yet, but the constant state of I-need-a-nap was ever-present. This situation with the DeLucas wasn't helping. All the worrying, all the fear. She wanted to believe the best because she wasn't sure she could handle it if Ryker got hurt...or worse.

Laney crossed her arms on the desk, making them a pillow for her head. Strong hands came to rub her shoulders.

"Relax," Braden told her. "Any minute he'll walk through the door and get angry because you're worrying."

Yeah, that was so like Ryker. She wished for that scenario more than anything.

"I swear, when you two aren't at each other's throats, you're both worrywarts."

Laney couldn't respond. She was too busy enjoying the massage and trying to wrap her mind around how she'd survive if something happened to Ryker.

Oh, she'd live and get along, but she'd be empty. Her child would be fatherless. She couldn't imagine anything scarier. Ryker had been in her life for so long, she truly didn't know how to exist without him.

When Braden's cell chimed, Laney jerked her head up and turned to stare as he answered.

"Yeah?"

Her brother's hard jaw, set mouth and grip on the phone weren't helping her nerves, but that was just typical Braden. As head of the family now, he was all business, all the time. Mac, their more carefree brother, was still down in Miami with his fiancée, Jenna. Those two had danced around their attraction for years…which reminded Laney of another stubborn couple she knew.

"Where is he now?"

Laney jerked to her feet, hanging on each and every word, watching to see if Braden's expression changed. Was Ryker okay? She wanted answers. Right. Now.

"I'll be waiting."

Braden pocketed his phone. "He's fine," he assured her. "But he was arrested. After some strings were pulled in the right direction, my contact with the Bureau managed to get him released. Ryker is being escorted by my acquaintance. I'm going to meet them just outside the city in a few hours."

Laney gripped the desk for support. "I'm going with you."

Braden put a hand on her arm. "You're going home. He's fine and it's late."

When she started to protest, Braden shook his head. "No, Laney. I don't know what's gotten into you. This is Ryker. You know he's fine. He'll be annoying you by morning, I'm sure."

What had gotten into her? Well, the father of her baby had been arrested, though the charges wouldn't stick because of their connections. He'd been set up in a trap that could've gone so much worse than what it had been.

How could she do this? How could she keep letting herself get all worked up over a man who kept pushing her away?

Finally Laney nodded. "Will you text me once you see him? Just to let me know he's really okay?"

After she grabbed her purse and keys, Braden kissed her cheek. "I will. Now go home and get some sleep."

Laney wouldn't sleep until she knew for sure. And

a text from Braden wasn't good enough. She wanted to see with her own eyes.

As she let herself out of her childhood home in Beacon Hill, Laney knew just where to go.

Seven

The last thirty-six hours had been a bitch. Ryker wanted nothing more than to get into his home and crawl between the sheets of his king-size bed. So much could've gone wrong in New York, but he refused to dwell on that. All he could concentrate on was the fact that he'd failed. One more dead end.

No scrolls. He hadn't even gotten to the mysterious damn trunk in the basement before he'd been caught off guard and cuffed.

Punching in his security code, Ryker let himself in. The sun was bright and promising a new day…and he was thankful for thick blinds. He hadn't slept since he left Boston. He sure as hell hadn't been able to relax when he'd been taken into custody. Not that he'd been worried. This wasn't his first run-in with the law, but he didn't have time for all this nonsense.

As soon as he stepped through his door and closed it behind his back, Ryker took in the sight before him. Without turning, he reached over his shoulder and reset the alarm. He wasn't about to take his eyes off the sleeping beauty perfectly placed on his leather sofa.

Laney wasn't quite lying down. She had her feet curled up to the side, her hands were tucked under her face, which rested on the arm of the couch. She looked so fragile, so small. But he knew she was neither. There was a vibrancy, a strength in her that terrified him. She feared nothing. He'd never found a woman who was willing to verbally spar with him like Laney. She wasn't afraid to throw back anything he dished out. She was absolutely perfect.

And she was the most beautiful sight he'd seen in days.

Ryker released the grip on his bag until it thunked onto the hardwood floor. He shed his coat and hung it up. She still didn't stir. Pregnancy was taking its toll on her. It wasn't like his Laney to be tired all the time.

Ryker froze. *His Laney?* Not in this lifetime. She'd never be completely his. But he was on a slippery slope and wasn't going to be able to hold on much longer. He'd told her before he was selfish, he'd proved that in Miami. But there was going to come a point when he wouldn't be able to turn her away.

Laney stirred, blinked until she focused on him, then jerked awake. The tousled hair, the slight crease on her cheek from where she'd lain, the flawless face void of any makeup staring back at him…maybe that time had come.

He started forward as Laney swung her legs off the side of the couch and stood. "I'm sorry. I didn't mean to fall asleep," she stated, tugging her long shirt in place over her leggings. "I just wanted to wait until you got home so I could see you were safe."

Something stirred inside him. Something primal. No one had ever waited to see if he was okay. Nobody had ever gone to the trouble of checking up on him. Oh, Mac and Braden checked in, but they were friends, brothers.

Laney was…special.

"I didn't think you'd mind if I used your code."

She'd only been to his house once, but every O'Shea had his code for emergency purposes and he had theirs. This was clearly an emergency for her. That primal feeling turned into a warmth he didn't want to recognize.

"But now that I can see for myself you're okay, I'll just go." She was adorable when she was nervous. "I'm sure you're tired and need to rest."

Ryker moved closer as she rambled, his eyes never coming off that lip she was biting. She'd been scared— for him. More scared than he'd ever seen her—for him. She was the most beautiful sight, and after the hellish past day and a half, he needed something beautiful in his life. He needed Laney.

"After we left things, and then we couldn't get in touch with you—"

His mouth slid over hers, cutting off her words. His arms wrapped around her waist, jerking her flush against his body.

Finally.

He felt like he'd waited forever to have her in his home, in his arms again. There were countless reasons why he shouldn't have been doing this, why he should've let her walk out that door.

But he needed this. He needed her, and he hadn't realized how much until he'd walked in and seen her curled up on his couch.

Laney melted against him, her fingers threading through the hair at his nape. Her mouth opened to his instantly, and Ryker didn't hesitate to take everything he wanted from her.

He wanted to devour her, wanted to take her into his bedroom and lay her flat out on his bed, taking his time the way he should've in Miami.

Laney was in his home, and this was one fantasy he'd had for way too long. No way in hell was he turning her away. He needed this. They needed this.

Before common sense or those red flags could wave too high, Ryker secured his hold around her waist, never breaking away from her lush mouth. He lifted her up, arousal bursting through him when she wrapped her legs around his waist.

"I didn't think you wanted me," she murmured against his lips.

Ryker spun and headed toward his bedroom. The sleep he'd needed moments ago was no longer on his radar.

"I never said that. Ever."

Laney nipped at his lips. "You push me away."

Ryker stopped, pulled away and looked into those engaging eyes. "Do you feel me pushing you away now?"

Her hips tipped against his as her ankles locked behind his back. "I wouldn't let you at this point. But what about tomorrow? Next week? What then, Ryker?"

On a sigh, he closed his eyes and rested his forehead against hers. "Right now, Laney. Let's concentrate on right now."

She hesitated a second longer than he was comfortable

with, but finally nodded. "I'm going to want answers, Ryker. I'm going to want to talk, not fight, about us."

About us. Those words terrified him and thrilled him at the same time. He'd worry about that conversation later. Right now he had the only woman he'd ever wanted in his bed actually here. He sure as hell wasn't going to talk, not when his emotions were raw. He had Laney and that was enough.

The second he crossed the threshold to his master suite, he hit the panel on the wall to close the blinds, encasing his room in darkness—much like the way he lived his life. Laney was the brightest spot he'd ever had, and he didn't need anyone to tell him he didn't deserve her, or their baby.

But heaven help him, he wanted both.

Laney tucked her face into the crook of his neck, her warm breath tickling him as he led her to his bed in the middle of the room. Easing down, he laid her on his rumpled sheets. He hadn't made a bed in…well, ever.

As much as he wanted to follow her down, he pulled back because he had a driving need to see her splayed out. He'd never brought another woman into his house, into his bed. If he thought too hard about this moment, he may let fear consume him, but he latched on to his need for Laney and shoved all else aside.

Her long shirt pulled against her breasts, her hair fanned out on his navy sheets and her eyes held so much desire, he didn't know if he was going to be able to take his time.

"If you are reconsidering, I'm going to kill you myself."

Ryker couldn't help but laugh. He reached behind his back and jerked his T-shirt over his head, flinging it across the room. Her eyes raked over his chest, his abs, lower. Pure male pride surged through him. He kept in shape and had never cared what anyone thought of him, not even his lovers, but he wanted Laney to care. He wanted her to…hell, he didn't know. There was nothing of worth in him, yet she wanted him. He was humbled and proud at the same time.

Laney sat up on the bed, pulling her shirt over her head as she went. Ryker was rendered speechless at the sight of her in a pale pink bra that did little to contain her full breasts. And when she reached behind her to unfasten it, staring up at him with those wide eyes, Ryker's control snapped.

With a need he couldn't identify, Ryker reached down and gripped the top of her leggings and panties. In one jerk he had them off and flung over his shoulder.

Laney lay back on his bed, a smug grin on her face. Ryker couldn't get his jeans unfastened fast enough.

"You think you've got me where you want me?" he asked, remembering he still needed to get his damn boots off.

She lifted one bare shoulder. "I've got you where you want to be."

No truer words were ever spoken.

After freeing himself from everything, he placed a knee on the bed beside her hip. Laney trailed her fingertips up his bare leg, sending shivers through him. Damn shivers. He was trying to keep some semblance of control here, but one touch from her and he was powerless.

Ryker glanced to her flat belly, worry lacing through him. He glanced up to see her smiling.

"It's fine," she assured him. "I promise."

He was clueless when it came to pregnancies or babies. Hell, he couldn't even deal with his own emotions, let alone care for another person. What was he thinking? Why was he letting his desire for Laney cloud his judgment?

"Hey." She reached for him, her fingers wrapping around his biceps. "Don't. Wherever you just went, come back. We'll deal with it later."

The war he'd battled with himself for years had no place right now. He couldn't deny her, couldn't deny himself. She was right. Whatever they needed to deal with could wait.

Laney eased her legs apart, tugging on him until he settled right where he needed to be. With his hands on either side of her head, he lowered onto his forearms so his hands could be free. He smoothed her hair away from her face, letting his fingers linger on her smooth skin.

"My scarred hands don't belong on you," he whispered, the words spilling from him before he could stop himself.

"I don't want anybody else's hands on my body," she purred, arching into him. "You're perfect."

Perfect. A word never associated with him before, let alone said aloud. Laney closed her eyes, blowing out a slow, shuddering breath. Ryker slid his body against hers, finally taking the time to appreciate how incredibly they fit together.

Laney flattened her palms against his back, urging him even closer. Her knees came up on either side of his hips as she let out a soft sigh. He couldn't take his eyes off her as he watched her arousal consume her. She could easily become a drug that kept him addicted forever.

But forever wasn't in his vocabulary. Forever wasn't a word for a man with his lifestyle.

"Tell me if I hurt you," he muttered. "I mean, with the baby…damn. I just don't—"

She leaned up, capturing his lips. "We're both fine."

Ryker captured her hips once more and rolled them over so she was straddling him and he was on his back. She sat straight up, her hands resting on his abdomen.

"I like this view better." He could look at it forever.

Damn that word for creeping into the bedroom again and making him want things he had no business wanting.

"You're letting me have control?" she asked, quirking her brow.

Ryker reached between them, rubbing his fingertip against her most sensitive part. Laney gasped, throwing her head back.

"I'm still in control, baby. Always."

Laney shifted, and in seconds settled over him, joining them, and Ryker's eyes nearly rolled back in his head. She was a vixen and she damn well knew it.

Her hips shifted, slowly. Too slow. Agonizingly slow. Enough.

Ryker gripped her hips between his hands and held her in place as he slammed into her at a feverish pace.

Laney's fingers curled into his bare skin, her nails biting into him. Perfect. This was what he'd missed. Her passion, her need for him that stirred something so deep within his chest, he refused to analyze it.

Laney tossed her head, her hair flying to cover part of her face. She clenched her eyes shut as her knees tightened against his sides. Ryker held his palm over her stomach a second before curling his fingers back around her side.

Mine.

The word slammed into him as Laney cried out her

release, and there was no stopping his now. Ryker's entire body trembled as he let go, Laney's pants only urging him on. He locked his eyes on her, shocked to find something in hers. Something much more than desire, much more than passion.

Damn it. Laney had love in her eyes. Love for a bastard who didn't deserve her, who'd betrayed her brothers. Love for a man who'd been told he was unlovable for the first twelve years of his life.

Ryker shut his eyes. He couldn't face this now. Not when he'd told her they'd talk later, not when he was feeling too damn exposed, and not when he knew there was no forever for them.

Eight

Monday morning had Laney heading to O'Shea's, the actual office in downtown Boston. Apparently there were some computer issues Braden needed fixed ASAP, per an employee's plea. Braden had told her this was top priority in an early-morning text.

Laney had only met the newest employee a handful of times, but based on what she'd seen of her and how she'd corresponded with her via emails and texts, Viviana was exactly the type of professional, poised person the business needed. The woman had been with them for nearly a year now and was proving to be an extremely loyal, trustworthy team member. She fit right in with the O'Shea family.

Laney let herself into the old building, which had been renovated into something of grand beauty back in the fifties. A few modern touches had been added to keep the ambiance up-to-date, and for security purposes, but overall, the building had been restored to its original grandeur. The old etched windows were kept, as well as the intricate trim and crown moldings. Scarred hardwood floors had been buffed and refinished to a dark, sparkling shine.

They wanted potential clients to feel at home. Because that's what O'Shea's was all about. Family.

Shaking off the cold, Laney turned and smiled at Viviana. The striking beauty was around the same age as Laney's brothers, but she could easily still be carded. She had glossy black hair, almost as if she had some Native American heritage. Her dark eyes and skin only showcased how gorgeous she was naturally.

"I nearly froze just walking in from my car," Laney stated, tugging off her gloves.

"Maybe I'll ask for a transfer to Mac's store in Miami," Viviana joked, her painted red lips parting in a stunning smile. "Just during the winter months. Boston can be brutal."

Laney nodded in agreement, recalling the snowstorm nearly a year ago when Braden and Zara ended up trapped together. Of course, if not for that storm, Zara may not be in the family now.

Laney couldn't imagine being trapped with Ryker. Actually, if their encounter two days ago was any indicator, their private time would be absolutely glorious. Maybe being trapped together would do them some good. Then he couldn't run away from what they shared and he'd have to listen to reason.

But Laney knew if they were alone, their clothes would be off and that would be the end of talking.

"We love you too much here to let you go," Laney replied, heading toward the back office. "Braden said the new program was giving you fits?"

Laney glanced at the framed images lining the walls. Ancestors in front of the store, some of her grandfather and father at the auction podium, another of her great-grandfather at his desk in the backroom...the same desk she was heading toward.

Viviana fell into step beside her. "I tried to go back through some records to find a piece we auctioned last spring in London, but the program shows a blank, like nothing was entered until two months ago."

Two months ago Laney had installed a simpler program; she'd put all the history of their auctions on there for easy access. Something was definitely wrong.

"Let me take a look." Laney moved into the spacious office and circled the antique desk her great-grandfather had found at an estate sale in Spain. This piece was part of O'Shea's history, passed down through generations. "Do you have any clients coming in this morning?"

Viviana crossed her arms over her plum suit jacket and shook her head. "Not today. I was hoping to get some pieces logged in to the system. We've already received quite a few framed pieces of artwork and several items from a recent estate sale Mac handled in Naples."

Laney settled into her comfort zone behind the screen. She pulled up the system she'd created and saw everything was up-to-date from the time she'd installed it. Then when she tried to retrieve backdated records, the files were completely empty. That was impossible. Everything should have been in chronological order just like she'd programmed.

"If you want to work, you can still get into the system

to add new items. You just can't go back." Laney didn't look up as she continued going from screen to screen to see what happened. All of her codes were still as they should be. "I'll let you know if I need you."

Laney's cell chimed from her purse, which was on the leather club chair beside the door. "Would you care to grab that for me?" she asked without looking up.

Scrolling down the screen, Laney dissected each and every entry she'd made. Nothing was off, but—

Wait. She scrolled back up. That couldn't be possible. She stared at the screen again.

"Something wrong?" Viviana asked.

Laney leaned closer to the computer, sure she was mistaken. But she didn't want to say anything to anyone until she could research things further. Braden would explode when he found out about the security breach. Still, she wanted to double-and triple-check everything before she went to him with this. There was no need to alarm anyone if she was misreading everything…but the odds of her being wrong were pretty much nil.

Her stomach turned. Who would hack into her system? Who had the balls big enough to go up against the O'Shea clan? How the hell had anyone gotten through all the security she'd installed?

The answer was simple. They weren't hacked. This was an inside job.

"Laney?"

Fury raged through her as she turned to look at Viviana, who held out Laney's phone. "You sure everything is okay?" she asked.

Laney nodded. "I think I've found the problem, but it's going to take some time to fix. I'm going to take this laptop with me. Can you use one of the others?"

Viviana's eyes widened for a second before she glanced around the office. "Of course. Is there anything I can do?"

Be on the lookout for the enemy?

"No. I've got it handled." Laney looked at her phone, still in Viviana's hand. "Oh, thanks."

She saw Ryker's name on the screen and opened the text. She'd left him sleeping the other night because she knew if she'd actually stayed, she'd want to spend every night there.

She had to make Ryker realize he wanted this. Perhaps if she wasn't so available, he'd ache for her the way she did for him. She wanted him so needy for her, so desperate to have her in his life, he'd ignore his demons and take a chance. She wasn't playing a game, she was simply opening his eyes to what they had.

Pulling up his message, she read:

We need to talk. Meet at Braden's now.

Laney closed the program and shut the laptop. "I need to go. Call me if you have any more issues, no matter how minor."

Viviana nodded and scooted back, and Laney headed toward the office door. "Of course."

Laney tossed her phone back into her bag. Pulling on her wrap coat, she knotted the ties before grabbing the laptop and sliding it into the side of her bag, as well.

"There haven't been any strange calls or emails, even from regular clients?" Laney asked as she slid the bag onto her forearm.

Viviana shifted, her head tipped as she glanced at the floor. "I can't recall any. It's pretty black and white here," she told Laney, looking back up. "You think someone has been messing with the system?"

"I think it's a possibility, and I want you to keep your eyes and ears open. Call me, not Braden or Mac, if you notice anything odd."

She'd figure out what was going on in the meantime.

"Of course," Viviana stated.

Laney headed through the main part of their office area and back out into the swirling snow. The streetlights lining each side of the street were decorated with simple, elegant evergreen wreaths with bright, cheery red bows. The garlands twisting around the poles ran from the wreath to the base. The city was battling the snowfall by keeping the sidewalks salted, the streets cleared. Laney absolutely loved her hometown of Beacon Hill and never wanted to be anywhere else.

As she climbed behind the wheel of her car, she wondered what Ryker wanted. Did he actually love Boston like she did, or did he love the lifestyle he led of traveling, going from one adventure to the next? Would he slow down, take fewer risks now that he was going to be a father?

Knowing Ryker...no. He would think he could do it all, as if he were invincible.

She headed toward her childhood home and pulled in behind Ryker's SUV. Large, menacing, just like the man himself. That whole dark, mysterious persona he oozed was so damn sexy, but there was infinitely more to Ryker. The layers that made up that man were tightly woven together, but she wasn't giving up on removing each one until she uncovered the very heart of him.

Grabbing her bag from the passenger seat, she got out of the car, careful where she stepped this time. Watching the ground before her gray boots, she started when a pair of black boots came into view.

"Easy." Ryker gripped her arms to steady her. "I came to make sure you didn't fall again."

Laney's heart flipped. She didn't want to keep sliding further in love with him, but there was no way to stop. Regardless of the baby, Laney loved Ryker. She'd love him even if they'd never kissed or slept together. Nothing could ever diminish her feelings for him.

"Well, startling me is not the way to go about helping."

Ryker took the bag from her arm and slid his other arm around her waist. "I wouldn't let you fall. Ever."

"If you keep tossing gallant gestures my way, I'm going to think you're trying to get all romantic."

Those dark eyes locked onto hers. "I don't do romance, Laney. I do reality."

Laney rolled her eyes. The reality was that she loved him, and he could ignore it all he wanted, but he had feelings for her, too. She wasn't offended by his words, not when his actions were booming louder than ever. Laney was optimistic that Ryker would come around... the question was how long would she give him before she finally told him how she truly felt? If she pulled out the cringe-worthy *L* word at this point, he'd sprint back into his steel shell and never come out again.

Ryker was vulnerable, not something she'd ever say to him or he'd ever admit, but the truth was glaring them both in the face. The don't-give-a-damn attitude, the rough exterior he offered to the world, wasn't who she saw. She looked beneath all of that and found the man he truly was...a kind, gentle and generous man with so much to give, one capable of so much love. It was a man he probably wasn't even aware existed. Or one he was battling to keep inside.

Regardless, Laney was about to rip his mask off and shove him in front of a mirror.

"Ankle okay today?" he asked.

"Just tender, but nothing I can't put weight on."

His arm didn't leave her waist, which was fine with her. She wanted his hands on her, and clearly he wanted them to be there.

"We have a problem."

Laney froze on the sidewalk, jerking her gaze up to his. "What?"

After the security breach, she didn't need more bad news. Dread curled in her stomach.

"We had a call from one of our contacts with the Bureau." Ryker ushered her toward the steps. "Let's get you inside. It's too cold out here."

"No." Laney placed a gloved hand on his chest. "First tell me what he wanted."

Ryker clenched his jaw. "Apparently someone is feeding them information. Intel only someone in our organization would know. They've discovered some pieces of art that are in our computer system, that only we have the log for. And I know you put those in like any other items we obtain legally, but they have a list of our back auctions."

Laney pulled in a breath, the air so cold her lungs burned. "This isn't a coincidence," she murmured.

Ryker's grip on her tightened. "What?"

"I have something on my laptop to show you guys. Let's get inside."

She could pull up any company document on a family computer, but she was most comfortable working with her own. She knew what documents and files to access right from the start. Time was of the essence.

As she turned, everything seemed to shift all at once. She tilted, thankfully against a firm, hard chest.

"Easy," Ryker told her, his arm around her waist tightening. "What happened?"

Laney held a hand to her head, shutting her eyes. "Just got a bit dizzy, that's all."

Before Laney could say another word, her world tilted again as she was swept up into Ryker's arms. "Put me down. I can walk."

"And I can carry you and your bag, so be quiet."

There it was. That emotion he held so hidden within him, one he didn't seem to recognize. If she thought for a second he didn't want her, she'd let it go. But when she saw a need in him, a need that matched her own, she couldn't ignore the facts...or let the best thing in her life slip right by because she was afraid to take a chance.

Laney wrapped her arms around his neck, nestling her face against the heat of his. She closed her eyes, relishing this pivotal moment. The baby would not be a tool in this path she was on to show Ryker how much she loved him, and that's not what this moment was about. Right now, he cared about her. He wasn't about to let her fall or get hurt. Laney only prayed by the time this was all said and done, that would still be the case.

She also refused to let him fall. She'd do anything to keep the man she loved safe. She was an O'Shea. The fact she was a female made no difference because she was brought up to be strong, fierce and resilient. Nothing could stop her from staking her claim.

"What happened?" Braden's worried tone brought her out of her thoughts. "Did she fall again?"

Ryker brushed by Braden and into the warmth of the house. "No. She started getting dizzy."

Ryker eased her down because it wasn't as if he could hold her forever. Shame that. Plus, if she clung to him too long, Braden would get the idea something was going on. Which reminded her that they were going to have to tell her brothers soon. Their unknown reactions terrified her.

"I'm fine," she assured them both, offering a smile. "See? Standing on my own two feet."

"Did you eat breakfast?" Braden asked, his brows still drawn together in worry. "Go sit in the living room, and I'll bring you something."

"No, no." She waved a hand, then opened the ties on her coat. "I ate. I must've just moved too fast, and with all that's going on with work, I'm just stressed."

Oops. Wrong choice of words. Ryker's eyes darkened, narrowed. His lips thinned.

"You'll be taking it easy. I'll make sure of it."

He delivered the threat in that low, sexy tone of his that left no room for argument. Laney merely nodded because now she was facing down two of the most alpha men she knew.

"Have a seat anyway," Braden told her, gesturing toward the living room.

Laney headed into the room that screamed Christmas: from the sparkly garland draped over the mantel, to the twelve-foot-tall noble fir standing proudly in front of the old windows, to the various candle stands, berries and other festive decor.

Quite the opposite of Ryker's house. Not one sprig of evergreen was to be seen there. A testament to what he came from. The child who didn't do Christmas had

turned into a man who didn't, and it was one of the sad-
dest things Laney had ever seen.

She took a seat on the high wing-back chair her mother
had fallen in love with at an estate sale when she and
Laney's father had first gotten married. Patrick O'Shea
had never been able to say no to his wife. Their love,
though cut too short in Laney's opinion, was something
Laney wanted. That love, the family, the bond was what
Laney dreamed of. And they weren't little girl dreams.
She was going into this situation with Ryker knowing
full well she could get hurt, but the chance of a love and
family of her own was worth the risk.

Weren't O'Sheas built on all the risks they'd taken?
A challenge was never avoided, but met head-on. And
conquered.

"Ryker told me you had a call from the Bureau," she
started, not wanting to waste any time. "I don't know
what all you found out, but Viviana's problem at the office was the system's backlog. I was looking into that
when I got Ryker's text."

Ryker leaned one broad shoulder against the mantel, crossing his arms over his chest. "Tell me what you
found."

Braden remained standing as well, right by the leather
sofa across from her. The tension in the room was palpable.

"When I go into the records, there is nothing showing from before I changed systems," she explained. "Everything should be in the files I added by year and then
broke down into months. Before October, there is nothing."

"Define nothing," Braden said between gritted teeth.

Laney faced him, staring into eyes exactly like her

own, exactly like their father's. "Not one document is on there. Don't worry, I have backups of everything at home. I'm not sloppy, Braden."

"I never said you were, but what the hell is going on and what does this have to do with my call from the Feds?"

"When I first started digging to see what happened, it appeared someone hacked into our system. But that would be virtually impossible."

There was no easy way to deliver such a statement, so she went for it.

"The only way someone could access the system is if they work for us. My security is so tight—"

"Not tight enough," Braden growled.

Laney straightened her back, squared her shoulders.

"Chill, Braden." Ryker's warning couldn't be ignored. "Respect."

Braden turned his attention across the room. "She's my sister, I can damn well say what I want."

"No, you can't." Ryker's sneer even made Laney shiver. "She's the best programmer I've ever met, and I know some shady bastards."

Even though she could've handled herself, and her brother was justifiably angry, Ryker's quick defense warmed her. He'd always protected her, but he'd never spoken back to Braden in such a manner.

"Who the hell are you to tell me?" Braden countered. "We may be facing a real issue here, not to mention the scrolls are who knows where. But the Feds are on our back and our system was hacked? Doesn't take a genius to figure out we have a mole."

The idea horrified Laney. They were so careful about who they hired. The background checks were extensive, their training and "babysitting" period was just as meticulous. Now the question was how did they narrow their search down to one office? They had branches all over the globe. Their main one, of course, was in Boston, and a year ago one opened in Miami and in Atlanta.

Could the traitor be one of the employees down South?

"We need to warn Mac," she stated, thinking aloud. "He needs to start scouring his crew while we look at ours. We clearly should start with our US locations. I doubt the threat is coming from overseas. That wouldn't make any sense."

Braden nodded. "I agree. What I want to know is how someone fractured your system."

Laney rubbed her forehead, wondering the same thing. Closing her eyes, she willed the slight dizziness to pass. Maybe she should get some orange juice or something in her stomach.

"I'm going to figure that out." Laney eased back in the chair, rested her elbow on the arm and opened her eyes. "I took one of the laptops from the office, and I plan on looking through its history. I'll do the same for the rest of them."

Braden's hardened gaze held hers. "I love you, Laney. I'm not doubting you. I'm shocked, actually. We've never had this kind of breach before, and the last thing I need is the Feds sniffing around."

Since Braden had taken over after their father's passing, the O'Sheas had been moving into more legitimate territory—which meant staying off the radar of the law. To her full knowledge, they'd been so careful. Minus Ryker and Shane's incident, there wasn't anything that she knew of that would cause this level of scrutiny...well, she still didn't know what happened to her ex.

What a mess. Having the Feds involved did not bode well for the O'Sheas.

"I promise you, there won't be a problem. I'll get this fixed, and we'll find out who the snitch is."

She risked a glance at Ryker, who looked even more menacing than usual. Those dark lashes fanned out over coal-like eyes, his hard-set jaw was clenched, his arms were crossed over that impossibly broad chest. Ryker was pissed, and she only prayed she could get to the bottom of this betrayal before he took matters into his own hands.

Nine

Laney had just grabbed a bottle of water when her front
door slammed. Because she lived in an old brownstone,
she didn't have that whole open-concept thing going on.
She liked her rooms cozy and blocked off into desig-
nated areas.

"Hello?" she called as she made her way to the front
of her house.

She wasn't too concerned about an intruder, considering she had alarms, cameras and an insane security
system she knew her brother and Ryker had paid quite a
bit for. They'd insisted on making sure she was safe the
second she moved out of the O'Shea mansion.

The bottle crinkled in her hand as she stopped in the
entryway to her living room.

"What are you doing here?"

Without taking his eyes off her, Ryker jerked out of

his leather jacket and tossed it onto the couch. "I'm making sure you're okay, and then I'm helping you get to the bottom of this damn mess."

Nerves stirred in her stomach. He was here because he cared, and he was here for work. Their worlds collided on so many levels, there was no way she could find separation.

"I'm fine."

"You were dizzy earlier, then you weren't feeling well when you were talking with Braden."

Laney twisted the cap on her bottle of water and took a drink. He hadn't made a move to come in any farther, but clearly he was staying since he'd taken off his coat. This was becoming a habit…one she would gladly build on.

"I was feeling a little light-headed while we were talking. It passed."

"You're not driving anymore."

Laney screwed the lid back on and cocked her head, sure she'd heard wrong. "Excuse me?"

Now he moved, like a panther to its prey. He crossed to her until they stood toe to toe, causing her to tip her head back to meet his intense, heavy-lidded gaze.

"You heard me."

"I did," she agreed. "I'm giving you the chance to choose different words."

A hint of a smile danced around those kissable lips. "I'm not backing down on this, Laney. Until your dizzy spells pass, I'll be your chauffeur."

Even though she knew he wouldn't back down, Laney waited a minute to see if he wanted to add anything…or retract such a ridiculous statement.

Finally, when he said nothing, Laney stepped around him and headed toward the corner of the sectional she'd been cozied up in. Well, as cozy as one could be while working on discovering who hacked into her family's computer system. Clearly the O'Sheas were smarter than to have all of their skeletons exposed for anyone to see. But there were items, especially in the past when her father was at the helm, that could be looked at twice. Some may find their "mysterious" auction pieces to be a red flag, considering the majority of them had been reported stolen.

Laney eased back into the curve of the couch and picked up the laptop she'd laid to the side.

"Glaring at me and using this whole silent predator vibe definitely will not change my mind," she told him without looking at him. She typed in the password for the laptop. "So, did you want anything else? Or are you ready to move on to work?"

Laney had just pulled up the system, but before she could go any further, a delicate pewter ornament appeared between her and the screen. Jerking her eyes up to his, she gasped.

"What is that?" She looked back to the ornament. "I mean, I know what it is, but—"

Well, damn. There she went, tearing up. She hated all these pregnancy-induced crying jags.

She reached out to take the likeness of a woman wrapping her arms around her swollen belly. The simple pewter ornament would look absolutely perfect on her white-and-silver tree. She clutched it against her chest.

But when she looked back up, Ryker glanced away, shoving his hands in his pockets. "I wasn't sure what to get. I mean, I didn't set out to get anything, but I was passing by that Christmas shop near the office."

"All Seasons."

He nodded. "Yeah. I knew you liked that place since you mention it every year."

Her favorite little shop because they literally transformed their store into a completely different place depending on the season. She could spend a fortune in there…and she had. A fact he well knew because he'd taken her there a few times when he felt she was in danger of being in public alone. Of course he'd kept his brooding self out front or waiting in the car at the curb.

"They have a tree in the window that reminded me of yours, and it caught my eye," he went on. He looked at his feet, the wall, the tree…anywhere but at her. "Then I saw this and…"

How adorable was he, being all nervous? This was definitely a side of Ryker Barrett she'd never seen before. Laney set the laptop aside and came to her feet. Tears flooded her eyes as she held tight to this precious gift.

She slid her arms around his neck, tucking her face against his. "This might be the sweetest thing anyone has ever got me."

Slowly he returned her embrace, and Laney wanted to sink into him. "You deserve more," he whispered into her ear.

She knew he wasn't talking monetary items. Ryker could buy her an island and a private jet to get there if he wanted. There was a fear in Ryker that allowed him to touch her, yet not get too emotionally involved. He felt he didn't deserve her, but she was just getting started in proving him wrong. He was everything she deserved.

"This doesn't mean you're driving me," she muttered.

Ryker laughed. The vibrating sensation bounced off her chest. "We'll talk about that later."

There wasn't going to be a later for that particular

topic, but he'd find out soon enough. They didn't have time to argue.

Laney pulled back, kissed him briefly, then shifted from his hold. Crossing the room to the tree, she hung her ornament right in the center, then stepped back to look at how perfectly it fit.

"I love it," she said, turning. "You didn't have to get me a gift, but it's my new favorite decoration."

Ryker nodded, which was about as much of a reaction as she was going to get from him.

"Now, we need to get to work because whoever is fighting us has chosen the wrong family to mess with."

Before she could settle back onto the couch, Ryker's arm snaked out and wrapped around her waist, pulling her against his hard chest. He closed the space between them, covering her mouth with his. Heat, instant and all-consuming, swept over her as she wrapped her arms around his neck.

All too willingly, she opened to him. He eased her back slightly, keeping his hold on her tight, protective. Laney threaded her fingers through his hair, wishing they didn't have to work, wishing they could go to her bedroom and use this kiss as a stepping-stone to something much more erotic and satisfying.

When he pulled back, nipping at her lips, Laney waited for him to say something…anything.

"I'm not complaining," she started when he remained silent. "But what's going on between us? You keep me in your bed the other day, you buy me the sweetest gift ever and now you kiss me like your next breath depended on it."

Ryker's hands slid to her hips where he held her still. "I have no idea," he stated on a sigh. "I can't put a label on this. I only know I did want you in my bed all day, I knew you had to have that ornament and just now my next breath did depend on kissing you."

Laney stared into his dark eyes, eyes that had terrified many enemies. Eyes she'd fallen in love with when she'd been only a teen. She'd seen him come and go many times while she'd been in high school. While her friends were out at the malls or movies with other boys, Laney was home waiting on Ryker to show for a meeting with her father. She'd get a glimpse of him as he'd come into the house. When she was lucky, he'd turn his gaze toward her, meet her with that intense stare for a half second before moving on to the study.

That split second had been worth skipping a night out with her friends.

"Don't fight whatever is happening," she told him. "And don't be afraid of it."

Ryker grunted. "I'm not afraid of anything, Laney. I think you know that."

Again, she wasn't going to argue. They didn't have the time. But he was so terrified of his feelings, he refused to even acknowledge them. Or perhaps he didn't even know they existed.

She eased back into her seat, set her water bottle on the cushion next to her and pulled the laptop back into her lap. Ryker grabbed the large ottoman from the accent chair and pushed it in front of her.

"Put your feet up."

Laney waited a second, but he merely raised a brow and continued to glare. Okay, no point in arguing. Propping her feet up, she started pecking at the keys. Ryker stood.

"It's going to be a while, maybe even days. Might as well have a seat."

"We don't have days."

Laney prayed she would find something that would lead them in the right direction. "You think I don't know that, Ryker?" She didn't even bother to spare him a glance as she worked. Time was of the essence—the only reason she didn't pursue that kiss. "I'm an O'Shea, a glaring fact my brothers and you often forget. I know what's at stake."

Laney ignored the silence as she scrolled through code after code. Let Ryker process her words because it was rather ridiculous how they attempted to keep her sheltered at all times, but expected her to twinkle her nose at the first sign of a computer problem. She wasn't naive; she knew exactly what her family did, what they stood for. She also knew Braden was doing his best to make sure they kept their reputation impeccable within the auction world while cleaning up their act on the legal side. Well, as much as it could be cleaned up. She knew Ryker had done things at her father's request…

She shut her eyes, forcing away any mental images. A shudder rippled through her.

"Laney?"

Instantly he was at her side. Sure. Now he chose to take a seat.

"I'm fine," she assured him. "Just a chill."

More like a clench to her heart. That was the part of her family's past she preferred to keep under wraps. She knew there were justifiable reasons for their actions, she even knew there were times it was self-defense. She'd been fifteen years old when she'd overheard a twenty-five-year-old Ryker describing a trip to Sydney to her father. Ryker had been telling Patrick about a guard who'd attacked him with a knife. Laney recalled standing on the landing of the house, curled up on the floor and holding on to the banisters in the dark. At that moment, she'd realized how dangerous Ryker's job truly was and what he put on the line for her family.

"I don't know how the hell you comprehend all that," Ryker muttered.

Laney kept scrolling, slowly, looking for any hint as to how their security had been breached. She knew the threat was on the inside. Which meant if she had to access every employee's computer, she damn well would.

Her mind kept returning to the timing. The newest stores had been opened a year ago in Miami and Atlanta. The Boston office had been around since the beginning. Where was the mole more likely to be?

Laney didn't know how long she searched. Losing track of time was an occupational hazard. Her stomach growled, and she waited for Ryker to make some snarky comment, but when he remained silent, she glanced over. The man was out. Head tipped back on the cushion, face totally relaxed. Laney wasn't sure she'd ever seen him this peaceful, this calm.

When Ryker was in work mode, which was nearly every time she saw him, he was hard, intense, focused. When they were intimate, well…he was exactly the same way.

Laney's hands went lax on the keyboard as she studied his facial features. His brows weren't drawn in, his mouth was parted just slightly, as if waiting for a lover's kiss, black lashes fanned over his cheeks. She could study him forever.

Forever. If she even said that word to him he'd build yet another wall to protect himself.

Without tearing her eyes away from him, Laney slid the computer off her lap and onto the cushion beside her. She tipped her head back on the cushion as well, needing just another minute of this. One more minute of nothing but Laney and Ryker. There was no outside world, there was no issue with work and there was no fear of telling her brothers that she was expecting Ryker's baby.

Given how fiercely he protected her, Laney knew he would be an amazing father. He doubted himself, but she'd be right there showing him how perfect he was. She wasn't experienced at being a mother, but she knew love. Between her love and his protection, their child would have everything.

Laney bit her lip to keep from tumbling into that emotional roller coaster that seemed to accompany pregnancy. She shifted her thoughts to what their baby would look like. Dark hair for sure since they both had black hair. But would the eyes be green or coal-like? Would Ryker's strong jawline get passed down?

Suddenly those coal-black eyes were fixed on hers. "How long are you going to stare at me?"

Ten

"You scared me to death," she scolded him, swatting his arm. He lifted his lids and couldn't help but smile.

Ryker had known the second Laney had stopped working. He'd heard her stomach growl and was about to say something, when he'd felt her shift. The sudden awareness of her eyes on him had him holding still. He'd felt the slightest dip in the cushion next to his head, and he wondered what she'd been thinking.

Then he'd worried where her thoughts were. He knew Laney had dreams of a big family. She had that innocence about her that would cling to romance and love. She had hope. He'd lost that when he'd been in diapers.

"Find anything?"

Laney kept resting her head on the cushion next to his. "Nothing new. We've already established that it was an inside job. Braden doesn't like hearing that one of his employees is a mole, but we have to find out who it is before they cause more damage."

Rage burned in his gut. There wouldn't be a hole deep enough for this bastard to hide.

"Don't." Laney's hand slid up his forearm. "I'm furious, too, but don't let it ruin this moment. I just want a minute more of no threats, just us."

Us.

"We're always threatened." Unable to resist, Ryker flipped his hand over and shifted to lace their fingers together. "The authorities who aren't on our side are always looking for things to pin on us. On me."

Laney closed her eyes. Ryker hated this. Hated wanting her with an ache that was indescribable. Hated that he couldn't have her fully because of who he was. Hated most of all that he was the one who put worry into that beautiful life of hers.

"I can't stand the thought of you being hurt, being a target." She met his gaze once again. The fear in those eyes gutted him. "I've known for years how much you put at stake, but now it's different."

"The baby—"

"And me." She leaned forward, resting her forehead against his. "Before the baby, before Miami. I started falling for you."

He'd known. Hell, he'd known for years, but hearing her say the words seemed so official and real. He couldn't have her committing herself to him. There was no future for them as a couple, only as parents to this innocent child. That's all they could share.

But, damn it, he couldn't hurt her. He couldn't reject this gift she'd just presented. Laney was everything perfect and pure in his life. She was that place in his mind he went to when he was on assignment and the world around him turned ugly. She'd been his salvation for so long…but telling her that would only give her false hope.

"I know you don't want to hear those words." She eased back, leaving Ryker feeling cold. "But I can't lie to you."

He didn't know what to say, so like a complete moron, he said nothing. Laney shoved her hair away from her face and turned to get her laptop, instantly diving back into her work. The moment was gone.

Ryker reached over, gripping her hand beneath his. Her fingers stilled on the keys. She kept her eyes on the screen, her throat bobbed as she swallowed. Nerves were getting to her, he needed to at least reassure her…what? What the hell could he say? Ryker had no idea, all he knew was he wanted that helpless look gone.

"I'm out of my element here, Laney." He decided to go with honesty. "You've been part of my life for so long, but—"

"I know," she whispered.

How could she know when he didn't know himself?

"No, you don't." Damn it, he needed to make her understand. "You can't possibly know what I feel. You have no clue what those words mean to me."

Her head dropped as she pulled in a deep breath. "I know you better than you think," she said quietly.

Silence settled heavily around them. Ryker had never been this close to a woman. He'd had lovers, mostly when he traveled and needed a stress reliever. The possibility of a serious relationship had never entered his mind. It had no place in his life.

"I know who you are," she went on, still not looking his way. "I've known all along."

Now she did turn, those vibrant green eyes piercing him right to his soul. Until now he hadn't even been aware he had one.

"I know full well why you're trying to keep me at a distance. I'm not backing down, Ryker. You need to know that I intend to fight for what I want, and I want you."

Laney's words should have terrified him. But damn if her fire wasn't the sexiest thing he'd ever seen.

"I'll consider myself warned."

Her eyes narrowed. "If we weren't in so deep with this traitor mess, I'd show you right now how much I love you. That will have to wait."

Ryker's body stirred. He'd never put his work second to anything or anyone before…but right at this moment he was seriously considering doing just that.

"Get that look out of your eyes." She laughed. "How about I keep working and you go see what you can find in the kitchen?"

Ryker came to his feet. "Because I'm all for equal rights, I'll cook for you. But I expect you to open doors for me and buy me flowers."

Laney laughed, the exact response he was hoping for. He couldn't handle tension…not with her.

"That wasn't sexist at all," she said, grabbing a throw pillow and smacking him.

That smile lighting up her face never failed to warm him in spots only she could touch. Guilt slammed through him. There was no way in hell Braden and Mac were going to allow their baby sister to have a relationship with Ryker, even if he thought he could risk it. No, Laney's brothers were looking out for her, and they would be justified by telling her *hell no* when it came to Ryker.

Baby or not, the O'Shea brothers wouldn't budge in

this area. They'd had him follow Laney's boyfriends over the years. Ryker had investigated worthless jerks, and he'd scared off the ones who posed any threat to Laney or the O'Sheas in general. Each time he'd had to intervene, Ryker had selfishly felt relieved that Laney wasn't going to be with some jerk any longer.

Now here he was taking that role…and Mac and Braden were going to have to be the ones to talk some sense into Laney because he sure as hell had no willpower where she was concerned.

And she was wrong. This baby did change everything. Ryker knew he'd never be the same again.

Dinner consisted of chips, salsa and, surprisingly, a taco salad. Apparently Ryker's favorite food was Mexican, and he'd made it happen. She hadn't known those ingredients were in her kitchen, but Ryker had worked a miracle and produced something amazing.

Hours later, Laney's eyes were crossing. She closed the laptop and glanced across to Ryker, who was on his phone, leaning against her newly decorated mantel.

"I'm waving the white flag," she told him around a yawn.

He straightened, shoving his cell in his pocket. "It's nearly one in the morning. You need to sleep."

"What about you? You need sleep, too."

Looking at him in her living room, all dark and menacing, he actually seemed to fit. Amid the sparkling tree, the garland, the Nutcrackers and especially the new ornament, Ryker worked perfectly in her living room, in her life. He'd been a sport and had hung the rest of her ornaments and even added the newly fluffed wreath to her front door. He did draw the line sprinkling the iridescent glitter across the silver and white decor on her mantel..

But he'd stayed. He'd brought her living room to life with Christmas, made dinner and put the empty storage boxes back in her attic. There was something to be said about a man who put his woman's needs first. And she was his woman. He'd figure that out on his own soon enough.

Ready to make good on that promise to fight for what she wanted, Laney set the laptop to the side and came to her feet.

"You need sleep, too," she repeated, slowly closing the space between them. "It would be ridiculous to go out in this weather."

His half-lidded perusal of her body from head to toe and back up sent shivers racing over her, through her. The man's stare was nearly as potent as his touch. She practically felt him when he licked his lips as if she were a buffet. And he could devour her anytime he wanted.

"I'm not afraid of snow," he told her.

Taking a risk that the hunger in his eyes was his weakness, Laney gripped the hem of her shirt and pulled it over her head, tossing the garment to the side. His eyes remained fixed on her, exactly where she wanted them.

"But why take the chance?" she asked, reaching around to unhook her bra.

In a flash, Ryker reached out, wrapping those strong hands around her upper arms. For a second she feared he was going to stop her. Then she focused on his face. Clenched jaw, thin lips, desire staring back at her.

"You want me to stay?" he growled. "Then I'll be the one doing this."

He tore away her bra, jerked down her pants and panties. She had to hold on to those broad shoulders as he yanked the material over her feet. Standing bare before him sent another thrill through her. He stood back up, his hands roaming up the sides of her body, over the dip in her waist, cupping her breasts. His thumbs brushed against their peaks.

Laney couldn't help but lean into his touch. But then his hands moved back down. His hands covered her stomach.

"No matter what happens with us, this is all that matters. I'll do everything to protect our baby."

Laney nodded. There was so much uncertainty between them, but the baby's security was top priority. Until the arrival of their child, Laney would show him just how much she loved him, how much he deserved to be loved.

"If that means you have to move to my house in London, then you'll do it." She started to say something, but his hard eyes stopped her. "I'm serious, Laney. We don't know what we're dealing with, and I'll be damned if I take a chance with our baby."

Fear fueled his words. She knew this unknown threat had him as worried as the rest of them. Now was not the time to bang her chest and be all independent. They were a team.

"I promise," she whispered as she went up onto her toes to slide her lips over his. "Anything you want."

Ryker's hands shifted to her backside. Pulling her flush against his fully clothed body, he growled. "I want to take you up those stairs and keep you locked in your bedroom naked for the next week."

Oh, if only...

"But all I can promise is right now."

He kept saying that. All of these "right now" moments were adding up. Did he notice? He would. One day he'd wake up to the fact they were it for each other. Laney dared her brothers to even try to stop her happiness.

"Then show me," she muttered a split second before his mouth came crashing down onto hers.

He lifted her with ease, carrying her toward the staircase as his lips demanded everything from her…and promised so much more. As if she weighed nothing at all, he took the four steps onto the landing. Just when she expected to feel him turn and head the rest of the way up, he stopped. Laney tore her mouth away, ready to ask him what he was doing, but she found herself being eased onto the built-in, cushioned bench.

She tipped her head back to peer up at him, the soft light from the lamp in the living room casting a perfect yellow rim around his frame. She had no idea what he intended to do, but he reached behind his neck and jerked his T-shirt over his head. After he tossed it behind him, he quickly rid himself of his black boots, sending them back down the steps with a heavy thunk.

Laney couldn't take her eyes off that impressive chest. Spattered with dark hair, a scar over his left pec and a tattoo of a menacing dragon over his right, Ryker was all man…and he was still stripping.

"This is the best show I've ever been to."

The snap to his jeans popped open, he drew the zipper down, all without taking his eyes from hers. "I don't want to hear about the time you and your friends went to Poppycocks."

Laney gasped. "You know about that?"

"Baby, I know everything about you, and I sure as hell am not getting into this now, nor are we discussing the fact I had to do damage control with your father and tell him you were at the mall."

Laney bit her lip to keep from laughing because Ryker clearly didn't find the humor in her sneaking into a male strip club when she was only seventeen. Those fake IDs she'd made for herself and her friends as a joke had come in handy.

Laney opted to keep her mouth shut and enjoy the view as Ryker ridded himself of the rest of his clothes. Unable to keep her hands still, she reached out. She needed to touch him, explore him. Every time they were together her ache for him grew.

Ryker took her hands before she could touch him. Jerking her to her feet, he tugged her until she fell against him.

"I'm calling the shots here. No touching."

Laney quirked a brow. "Then this night is a total bust if I can't put my hands on you."

Strong arms banded around her waist, and instantly she was lifted once again. Laney wrapped her legs around him as he continued up to the second story.

"I'll tell you when you can touch me," he ordered. "I'm going to lay you down and do this right. We're always in a hurry."

Laney rested her head against his shoulder. "Does this mean you're staying all night?"

He reached the double doors to her bedroom and shouldered them open. Looking down into her eyes, Ryker nodded. "I'm staying. Saying no to you is becoming impossible. I don't know what the hell that means, but for now, I'm staying."

Laney knew exactly what that meant. It meant Ryker was hers, and he was finally, *finally* coming around.

Eleven

Ryker rolled over in bed. The canopy with white sheers draped all around the posts was definitely not his bed. This was Laney's world, a world she'd graciously let him into.

No. Scratch that. A world she'd woven him into, and he was getting to the point where he wasn't sure if he ever wanted to leave. It would be the smart thing to do, but he had needs, damn it…and he wasn't just talking physical.

He had no clue what time it was, but the sun wasn't up yet. The soft glow from Laney's phone had him squinting to see what she was looking at.

Baby furniture. Something twisted in his gut. All this time he'd been worried about their safety, about how he'd handle Mac and Braden. The reality was this child would need things. Probably lots of things he had no damn clue about. But he'd learn. He refused to be a deadbeat dad like his had been. Ryker would go out of his way to make sure his child, and the mother of his child, was comfortable and wanted for nothing.

Ryker slid an arm around Laney's waist, flattening his palm on her stomach. "I'll buy whatever you want," he murmured, nuzzling the side of her neck.

The warmth of her body penetrated him, never failing to warm areas that had been iced over for years.

"I can get the things for the nursery." She scrolled through a variety of white cribs. "I really want yellow and white, no matter the sex. I can always add accent pieces once we find out what we're having."

Ryker swallowed. This was a conversation he never, ever thought he'd be having...especially with his best friends', his *employers'*, little sister.

"Do you care what we have?" Laney turned her head slightly to look at him.

Ryker eased back. "I hadn't thought about it, actually."

Blowing out a soft breath, she turned back toward her phone. "No, I'd say you haven't. This isn't something that excites most men, and when you weren't wanting a baby at all—"

Ryker lifted enough to roll her beneath him until she was on her back and staring up at him. He rested his hands on either side of her head.

"A baby may not have been on my radar before now, but that doesn't mean even for a second that I'm not excited about this life, Laney."

Her face lit up. Her brows rose, a smile spread on her lips. "You're excited?"

Hell. He hadn't realized he was excited until he'd said the words aloud.

"I am. I'm scared as hell, though. I haven't thought

about the sex because it doesn't matter to me." Ryker kissed her softly. "All that matters is you two are safe, healthy, happy. That's my goal here, Laney."

Cupping the side of his face, she stared back at him. Her brows were drawn in, the happiness in her face vanished.

"I'm scared for you," she murmured. "When Braden and Mac—"

He silenced her with his lips. "I'm not worried about them."

"They won't like this." She blinked as moisture gathered in her eyes. "They'll blame you, and I've been half in love with you my whole life, and Miami was—"

"Amazing." He nipped at her lips, her chin, along her jawline. "Miami had been coming for a long time. There was no way I could've avoided you forever."

The screen on her phone went dim, plunging the room into darkness. He settled perfectly between her spread thighs.

"I can resist many things in this world, but you're not one of them." He ran his lips along the side of her neck as she arched her body against his. "I'm only human, Laney. And I can only ignore my body for so long. I've told you before, I'm a selfish bastard."

"No, you're not. You're one of the most giving people I know." Her arms and legs encircled him as he slid into her. "You know this is more than just the baby and chemistry between us, right?" she asked.

Ryker stilled for a second before moving his hips slowly. "I can admit that, yes. But beyond that, let's just—"

"I know. Concentrate on now." She returned his thrust

with a quicker pace. "I'm all for what's happening right now."

But they would get back to this topic later, he knew.

Ryker framed her face between his hands again and covered her mouth with his. He'd never wanted to take his time like this, never wanted to enjoy the process of getting to the climax. Fast and frantic had been just fine with him. Slow, passionate…that meant getting more emotionally involved.

And God help him, he had plunged headfirst into this…whatever this was…with Laney.

Her nails bit into his back. She opened her mouth fully for him, completely taking him in every way she could. There was a fire, a burning for her that hadn't been there before. The all-consuming need he'd had in the past was nothing compared to right here, right now. She was taking him and wrapping him into her perfect world where she believed such things as love actually existed.

Ryker tore his mouth from hers, ran his lips down her neck, to one perfect breast. Her hands came up to his head, as if to hold him in place. Her soft gasps only fueled him further to make sure she had everything she wanted.

"Ryker…"

He eased back, then pushed forward hard. Once, twice. Her entire body shuddered beneath his. It was almost too much to bear as Laney cried out his name, arched beneath him and came undone all around him.

And it was all Ryker needed to follow her over the edge.

The papers for the new property had been signed a few days ago, the contractor had been hired and Laney couldn't wait to get her hands dirty and dig into the process of renovating the old, neglected building in Southie.

Right now, though, she was having a difficult time breathing in the damn dress she'd purchased for O'Shea's annual Christmas party. She'd thought it was fine in the store, but, the overflowing cleavage and the slight pull of the emerald green satin at her waist gave her pause. She hadn't noticed her midsection getting any larger, she was only eight weeks pregnant now, but something had happened overnight because she was seriously worried about popping that side zipper.

"Being so gorgeous and built like that should make me hate you."

Laney spun to see Jenna, her arm looped through Mac's. Crossing the ballroom, Laney threw her arms out wide.

"I'm so glad you guys made it in." She hugged her brother before turning to Jenna, taking in the gorgeous red dress that highlighted her curves. "Like you're one to talk. You look stunning."

Jenna had a voluptuous figure, not model-thin like some women felt they needed to be. Jenna was a beautiful woman and looked even more striking now that she was in love. Mac, Laney's globe-trotting playboy brother, had finally been tamed by his best friend when he had to pose as her fiancé. Laney would've given anything to see the moment her brother realized Jenna was the one. She had seen this coming for years and couldn't be happier for the two of them.

"I was worried the snow would delay you all getting here."

Mac shrugged. "I checked the area before I took off."

Her brother doubled as a pilot. "I was confident we'd be safe. If not, we could've gone into DC and rented a car."

"He'll fly in almost anything," Jenna joked. "He's had me white-knuckling it more than once, but he assures me he has everything under control."

Mac's pilot's license came in handy since he hated Boston winters and was now living it up in Miami.

"Next year I vote we move this party to my house," he suggested. "Too damn cold up here."

"Are you complaining already?" Braden stepped into the room, Zara by his side. He slapped Mac's shoulder. "You haven't been in town an hour and already a hater."

Laney noticed Zara scanning the room and tuned out her brothers' banter. "I came a little early and made sure all the centerpieces were set up like we'd discussed. I hope you like them."

Her sister-in-law smiled. "They're beautiful."

"You're beautiful," Laney countered. "That gold dress is perfect on you."

"I think we all look amazing." Zara continued to look around, her brows drawn in a frown. "Is Ryker here? I thought he told Braden he'd be here early."

Laney's heart quickened. It had been several days since he spent the night in her bed. He'd gone out of town on business to acquire some authentic pieces for the spring auction. He'd only gone to Toronto, then to Chicago, but she hated not knowing he was in town. Not that she ever felt at risk, but she definitely felt safer knowing he was around.

"He's in the study," Braden stated. "He…had to take a call."

A call? Why had Braden hesitated? Laney knew Ryker's personal life was technically none of her business, but she still wanted to know what was going on. And if Braden had been in the study with Ryker, then the call was most likely business…in which case she still wanted to know.

"The room looks amazing," Jenna said as she pulled away from Mac's side and started walking around. "The lights, the tables, all of it looks magical. You all really know how to treat your employees."

"Loyalty deserves to be rewarded," Mac stated simply. "And O'Shea's wouldn't throw a cheap party."

"Neither would I," Zara chimed in. "I totally use you all to boost my own company."

Braden smiled, leaned down to kiss his wife on the head. "You do an incredible job. You don't need us."

Her brothers had found two amazing women to share their lives with. Laney wanted to tell them all about the pregnancy, but she wasn't ready. Beyond the fact that she worried how they'd treat Ryker, Laney wanted to tell Zara privately so she didn't have to absorb the news around others. Zara would most likely be elated, but Laney didn't want to take any chances. The miscarriage was still fresh, but did that loss and ache ever really go away?

Laney prayed she never had to find out.

She pulled in a breath, as much as her dress would allow. "I'll be right back."

She wasn't going to make up an excuse to leave the room. The guests weren't due to arrive for another hour, so her presence wasn't needed at the moment.

The foursome continued talking as the caterers entered through the side doors to set up the food tables in the back of the room. Laney saw her chance to slip out. She headed toward the wide, curved staircase and made her way up to the study. Nobody would think twice about her and Ryker talking.

Once she reached the landing, she glanced over her shoulder to see that she was still alone. She didn't hear Ryker on the phone as she approached the study, then she realized the door was closed. Laney turned the knob slowly as she pushed the door open a crack. When she peeked inside, she didn't see Ryker on the phone at all. His hands were on the desk, his back to the door, his head bowed.

Opening the door wider, Laney let herself in. Her heels were quiet on the carpet, but the shift in the full skirt of her dress pulled Ryker straight up. He spun and froze. Laney stilled, as well.

She'd seen him in a tux before, but something about seeing him now that she knew him so intimately…damn, he was one sexy man. His all-black tux played up the menacing male he was on a daily basis, but the expensive cut screamed money and class. Ryker was every type of fantasy man wrapped into one delicious package.

And something was troubling him. His tight face, clenched jaw and worried eyes stared back at her.

"What's wrong?"

Shaking his head, he pushed off the desk and walked toward her. "Nothing now that you showed up wearing this killer dress."

As much as her ego appreciated his approval, she wasn't letting his compliments distract her from digging deeper.

"Tell me." She stepped back when he stood right before her. Touching him now would get them nowhere… except naked, which was a bad idea, considering her family was downstairs. "Something happened."

Raking a hand over the back of his neck, Ryker blew out a sigh. "Nothing for you to worry about."

When he reached for her, Laney held up her hands. "No. You're not blowing me off. I do worry, Ryker. It's what happens when you care about someone."

"It's just work, nothing I can't handle." He moved lightning-fast and wrapped his arms around her, pulling her body flush with his. "You didn't tell me you'd look so damn sexy tonight. I'm going to have a hard time keeping my hands to myself."

Laney wanted his hands all over her, but she also wanted to know what he was hiding from her.

"You better keep your hands off. If we expose ourselves here, you and my brothers will have a fight and that's not the atmosphere we want for this party."

"I'll just have mental foreplay until I can get you back to my bed tonight."

Laney lifted a brow. "Your bed?"

He slid one fingertip up her arm, across her collarbone and down to the V of her plunging neckline. "My bed. Where you belong."

Laney could barely process the meaning of those words for all the delicious tingles shooting through her. Finally, he was coming around and admitting he wanted her. They were making progress and she was going to continue to build on this, to show him exactly what they could be together.

Ryker's eyes held hers, so much desire and passion staring back at her. She couldn't get to his house soon enough.

The click of the door had Ryker easing his hand away and crossing his arms over his chest. Laney took a step back.

"Everything okay?"

Laney kept her back to Mac, who'd just come in. Her eyes stayed on Ryker, who was looking over her head.

"Yeah. Laney was just following up on an email she sent me earlier."

When Ryker moved around her, Laney turned in time to see the one-armed man hug between the two.

"I hear we got the Feds on us now." Mac shoved his hands in his pockets and rocked back on his heels. "If you all need me here, let me know. I doubt the source is coming from down South."

Laney shook her head. "I disagree. I think the timing is too coincidental, since you opened two new stores and now we have a mole."

"We can't rule out anything yet," Ryker, the voice of calm and reason, interjected. "I'll pursue every angle, and Laney will dig deeper to get to the bottom of this. She's been losing sleep over it."

Mac's eyes darted to her. "You can't take on all of this by yourself."

Guilt hit her hard. "I set up the system, I did background checks on every employee. By default, the blame comes back to me."

"We don't work that way," Ryker told her, his gaze hard. "We're a team. Remember?"

The burn in her throat, the prickling sensation in her eyes came out of nowhere. Now was not the time to cry. But damn him for reminding her of that fact.

"He's right," Mac agreed, oblivious. "We're all in this together, and we'll get out of it together. We just have to pool our efforts like we always do."

Laney pulled in a shaky breath and nodded. "You're right. I still feel responsible, but I will get to the bottom of this. I just need more time with the computers to eliminate our main office as the source of the snitch."

"Not tonight," Ryker told her. "Tonight we're all taking a few hours off and not worrying about work. We have enough Feds in our pocket to hold them off for a bit."

Between the Feds and worrying about the baby and when to drop that bombshell, and trying to analyze Ryker's sudden change of heart about sleeping with her, Laney had a headache. No surprise there.

She rubbed her forehead and closed her eyes for a moment. The guys continued to talk, and she willed the oncoming migraine to cease. Maybe it would help if she ate something. The caterer they'd hired was the best in the area. Laney's mouth watered at the thought of the filet mignon on the menu, and the chocolate fountain and fresh fruit sounded amazing, too.

"Laney?"

Ryker's worried tone had her opening her eyes, offering a smile. But the smile was moot when she started to sway.

Instantly Ryker took one of her arms and Mac had the other.

"You all right?" Mac asked.

Laney nodded. "Just getting a headache. No big deal."

She glanced between her brother's worried expression and Ryker's questioning gaze. She knew where Ryker's mind was, but she couldn't reveal too much here.

"I'm fine, I swear. I just need to eat, that's all."

Ryker's grip on her elbow tightened. "Then let's go downstairs and get you something."

Nodding, Laney pulled from both strong holds. "I can take care of myself. I'll just go into the kitchen and grab some crackers to hold me over."

"No, you'll eat more because when guests arrive, you'll be talking, and you'll forget to get a plate for yourself."

Laney stared at Ryker and he glared right back. While the whole protective thing was cute and sexy, she couldn't stay around him during this party. Their guests—her family—would be on to them in a second. Laney saw how Zara and Jenna stared at their men, and Laney knew for a fact she had that same love-swept gleam in her eye.

"I'll grab some fruit or something, too," she assured him. "I'm fine."

Without waiting for another argument, she turned from the guys and headed out of the room. Once in the hallway, Laney leaned against the wall, held a hand to her stomach and took a moment to relax. She needed to stay focused on finding who was betraying her family, but she couldn't neglect her body. This baby was everything to her. She'd wanted a family of her own since she could remember, and she'd been given this gift. It might not be how she had pictured things would fall in line, but did life ever really work that way?

Laney pushed off the wall and headed downstairs. She needed to get a hold of herself and put on her game face. This night had to be about the company and her family. And discovering the traitor in their midst.

Twelve

Ryker moved about the room, never straying too far from Laney. That damn dress was going to be the death of him. He wasn't sure if he wanted her to leave it on later when they were alone or if he wanted to peel it off of her. Those curves, the breasts that threatened to spill out and the fact she was carrying his baby were a lethal combination.

"You think our betrayer is here?"

Ryker gripped his glass of bourbon and nodded to Braden. "Yeah, I do. I think the bastard wants to keep close, thinking if they didn't show up, we'd see it as a red flag. They'll act like the doting, perfect employee."

"Damn it." Braden took a sip of whatever he was drinking, *Scotch by the smell of it*, Ryker thought, and let out a sigh. "I knew they'd be here. When I find out who I opened up my home to, my family to, they will be sorry they ever crossed us."

Ryker scanned the room. Laughter, chatter, hugs, everything seemed like a regular O'Shea's Christmas party. Women wore glamorous gowns and the men wore their finest suits. The tradition had been started decades ago. Before the O'Shea clan had taken him in, he never would've dreamed this was where he'd end up. A boy from a broken home with a deadbeat, druggie father had turned into a billionaire by simply being loyal and valuing what family was all about.

And Ryker would do it again even without all the money.

Zara joined them, swirling her glass of wine. "I'd say this party is another success."

Braden nodded. "Of course it is. I married the best event coordinator in the world."

Ryker listened, but his eyes were on Laney. She was chatting with Viviana and whoever her date was. Some guy with a beard and an expensive suit. Ryker had never seen the man before, but he'd met Viviana and knew the family trusted her. Laney hugged the woman and turned, her gaze catching Ryker's. His heart kicked up as she made her way across the floor. The way her body shifted, the way that dress hugged her until mid-thigh then flared out, those creamy shoulders exposed…he was going to have to think of something else because Laney was seriously killing him. And from the smirk on her face, she damn well knew it.

"Feeling better?" Braden asked when Laney stood before them. "Mac said you'd gotten dizzy or something earlier."

"I'm fine."

"You're not taking care of yourself," Braden added.

"This is the second time this has happened recently. Have you been to the doctor?"

Laney nodded. "I have, and I promise I'm perfectly healthy."

Ryker hated this. Hated lying to the only people he truly cared about.

"Have you tried this white wine?" Zara asked Laney. "It's the best I've ever had. I already asked the caterer the name, and I'm going to order it for my next event."

Laney shook her head. "Wow, it must be good."

"Let me get you a glass," Zara stated.

Ryker froze at the same time Laney's eyes widened. "Um, no. I'm just going to have some water for now."

Zara's brows drew in. "Are you sure?"

"Positive."

Ryker needed to move this conversation in a different direction. Laney was uncomfortable, and that was the last thing she needed.

"Braden, are you—"

"Oh, Laney." Zara's words cut him off. "Are you... are you pregnant?"

The last word was whispered, and Ryker gritted his teeth. He scrambled for a defense, but he couldn't outright lie. It wasn't as if they could keep the baby a secret forever. Damn it, he wanted, needed to come to Laney's aid here, he just had no idea how.

"Laney?" Braden jerked his attention to his sister. "Are you?"

The party went on around them, but the silence surrounded their little group, blocking everything else out. Ryker opened his mouth, not sure what he was about to say, but Laney's one word response cut him off.

"Yes."

"Oh, honey." Zara stepped forward and hugged Laney. "I'm sorry. I just blurted that out because I recognized the symptoms. I shouldn't have said anything."

Laney returned the embrace. "It's okay. I was waiting to tell you all. I wasn't sure how you'd take the news."

Zara leaned back. "I'm happy for you if you're happy. Braden and I are confident we'll have children, so don't worry about me."

Laney's smile widened as she turned her attention to Braden. "Well, do you have something you want to say?"

"Who's the father?"

His low, anger-filled tone cut right through Ryker. To Laney's credit, she didn't even flick a glance his way as she continued to smile.

"Right now we're just keeping things low-key. I'm not ready to say who the father is just yet."

Part of Ryker was proud of her response, honest but still keeping their secret. The other part of him, the bigger part of him, hated the fact he was kept out of the equation. He wanted to be part of this child's life from the start. Not hidden in the background.

And he sure as hell didn't want Laney defending him. That wasn't how this was going to work. He may not know where the hell they were headed, but he wasn't going to hide behind a pregnant woman.

"I'm the father."

He ignored Laney's gasp and concentrated on Braden...who slowly turned his eyes to Ryker.

"You're lying," he stated in a low, threatening tone. "You'd never do that to me."

Laney reached forward, putting her hand on Braden's arm. "Don't. Not here."

Braden shrugged her off. "I will kill you myself."

Ryker clenched his fists. "You can try."

"No bloodshed." Laney stepped between them, her back to Ryker. "Now is not the time to discuss this."

Zara tugged on Braden's arm. "She's right. You need to step back, and we can all talk after the party."

Braden's hard eyes never wavered from Ryker's. This was his brother and he'd betrayed him. Ryker didn't blame Braden for wanting to kill him. Whatever Braden, and Mac, threw his way, Ryker knew he deserved every bit of it. But the worst part, the scariest part, was the possibility that he'd no longer be part of the family.

Braden shifted his attention to Laney. "What the hell were you thinking?"

"My personal life is none of your business," she spat.

"What is going on?" Mac moved to the group, Jenna right on his heels. "You all are causing a scene."

"Laney's pregnant and Ryker is the father." Braden delivered the blow to Mac in a disgusted tone, but never took his eyes from his sister. "She was just about to explain what the hell she was thinking."

"I wasn't about to explain anything to anyone," Laney said, lowering her voice. "I don't owe any of you a defense. And I sure as hell am not getting into this here."

When she turned away, Braden reached out and snagged her arm. Ryker saw red.

"Get your hand off her," he gritted out. "Or I won't care what type of scene we cause."

Braden's anger was palpable. Ryker would gladly take the brunt of his rage, but he refused to have Laney shoulder the blame.

"This isn't the place," Mac stated. Ryker glanced to him, but was met with equally angry eyes. "But we are going to talk when this party is over."

Ryker nodded in agreement. Laney jerked free of Braden's grip and gracefully walked away. She wasn't going to cause any more of a scene than necessary, and he applauded her for her poise and determination. Ryker, on the other hand, was ready to throw his fist through a wall.

"Come on, Braden. You have a party to host." Zara wrapped her arm through his. "Getting angry isn't going to change a thing."

Braden remained still for several moments before being led away. Ryker turned to Mac and Jenna.

"You want to say something now?"

Mac's jaw clenched. "Later. I'll have plenty to say later."

"What your sister and I do is none of your concern."

Mac's sneer indicated otherwise. "You got my sister pregnant. I'd say every bit of this is our business, *brother*."

The parting shot did the damage Mac had intended. He walked away, leaving Ryker feeling even more like a bastard than he already did. He'd never thought he was good enough for Laney—and her brothers had just hit that point home.

There was no certainty how things were going to go down, but Ryker vowed to keep Laney safe. He'd told her he wouldn't let her get hurt, and he damn well meant it.

Oh, he wasn't concerned her brothers would physically harm her. No way in hell would they do that. But words could cause more damage than any actions, and tensions were running high.

Ryker felt for the souvenir penny inside his pocket, the reminder he needed right now. Family was everything to him, and he'd slashed right through that shroud of trust.

Now he had to pick up the pieces and make some vain attempt to put them all back together.

Laney's nerves were shot. She didn't have the energy to argue with her brothers, and she was furious at Ryker for dropping their bombshell the way he had. She'd had things covered, she was trying to keep him out of the hot seat until her brothers had a chance to process the pregnancy.

And she could think of so many other times that would've been more appropriate.

The caterers were gone, the room now a skeleton of a beautiful Christmas party. The employees had all mingled, chatting about the upcoming spring auction, the biggest one of the year. Laney had tried to zero in on who she thought could be capable of betrayal, but after the intense scene with her brothers and Ryker, she had lost focus.

"I'm so, so sorry, Laney."

Laney turned toward the doorway to the ballroom leading off the foyer. Zara had her hands clasped in front of her as she worried her bottom lip.

"None of this is your fault." Laney moved toward her sister-in-law and let out a sigh. "I have no idea where the guys went, but I hope Ryker is still alive."

Zara nodded. "Braden and Mac are outside, and I saw Ryker go up to the study. Jenna is finishing up in the kitchen, but I wanted to slip out and see you without the others."

Tears pricked Laney's eyes. "I was so worried how you'd take the news. I didn't want to bring back all of those memories."

Zara reached out, taking Laney's hands in hers. "The

memories are always there. The hurt will never go away, I imagine. We are trying to have another, and my doctor says he sees no reason why we can't get pregnant again. Don't worry about me, Laney. This is a special time for you and Ryker."

Laney blinked back the burn and moisture. "I don't know what Braden and Mac are going to do. I mean, they're all like brothers, they're best friends. Ryker needs them in his life. He had no one before coming here. He—"

"You love him," Zara said softly.

There was no denying the truth. "Yes."

"Then fight for this. Your brothers are in a state of shock, and most of their anger stems from getting caught off guard. Make them see how much you care for Ryker. Does he feel the same way?"

And wasn't that the question? How did Ryker feel? The man was so closed off. She knew full well how he felt about their physical relationship, and she was almost positive he had feelings for her, but she wanted him to say it. To admit how he felt and stop hiding from everything.

"It's okay." Zara squeezed Laney's hands. "Go on upstairs. Your brothers will be up shortly, I'm sure."

Laney wrapped her arms around Zara. "I'm so glad you're in our lives."

Returning the embrace, Zara whispered, "Me, too."

Pulling herself together, Laney made her way upstairs. She wasn't ready for this talk, didn't think she'd ever be. She knew going in that harsh words were going to be exchanged, some things that could never be taken back. But she wouldn't let her brothers blame Ryker. That was an issue she refused to back down on.

When she eased open the study door, she saw Ryker

across the room, facing the floor-to-ceiling windows behind the desk. With his hands in his pockets, he looked as if he didn't have a care in the world. Laney knew different. He carried everything on his shoulders.

She closed the door at her back, and the click had Ryker glancing over his shoulder.

"You need to leave," he told her, turning back to look out the window. "I've got this."

Yeah, carrying the entire weight, as if this pregnancy was one-sided.

"We're a team, remember?"

She moved across the floor, nerves swirling in her stomach. If he shut her out now, Laney didn't know how she'd handle his silence.

"Why didn't you let me manage things earlier?" she asked as she came to stand beside him. When he didn't look at her, Laney's heart sank just a bit more.

"I don't want you to think I was keeping your name from them for any reason other than it wasn't the time or place to get into this."

Ryker whirled, eyes blazing with fury. "I'm not hiding behind a woman. You think I was just going to stand there and let Braden speculate? How would that have worked out for either of us when he did find out the truth? If we'd let that go, his rage would've been worse."

Once again, Ryker was the voice of reason. Plus, it wasn't his style to let a woman take the fall, especially her. She should've known he wouldn't stand by while she made excuses and skirted around the truth.

"I just want to go home with you and be done here," she whispered.

"I'm not sure that's the best idea right now."

Laney froze. "What? Don't even tell me you're letting them come between us already."

He turned back to stare out at the dark night, illuminated only by the glow from the patio lights below. "I've told you before there is no 'us.' Their reaction should have told you that."

Laney crossed her arms over her chest. "And we're not going to fight them on this?"

The muscles in his jaw clenched. His silence might as well have been shouted through a bullhorn.

The door to the study opened, then slammed. Laney glanced up to see her brothers. Furious over Ryker's stance, Laney had had more than enough.

"If you're going to come in here and beat your chests over how you're supposed to protect me and Ryker knew better, save it." Laney glared across the room as her brothers started in her direction. "I'm expecting a baby. We didn't plan it, but your anger won't change a thing."

Mac stopped behind the leather couch and rested his hands over the back. "Maybe not, but we're still pissed. We're family, Laney. Ryker crossed the line."

Laney rolled her eyes. "I assure you, he didn't make the baby himself."

"So what now?" Braden asked, his eyes on Ryker. "What do you plan to do with my sister?"

Laney stilled, her back turned to Ryker as she waited on his response.

"I plan on helping her raise our baby and continuing to keep her safe. This changes nothing."

Laney's heart broke. Cracked right in two, then splintered into shards on the ground. She wasn't going to beg anymore. She'd tried to show him how perfect they'd be together, but clearly he wanted to keep that bit of distance in place so he could hold together the only family he'd ever known. She understood his fear, admired him for clinging to what he'd built, but to throw away her love was the last straw.

Laney turned to face Ryker. "You're right. This changes nothing. We're going to have a baby, but that's all."

Those dark eyes stared back at her. Lips thinned, jaw clenched, he was seething. Laney continued to stare, tipping up her chin in defiance. If he wanted to expand, then he needed to do so now. If he wanted to come to her "rescue" like he always had in the past, he needed to say what he felt. Why did have to be so set on doing the right thing? He was human, and they were attracted to each other. He'd showed her with his actions that he cared. Why was he choosing her brothers over her—again?

"We have too many problems going on right now for you two to be at odds," Mac cut into her thoughts. "Laney, are you feeling okay? Are you sure you can keep working?"

Throwing her arms in the air, she spun. "For heaven's sake, I'm pregnant, not terminal. I've had a few dizzy spells, but that's all normal."

Braden ran a hand over the back of his neck and glanced toward the ceiling. Laney waited for the backlash.

"Don't take this out on Ryker—"

"Stop, Laney."

She glanced over her shoulder. Ryker had turned from the window. His dark eyes held her in place, and she wanted to say so much more. She wanted to beat some sense into him until he relaxed his moral compass. He was so damn worried about getting shut out, he was literally letting her slip away.

"I'll handle my end," he told her.

His end? So they were on separate sides?

"Yeah, I guess you can." She swallowed the hurt, ignoring the threat of tears. She had no time for tears, she was too angry. "I'm going home. I'm tired, I've had a long day."

Gathering the skirt of her gown in one hand, she marched toward the door.

"Laney."

Ryker's voice stopped her.

"I'll drive you home."

Letting out a humorless laugh, Laney turned. "Like hell you will. I can handle this myself."

Throwing his words right back at him should've made her feel marginally better, but she only felt empty. She shot a glance to each of her brothers.

"If I come across any new leads on the mole, I'll let you know."

She couldn't be in this room another second, and at this point she didn't care what they did to one another. They were all morons. Laney wondered how the hell she'd been cursed to be surrounded by idiots. Not one of them was thinking beyond this moment. Her brothers weren't looking to the future, to a new generation of O'Sheas, and Ryker was being so damn stubborn, she was getting another headache thinking about it.

By the time she got home, all Laney wanted to do was soak in a bubble bath and think about her precious baby. Designing a nursery in her head was exactly what she needed to relax. No work, no men, just sweet little baby thoughts.

Thirteen

Ryker's eye throbbed. He'd deserved the single punch to the face…hell, he had expected so much more. Braden had delivered the blow, and Ryker hadn't even attempted a block.

How could he fault them for being protective of Laney? Ryker had done several interventions on her behalf when she'd been with men who weren't appropriate. He expected nothing less from Braden and Mac.

But Ryker had hurt her. He'd lied when he said the baby changed nothing. This baby changed everything. He'd been void of emotion for so long, something uncomfortable kept shifting in his chest, and he was scared as hell. Not that he'd ever admit such a thing aloud. He'd meant what he said when he'd told her there was no "us." Even so, he couldn't seem to stay away.

Though it was late, Ryker found himself standing outside Laney's house. It was time for damage control. He didn't text her first, nor was he about to knock. He knew O'Sheas hurt deeply and wanted to be left alone.

Too damn bad.

Ryker let himself in, punched in her security code and locked the dead bolt behind him. The Christmas tree lit up in the corner drew his attention to the pewter ornament hanging front and center. She'd genuinely been surprised and happy when he'd given that to her. He'd never seen her smile like that, at least not directed his way. He wanted to see that again. He needed to know he hadn't damaged something inside her.

Damn it. He raked a hand through his hair. He knew more than most how deeply harsh words sliced, and once they were out, there was no way to take them back.

"What do you want?"

Ryker glanced up the staircase. Laney stood on the landing, belting her robe, her damp hair lying across one shoulder.

He remained where he was, though everything inside him demanded he rush up the stairs, grab her and beg for forgiveness. Pride wouldn't let him…the same damn pride that was making her hurt.

Why did he have to be such a bastard? Why didn't he have normal feelings like everyone else? He'd been fine with his callous ways…until Laney.

"I came to apologize, though I doubt you'll accept it."

Crossing her arms over her chest, she nodded. "You're right. Which brother hit you?"

"Braden."

"Neanderthals," she muttered before starting down the steps. "I should get you some ice."

Ryker paused. "You're going to play nurse after what happened?"

Laney reached the landing, her hand braced on the newel post. "Braden had no right to hit you because we slept together. That's none of his business. But don't mistake the bag of ice as my forgiveness."

Even when she was pissed, Laney wanted to help. She managed to do things to him, things he never thought possible. She made him feel as if he actually had a heart. Problem was, he had no idea what the hell to do with it.

When she reached the bottom step, Ryker pivoted just enough to block her. With her up just those few inches, she was at eye level and right where he wanted her to be.

"Don't make this more difficult," she whispered, biting her bottom lip. "I'm tired, Ryker. You said enough earlier."

Jasmine. She'd used some form of Jasmine soap or shampoo, or whatever other potion women used. And she smelled absolutely delicious.

"I didn't mean those words the way they came out," he told her, clenching his fists. He wanted to reach for her, was desperate to touch her, but he didn't want his other eye blackened. He may be desperate, but he wasn't stupid.

"Yet you waited until we were alone to tell me that." She quirked a brow. "Your apology is accepted, but the damage is done. Do you want ice or not?"

"No."

"Fine. Then let yourself out and reset the alarm. I'm going to bed."

Before she could turn, Ryker placed his hand over hers on the post. "I'm lost, Laney. I have no idea what the hell I'm doing."

Her hand relaxed beneath his, giving him a minor

hope she wasn't ready to shut him out. If there was ever a time to spill his thoughts, it was now.

"I can't lose any of you," he went on. "Do you understand that? You're all I have. Braden and Mac are my brothers. I have no idea where this is leading between you and me, but I have to have some stability. I know you think I'm some superhuman, unfeeling bastard right now, but I feel…too much."

Laney's eyes closed, and Ryker had no idea what she was thinking. Everything was new to him. He'd been infatuated with her for so long, but never thought anything would come of it. Yet, here they were, expecting a baby and trying to wade through this mess he'd made.

And she loved him. Words he could never, ever forget.

"I can't do this with you." Her misty eyes landed on his, touching him right to his soul. "You know how I feel and when you do this push-pull. I have no idea how to react. I get that this family is yours, I completely understand you can't lose us. But are you willing to ignore everything between you and me?"

The hurt in her tone destroyed him. Ryker couldn't stand another second, he had to offer some comfort, but he knew the comfort was mostly for himself.

Taking her face between his hands, he stared directly into those vibrant green eyes. How could she pierce him so deeply? Nobody had ever even come close to touching him the way Laney had. But if he risked everything, *everything*, and they fell apart, it would kill him.

He eased forward, resting his forehead against hers and pulling in a deep breath. "I need time."

"I've given you most of my life," she whispered. The direct punch hit its mark.

"I'm new here, Laney. I can't mess this up, for you, for our baby. Just…don't give up on me."

Silence settled heavily around them, and Ryker hated the vulnerability he was showing. But this was Laney, and he was starting to see exactly what it would take to keep her waiting until he figured out his jumbled emotions.

She didn't say anything, didn't touch him in return. Ryker knew he wasn't done baring his soul. Stepping away from her, because he couldn't slice himself wide open *and* touch her, he started pacing her living room.

"I had the sad, clichéd childhood," he began, ignoring that instant burn to his chest when he thought about those first twelve years. "My father was a user, a man-whore, a worthless piece of trash who never should've been allowed to keep a child. I witnessed more by the time I was five years old than most people see or hear in a lifetime."

Ryker stopped in front of the mantel, catching Laney's gaze in the large mirror hanging above the greenery. "He'd leave me alone for days. I stole food to eat, I got myself ready for school, I picked fights on the playground so I could go to the principal's office."

Bracing his hands on the mantel, Ryker lowered his head. "I just wanted any contact with a male adult. I didn't care if it was negative. They'd try to call my dad, but of course he never answered. Half the time our phone bill wasn't paid anyway. So I'd stay in the office and finish my schoolwork, which was what I wanted. I wanted to be left alone to do my thing."

Pushing off the mantel, he started pacing again. He'd never let his backstory spill out like that. But now that he'd started, he wasn't about to stop. Laney deserved this part of him, she deserved it all, but this is all he could give for now.

"When I saw your brothers in a fight, I was all too eager to jump in. My dad had been gone for nearly a week, and I was pissed. I needed to take my aggression out on someone."

"How did nobody notice this for twelve years?" Laney's quiet question broke through his thoughts.

"People are so wrapped up in their own lives." He shrugged and reached for the ornament he'd given her. He rubbed his thumb over the roundness of the silhouette's belly before letting it go to sway against the branches. "I was so skeptical about meeting Patrick, but the second I saw him, I knew he was one of the good guys."

Laney let out a soft laugh. "Only a select few would lump him into that category, but I agree. He was the best."

"From the second I came to stay with you guys, then started working with your brothers, I felt like I had a place, a real home. Braden and Mac treated me like family. You were so young at first, I ignored you. But once you got to be a teenager, I was looking at you in ways that I shouldn't. Had your dad had even the slightest idea of what my thoughts were, he would've killed me himself."

"You never looked at me twice," she stated.

Ryker threw a glance over his shoulder, just in time to see one of her cats dart up the steps and disappear. "I looked. I fantasized. My penance for lusting after you was to watch you grow into a beautiful woman, to see other bastards on your arm. Then when we saw how eerily good you were with computers, I realized my penance had just begun."

He moved to the wide window in the front of the

house. Staring out onto the darkened night, with only a street lamp lighting a portion of the view, Ryker was forced to look at his own reflection. Fitting, considering he barely recognized the man who was spouting off his life story.

Slipping his hand into a pocket, he pulled out the penny. "I have been just fine keeping my distance from you. I mean, I wanted you, but I knew you were on another level, and nothing between us could ever happen. I've never forgotten where I came from, no matter how much money I have in my account or how many houses I own."

When he turned, he found her exactly as she'd been moments ago. Standing on that bottom step, her hand on the post, her eyes never wavering from him.

Holding up the pathetic piece of metal, Ryker walked forward. "I keep this ridiculous reminder in my pocket of what I came from. I've had this with me every single day since I was ten years old."

He stood only a few feet away, but held the penny out for her. Laney took it, examined it.

"This is one of those flattened pennies with your name on it." She brought her eyes back to his. "What's this from?"

"My dad was actually sober for a few hours one time." How sad was it that Ryker could pinpoint the exact hours his dad had gone without a drink or a fix? "There was a carnival outside the city, and he took me. He got this with my name on it, maybe because he felt he owed me something. I have no clue why, but this was the only thing he'd ever bought for me. This was the only time in my childhood he'd actually taken me anywhere."

Laney's eyes filled as she clutched the penny in her hand. "Are you worried about being a father?"

"Hell, yes, I am." Ryker rubbed the back of his neck, glancing to the floor before going on. "What do I have to fall back on? What part of my past says I'm ready to help raise another human being? I won't leave either of you, but I'm scared as hell, Laney."

"You're not afraid," she countered, her voice softening. "You're refusing to accept what already is. You have all of these wonderful emotions inside you. I know you care for me, I know you care for this baby. If you'd let yourself relax, you'd see there's so much more than fear. Fear is a lie. If my father showed you nothing else, he showed you that."

"There can't be animosity between your brothers and me, or them and you. There can't be. This family needs to be unified, and I swore to your father we'd find those scrolls, we'd keep this family going. I promised, Laney."

Still clutching the penny, she crossed her arms and nodded. "And we'll continue to do just that. My brothers aren't part of what you and I have going on. You need to understand that because if you don't, then we have nothing."

"If I were Braden, I would've killed someone like me."

Laney's hard stare held him in place. Damn, when she got that look, she was every bit Patrick O'Shea's daughter. She meant business—and she was sexy as hell.

"Braden's not going to harm you. Well, other than the black eye."

"You're aware of the man I am, what I've done to keep your family safe."

Laney nodded. "I'm not naive."

"You never ask me, you never look at me as if you disapprove."

Laney shrugged. "I know my father had his reasons.

I know Braden wants no more violence and that you had to take care of Shane because he tried to hurt me." She swallowed, bit her lip and pushed on. "And I know when my ex disappeared—"

"I didn't kill him. I couldn't. I sent him away with a fat check and a promise that if he returned, he would be finished."

"I thought you…"

Ryker nodded. "I know what you thought. I let you think that because I was trying to keep some wall between us, but it didn't work."

Laney blinked, glanced around the room as if trying to process what he'd just said. "I'm glad you didn't hurt him, but why didn't you? You hated him."

Hate was such a mild term for the man who'd verbally abused Laney. The guy was lucky he was still drawing breath in his lungs.

"I didn't want you to look at me like I was a monster."

"I could never look at you that way."

Ryker took a step forward. "I couldn't take the chance."

Laney uncrossed her arms, handed the penny back to him and pulled in a breath. Ryker shoved the memento back into his pocket.

"How much did Braden give you to send Shane away?"

"He didn't give me the money."

Her perfectly arched brows drew in as she tipped her head. "You used your money?"

"I'd have paid him every last dime I had to leave. I didn't want to have his blood on my hands, and I wanted him out of your life."

Laney pushed her hair over her shoulder and clutched

the V of her robe. She'd looked so damn gorgeous earlier in that red ball gown. She'd nearly stopped his heart and was the envy of every woman there; she was also most likely most guys' fantasy tonight.

But right now, she stood before him, void of all makeup, wearing nothing but her silk robe and smelling like everything he didn't deserve.

"Don't shut me out," he murmured. "I need time, and I know it's not fair to ask, but…just don't push me away, even when I'm being a selfish bastard."

It seemed as if an eternity passed as he waited for her to say something. Instead, she reached out, took his hand and turned to go up the steps.

"Laney."

She stopped but didn't look back at him. Ryker moved up to where she stood, lifted her in his arms and carried her the rest of the way.

"This is more," he told her. "Just let me catch up."

When she laid her head on his shoulder, Ryker knew he was breaking ground on learning how to live with a heart that actually feels. Now if he could only figure out a way to make sure she didn't get hurt…and prove to Braden and Mac that he wasn't just messing around with their baby sister.

Fourteen

Laney was no closer to finding the traitor than she had been three days ago. Her family was counting on her. Their reputation, their...everything hinged on her finding the person who dared go against them. Until they knew who was behind the leak to the Feds, they were each taking turns manning the main office. Laney still wasn't convinced this was where everything went down; the clues the internet was giving her could be deceiving.

Mac and Jenna had decided to stick around through the holidays and definitely until this mess was cleared up.

Working in the office of her ancestors, Laney started looking at keystrokes with a program she'd downloaded. Every laptop in the office had to be checked. They had eight. The Boston office had to be ruled out first. Even though the new offices seemed coincidental in timing, if someone were going to attack, they may do it from close range where they could keep an eye on most of the key players.

Laney reached for another cracker. Normally she'd scold anyone for eating around their computers, but time was of the essence and her little one demanded some food.

"Anything?"

Laney didn't spare Braden a glance as he stepped into the office. "Not yet."

"How are you feeling?"

She hadn't seen him in three days, since the night of the party. He'd texted her to talk work and ask if she was feeling okay, but that was it. Ryker's name wasn't mentioned, and Laney was perfectly fine with that. The more her brothers stayed out of her personal business, the better.

"Hungry. I'm either tired or hungry. It's a cycle."

"Zara is out running errands. I'll have her bring you something."

Laney shook her head. "No need. I practically packed my kitchen in my bag because I knew I'd be here all day and evening."

Braden took a seat across from her. "You can't work yourself to death. You're expecting. I know how tired Zara was."

Her fingertips stilled on the keyboard as she glanced over the screen. "I'm sorry if this hurts you."

Braden shook his head. "You being pregnant isn't what bothers me."

Laney tried to keep the anger at bay. If they were all going to move forward, they had to stay levelheaded and remain calm. And after Ryker had spent the night simply holding her, Laney had a newfound hope that things would work out. They had to.

"You don't want to hear this, but Ryker and I aren't just fooling around."

Braden crossed his ankle over his knee and curled his hands over the sides of the chair. "No, I don't want to hear that my best friend, a guy I call my brother, is taking advantage of my sister. It doesn't sit well with me."

"You think that's what this is? That he's some sex-crazed maniac and I'm his poor, unsuspecting victim?" Laney shook her head and reached for another buttery cracker. "You have no clue, then. I love him."

"Damn it, Laney." Braden jerked forward in his seat, his hard stare holding her. "You're going to get hurt. A guy like Ryker doesn't do relationships. Have you ever wondered why he hasn't had a woman around us? That's not his style."

"It wasn't your style, either, until you got trapped with Zara. Now look at you."

That narrowed gaze didn't intimidate her. She took a bite of her cracker. "If you're done throwing your unwanted opinions around, I have work to do."

Braden came to his feet and blew out a breath. "You're going to get hurt," he repeated, his tone softer now.

"I'm a big girl."

She refused to look at him, refused to give him the power over her, because he had no say in how she handled her emotions or what she did with Ryker.

When he stormed out, Laney let out a breath. *That went well.*

Her cell chimed, but she ignored it. Braden was here, so if there was anything pressing going on, he'd know. The more she looked over this laptop, the more she was convinced it was clean. She'd just shut it down when her cell chimed once again.

Leaning over, she dug into her purse and fished it out of the side pocket. Giddiness burst through her when her contractor's name appeared.

She swiped her finger over the screen to open the message.

Inspections all passed. Moving forward on reworking the electrical.

Finally. Some good news. With the initial building inspections passed, she could push forward and hopefully come in ahead of her original spring opening.

After Ryker had shared his story with her the other night, she was even more determined to raise awareness for children who didn't have a proper home life.

She may not be able to help them all, but if she even helped one, then that was one less child who would doubt his or her self-worth. These kids needed to know someone cared about them, genuinely cared, because that was the struggle with Ryker right now. He didn't know what to do with the love she offered.

Laney sent off a quick reply that she'd be by tomorrow to discuss lighting and a few other questions she had regarding the kitchen area and the rec room.

She was making headway with the project, and possibly with Braden since he didn't seem so full of rage. Now if she could only figure out this puzzle of who was betraying her family. She didn't feel a bit sorry for the person on the other end of this investigation. Whoever had gone against the O'Sheas deserved everything they had coming.

* * *

Ryker had a sinking feeling, and he never ignored his instincts.

As he pulled in front of O'Shea's, he killed the engine and let his mind process all the intel that had come in regarding the scrolls. There were obvious dead ends, so he dismissed those immediately. But there was something eating away at his mind. It only made sense for the works to be fairly close. They were last known to be in Zara's home, or the home that the O'Sheas had lost in the Great Depression. If they had gotten out, word would've traveled.

Braden had searched, Ryker had searched. There wasn't a square inch of that house that had gone uncovered. But Ryker couldn't help but wonder if he'd missed something.

Zara's house sat empty now, well, save for her grandmother's things, because Zara had moved in with Braden. But Ryker wanted to go back in. He refused to give up. He'd been all over the damn globe on hunches, on veiled hints, but nothing had turned up. Frustration and failure were bitter pills to swallow, so he was going back to the point of origin, starting at square one. Because he was fresh out of leads.

Now more than ever, he needed to find those heirlooms. He needed to prove his family loyalties.

He stepped from his SUV, pulling his leather coat tighter to ward off the bitter chill. As soon as he stepped into O'Shea's, Braden's glare greeted him.

"Your eye looks better," he commented before looking back down at a stack of folders on his antique desk.

Ryker didn't take the bait. His eye still hurt like a bitch, but he had no right to complain.

"I want to get back into Zara's house," he said instead.

He moved farther into the spacious lobby area, complete with a Christmas tree that Laney no doubt had a hand in putting up. It had the same damn glittery nonsense she'd wanted him to put in her house.

"That resource is exhausted if you're referring to the scrolls." Braden dropped his pen and eased back in his leather seat. "Why do you need back in?"

Ryker shoved his hands in his pockets. "There's something we're missing."

"You're wasting your time."

"It's my time to waste." He refused to back down on this. "You know I'll just go in regardless. I'm merely telling you for courtesy."

Braden slowly came to his feet. Ryker didn't move, didn't bother to get out of the way when Braden came around the desk and stood toe to toe with him.

"Oh for pity's sake. If this is another pissing contest, count me out."

Ryker caught a glimpse of Laney in the doorway to the back office. Her hair was tied up in a loose knot, and her outfit consisted of an oversize gray sweater, black leggings and brown boots. She looked so young. Granted, she was ten years younger, but the simple outfit had her appearing almost innocent. His heart slammed against his chest as he took in the sight.

He offered her a smile. "I'm just letting your brother know of my plans for the evening."

Rolling her eyes, she moved toward them. "Braden, I think I found something. If you can stop being a bully for two seconds and come look?"

She'd barely gotten the words out before Braden and Ryker were in motion. Once in the office, Laney settled back into the seat, and Braden took one side of her chair while Ryker took the other.

"I found an encrypted email. I had to dig, and the person tried to delete it, but here it is."

"Open it."

Laney shook her head. "I can't. That's the problem. But the subject is damning and it's from the general computer at the main office."

She pointed to the bold header: BACKLOG

"And look at the time and date." She pointed to the screen—it was as soon as the new system was in place. Hours after it had been implemented, in fact. Then they had clearly sent the email and quickly covered their tracks.

The mole was good, but Laney was better. This was the break they'd needed.

"Bastards." Braden slammed his hand on the desk, making Laney jump.

"It's a start," she said, attempting to console him, but there was no calming him. This meant war for whoever did this. "The email wasn't from our internal system, and the account is fake. I just have to dig to find who set it up."

"You can do it." Ryker placed a hand on her shoulder and squeezed. "We all know you can. We're just frustrated and need to get this sorted out before the Feds find something incriminating."

Braden threw up his arms. "They have our sales records. If they search through each and every item, they're going to find questionable pieces."

Feeling a surge of loyalty and protectiveness, Laney glanced up at her brother. "If they searched each piece, they would have speculation at best. I have nothing in the program that indicates where the pieces came from. All of that is stored at my house, in a safe that even you two couldn't crack."

"I'd shoot it." Ryker straightened. "So, you're going to work on this, and I'm going to go back to Zara's tonight. Are you staying with her, Braden?"

Laney leaned back in her seat, looking up at the two men who seemed to be having some sort of staring showdown. She crossed her arms and waited for the testosterone to come down a notch.

"I'm not leaving her alone in her state," Braden replied. "You go. I'll make sure she's fine."

"With all this going on, I think it's safest if she's with one of us at all times."

Braden nodded. "That we can agree on."

Laney jerked to her feet, sending her chair flying back and crashing into the wall. "*She* is right here. And *she* can take care of herself."

They both stared at her as if she'd lost her mind. "I'm serious," she went on. "I don't need a babysitter, and nobody has threatened us with physical harm."

"You're pregnant," Braden growled. "You're automatically vulnerable."

Laney turned to face her brother fully. "You know I'm capable of taking care of myself. Stay all you want, but when I leave, I won't be needing a shadow."

Braden glanced over her shoulder toward Ryker. "Will you tell her? Maybe she'll listen to you."

"She won't listen to me. I ignore her wishes when it comes to things like this anyway."

Yeah, which was how he'd ended up tearing her dress off in a Miami hotel room. He'd been worried for her safety…and then she'd been plastered against the wall, panting his name.

Ryker took her arm, urging her to look at him. Laney shifted her attention. "What?"

"Just listen. For once. I'll be back later. Go to my place. I'll meet you there."

Braden practically growled behind Laney. "Can you two not talk like this?"

"Leave the room," Laney spouted over her shoulder. "I'll go home. If you want to come there, you can. I have too much to do."

Ryker nodded. "I'll try not to be too late."

Once he was gone, Laney glanced back at her over-bearing babysitter. "You know your hovering and child-ish attitude aren't going to make my feelings for him go away."

"I've thought about this. I don't like feeling betrayed, but there's so much more at stake. I want you both to real-ize what's at stake if you fall out. We need him, Laney."

"You think I'm not aware of that? I can't help who I fall in love with, Braden."

He blew out a breath and pulled her into his arms. "Damn it, Laney. I love you both and don't want either of you hurt—even if I'm still pissed at him."

Laney sank into his embrace. "I don't think it's me you have to worry about."

Fifteen

Ryker searched the obvious hiding places at the former O'Shea home once more: closets, cabinets, old trunks. He made his way to the secret tunnel Zara had showed them. The space was rather small and had no shelves, just a chair in the corner. The tunnel could be accessed at one end from an opening at the kitchen and at the other end from the long hallway. Ryker knew if those scrolls were still here, they'd likely be someplace "hidden" like this where no one would think to look.

He ran his hands over the walls. He'd never thought to look for another secret passage. Who knew what surprises this house had concealed? He covered every square inch of the walls, then worked on the baseboards, the floorboards. The tunnel was clean.

He'd been there for five hours and had covered the basement and main floor. There wasn't a loose floorboard to be found. As he went up to the second floor, the steps creaked, groaning against his weight. He froze. Old steps were bound to crackle and settle, but he'd never explored the stairs. Hadn't even crossed his mind—until now.

Ryker went back down the steps and started there. He knocked on the boards, curious if any were loose or sounded different from the others. He tapped each post on the banister, as well. He'd nearly made it to the top when, two steps from the second-floor landing, he hit pay dirt.

He'd been excited before on other hunts only to be deflated when nothing happened. But he was damn well going to devote every bit of energy he had to fulfilling Patrick's dying wish. Ryker owed him at least that—especially because he hadn't been able to stay away from Laney. That was a debt he'd never be able to repay.

Wrapping his fingers around the outside edge of the wood, Ryker gave a slight tug. The wood creaked as it started to give way. The banister that rested in that particular step splintered. Ryker jerked it out, tossed it down the steps…he'd pay to have it repaired later.

His heart accelerated as he gave the board another pull. Finally it ripped free from the step. He eased down another stair and pulled out the minuscule flashlight he'd shoved into his pocket before coming here.

Bending to get a good view, his chest clenched as he spotted something inside. No way could this be the scrolls. The odds that they'd been right under their noses the entire time was pretty nonexistent. Yet something had brought him back to the old house.

Ryker slid the end of the flashlight between his teeth,

then, using both hands, he reached into the space and tugged out a metal box.

Sinking back onto the step, his back against the wall, he stared at the box as if it held every answer he'd ever wanted. Was this them? He wanted to rip into this box to see, but at the same time he wanted to wait, to hold on to the hope he felt right at this moment. If these were the missing scrolls, Ryker had just accomplished what no one else had been able to.

Zara couldn't have known about this hiding spot in the steps or she would've told them. Which made him wonder if her grandmother even knew.

He set the flashlight aside and pulled the lock-pick kit from his jacket pocket. The box was definitely an antique, turn of the twentieth century, if he was guessing right. He'd been working with and acquiring for the O'Sheas long enough to know antiques. This box may be the one the O'Sheas had used before the scrolls had gone missing.

Carefully he went to work on the old, rusted lock. The box was long but not very wide. Ryker wondered if the scrolls could even fit in something this size. Suddenly the lock clicked and the lid flopped open. Most old locks were harder to pick. Clearly this was meant to be.

"Damn," he muttered. There were tubes inside the box. Nine tubes to be exact. Nine tubes that possibly held the nine scrolls.

Ryker couldn't get into one of the tubes fast enough. He'd barely pried the lid off one when his cell went off.

He ignored it. Nothing was more important than this right here. He didn't want to pull anything out, because if these were the scrolls, they'd be beyond delicate. But once the lid sprang free, he grabbed the light again and angled it inside the cylinder.

This was it. He'd found them. Finally.

There were no words, there was nothing but a sense of accomplishment unlike anything he'd ever known. He'd done it. After years, decades of hunting, Ryker had been the one to find the heirlooms so important to the O'Shea family.

Quickly, but with care, he put everything back into the box.

Glancing at his watch, he realized he'd been at Zara's longer than he first thought. It was late, dark, but there was no way he could let this moment pass. He had to let everyone know.

He sent off a quick text to Mac, Braden and Laney, telling them all to meet at Braden's. Mac should already be there, since that's where he was staying, and Laney…well, who knew where she would be. He hoped at Braden's so she could be safe, but knowing her, she went home and was up to her chin in jasmine-scented bubbles.

Ryker had procured many pieces over the years. He'd traveled all over the world. He'd learned languages, used disguises, made enemies all in the name of loyalty and love for this family.

And he was finally coming home with the one true gift he'd always longed to deliver.

"How the hell had we missed this?" Braden asked.

Laney couldn't take her eyes off the tubes. Nine of them lay on Braden's desk. And they were all there to witness this important moment in the O'Shea family history: Mac, Jenna, Braden, Zara, Laney—and Ryker.

She'd never in her life seen him so excited. The pride on his face... Laney couldn't put into words the transformation.

She'd had news to share with them about some antiques at an old estate not far outside the city that they needed to acquire, but that could definitely wait. This moment had been a long time coming. Decades. And here they all were gathered around her father's old desk. Laney couldn't help but feel as if he were here in spirit.

Tears pricked her eyes, but she blinked them away.

"I never even knew that step was loose, let alone came apart," Zara stated. Shock laced her voice as she, too, continued to stare. "I'm sure my grandmother didn't either or she would've told me. She was only a baby when she went to live there."

"Dad was adamant that there were no hidden areas," Braden chimed in. "We knew of the small tunnel that led into the kitchen, but nothing like this."

Braden turned his attention to Ryker and slapped a hand onto his shoulder. "You did it."

Ryker nodded, not saying a word. He may have appeared to have it all together in that typical Ryker fashion, but Laney knew that inside, he was trying hard to keep his emotions in check.

"I had to," Ryker finally murmured, his eyes fixed on the layout. "I owe you all—"

"Nothing," Braden confirmed. "I know I was pissed at you for the whole Shane incident—and I won't even get into Laney—but I see why you took matters into your own hands this time. If you do it again, though, I'll kill you."

Ryker's mouth twitched, but he merely nodded.

"But this is something I honestly never thought would

happen in my lifetime." Braden's voice grew thick with emotions. "Dad would be so damn proud of you."

A tear trickled down Laney's cheek. Zara wrapped her arm around Laney's shoulders, giving silent support. They were all feeling years' worth of frustration, hope, determination, all rolled into this moment. So many leads, so many cities… Ryker had single-handedly trekked all over the globe in an attempt to bring these home where they belonged.

"We need to get these in the safe," Mac chimed in. "Nobody can know they're here, and the security should probably be bumped up."

"I'm already on it." Work mode, that's what Laney could concentrate on. She swiped her damp cheek. "I have an alarm you can put on just the safe. It's sensitive but necessary."

Braden nodded. "Great. How are you doing on the search for our mole?"

"It's got to be one of the employees at the main office." A sick feeling settled in her stomach at the thought of anyone doing this to her family. "That narrows it down to six. Viviana is the newest employee, but I almost feel she's too obvious. Maybe whoever is doing this is using the timing of her coming on board."

Braden carefully capped the narrow tubes and placed them all back into the shallow box. "Keep everyone working on a regular schedule."

"What?" Mac questioned.

"Keep the enemies close," Ryker added. "Now that we know it was one of them, Laney can keep an eye on everything they're doing on our system."

"And they won't have a clue," she added with a smile.

"This is my favorite part of work. Oh, also freezing assets. I do enjoy knowing our enemies are broke."

Jenna laughed. "I'm so glad I'm on your good side."

Laney couldn't help but widen her smile. "You're safe. The DeLucas on the other hand…"

"What did you do?" Braden asked, his hand resting on the now-locked box.

With a shrug and a surge of pride, Laney met the questioning gazes of her brothers and Ryker. "Merely closed some credit cards, possibly drained their off-shore bank account."

Ryker's eyes widened, his nod of approval giving her another burst of excitement. No way was she going to let them get away with the petty little game they played with Ryker. Braden said no more violence, fine. She didn't get involved with that part anyway. But she could sure as hell ruin someone's life. Hard to keep being a jerk when you were broke and powerless.

"I swear, you scare me sometimes," Braden added. He came around Ryker and gave her a brotherly hug. "Just be careful. I know you make sure things can't be traced back to you, but I still worry. Especially now that you're pregnant."

Laney patted his back, meeting Ryker's gaze over Braden's shoulder. "I'm fine. The only time I'd ever been in physical danger was with Shane."

And thanks to Ryker, Shane was a nonissue.

Laney stepped back, smoothing her sweater over her torso. "Since we're talking work, I have a house out in Bradenton that has several antiques that could be of interest. The owner actually called me today asking if we could come look and discuss adding them to the spring show. I'll give you a heads-up. The price they're wanting is a bit over what I would estimate. But I haven't seen them."

"I'll go." Ryker shoved his hands in his pockets. Laney wondered if that penny was still there after his emotional purging session the other night. "Now that the scrolls have been found, I won't be so tied up and consumed with them. I'll do something normal for a change."

Laney held her breath while Mac and Braden stared at Ryker. After all that had happened—her pregnancy, finding the scrolls—Laney prayed her brothers kept Ryker in their brotherhood.

"You do that," Braden finally said. "Good change of pace for you, and it's only thirty minutes away."

Laney let out the breath she'd been holding. "I'll let them know you'll be there the day after tomorrow."

"All this excitement has me exhausted." Zara circled the group until she came to stand next to Braden. The look she gave her husband implied that she was more than ready for their company to leave. "Ryker, thank you, and please don't think a thing about tearing up the staircase."

Shifting in his stance, Ryker rubbed a hand over the back of his neck. "I'll fix it, you have my word."

"I'm going to head on home," Laney told them all. "I'm pretty tired, and it's way past my bedtime."

She gave her brothers a hug, said her farewells to Jenna and Zara, and when she turned to Ryker, there was no mistaking that hard look he gave her.

"Fine. You'll drive me home, and I'll get my car tomorrow. You don't even have to say it."

"Just to make sure she's safe," Mac chimed in.

Laney whirled. "Not now. We've had a good night. Let's not get into another pissing contest. His eye still hasn't healed."

"I can speak for myself," Ryker added. "I'll take her home, and from that point it's nobody's business."

Braden opened his mouth, but Zara elbowed him in the side. "You love them both. Let them figure out their own relationship."

Braden kept his eyes on Ryker, but Ryker only let out a slight grunt. "I get it," he said, holding his hands up. "If I hurt her, you'll bury me, nobody will find me. You all are the only ones who would look anyway."

Laney placed her hand on Ryker's arm. "Braden and Mac will get over it. We're having a baby. Let's focus on that for now."

She couldn't help but borrow his earlier verbiage. Everything that was happening between her and Ryker was going minute by minute. That's the only way her brothers could take it, as well. Besides, how could she tell them what was going on, where she and Ryker were headed, when she didn't know the answers herself?

Silence surrounded them, and Laney was beyond done with all this veiled testosterone tossing.

"Get her home safely," Braden finally said before Laney could open her mouth.

"That's what he's done for years." She had to remind them of how loyal Ryker truly was. And wasn't that ridiculous? He'd been around for decades and had proven himself over and over. "Ryker isn't the one who betrayed you. Remember that."

Laney marched from the room. Still thrilled about the scrolls, she tried not to let her brothers' archaic attitude ruin her mood. She didn't care where Ryker took her, his house or hers. She intended to show him just how thankful she was about his discovery.

Sixteen

Whether it was due to the euphoric state of finding the missing scrolls or the fact that he held Laney until she fell asleep, Ryker didn't know, but he'd been unable to relax in her bed. Last night, after they'd left Braden's house, Ryker had every intention of going to his place, but Laney had nearly crawled in his lap in the car, suggesting they go to her house because it was closer. Who was he to argue?

Now he wished he were anywhere else. As he sat in the middle of one of the spare bedrooms, Ryker glanced at all the pieces to this crib. How did all of these damn pieces go together? The picture on the large box in the corner showed what he should end up with, but he'd never built a crib before. Hell, he'd never built anything. His hands had always been used in other not-so-innocent ways.

Ryker glared at the directions, trying to make sense of the pathetic diagrams. Why the hell didn't the company just send someone to assemble the damn thing when you ordered it?

He'd known she'd been looking at furniture, but until he'd walked past the spare bedroom this morning on his way to get coffee, he'd had no idea she'd actually bought a crib. He couldn't sleep and didn't want to wake Laney, so he figured he'd give it his best shot.

He'd stood in the doorway so long just staring. It had never occurred to him where the nursery would be—her house or his. Both? This was where things started to get even murkier. He didn't want to concentrate on all the reasons this path he was on could go wrong.

Yet he couldn't help himself. The level of comfort he was settling into with Laney was hinting at something so much more. He'd spent nights in her bed, the selfish jerk that he was. Ryker just couldn't tear himself away. He'd mentally pushed Laney away for so long, for so many reasons—his childhood was crap and didn't know how to do a relationship, her father had trusted Ryker to always do the right thing, Laney was ten years younger. The list went on and on, pounding away at Ryker's mind.

Frustrated at his insecurities, he pulled over two of the long boards and a pack of screws. That took no time to put together. Perhaps this wouldn't be such a pain and he could have it done by the time Laney woke up.

The sun hadn't even come up yet, so hopefully she'd sleep a little longer. She needed it. Their baby needed it.

Maybe if this crib got assembled, and didn't fall apart, he'd take her out to pick out something else she wanted. He hadn't gotten her a Christmas present. Hell, what would he even get her? She was all sparkles and grace, and he was a wolf in an Italian suit when his leathers wouldn't suffice.

Their worlds may have collided and run parallel for the past several years, but that didn't mean they were on the same playing field.

By the time Ryker got to the sides of the antique, white sleigh-style crib, he was ready to chuck the entire thing out the window and buy her one already assembled.

"I was going to have someone come in and do that for me."

Ryker jerked around. Laney stood in the doorway, her silk robe knotted around her still-narrow waist, her dark hair tousled all around her shoulders. A lump settled heavily in Ryker's throat. How could he take the mob princess and attempt to fit into her world? Not physically, but mentally. He was a damn mess inside, and he didn't need to pay anyone to tell him that.

"Why aren't you asleep?" he asked before turning back to the mayhem that posed as a baby bed.

He wasn't sure how long he'd been in here, but he needed a break. Ryker came to his feet, brushing his hands on the boxer briefs he'd slept in.

"The bed was lonely," she told him, raking her bedroom eyes over his nearly bare body.

Her smoldering looks never failed to make his body stir. The need for her had never been in question. If all of this was physical, if she wasn't Patrick O'Shea's daughter, hell, if she were anybody else, none of this would be in question.

"What's that look about?" She tipped her head to the side and crossed to him. "You found the scrolls, but you still look as if the weight of the world is on your shoulders."

Maybe because it was. The baby, the need to want Laney in his life more… Ryker wasn't even getting into how Braden and Mac still didn't approve. That he could handle. It was the rest of it he wasn't sure of.

"Ryker?"

He closed his eyes and willed his demons to stand down, but they were rearing their ugly heads even harsher than usual.

"We need to take some time—"

"What? Are you seriously going to tell me you need time?" Laney crossed her arms over her chest. "Don't be clichéd, Ryker. I already told you I was waiting for you, that I'd be here for you."

At least one of them was strong right now.

He ran his hands through his hair, his eyes burning from lack of sleep. "I can't get this damn thing together."

"The crib?" Her brows drew in. "This isn't a big deal."

It was everything.

"Do you know my father threw a glass table at me when I was seven?" he asked, needing her to understand. He ran a fingertip along the scar on his chest. "A piece ricocheted off the wall and hit me here. That wasn't the only time he lost his temper, Laney."

"And you think this is going to change how I look at you? Because you're nothing like him."

With a snort, Ryker shook his head. "I'm exactly like him. You do know what I've done for your family for years, right? When you were learning to write cursive in school, I was already doing all the dirty work."

Her eyes narrowed. In a move he didn't predict, she reached up, planted her palms on his bare chest and gave him a shove.

"If you're going to be a coward and worry about losing

your temper with me or our baby, then get out. I won't wait around for you when you're acting like this. I know the man inside, but clearly you have yet to meet him."

Her rage shattered him. "Are you willing to take the chance? I've never done the traditional family thing, and I have one good memory of the first twelve years of my life. That's all."

"Then you should be more determined to make memories with your child."

Could he? Was that even in him? He had no clue what children wanted. All he knew was what Laney deserved.

If you love it, set it free.

He stared at her, willing his feet to move, to go into her bedroom and get his things so he could leave. But the pink in her cheeks, the hurt in her eyes and the grim line of her mouth were hard to ignore.

"You have to know I'm distancing myself for the sake of you and the baby." He wanted to reach out and touch her. To let her know he did care, too much, but he had to get inside his own head and sort things out. "I need to know you're safe. That's been my role for so many years, but now I need to know you're safe from me."

"Safe from you? Then stop hurting me," she cried, tears filling her eyes. "You can walk out that door anytime, but don't think it's revolving. You know I love you, damn it, you love me, too. I can see it. You wouldn't be so hell-bent on pushing me away otherwise."

Now he did reach for her, taking her hands in his, holding tight when she tried to jerk away. "There's so much inside me that I need to deal with. Everything hit me so hard all at once…"

Damn it. He shook his head, glancing down to their joined hands. "Your father, your brothers have been the only family I've ever loved. But there's still that demon inside me that is the twelve-year-old boy who wasn't given love and security. I need to get that under control before it controls me."

"It's already controlling you." Now when Laney pulled, he let her go. "You have shut yourself off from real feelings for so long you have no idea how to handle them. You found the scrolls, fulfilled your promise to my father, and now you have all this space in your mind that is filling back up with doubts."

She was so dead-on. There was nothing she hadn't hit directly.

Pulling the V of her robe tighter, she glanced away. "Just go, Ryker. You want to. You want to run and hide and be secluded from anything that threatens you to step outside of your comfort zone."

Damn it, she was his comfort zone. He just knew if he stayed in that space too long, he'd end up destroying it if he didn't get a handle on his past.

"For now, this is for the best." He leaned down to kiss her on the head, but she stepped away, her eyes blazing at him.

Swallowing back his emotions, he moved around her and went back to her bedroom to get dressed. He only prayed he was making the right decision because he wanted Laney, wanted their baby. But he couldn't pull them into his world when he couldn't even handle living in it himself.

So maybe going back to Southie wasn't the best of ideas. But Ryker figured if he wanted to rid himself of the past, he'd need to tackle it headfirst.

So here he stood outside his old apartment building.

The place looked even more run-down than he remembered, and he hadn't thought that was possible. The gutter hung off one side, the wooden steps were bowed, the railing half gone. There was no way this could be deemed livable because if this was the outside, he didn't want to know what the inside looked like.

Snow swirled around him. The house next to the apartments wasn't faring much better, but someone had attempted to brighten it up with a strand of multicolored lights draped around the doorway.

Shoving his hands into the pockets of his jeans, Ryker stared back at the door that led to his dilapidated apartment. For the first twelve years of his life, he'd called this place home. He hadn't known anything different. Much like so many of the kids in this area. Granted, some kids had a happy home life because money wasn't the key to happiness. Having a home that was falling apart was definitely not the same as having an addict father who didn't give a damn.

The penny in his pocket brushed the tip of his fingers. Ryker honestly had no clue where his father was now; he didn't much care, either. Most likely the man had killed himself with all the chemicals he put into his system.

Ryker had actually shed tears after Patrick's death, but felt absolutely nothing when he thought of his biological father.

This place did nothing but bring back memories Ryker hated reliving.

He turned, heading down the street. He'd parked a block away, needing the brisk walk. Keeping his head low to ward off the chill, he headed back to his SUV, which stuck out like the proverbial sore thumb. When he was a kid, if this big, black vehicle had come through, Ryker would've thought it was the president himself.

He'd just stepped off the curb and crossed the street when he noticed movement out of the corner of his eye.

"Mr. Barrett?"

Ryker glanced toward the old building that had sat vacant for several years. It used to be a store of sorts, then a restaurant, and he'd just assumed it would be torn down.

"I thought that was you."

Ryker eyed the man who was unlocking the door to the building. After getting closer, Ryker could see it was Mr. Pauley, a popular contractor around the Boston area. The O'Sheas had used him a few times in the past. The truck behind Ryker's vehicle bore the familiar emblem from Mr. Pauley's company.

"How are you doing, Mr. Pauley?" Ryker called.

"Good. Good. Did you come by to check on the property?"

Confused, Ryker stopped by his car. "Excuse me?"

"Miss O'Shea said she'd be by today." He tugged the door open and held it with his foot as he shoved his keys back into his coat pocket. "I figured since you were here, she sent you."

Miss O'Shea? Laney? What the hell was going on?

Ryker was an O'Shea by default, so there was no questioning why the contractor would think such a thing. Everyone around the area knew full well who the infamous family was, and who Ryker associated with and now called family.

Deciding to play along and figure out what Laney was up to—though after this morning he had no right—Ryker headed toward the open door. Once the two were inside, Ryker glanced around. The place was empty, save for the cobwebs that could only have come from tarantulas, some old boxes and some loose flooring.

"As I told Miss O'Shea the other day, I'm reworking the electrical." Mr. Pauley walked through the space and kept talking as if Ryker knew exactly what was going on. "I'm not sure about the kitchen. I may need to rewire some things in there, especially for the appliances she's wanting to use. This building is definitely not up to par for the two ovens she's suggested."

What the hell was Laney going to do with a building in Southie? Ryker continued following the middle-aged man toward what he assumed was the kitchen.

"She's got in mind she needs to crank out several meals a day. I admire her gumption, but this is going to take a lot of money to keep going."

Glancing at the cracked countertops, a rusted refrigerator, a sink that used to be white, Ryker started spinning ideas in his head. And all of them revolved around the perfectly generous Laney.

"But if anyone can help these kids it's her. Patrick was determined to save people." Mr. Pauley glanced back to Ryker with a side grin. "Anyway, this outside wall would be the best location for the ovens, but the wiring is all off. It can be run here. It's just going to cost more than the initial estimate I gave her. Same with the ventilation. Not much more, but—"

"I'll cover it."

His head was spinning, his mind racing over what could have possibly gotten into Laney's big heart that made her want to do this.

Damn the emotions she forced out of him. She wasn't even here and he was facing things he didn't want to. He was feeling so much…and he wasn't as afraid as he used to be. She'd come into his old neighborhood, she was renovating this old building to help kids...just like he used to be.

But he'd told her about his sordid childhood only days ago. There was no way she could've set things in motion that fast—no matter what her last name was.

Something twisted in Ryker's chest, some foreign emotion he almost didn't want to put a name to. The weight of this newfound feeling seemed to awaken something so deep within him, Ryker wondered how long he'd suppressed everything that was bursting through him now.

His entire life.

Ryker tried to focus back on what Mr. Pauley was saying as he pointed and gestured toward various parts of the spacious area that would become Laney's ideal kitchen.

Whatever Laney wanted, he was completely on board.

Seventeen

For the second time in as many weeks, Ryker had made a purchase at All Seasons. Now he stood outside Laney's house feeling like a fool. Perhaps this wasn't the way to go about things. Maybe he'd blown his chance when he flipped out over the crib and let all those doubts ruin what they had going on.

Since he left yesterday morning, she'd only texted him once, and that was to remind him of the home in Bradenton. He hadn't gone yet; there were more pressing matters to attend to.

For the first time in his life since becoming part of the O'Shea family, he was putting work on hold.

Because he didn't feel like he deserved to walk right in using his key, he rang the bell and gripped the shopping sack in his hand.

He didn't wait long before the door swung open. Laney

didn't say anything, and he waited for her to slam the door in his face. To his surprise, and relief, she stepped back and gestured for him to come in.

The warmth of her home instantly surrounded him. She had a fire in the fireplace, her tree sparkled with all the lights he'd put on it. This was home, a perfect home for their child to be raised in.

"Did you get to the estate?" she asked, brushing past him and heading back toward the kitchen.

"This is more important."

Laney stopped in her tracks, just as she hit the hallway off the living room. Her shoulders lifted as she drew in a breath and let out a deep sigh. When she turned, Ryker didn't waste any time moving toward her. He was done running, done hurting her, hurting them.

"I brought something for you." He extended the sack, smiling when her eyes caught the name on the side. "You can open it now."

She quirked a brow, kept her eyes on his and reached for the bag. Laney fisted the handles and stepped aside, sinking into the oversize chair. With the bag in her lap, she pulled out the tissue paper. Ryker shoved his hands in his pockets, waiting for her reaction, hoping he'd gone the right route in winning her back.

When she gasped and pulled out a white-and-gold stocking, her eyes immediately filled. That was a good sign...wasn't it?

"There's more." He nodded toward the bag and rocked back on his heels.

She pulled out another stocking, then another. Tissue paper lay all around her, the stockings on her lap as she stared down. Ryker couldn't see her expression for her hair curtaining her face.

Unable to stand the silence, he squatted in front of her.

"I don't have a fireplace," he started, reaching for one of the stockings. "I was hoping we could hang these here."

When she tipped her head to look at him, one tear slid down her cheek. "You put my name on one and yours on the other."

Ryker lay the smaller stocking over the larger ones. "And this will be for our baby. We can have the name put on once we know it."

"How did you…this…I don't even know what to say."

Speechless and in tears. Ryker was taking all of this as a very good sign. But he also knew Laney wouldn't be so quick to let him fully in. He'd been so back and forth, he needed to lay it all on the line and explain to her just what he wanted. Holding back was no longer an option.

"I hope you don't mind. I made a few adjustments to your plans with Mr. Pauley."

Laney's eyes widened as she sat up straighter. Her mouth formed a perfect O, and she continued to stare.

"I went back to my neighborhood, thinking maybe I could settle those demons once and for all." Before he would've gotten up to pace or avoided looking at her face, but he reached for her hands instead. "Mr. Pauley thought I was there to meet with him since you mentioned going by today."

"I…I called him a little bit ago but got his voicemail."

Ryker squeezed her hands. "Why did you start this project, Laney?"

"I wanted to make a difference for some kids." She glanced down at their hands, a soft smile adorning her mouth. "I started this before you ever told me the full story of your childhood. I'd heard enough over the years and always wanted to do something of my own. When I thought about what you went through, I would get so upset. I thought opening a place for kids to come after school would be ideal. They can get help with home-work, we can feed them. In the summer, they can play basketball, interact with other kids and hopefully stay out of trouble."

She kept talking until Ryker put his finger over her lips. "You humble me, Laney O'Shea. Those kids are going to love this, love you."

Reaching out, he tipped up her chin with his finger and thumb. "Not as much as I love you."

The catch in her breath had Ryker easing forward, closing the space between them as he covered her mouth with his. He stole only a minor taste, promising himself more later.

"I do love you, Laney. Maybe I always have, but I was damn scared of it." She laughed, her eyes sparkling with more unshed tears as he pushed on. "You knew it, and I'm sorry it took me so long to catch up. But I have this past that sometimes threatens to strangle me and I... I'm working on it, but I can't work on my own. I need you, Laney."

She threw her arms around his neck, crushing the stockings and tissue between them. "I don't want you leaning on anyone else. Because I need you, too."

"I want to be here, with you." He eased back but didn't let go. "Your house is warm, it's perfect for our baby, for us. Our family."

"You want to move in here?" she asked, her eyes wid-ening. "My brothers—"

"Aren't welcome. This is about you, me and our baby. Your brothers have an issue, they can take it up with me. I love you, Laney. I've never loved another woman. I want to be a team with you. All of the things I worried exposing you to, you've understood all along."

Laney's hands framed his face as her eyes searched his. "All of this came from you discovering my project?"

"The project just opened my eyes," he told her. "But why didn't you tell me?"

Laney shrugged, nibbling on her lip. "I didn't tell anyone. I told you I wanted something just for me. I'll tell the guys later, but I didn't do this so you all would be proud. I'm doing it for the kids."

Ryker settled his hands on her belly. "You're going to be the best mother. I can't wait to be a family with you."

Laney rested her forehead against his. "We're already a family."

Epilogue

"And who are you again?"

Ryker wasn't about to let just anyone into Braden's home. They were in the middle of a celebration. After a month of tiptoeing around the fact he and Laney were living together, the brothers had finally come to realize that Ryker and Laney were a done deal.

But it wasn't so much their relationship they were celebrating. Zara was pregnant again, and Mac and Jenna were closing in on their wedding date. There was plenty to be happy about…except this visitor at their door.

"I'm an investigator. Jack Carson."

Investigator. More like a nosey jerk with too much time on his hands.

"And what do you want?" Ryker asked, curling his fingers around the edge of the door and blocking the narrow opening with his body. "We have attorneys, so if you have an issue—"

"There's been a fire at the home of Mr. and Mrs. Parker in Bradenton."

Ryker froze. "A fire?" He'd just talked to them two days ago. They were still haggling over prices for their antiques. The young couple with a new baby had inherited the estate and all its contents, and they were hoping to earn some money by selling the larger pieces.

"You seem stunned by the news," Carson stated. "You wouldn't know anything about the fire, would you?"

Shocked, Ryker bristled. "How the hell would I know about it since you just told me? Are they all right?"

The investigator's eyes narrowed. "They were killed. Only the baby survived because the nursery was in the back of the house."

Ryker's gut clenched. The thought of an innocent baby without a mother and father was crippling.

"I hate to hear that," he said honestly. "Why are you here telling me this?"

Braden came up behind Ryker and eased the door wider. "Something wrong?"

Ryker nodded to the unwanted guest. "This is Jack something-or-other. Claims he's a PI."

"What's he want?"

Jack went on to explain the fire while Ryker studied the man. There was something about him that was familiar. Despite the expensive suit, the flashy SUV, the man smelled like a cop. But cops didn't make this kind of money, neither did the Feds. This guy was definitely suspicious...and ballsy for showing up here.

"That's terrible," Braden replied once Jack was done with the story. "I'm not sure where we fit in."

"We're just trying to find who set this fire because it appears to be a cover-up." Jack's assessing eyes kept shifting between Ryker and Braden. "There was a robbery, and most of the antiques were wiped out. The couple actually died from gunshot wounds."

Ryker remained still. "Why don't you quit dancing around the reason you're here and just spit it out."

"The O'Sheas had been talking with this couple, correct? About taking some of these antiques to auction?"

Ryker narrowed his eyes. "Our business is none of your concern."

"It is when there are two dead bodies."

Braden took a step onto the porch. Jack instantly backed up, but merely crossed his arms as if he was bored.

"Get the hell off my property," Braden growled. "If you have a problem, take it up with our attorneys. We don't talk to random strangers accusing us of something we know nothing about."

Braden took a step closer, and Ryker wondered if he'd have to step between these two.

Nah. It was nice seeing Braden get so fired up.

"What cop sent you?" Braden asked.

Jack remained silent and tipped his head. The cocky bastard was seriously getting on Ryker's nerves. Having had enough of this nuisance, Ryker stepped onto the porch and wedged a shoulder between the two.

"While this is fun and all, we actually have lives to get back to," Ryker told Jack. "So you're here of your own accord? No Fed or cop sent you? Then get your nosey ass off the property."

Clenching his fists at his side, Ryker tried to compose himself. But if this guy didn't budge soon, he wasn't going to be responsible for his actions.

Finally, Jack nodded and walked back to his car as if he'd been here for a flippin' Sunday brunch. Arrogance was a hideous trait to witness.

Once the guy was gone, Ryker turned to go back inside, but Braden hadn't budged. He was still staring at the spot where Jack's SUV had been parked.

"Don't let him get to you," Ryker stated. "It's a shame about that couple, but they can't pin any of that on us when we didn't do it."

Braden shook his head. "Did you see his eyes?"

"What?"

Braden looked to Ryker. "That guy. Did you look at his eyes? They seemed so familiar."

Ryker agreed. A shiver crept up his back. He didn't like when he got this feeling. Things never ended well.

"I don't think he was a PI." Braden ran a hand over the back of his neck and started heading toward the house. "We'll talk to Mac later, but for now keep this little visit between us."

Ryker fell into step beside him. "We need to watch our backs. Who knows who the hell this guy is."

It was hard for Ryker to put the mysterious man out of his mind, but when he walked into the house and Laney met him in the hallway, he found himself smiling. She had the slightest baby belly, only visible when she wore something tight. Today she had on a body-hugging dress with tights and boots. She was so damn sexy.

"I wondered where you went," she told him. "Who was at the door?"

Braden moved on into the living room, leaving Ryker and Laney in the foyer. "Nobody important," he replied.

They hadn't discovered the mole, yet, but it was only a

matter of time. Ryker wasn't giving up on bringing down the culprit who was hellbent on destroying the only family he'd ever known.

Laney's arms looped around his neck. "If you're done celebrating here, I'm ready to go home and celebrate privately."

Ryker whispered in her ear exactly what they would be doing in private, and Laney melted against him.

This was his woman, his forever family. They'd been his all along…all he'd had to do was reach out and claim them.

* * * * *

LET'S TALK
Romance

For exclusive extracts, competitions
and special offers, find us online:

f facebook.com/millsandboon

🐦 @MillsandBoon

📷 @MillsandBoonUK

Get in touch on 01413 063232

For all the latest titles coming soon, visit
millsandboon.co.uk/nextmonth

MILLS & BOON

THE HEART OF ROMANCE

A ROMANCE FOR EVERY READER

MODERN

Prepare to be swept off your feet by sophisticated, sexy and seductive heroes, in some of the world's most glamourous and romantic locations, where power and passion collide.

HISTORICAL

Escape with historical heroes from time gone by. Whether your passion is for wicked Regency Rakes, muscled Vikings or rugged Highlanders, awaken the romance of the past.

MEDICAL

Set your pulse racing with dedicated, delectable doctors in the high-pressure world of medicine, where emotions run high and passion, comfort and love are the best medicine.

True Love

Celebrate true love with tender stories of heartfelt romance, from the rush of falling in love to the joy a new baby can bring, and a focus on the emotional heart of a relationship.

Desire

Indulge in secrets and scandal, intense drama and plenty of sizzling hot action with powerful and passionate heroes who have it all: wealth, status, good looks…everything but the right woman.

HEROES

Experience all the excitement of a gripping thriller, with an intense romance at its heart. Resourceful, true-to-life women and strong, fearless men face danger and desire - a killer combination!

To see which titles are coming soon, please visit

millsandboon.co.uk/nextmonth

JOIN US ON SOCIAL MEDIA!

Stay up to date with our latest releases, author news and gossip, special offers and discounts, and all the behind-the-scenes action from Mills & Boon...

 @millsandboon

 @millsandboonuk

 facebook.com/millsandboon

 @millsandboonuk

It might just be true love...

GET YOUR ROMANCE FIX!

Get the latest romance news,
exclusive author interviews, story
extracts and much more!